ELEPHANT

PAUL PICKERING is the author of six novels, *Wild About Harry*, *Perfect English*, *The Blue Gate of Babylon*, *Charlie Peace*, *The Leopard's Wife* and *Over the Rainbow*. *The Blue Gate of Babylon* was a *New York Times* notable book of the year, who dubbed it 'superior literature'. Often compared to Graham Greene and Evelyn Waugh, Pickering was chosen as one of the top ten young British novelists by bookseller WHSmith and has been long-listed for the Booker Prize three times. The novelist J. G. Ballard said Pickering's work is 'truly subversive'. As well as short stories and poetry, he has written several plays, film scripts and columns for *The Times* and *Sunday Times*. He lives in London with his wife and daughter.

ELEPHANT

PAUL PICKERING

SALT

CROMER

PUBLISHED BY SALT PUBLISHING 2021

2 4 6 8 10 9 7 5 3 1

Copyright © Paul Pickering 2021

Paul Pickering has asserted his right under the Copyright, Designs
and Patents Act 1988 to be identified as the author of this work.

First published in Great Britain in 2021 by
Salt Publishing Ltd
12 Norwich Road, Cromer, Norfolk NR27 0AX United Kingdom

www.saltpublishing.com

Salt Publishing Limited Reg. No. 5293401

A CIP catalogue record for this book is available from the British Library

ISBN 978 1 78463 225 0 (Paperback edition)
ISBN 978 1 78463 226 7 (Electronic edition)

Typeset in Neacademia by Salt Publishing

Printed and bound in Great Britain by Clays Ltd, Elcograf S.p.A

For Alice

"I loved you without hope, a mute offender;
What jealous pangs, what shy despairs I knew!
A love as deep as this, as true, as tender,
God grant another may yet offer you."

ALEXANDER PUSHKIN.

ONE

"ELEPHANT!" I MET my elephant under a green Christmas tree hung with red candles and silver bells and high as the roof at a ball in the Tsar's Palace outside St Petersburg. It was a small, silver elephant. I was an ornament too. I was one of the twenty children in sailor suits from the Imperial Nursery placed under the tree with the presents. I was already so excited my breath became hiccups. The kind of hiccups you get from drinking apricot juice too quick. ELEPHANT. If you are silent for a long time words become more your friends, not less. The dancers, the women in white dresses, the men in white uniforms with blue sashes, were part of the music itself and whirled near, ONE-TWO-THREE. I had not spoken much for the first five years of my life but this is a story beyond language and numbers that I write grown and educated and fearing not merely death but this story's total annihilation. Even then I said things from dreams the woken did not want to hear. They were upset when I said JESUS IS DEAD. I was sitting on the floor in the great, mirrored ballroom of the Tsarskoye Selo palace that was also blue and white like a cake. The orchestra was playing loudly and the dresses of the young ladies caught my face and made me giggle. SLAP-ONE-TWO-THREE . . . SLAP-ONE-TWO-THREE

. . . I was there on the warm wood floor in the creamy electric light surrounded by flashing sequins in an ocean of white satin and petticoats. There were floor to ceiling mirrors on the Christmas-tree side of the ballroom and French windows on the other, looking down to a lake, but between several of the windows there were gold-framed mirrors, so the waltzers were carried on into endless bending reflection that my tutors call INFINITY. The word was in my dreams and I asked them what it meant. The elephant and I were in the mirrors' INFINITY too. The elephant was as little as my fingers and had red jewels for eyes, a heavy silver bauble on a dark green pine needle branch, and I began trying to draw it with my wax crayons on a piece of paper covered in my writing. Clever men came to see me, even the Holy Man with deep-pit, fall-into, midnight eyes, and listen to me and get mad and shout but come back. They didn't like it when I ran round like a jumping jack. The pine needle branch ended in a candle and I blew out the candle and took the elephant off. The air smelt of smoke, the scented candle and pine needles. The elephant was free! In between drawing the elephant I was writing WORDS I now know the full meaning of. I was so happy I had not even had any sweets or anything to eat. NO ONE GOES TO HEAVEN was another thing I told the ladies. There were a lot of orphans in the Imperial Nursery that the old cleaning women who worked there called "bastards", *ubliduki*. It is a bad word. I am not *ublyudok*. The nice women at the Imperial Nursery who smelt of good soap told me that my family had died in the war in the East and I was in St Petersburg because I was a minor prince (there were lots of us ornaments and bastards). THERE IS NO HELL, I shouted one night. A few of the boys and girls had been just collected on the Tsar's travels because they were pretty. The ladies said I was pretty. I had been on a burning train with my parents and was saved by a nanny. I had howled like a wolf, literally like a wolf, when I got to the Imperial Nursery but then stopped and smiled and smiled. The ladies said I had been buried for days under dead passengers hearing the wolves sing their hunger songs and then them fighting over the bodies on top of me; important people, politicians and a German moral philosopher, a kind of teacher, the ladies in the nursery told me. Often I surprised them with words I did not understand from my dreams. The ladies said I was possessed when I shouted: THE DARK RIVER FLOWS TOWARD GOOD. Then they decided I heard the words when the wolves were eating the moral philosopher and mimicked them like a phonograph or a parrot. But the ladies knew that wasn't true and it frightened them. I do not remember the burning train, which is strange, nor the fire or the smoke, or the Chinese Boxer rebels attacking, or the singing wolves eating my mother and father. I learned many cheerful songs in the Imperial Nursery yet I found it hard to remember my parents. Except when they went out to dances like this one and kissed me, and my sad-eyed mother smelt of perfume and lipstick and face powder and her furs of snow. The last time was in the dead of night, in candlelight. The old ladies said my parents had been murdered on that train. I hope it was before the wolves started their dinner. Perhaps my parents were going to a ball. With INFINITY mirrors, so they waltzed forever. I remember my mother saying to promise her to say my prayers and sleep tight. We were in the far, far East where you needed prayers. I then whirled across the ballroom with the silver elephant and sat on the floor by one of the food tables and began to write more words on my paper and draw. That is how I got into trouble with the Tsar.

TWO

THE PLANET-WIDE NEW York sky was turning red on 20th and Broadway and Natasha wanted to get home so she could read again the start of the boy's story she had received by email.

"God and his lovin' angels bless you, girl."

Natasha had reached into her suit pocket and taken out two single dollar bills of coffee money and put it in the Styrofoam cup of a large black woman in an orange tracksuit and light blue mask sprawled on the pavement a few doors from the house Natasha lived in on 20th. She knew she should not do this in New York, but more poor people were on the street due to the pandemic. Her day in Columbia University's Low Library had been an ordeal. The acting chief librarian, a woman brought in because of the pandemic who bred and "showed" Toy Poodles, had said Natasha was probably not emotionally suited for the job, after catching her reading Nabokov. For the acting chief librarian, a library was a penitentiary for books and ideas and the woman was glad that no one could borrow any of them now. A drug deal was in play two doors on, yet outside Natasha's doorway there was no one. There never was. The house was forbidding, a dark, dirty brown, even for a brownstone, that had never been renovated in a now fashionable area. Looking about her, she took out her keys and opened the front door and, being the only one in the building, scooped the post off the rotting mat. There was one envelope that made her heart beat faster. There had been a little cage to catch the bloody syringes and lighted cigarettes, but it had disappeared. The hallway was dark and carpet-less with a small window over the door and none at the back, and today she bi-passed the old, unreliable, expanding-metal-door elevator, so easy to trap your fingers in, and ran up the stairs, two at a time. On the first floor was the creepy apartment where she had first stayed, crammed full of a dead artist's unsaleble pictures, in which you could hear the rats in the spaces behind the cream-painted walls and she had sung to them in the shower and recited her poems. She got to the top and undid the complicated locks on her apartment door. Perhaps the big, A4 envelope was from him, the man in Paris, the man who had been going to take her away from everything. She tore open the brown paper as she got inside. It wasn't from him. Someone, probably a student who mistook her importance, had sent her the first few pages of the boy's story photocopied, in case she did not read her emails. She went into the bedroom and put it on the bed underneath the skylight and then showered to wash the day out of her head.

Natasha towelled her hair and threw herself back on the bed and quickly read the pages.

The sky had turned fresh-blood red in the setting sun as she finished and lay back on the pillows, looking up at the skylight on that hot summer evening, a Paisley silk robe of blues and purples under her body. It had once belonged to her poor mother.

She had read the pages again, transported to Tsarist Russia and fascinated by the boy and his strange dreams and his way with capital letters, creating an emotional code, with words and phrases having an almost magical significance, using language as a game that released him from time and history.

Who had sent her this?

Natasha had hardly slept the night before but had dreamt. She tried to note the dreams down in a book she kept by the bed like Nabokov, but was not so tidy. *Nabokov, Dreams and Time* was the title of her doctorate. Last night she had dreamed of butterflies. A dream she had had many times before. In Natasha's dream there were trays and trays of butterflies she instantly knew had been caught in nets, killed in a killing jar of bruised laurel leaves and then pinned onto cork and labelled, behind thick glass, in cases and framed in what must be in a museum because the air smelt musty and of furniture polish and mopped stone floors, like the Smithsonian in Washington, with its huge African Elephant in the entrance hall. In the first of the cases were exotic blue butterflies from the tropics as big as a hand, certainly as big as her hands, and she was consumed with sadness that a man had gone to Brazil, or some other end of the earth, to entrap and kill such a creature in his moments off from colonial duty. In the dream were stone arches of vast inner spaces of the museum sculpted with pineapples and held aloft by giant Negro slaves and there was a thick red carpet. Red was a trigger for her imagination, always, and she experienced everything about the butterflies and the tightly locked cases in an instant. The blue butterflies were not ones she recognised, but as she was about to turn away one of them moved, slightly. She looked back and there was a fluttering of the butterfly's deep blue wings that became a strong vibrating of both wings; panicky bursts of energy, even though she could see the pin that held the insect to the cork. Natasha could not breathe. More butterflies began to move and the butterfly that had started to flutter first pushed at the cork with its long legs and unpinned itself, beating its wings strongly to press the pin from its body, bleeding liquid.

The other butterflies imitated the first and she was about to go and try and fetch someone or at least record the moment on her phone, when the glass front of a case smashed with a crack like a pistol and she was surrounded by butterflies, this time blood red. They flew around her head, turning the museum into a carousel with Natasha at the centre. It was not long before all the cases were exploding and she was in a storm of many colours; a phenomenal resurrection. But it was beyond that. She felt inside the instant of the thousand, thousand butterflies that flew up into the darkness in the grey granite halls. It was a dream of beauty and colour and, above all, of freedom and rebellion.

It was the red in the clouds that had triggered her recollection of the dream.

Above her, a few New York clouds were still porcelain white and blue on the tops, cresting like waves, and then shades of pink and sanguine crimson underneath, as if in early summer, the summer of the lockdown, the seedy modern plague, an even more apocalyptic event had arrived to crystallise the unnamed anxieties of her generation.

A plane high above turned silver and gold, flashing briefly in the brighter light further up before disappearing into a cloud.

A slow, shabby, coat-winged bird, perhaps a heron, made its shaky way north, up Broadway, to Central Park and the ponds of Strawberry Fields, or possibly the reservoir. The sunset was strawberry now. She loved strawberries with a passion. She loved the colour red. For her it always meant change.

It was the colour of the old candlewick counterpane pulled over the head of her father, dead a year ago. One side of his face was red too, from the settled blood when they found him.

The cool, defining breeze off the ocean, redolent of ozone

and another ocean, the Pacific, and her childhood, of kelp and pounding surf and catching crabs, was blowing through the cracks in the skylight. She liked the sensuality of the boy's writing. Natasha's own senses had mixed together since she was four. She saw letters as colours, Grapheme-colour Synaesthesia, like Nabokov, and, like the writer and catcher of butterflies, she had vivid, colour-haunted dreams that predicted the future. Nabokov thought the future had already happened and time was flowing in the opposite direction to the one presumed, in fact backwards, and one was quite right to be anxious about history known about, but never experienced in tooth and claw. The bad times full of pestilence and war were behind us all, but what if time was heading in that direction, making us boats against the current? The man in Paris said her generation were all so anxious because time was surging tidally back and connecting to the trauma of World War Two. Natasha loved the dandelion-seed sensitivity of the poet Emily Dickinson, to whom Natasha had been compared, and her timeless line: "I heard a fly buzz - when I died."

She had just made her decision on her twenty-seventh birthday to quit writing poetry, after winning three national competitions and getting a Pulitzer nomination, and take a job and support her sick mother. He, the man in Paris, had wanted her to continue writing, wanted her to be his dependent, an exotic animal he could keep in a house or a flat somewhere and show off at dinner parties. Natasha rubbed at her pubic hair which was still sharp and spiky and had not grown fully back. She saw herself projected, unpinned, like one of the museum butterflies, onto that familiar, infernal sky, her blonde hair cropped in protest at what had gone down in Paris, her blue eyes that her mother said were panicky, her amused, half-smiling mouth that made her teachers think she was not taking things seriously enough, and her too long, slender, six-foot-in-her-Bobby-socks body. She looked at her computer on the old brass bed next to her and the email she had written in total weakness.

From: NatashaA@gmail.com
To: TMP@pictec.org

Paris? What happened in Paris . . . ? Why?

Natasha gazed, trembling, at the email still in the Draft folder before deciding not to delete. She had not written more. It was going to come out all wrong. It was a month now, since Paris. For her that particular piece of time meant everything. She knew she should get on with designing the creative writing class for the next semester at Columbia University where she was nominally only a librarian, allowed to do a bit of teaching. Instead, she turned back to the boy's story. A truck horn sounded down below. One way or another she had to get away from thinking of the man in Paris. She opened the small bedside cabinet drawer and felt for her headache pills, which were not there. Instead, she found three loose tablets. They were all red and different sizes. Maybe if she took them she would grow like Alice. She left them. She had finished with all that, too, even though it was that kind of day. The truck horn sounded again. The skylight was all a magnificent ruby now, and gold. She had meant to go running. Up to the reservoir with the raggedy clothed heron, where bright blue jays fought over the trash baskets, but no way after dark. She began to read the three pages again. Here was a soul not unlike herself who lived, as she did, on the precipice of one age changing into another. The boy appeared to have all the nostalgic innocence of a rebel on a path of discovery, even though Natasha's rebellion and wanderings were over after what had happened in Paris and to her father and mother. After Paris. That's what her life was now. Her computer beeped and she half expected it to be the man in Paris. But she saw she had another packet of the boy's story sent from an anonymous email. She lent back on the pillows and read.

THREE

"**H**E SPOKE!"

A princess with blonde ringlets at the ball clapped her hands and bent over me, all in white like a swan. "ELEPHANT," I said again to the little silver animal that was mine now. Then I read the words written on the paper I was drawing on. There were drawings of the dead Tsar, all with blood everywhere, and his family. READING IS ESSENTIAL FOR FREEDOM.

"He spoke, the little man spoke. He said something clever."

"No, he couldn't have. He's an idiot, that one. He speaks rubbish. He's an idiot."

"You're an idiot. All the Tsar's cavalry are idiots! No one says anything intelligent in Russia anymore."

I liked the sound of the word IDIOT. I liked words. They were in my own head. They are jewels and do not need to have anything to do with other people. You can hide in words or let them explode like fireworks. They were my TOY SHOP.

No one seemed to know who I was or, indeed, what I was. To a few of the women at the Imperial Nursery I was a MONSTER, who had hardly spoken for the first years of his life, and when I did, I said too much that was unsettling, and quite often advised I should not be allowed to play with the rest of the Imperial Family, and that my outbursts had me bound for the public asylum. Others said I had joy in my heart, so I did not care. JOY!

I loved the Imperial Nursery, which smelled of biscuits and fresh-baked bread and the face powder of the ladies. Mostly they called me *Mishka*, little bear, and they called every boy that or little prince and there were lots of tiny princes and princesses. A few times they called me *Pasha*. There were thirty-two girls and boys, many who did not seem to belong to anyone but themselves. The matrons, even the strict ones, said I was a very beautiful boy, I am not boasting, as I write this many years later, but I was famous for my large green-blue eyes and a smile that quivered and broke out from a dimple in my cheek, like so much sunshine from behind a cloud. My nose is long, like Mr Gogol's the women said, and my ears a little pointed, I have a wide mouth and haystack-coloured hair. I smile a lot. There were those who were unnerved by that smile but I do not mind. The day of the elephant on the Christmas tree was my earliest complete memory and the start of my life. I was not sure of trusting my dreams and imaginings about burning trains and singing wolves, based on the ladies' stories. Before the Christmas ball I only remember snatches of bouncing a ball against a door and chasing grasshoppers through the warm summer meadows outside St Petersburg, counting which had red flashes in their wings and which blue, on nights when every tree and flower and bulrush hummed and crackled with life.

I did not mind at all being brushed by the silken dresses. ROBES in French. I felt part of the whirling mass of them.

With the crayons that I had taken from my tutor's desk, I sat there in my white silk sailor suit, drawing. The girls smiled at me as they passed and so did most of the officers, hot from the modern heating in their blue and white cavalry jackets, as the orchestra played and played and the huge windows looked out onto the gardens and down to the frozen, moonlit lake.

The white gowns battered me gently in the face and I chuckled until I stood up and shouted out: "TOUT EST MOI ET JE SUIS TOUT." Everything is me and I am everything. I loved the word TOUT. We learned French as well as English in the Imperial Nursery. TOUT sounded like the happy breath of God.

"He spoke again," said the princess, clapping her hands. She was a minor princess with a long neck and kind eyes. "The little man spoke in French."

Her partner pretended a yawn.

"His tutor is French. All tutors used to be French. Now most of them are English, thanks to the Tsarina, don't forget. We are all meant to speak English now as the court language. I thought this one was meant to be mental?"

The princess looked at him with failing patience.

"This little one who you thought to be an imbecile is imperfectly quoting Baudelaire."

'Who?" said the officer. The princess hit him with her fan.

She reached for what I had been inscribing and drawing on the piece of paper on the ballroom floor. The ladies said the ballroom had come all the way from Paris and was a copy of one in the palace at Versailles.

"And he's been writing too. Clever boy! He is a prodigy! A miracle!"

She then read my words and saw my drawings. She went very pale and gave a strangled little cry and scooped me up and took me to the side of the dance floor under the mirrors as high as the room. The dancers did not look into them or think what they were. I do not suppose for one moment the

13

princess wanted to get me into trouble, but her stern mama came over to see what the commotion was about and was horrified. I laughed. Her mother looked as if she had swallowed a PIKE FISH. It may have been to do with the nice princess being German. The fleshy mama then summoned other ladies and then gentlemen and dancers. It was the fifth year of the twentieth century and there had been a revolution that didn't work but which everyone talked and talked and talked about. More grown-ups read what was on the paper and stared back at me with increasing alarm. I was then rushed in the arms of one of the soldiers to the Amber Room, which was away from the festivities, where the Imperial Family were.

AMBER was a good word.

It was a room where the walls were solid amber and was given to Peter the Great by Frederick the Great, or that's what an old Imperial guard had said who showed us around. I loved the room because there were flies and bits of plants embedded in the transparent honey-brown stone. It was meant to make you young and live for ever. Like the dead flies. If you told a fib there, though, you got caught up in the walls, with the flies. "That's like Russia," one of the ladies had said and giggled behind her hand. 'Everyone caught up in lies."

The Tsar was standing by the wall, to which were fixed a number of paintings, one upside down. Even I knew that. It was a pretty landscape of a lake that looked like the sky and was an easy mistake to make. But as Catherine the Great herself had hung them, no one was going to point this out.

"So you can talk?' said the Tsar, in Russian. The Tsar was a tall and awkward man and the room was too small for him. His fists were clenched. From one protruded a cigarette. He had headaches probably because of the revolutions, the ladies said, like spinning round too much. I felt sorry for him. We were all taught to love and say prayers for him every night, the Tsar.

I smiled up.

"Yes," I said.

"Perhaps it was your silence that confused us in the past?"

He was not a clever man in most ways and what he said was not a joke. But everyone laughed.

"No, sire," I said. He was not used to the word but I was not going to tell a lie in the Amber Room and be caught in the walls with the flies and the lies forever.

He looked surprised at this reply and the Tsarina, who was sitting down by an enormous vase of white silk imitation flowers, lit a cigarette in an ebony holder and said in English, "Perhaps the boy is possessed by the devils who are loose in our sacred city."

She rocked back and forward and hugged a black silk shawl patterned with great red roses over her white ball dress. She must have been a beautiful woman, now with dark lines under her eyes and I always thought of her as Mama, as did many of the other children at the court. The ladies said she was German but had been brought up in England by Queen Victoria. Underneath her perfume she stank of sweat and mice.

"How can you speak in French?" said the Tsar. "I gave orders that the court language is English now. That is what is taught in the nursery."

I shrugged, possibly in a French way.

"One of my teachers in the nursery is French."

I saw from the expression on the faces in the room that this was now regarded as unspeakable. It was the language of the revolution, I heard a lady say. REVOLUTIONS ARE IMPOSSIBLE. IDEAS DO NOT BURN, I had said to the

15

ladies one night when doing cartwheels. Revolutions. It echoed in my dreams. I dreamed a lot. I did not say this to the Tsar.

The Tsar came over and peered down. He had a monocle. He assumed a stern expression and cast a shadow over me. He was wearing an ornate military uniform in white and blue and several military orders, including that of Saint Anna, around his neck.

"And you can read?" He made it sound like an insult. I was frightened now.

"I try, sire." I answered in English.

"In French?"

"The language of chaos," said the Tsarina. "It is how the Jews communicate with each other. The city is full of Jews! Jews! Christ protect us. It is full of these revolutionaries. They breed like rats and all shout at each other in French. It is despicable and the work of Lucifer." She began to pray.

The Tsar was unnerved.

"In French?" he repeated.

I did not reply. Everyone was staring at me. More men in grey suits had come into the small room.

"So you know the words of French poets . . . but who told you to write this? The words on this paper? Was it one of your tutors? It seems I am surrounded by spies that come into my palaces with the ease that worms get into the timbers of a boat."

The Tsarina looked up and blew a cloud of smoke.

The Tsar held the piece of paper in front of me. On it, in my shaky handwriting in capitals, were the simple words I had dreamed: LE TSAR DOIT MOURIR. The Tsar must die. The words TSAR and DOIT in particular pleased me. DOIT t the same letters as IDIOT in French.

told you to write the Tsar must die?"

He paused and then stepped forward and snatched the silver elephant I was holding in my hand.

"A thief as well, I see. That was on my writing desk. No one comes near my writing desk. How did you get that, my little thief?" he said, angry. To me, it was as if God himself was angry. He then hit me across the head with a pair of white kid gloves. It was not at all hard but I started to cry. He was about to hit me again but the very brave princess, who had discovered me writing amid the waltzing of the ball, put herself between me and the Tsar.

I was in a lake of tears. I wanted the elephant.

"This is not the way, Your Imperial Highness. He is an innocent child," said the princess.

"No one is innocent these days,' said one of the generals, who had shuffled into the room and was pouring himself another glass of champagne. The Tsarina then actually laughed.

"He cannot be one of yours, Nicky. Whoever heard of a clever Romanov?" she said. "We are doomed. It is prophesied in the words and drawings of a child. Fetch me the Holy Man. He can make preparation for the boy to be exorcised and healed."

The Tsarina got up from the chair and came over to where I stood. She crouched down and took my arms, gently.

"Everyone leave," she commanded. When they were gone she lit another cigarette with a candle on a small table. She turned to the Tsar.

I was alone with them in the tea-glass coloured room.

They both knelt down by me. Their faces were very close to mine. Suddenly they were different.

"Dear one . . . Look at this boy, for God's sake. What do you see?"

I was really frightened now.

"I see what you see," he said wearily, as she stroked my hair. "I know he looks like poor Alexei. Not too much. What are you thinking, my darling?"

Then with a glint in her eye, she said: "I will ask the Holy Man what he advises."

The Tsar tugged at his collar.

"His parents died in the East. The minister said so. He is not related to us."

"Everyone is related to us," the Tsarina said, with a knowing laugh. "I will tell the Holy Man."

My tears stopped. Did they mean I was somehow one of the Imperial Family? How could that be? I was excited and scared and my lower lip started to quiver. I wanted to be part of a family. Any family.

She then stood and left and the Tsar stood too. But he remained, staring at the floor.

"Not the fucking Holy Man," he said quietly in Russian, holding his head. "Oh please, not the fucking Holy Man. I'm getting one of my headaches."

At this, the princess who had saved me hurried into the room, curtsied and rushed me out. She hid me under a table for the rest of the ball and her beaux, of whom there were several, brought me nice things to eat and even a sip of iced champagne, which made my head dance with the music and the colours. They all waltzed and waltzed except for a pause when a very beautiful ballerina did the 'Dance of the Sugar Plum Fairy'. I saw her searching around the base of the Christmas tree as if she had lost something among the presents.

Afterwards, the dancer came over to me and reached down to kiss me, not just once but again and again and again, and her lovely face contorted with great sadness and she burst into tears and left the room.

SUGAR PLUM FAIRY was in my head.

A few of the officers laughed and whispered. Christmas presents were handed out. I did not care. I only wanted the elephant that had been taken from me.

The princess, who had gone after the dancer, returned with a flower from her dress. I did not want the flower, I wanted my elephant. I trusted the elephant.

I still saw the anguished look of the SUGAR PLUM FAIRY.

"She was too upset by the emotion of her performance to remain with us. Don't worry a bit about the Tsar," said the princess, with a wink. She gave me a kiss on the forehead and her skin had the scent of hyacinths. "I'm sorry if I got you into trouble. This is all about more than you can know or understand. Do not worry. It will be forgotten by morning. They'll all get drunk and forget. They'll be glad they have a prodigy. The Tsar has plenty of other things to worry about, like the war with Japan. It will all blow over. You just see."

I did see. But I wanted the elephant the Tsar said belonged to him. I needed the elephant.

FOUR

THE NEXT DAY after her dream of the rebel butterflies, after seeing the fiery red sky that set ablaze her thoughts about the boy in the manuscript, Natasha went for a run up Fifth Avenue and into Central Park. She ran in an easy lope, dodging people and hurdling a drunk near the Hans Christian Andersen statue, past the zoo, past two Audubon perfect blue jays fighting in a trash basket, and around and around the creamy, light brown water of the reservoir, looking like milky chocolate behind a high fence, with other morning pilgrims. Natasha liked the oily sensuality of the still water and the fallen leaves, almost a piece of wilderness if you got up close to the fence, until you looked up and saw the city, the lunacy of American Gothic shouting from Art Deco skyscrapers. Running was as close as she got to her butterfly moment in her dream. A girl she knew from Columbia waved and shouted "Hi" but mainly the runners were a closed sect. They were further entrapped by their Bluetooth earphones and several of the girls wore veil-like black masks. Natasha then ran back through Strawberry Fields, past the little rowing pond, wondering what had happened to the shabby heron.

When she got back to the apartment on 20th she showered. It was a better shower in the top flat under an opaque skylight. There were no rats behind the walls. The apartment she had been in first in the old building, which belonged to a friend's family, was still entirely full of the former artist tenant's paintings. These were all a uniform light grey and showed a hardly discernible image within the paint and under layers of varnish. The effect was to suggest, whatever the image was, that it was very important. There were a few more conventional Miro-like works propped against the walls and a pile of magazines with interviews about the artist. The artist, Gannin, a Russian, had sold no work before his grey period, one interview in the *New York Times* magazine said, and enjoyed brief and intense notoriety, as before producing them he had cut off both of his hands under local anaesthetic using a sheet metal cutter in a Queens foundry and had nearly died on the way to hospital, where he thought they could be sewn back on. (He naively trusted the correct position of the future in time in New York traffic.) Natasha had not believed the story at first and had looked up the newspaper files. A magazine cover showed the artist smiling at a table with his hands in front of him. He had been preparing with assistants for another show when he died of a painkiller overdose in the high-ceilinged room containing the paintings. When Natasha heard the rats behind the boards and tiles in the shower it sounded like someone was in the main room, the "gallery", with the hot lights, where no one ever came. Natasha was not superstitious, but she did not like to think of the return of the artist, or even worse, just his scorned hands. She, too, had stopped her art, her poetry. She put on a clean red tracksuit and, feeling she might have pulled a hamstring, went down in the old, slow elevator that had been mysteriously cleaned and smelled of metal polish and beeswax, and hurried to the Korean diner across the road.

Natasha did not need to order. The waiter, dour, surly but almost annoyingly attentive, brought her black coffee and a glass of iced water, and then in no time at all, two eggs, sunny side up, by a mound of perfect hash browns. She smiled and thanked him and he turned his back and walked away, but not before a curt nod, the equivalent of three sonnets and several bouquets of long-stemmed red roses. She ate quickly but before she had finished her phone went ping. It was a friend from Harvard. Natasha felt a sad and appalling nostalgia. Now the dream times, the good times, seemed over, especially after Paris. She looked down at the email on her phone.

From: (ChiChiChica) Froment@fas.harvard.edu
To: NatashaA@gmail.com

Hi there, Nash, how are you? How is your marmalade cunt? It does taste exactly like marmalade. I part read the pages you sent and yes, I would say it may be the beginning of something Faustian and unsettling and a little bit Schopenhauer. Please tell me you wrote it, my darling. Or are you saying that the boy is real? That he wrote these first pages of his own history? He is a total love, I give you that. But all this is distraction. Hallucinations! Elephant is another name for PCP or angel dust. Tell me you have not been cramming down the pills? Now let's get down to the real stuff. Why don't you come back to me this instant and let me wrap my eighteen hundred arms around you again? Your prince charming has let you down. He has not only let you down he beat the holy shit out of you and worse. I do not understand why you feel you need a man when you have little me. No llores, mi querida. I still think you should report the grand shit to the police. You say it is not rape but it sounds like rape to me. Blood all over your blouse? Blood! All over a wrecked 1000-dollar-a-night room? That is not fucking consensual. Rape is as bad as murder in my book and I am still thinking

22

of going back to Juarez and getting my half-brother's gun and shooting your man in Paris down dead by a nameless wall somewhere. Hey, Chica, where you goin' with that gun in your hand! Love is dangerous. I think Pushkin, who you admire so much, thought of love as a charging elephant. Elephants again! Come home to mummy. I got the case cracked and the Martini shaken to its existential core. There is no elephant in the room in this Russian tale. Nothing obvious. It's worse than that. What darkness! Singing wolves! Terrifying! Cool! Run to me, Natasha. I can get you a job here any time you want and we can pop champagne corks into the happy Charles River and get up close and personal in the Lilac Arboretum and eat a peach or two. They need minds like yours. It's all getting stale. I need you. Harvard beats fucking in fucking New York. You can have excitement and civilisation. You only went there because of the man. The Man. Leave all that, Natasha. Come back to me now. You know I love you.

Reloveution! ChiChi
Dr Martha Froment
Gurney Professor of English Poetry and Liberal Arts
Harvard University
Cambridge, Boston.

Natasha shook her head and ran her fingers through her short hair. What happened in Paris had gone nuclear, but it was not what ChiChi said. It was endearing that ChiChi exaggerated so much in her personal secret life when her academic one was so non-generalised and exacting. There was a desperation in her frenetic energy. A wanting to be dumbly young again. Natasha doubted that ChiChi had any Mexican relatives at all. Natasha was late. She paid and ran across the road, getting honked at by a yellow cab. She skipped up the steps of the building and inside, not wanting to push her hamstring too far, closed the heavy door of the elevator and pressed her floor button. The light above her head flickered and for a moment there was a clicking sound but nothing happened. In Paris there had been a similar elevator and anger and blood and now it was time for reality. The light flickered again and there was more clicking before the elevator ascended fitfully and she reached the top floor. Inside, she changed into her work clothes, a blue suit. She could not get Columbia to pay her as a lecturer. Perhaps they had heard from her friends that she had given up on her poetry. But her mom was sick now after what happened to her dad. Natasha wished he hadn't gone and that she had been nicer to him. Her mother had loved dancing all her life in small parts in the chorus and musical theatre. The day she heard about what had happened to her husband she stopped dancing. Then her mother had stopped moving and talking and smiling and there was worse to come. Natasha helped pay the bills for the nursing home. She sighed.

Natasha's poetry had survived assaults by post-modernism and post-structuralism and all manner of academic strait jackets. It had survived the unexpected affair with ChiChi. But there had been something poetic from the start in what Natasha felt for the man in Paris, and she had written less. She had written less too after her father died, no line seeming sufficient to embrace the loss and absurdity. But, if she were brutally honest and she tried to be, it was love, in the main, in its full unpredictable flow that came between her and the blank page. Stretching her naked body on a cold, white sheet, her cries of ecstasy substituted for rhythm and syntax and the horizontal line she put instead of the period point. You cannot write poetry when you are making love, and she and the man in Paris never stopped.

Natasha looked at herself in the mirror and smiled. Her hair was convict-cropped. Genet said there was a close relationship between convicts and flowers, the fragility and delicacy of the latter for him complimenting the brutal insensitivity of the former. Natasha's hair probably made her look like an anarchist who might place a lighted cigarette or two in prized first editions of bourgeois literary gods like Emerson and Thoreau. She had to get herself focussed and on track. She had to learn to switch off and just work, like when she was running. Anyway, her poems were not that good, she thought, and she didn't want to be like the handless artist, reaching for sensation.

With her low heels in her bag, Natasha headed down the stairs in her trainers and up 20th. She liked West 20th and how it crossed 6th with the old Limelight Club in the blackened church on the corner, now a Chinese restaurant. She preferred that way to the subway on 23rd instead of going down to Broadway. She quickened her pace, dancing around an arguing couple as more people pin-balled towards her, only socially distanced by their clothes. She thought of ChiChi. It was not rape. She hurried on as a taxi had stopped and two cars behind were already honking their horns and windows were being wound down as a New York minute was being wasted. A cop by a burlesque bar turned away. There was a cold, gritty wind from the river. She had met the man in Paris here at a gallery opening and he talked to her all night as if she was the only person in the universe, talked of how her poetry was so important, not just for herself but the world, and something shifted, changed her, changed everything. He was the first man to talk to her like this and he wrote himself into every hope and dream and atom of her being. The man in Paris who had not called. She shook herself and quickly disappeared down the subway, trying to give her dreams the slip. The man in Paris not calling was like a hot knife in butter. On the train she started to read the Russian story again. Always when there was trouble she hid in stories. Her grandmother had died when Natasha was seven, a woman she dearly loved who had taught her to draw and, more significantly, to love poems. Her grandmother had taken a whole winter to die at the turn of the millennium but had been so cheerful on a bed that was put up for her on the ground floor of a small house in San Francisco. No one told Natasha her grandmother was going to die, but she picked up the entire thing from the whispering adults. To keep everything at a distance, at a manageable distance (she constantly felt like crying), she read 101 *Dalmations* again and again. In all she read it nine times, lingering over the twilight barking and the hot sugary tea and toast, and the triumph over death and evil. It was not the crummy Disney version but the original novel by Dodie Smith. Books became an extension of Natasha's dreams, as did her own writing. They stopped time rushing at you. There was no warning, no protection, when her father died, which was typical. The Russian boy had dreams. The trouble was deciding if they only existed on paper. Could the story she had been reading really be true? Natasha wished she had more to go on. She was hooked already and whoever sent the pages to her realised how it worked with the reader. Dickens knew the addictive power of having his work serialised in a newspaper. The subway train stopped and the lights dimmed and flickered like the lift she tried to avoid in her building.

"Is this a metaphor, I ask myself?" said the striking, tall, obviously gay man next to her, dressed like Sherlock Holmes but without the silly cap.

She knew enough of the city not to reply. The lights came fully on again and they sped on down the long, dark tunnel. She put the manuscript away. Natasha had a tendency to look for too many metaphors. Later that day a new "packet" of the boy's manuscript appeared on her computer.

FIVE

WHEN ONE OF the ladies took me back to the Imperial Nursery from the Christmas Ball everyone was very quiet. I could smell incense and as I went up to the little dormitory where I slept I heard a papa saying prayers. I thought it was because of me and he was praying for my soul. That it was for stealing the Tsar's elephant. But he was just blessing a child whose new "parents" were taking him away the next day. I wished I had real parents. Any parents. I had been crying before and the tears came again. The hairs at the back of my neck stood up. I felt a presence behind me. I saw a worried expression on the nice face of the old papa who was swinging his incense holder to make the place smell nice.

"You are not meant to come here . . . You are not meant to be in here," said the lady with me to the person behind us. There was a shaking fear in her voice. A man spoke with authority:

"Leave, priest. This boy does not need you. Leave, all of you. Except you, little one."

He clapped his hands.

"I am not leaving," said the lady who had just spoken.

I turned and towering above me was the Holy Man. He had come to see me before after I had said things from dreams.

He had very long, black greasy hair and a beard. He came and picked me up and held me very near to his face. "I see your future. It has been promised, I see." I did not understand him. He smelt of sweat like the Tsarina but not of mice and there was also a curious scent like cooking cloves and pinecones and chocolate all mixed up. His face was white and thin. Then you looked into his eyes and thought you could see forever, a thousand leagues, into the endless forest, all the way to China and all in a glowing dark. You could not look away. It was not frightening but you knew, you just knew you should not be doing it, taking the step into the forest. He spoke again and his voice was deep and measured like a priest, "Kiss me. Kiss me, Pasha. When I came before we talked of power and how we distract ourselves with rosebuds and ballerinas and elephants."

I let him lean down and kiss me on the lips.

The lady shouted hoarsely:

"Get out, Rasputin! You are Satan's animal! Guards! We cannot have this madness in Russia, please God."

The Holy Man did not even seem to hear her. He smiled at me in the kindest way. He had been kind to me when he came to see me in the past, sometimes with others, teachers who said they wanted to learn from me, who argued with me, but the best times were when he came alone and put his arm around me and I felt calm and at peace. His hands warmed yours like the wonderful tiled stove in the Imperial Nursery kitchens. He had a deep voice that was brown like forest honey and made the world tremble but then he smiled like sunshine. I was not afraid of him and would have gone anywhere with him. He had an immense and gentle soul. He was the only adult to treat me as an equal or as if I had any value. I remember exactly his words as if he had written them on my most secret self, though at the time I did not fully understand.

"Remember what you told these dear ladies after your dreams? What you then repeated to me about the world being like an endless river of dark fire?"

"I do," I said.

"Well to myself and the learned others who came to see you, wise men, Magi, that was an image that explained the dark power of creation and our disintegrating modern times. The little houses you saw on the shores are our flimsy, ape-like ideas. All on our way to a murder! Our own. How deliciously funny. None of us escapes our fate. Not even a Tsar."

I nodded. I noticed the lady was trembling. The very WORDS were dangerous. Rasputin ignored her.

"With your brilliant image of the dark river you described how our lives really are, without recourse to boring gods and angels. Angels cannot stop the fire that is coming. The ancients used to prize the wisdom of children, those closer to birth being more at one and sensitive to the un-reasoning forces of the universe. The elders of the temple invited Jesus to talk with them. In so-called primitive Africa they still listen closely to special children, like yourself."

He stared deep into my eyes until it hurt.

"We may not see each other again in this world, so promise me something. Let us make a holy pact. A bargain. You must promise that you will try to discover if there is a meaning to life beyond the dark river, our pathetic mud huts on its banks and a miserable, ridiculous death. Do this, my child, and I guarantee you will find enormous happiness. Enormous![he used the word *ogromnyy*] This excitable lady thinks I am the Devil, or at least one of his black, twinkling imps, and, unlike God, the Devil always keeps his promises. If you do not do this I will take what used to be called your soul and crunch it down for my afternoon tea with French marzipan cakes, or the world will. Munch, munch! Do you trust me, my dear? Do you promise to find a meaning beyond the dark river? Do you swear?"

He was grinning and I laughed: "I swear," I said, and he kissed me on the lips again to seal the bargain.

The lady I was with screamed, began to make the sign of the cross, and fainted. The Imperial Nursery did not approve of public diabolic bargains involving their children, just private ones with childless couples.

Then with a booming laugh that echoed to the kitchens, Rasputin slipped away before the reluctant guards finally came.

The next morning I ate my meat pancakes at breakfast in silence while a boy across from me said the penalty for theft was having my arm cut off. The penalty for theft from the Tsar was to have all my limbs cut off and be thrown in the river, with curses, by the Peter and Paul Fortress. My miserable, ridiculous death was coming sooner than I, or even Rasputin, thought and without any happiness. A lovely girl who was my friend told the boy, who had a head cold, and whose nose was running with green snot, not to be so nasty. The girl and I had cuddled together in her dormitory bed like grown-ups. At that moment a man came to take me to the Tsar's study and I felt I was going to cry but bit my lip so I did not.

When I eventually saw the Tsar, I was ready to be dismembered. But he was in a very good mood.

The silver elephant he had accused me of stealing was on the desk in front of him with a red ribbon through a ring on its back. The Tsar put it in his pocket.

"I have had an idea," he said. He had a very boyish smile

this morning. He had several advisors in the room with him and they looked at me, a little askance. They appeared very worried at his idea of an idea.

I smiled at him and nodded. I don't think he had ideas very often.

"Come with me, little one. Bring him, bring him. Do not stand on ceremony."

The Selo palace was surrounded by beautiful gardens. It was built by Peter the Great and by his daughter Catherine who both spent time there and, in their passion for the exotic, established a menagerie to rival those in London, Paris and Berlin, said our tutors. The animals in the Imperial Zoo had a better time of it because they were not constantly being spied on and teased by the public. In Selo they lived a life of no wanting. They were purely there to be studied and drawn by a small number of scientists and artists and for the occasional polite amusement of the Imperial Family.

There was a delight on the Tsar's face that took him back to being a child again and in that moment I loved him very dearly. Today, he was wearing a peasant shirt, buttoned at the side of the neck and with a belt around his middle. Over this he wore a fur-lined greatcoat. There were dark rings under his eyes. I felt a sadness in him and a foreboding. He just wanted to play, as I did.

He sat down in the snow by the very large cage of an old lion that knew him. I sat on his greatcoat. He was so pleased to be there he kissed me, everyone kissed everyone three times on the cheek, but this was a tender kiss on the forehead and I was glad. The day was a cold one and there was a gentle sleeting but it did not seem to bother the Tsar. The cold did not upset the lion either and the huge cat put his head against the bars and, to my surprise, the Tsar reached in and tickled the cat's ears and his nose. The lion purred, so loud you felt it inside you.

"They're not like us," said the Tsar, gently. "They do not think like us," he said, and the lion purred louder at the sound of his voice. "Our brains select what we see and edit and exclude things. But the lion here lets in everything. That's why he's easily scared, easily angry, can behave strangely. He sees too much. If we could talk to him, if we had a common language, we would still not understand him because of how he sees the world. He sees it all at once and without any filter or time. There are people like that. Poets. Perhaps you are like that?"

He was silent and continued to play with the lion.

I plucked up courage and spoke.

"Please, sire. Are you going to have my hands and feet cut off and throw my body in the Neva River? For stealing your elephant? If so, I'd like to say goodbye to the princess first."

He laughed at this and so did all of his attendants but then he grabbed me and hugged me to him. Really hugged me passionately, with tears in his eyes.

He produced the silver elephant from his pocket and put the ribbon round my neck.

"It is now yours."

I looked at it, disbelieving.

Then I threw my arms around his neck and kissed him on the cheek.

"Oh, thank you, thank you, Papa!"

He laughed.

"I am not vexed with you at all, dear one. I'm not vexed. Indeed, you may be of great help to our family in the future. You may be of eternal help. But I want you educated away from St Petersburg. Away from the Imperial Family. You'll understand your relations to us better when you grow up."

He saw I was upset and he sent the others away and led me around the cages and animal and birdhouses, my little hand in his long, cold one. He was trying to smile down at me. I so wanted him to be my father in that moment.

At last, as the winter light was starting to fade, in an area of fields protected by a high wooden fence we came upon a herd of elephants. I liked the sound of the word in Russian. SION. Like the city of Jerusalem.

I was amazed at the great, grey creatures and their curtain-like ears. I had seen the tame Indian elephants in the circus but never anything like these. They had tusks as long as a lion and stood above us, massive as a house.

The ground shook as they walked, even with the cushion of snow.

There was a baby one and I laughed.

"These elephants are from Africa," said the Tsar, his breath showing like steam. "Their Latin name is *Loxodonta Africana*. In an African language they are called *Temba*." I wondered whether the Tsar wanted me to call him father. The Tsar liked all the children of the Imperial Nursery to call him father when he visited.

"Are they not very cold, sire?" I said. The elephants looked as if they were patiently waiting for the next train back to Africa.

He shook his head.

"They've been here since Peter the Great. They have warm stables now electrically heated and lit like the palace, which they go into when it is very cold. Just like human beings they become used to anything, don't they? Throw one an apple. These animals have never seen Africa but they carry it in their hearts and dreams. They are wild and no one can tame them, it is said, but they seem happy here. Two elephants were a gift to Peter the Great along with a black slave. An African. A remarkable man who became most educated and ended up as a general, not that all of those men are educated. We are trained not to expect the unexpected though Peter the Great always did. The black slave, the general, Gannibal, is the ancestor of our poet Pushkin for whom St Petersburg was a new Jerusalem. Look here. Pushkin!"

He reached for the little elephant around my neck that I was holding tight in both hands. I did not let go but he pushed on the trunk and it went up and a little piece of paper shot out from the elephant's bottom. I laughed. On the tiny paper was writing. He read it out:

> "I loved you without hope, a mute offender;
> What jealous pangs, what shy despairs I knew!
> A love as deep as this, as true, as tender,
> God grant another may yet offer you."

He shuddered. He then began to laugh to himself and I did not know what he had been talking about, I had no clue. Great things were going on I did not understand.

The nearest elephant put up his trunk and let out a trumpeting blast that made me jump and the Tsar laugh more. He rolled the little poem up and put it back in the elephant and clicked the trunk shut.

"When am I to go, sire? Please do not send me away. What exactly is your purpose for me?"

The Tsar then grabbed hold of my shoulders though did not look me in the eye.

"Elephants . . . Has anyone mentioned them to you?

Laughing at me? In French? Elephants? Ballerinas?" There was hurt in his eyes.

I thought it better not to reply and he sighed. I hid inside the word ELEPHANT.

His long back was then turned to me and he was suddenly walking away, surrounded quickly by his attendants and advisors. His advisors were excited but not in a good way and I saw that back, which had straightened among his beloved creatures, bend as if again under a great weight and the spring go out of his step.

He was helped into his greatcoat that he pulled around him.

There had been news from the fleet off Japan. I overheard the others talking, talking. There was no longer a fleet off Japan. Poor Tsar. I was sad for him. He did not understand, or had been distracted by elephants and rosebuds and ballerinas from the river of fire.

SIX

NATASHA WAS WOKEN by an alarm on her cell-phone and then there was the sound of the door phone buzzer at the apartment door. She got out of bed and pressed the speaker button.

"Mail man, got a parcel for you. Lemme in. Got to sign for it quick. Parcel for you, lady."

She pressed another button to let the man in downstairs.

She sighed, the parcel was probably for her talented and generous girlfriend, who worked in the Brill Building on 49th and whose parents owned the whole building on 20th as an investment. Natasha had told the girlfriend something about Paris. She said she did not want the man coming round, trying to get her back. Yet, she had dreamt about him just that night.

Dirty rain drizzled down the old, leaky skylight that had cracked panes here and there. She yawned and kissed her teddy bear, Demetrius, named after the first great librarian at Alexandria, that her mother had given her after Natasha's final row with her father a year and a half ago. She caught her reflection in a large mirror by the door: she had to get fitter. She thought of her dream of the man in Paris. She did not think she was fucked up about sex. She had had a very happy childhood, although perhaps one defining moment of power and embarrassment stuck in her mind. She had become infatuated with a neighbour's sensitive, poet son, who his father thought was gay and therefore made play football, which he hated. She had been very fond of the boy, though not in love with him and they kissed and caressed in the back of an old Ford pick-up truck until eventually things went all the way and it became their special place. One day his parents came back suddenly about an hour after they had gone out and Tad, as the boy was called, grabbed his clothes and ran out of the garage to head them off and switched off the lights. Unfortunately, he grabbed Natasha's stuff as well, her short, blue summer dress too, leaving her naked on the long, cold, torn leather back seat. She got out of the truck being careful where she put her bare feet in the chaotic garage. There was a lot of slamming of car doors outside but then the fluorescent lights all went on and she was face to face with Tad's father. She stood there in the unrelenting glare and the man had seemed to shrink. He was very like his son but bigger with a shock of black curly hair. He just stared at her among the racks of car magazines, old copies of *Playboy*, a gun rack with two shotguns and a rifle and another shotgun that had been taken apart on a bench, the mouldy head of a stuffed deer, college football pennants, the smell of engine grease, old hunting boots, broken fishing rods and tins of Valvoline Motor Oil and brake fluid. Natasha was still flushed from lovemaking and Tad's father quickly threw her the blue dress his son had taken. Every time she stood naked she thought of the power of that moment. Before that she had felt self-conscious, embarrassed and afraid in the male gaze. That night she not only stood taller than Tad's father, she was stronger inside. Natasha had half-smiled at him, and, in a moment of inspiration she could not explain, put her hands on her hips. Tad's father's disapproving, terrified look, before he fled, seemed to affirm her apartness and the fact she was already a published poet and an outer-space alien to people like him and his dumb Americana fetish objects, and that was why she had dreamed of breaking totally away with the man in Paris. She had not told any of her friends about the encounter. The only person she had told was the man in Paris and he had been silent for a long time. He then said: "If you spell your name the wrong way round it becomes Ah, Satan."

Natasha surveyed herself again in the mirror. Maybe she was in good shape, she was too critical, and pictured the face of a man she had recently met in New York. But she wasn't dating after what happened in Paris, not yet. Maybe she should go back to ChiChiChica. But that would mean going back to Harvard. She rubbed a white scar on her hip bone. That was Paris too.

There was a knock at the door.

"Parcel for you. Have not got all the days of creation." The accent was foreign and the man out of breath.

She went back into the bedroom and wound a sheet around her but then hesitated and put an old woollen dressing gown over it and went to the door and took the key off the hook. It was one of those doors that lock in the centre and cantilever bolts spider out to the doorframe. She peered through the little spy hole in the door. She was taking no chances. A tall man with a small head, an even smaller hat, a bow tie and a long tweed coat was holding a brown paper parcel wrapped up with hairy string.

No one wrapped up packages like that these days. Natasha believed the deliveryman to be innocent and turned the key in the lock. When she pulled open the door a little he smiled, showing yellowing teeth, and pushed the package through. The brown paper smelt of summer rain.

"Do you want me to sign?" she said. He nodded and she signed. The man laughed, stared at her in wonder and nodded and then ran down the stairs.

"I need a sign. Don't we all?" he shouted back up the stairs.

Natasha was interested in signs too.

After finishing her doctorate at Harvard on Nabokov she had ended up for a brief moment as number two in that university's peerless library where time stopped in a good way when she was a student. Nabokov had been a fan of a crazy flyer called Dunne who had proposed that our experience of time as a straight line is an illusion brought about by human consciousness. He argued that past, present and future were continuous in a higher-dimensional reality and we only experience them sequentially because of our mental perception of them, a theory that now fitted in with Quantum Physics. Nabokov had been converted when he realised dreams, in a period of rapid eye movement lasting only instants, can seem like years and in this world of distorted time we may glimpse the future flow back to the present. In one dream his Uncle Basil, who had left him a fortune wiped out by the revolution, appeared to him and said in a matter-of-fact mutter: "I shall come back to you as Harry and Kuvyrkin." Forty-two years after the fortune's loss, Harris and Kubrick Pictures approached Nabokov with an attractive offer of a handsome sum to buy the film rights to *Lolita*, at once restoring much of his lost fortune. Natasha had felt on the edge of a great breakthrough, but no one was that interested.

One day, after the release of sexual rapture, when they were still in New York, the man in Paris had teased her relentlessly about the absurd possibility of hiding as a librarian, like Lara in *Dr Zhivago*. He quoted Heidegger at her and said she had once dwelt in her own poetry and now was considering dwelling in other people's books: "You are an artist, Natasha. You show the world anew. What does it take to make you realise this?"

The other thing he teased her about was being in love with Pushkin and that the duellist would come and kill him one day. Natasha had said she hoped so. A week ago, she had gone out for a meeting with an old teacher from Sacramento University. His new book was called *The Migration Myth*, about how migration was not only good but was one of the most important phenomena of the century, the other two being the End of Work and Climate Change. He was a sweet, if troubled, man and she had not had an affair with him in Sacramento or even kissed him because he was married with two cute-as-buttons boys. He said he was surprised how much she had changed.

Natasha came from a small town outside Sacramento and had always wanted to change things for the better, like every-one in air-head California. But to do so people needed to realise you had to get the books in order to see where you were. Her mother's sister had worried about Natasha coming to New York because she too readily told people what she thought. "Never open the door to strangers or accept things from people you don't personally know. Or say stuff like you do. Certainly not to strangers." She said strange stuff early on, like the boy in the story. AMERICA DON'T DREAM NO MORE, Natasha had told her prissy, suit-and-bow-tie Third Grade teacher, aged nine, and, ONLY POETS SHOULD BE PRESIDENT, sounding like her father and his friends. She did not explain to her aunt that most times she was a total stranger to herself. On the shelf above her bed she had put a photograph of her father and mother smiling impossibly wide when she had become an All American Track Star at college. She was smiling too. It had felt phoney. She had to force that smile even though she wanted the award. She wanted more. She wanted everything.

One of the things she had found among her father's papers, which she had not expected, was Dunne's book *An Experiment with Time*. Her father was a mathematician, not a physicist, but was interested in Heisenberg's Uncertainty Principle, that one can never measure anything without changing it, which led on to much weirder things he used to talk about over cornflakes at breakfast, about energy and protons which appeared from nowhere. It had to do with the multidimensional nature of time and infinity, he said. "Once you start talking of infinity, the natural laws go out of the window." When she was a little girl, her father, James, wore lumberjack shirts and played the guitar and had the sweetest smile, but after a small paper in an obscure journal he was snapped up by the US military and in three years became thin, withdrawn and distracted. He could not sleep and her mother, Cecilia, tried to tidy round him and go on as normal. He did not, could not, talk about his work but developed obsessions, probably to try to ground himself and get back to the human, and the major one was for the novelist Steinbeck and his book about the Great Depression in Monterey, *Cannery Row*. At times her father, who was sometimes called Doc, thought he was the marine biologist in the book. For emotional not investment reasons he bought a crazy hotel in Monterey, which Steinbeck had written about, an old canning factory outside town full of drunks and street people, where her father went to stay alone and talk and play guitar more and more, without her mother. Then one day her once amazing father James fell from a second-floor window. No one thought this strange as he had a reputation for clumsiness and other-worldliness. Her mother went to the hotel, which she had only visited once and tried to make light of, where she found the suicide note the police had overlooked. She had burned the four single-spaced pages because they contained "terrible things" she refused to tell the police or anyone. All she would say was that he could not be part of the world's destruction. She threw these ashes with his into the Pacific. Her mother hardly said another word for a month, then all of a sudden started talking faster, not making sense, and began to run for no reason, including into traffic. She had to go into a home. In the home she said nothing at all.

Natasha pulled open the brown paper parcel, which contained another "packet" of the boy's story, and there did not seem to be a note. She took off the dressing gown, threw the sheet on the bed and pulled on some clothes. She sat on the bed and started to read the photocopied, mostly light-duck-egg blue pages in purple ink, though a few, here and there, were white, all written in a clear old-fashioned, copperplate hand. Had someone read her dissertation and therefore sent her this? She had no Russian ancestral connections she knew of except her Christian name. Her surname was Foster. At school she was embarrassed about her name, but her parents never really did explain and she attributed it probably to an obscure composer friend or perhaps her father's fascination with Russian literature. She had always thought her family originally came from a pretty and dead town in England, but it did not matter to her. Once you were threaded through the eye of California's needle, all identity was lost. There was no dwelling there. Just Freeways. She had always said she liked that.

This next "packet" of the manuscript astonished Natasha. She warmed to it. She read it as the rain drummed on the skylight, then placed it neatly on the bed and stared at the pages. Why had the typed pages been emailed to her at first, then the same section of the handwritten photocopied manuscript delivered? Was it to prove the story was true? Or perhaps it was some kind of sophisticated joke her friend, who lent her the apartment, who worked in the Brill Building, was playing on her. The kind of people who worked there always had time for things like that. It was, after all, the home of *Saturday Night Live*. Natasha tried not to watch television. One girl's job, her friend had told her, was to look after Paul Simon's New York wigs. Natasha did not understand such people. They might as well be from another planet.

After lunch she picked up the partial manuscript again.

Who writes what in its total form would be hundreds and hundreds of pages by hand, not typed, not word processed, for fun? And all of the Russian names were right and the locations, she had begun to check. She had an overwhelming sense of the power and, at least, fictional truth of the story. Even with what she had read. The boy's story deeply affected her. She felt he was trying to tell her the secret of the world.

It was then that Natasha's phone started to vibrate.

A process of downloading was beginning. She tried to switch off the download but dropped the phone on the wooden floor and it shot under a heavy dresser. When she finally reached it, the download was complete.

She had a new app. It was an elephant with large ears on a blue background. So, perhaps the story was a joke.

She scooped up the brown paper of the parcel to put it in the trash and a card fell out. It was an invitation to a tea party on the Upper East Side. The invitation was both in English and in Russian.

"Darling Natasha, Little one! Expert on our literature. It will be our great honour to see you for tea and cakes in our apartment on Friday, August 25, at 6.30pm. With love and hope, Nadya."

There was no telephone number or email address, but a

picture of an icon was reassuring, she supposed. No one had called her "Little one" in a long time.

She picked up her phone with the new elephant app and put it down again. It took her an hour to decide but eventually she clicked on the elephant.

Natasha's phone then started to make a strange, ethereal, singing sound.

SEVEN

THE UNEXPECTED MANUSCRIPT: PACKET IV

TWO WEEKS AFTER my meeting with the Tsar in
his private zoo, I had been driving in a heavy wooden
sleigh for two days and nights through thick forest with trees
so weighed down with snow their branches were twisting and
breaking, like bent old women, or witches, and then onto the
endless steppe when I first saw the palace, my destination and
new home, in the pink light of a gentle, windless dawn. My
face and nose were sore with the cold. My eyes ached. Yet I
was beyond glad. I felt a joy at that new dawn. The new moon
and stars were still bright in the glowing, raspberry sky.

After the excitement of the Christmas ball, here was where
time stopped.

In the distance was the place I knew later as Mikhailovskoye,
which was in the Urals, many miles from a town called Perm,
and not quite Siberia, where I had read there were strange and
wonderful beasts, half-human, half-animal. And I wanted to
see a tiger, not in a circus or a zoo, but walking about in its
own forest because I had read a storybook about one. TIGER
was a thrilling word. This was a real adventure for me as
none of the ladies from the Imperial Nursery were allowed
to come with me. All of the women who dealt with me had
cried and the princess from the ball came to see me off on the

special station at Selo, a terminus of red carpeted platforms and polished brass door handles just for the Imperial Family, the journey had begun by rail, and the princess cried too. I cried, but inside I was excited.

I looked up out of my ice-stiff wrappings of wolf furs and I shouted to the sleigh driver that I was sitting next to: "Where is Siberia?"

He glanced down at me and pointed with his whip beyond the palace.

"I want to go there one day," I said, and the man turned as he brought the horses to a halt. His moustache and beard had frozen on his face. He was so covered in snow he seemed to have become part of the last smoking, whirling blizzard.

"I'm sure it will be so if you have been sent this far at so young an age," he said, with a smirk, taking a swig of vodka from a flask by him and continuing on.

At first sight the frozen palace seemed even bigger and grander than the one at Tsarskoye Selo. There was an elegant bridge too, over a river.

Then I looked again.

"But that's . . ." I began.

The driver laughed.

"Not what it seems? What is?"

When we got nearer I saw clearly that the bridge was not a real bridge but a single, painted wall made to seem like a bridge.

Instead, we went over the frozen stream by way of a ford. This did not dismay me at all as I was eager to get to the palace. And I thought after a few days on this adventure and punishment I was going back to St Petersburg to take up my life in the gold and marble palaces again. The sleigh took me closer and closer and I pushed back the wolf-skin cover to see better and leaned forward.

Before me was a great house, part European, part Russian with delicate towers and tulip domes.

The horse slowed.

"No!" I cried out. My voice shrill and making smoke in the cold air.

The sleigh driver laughed again. It was not a nice laugh.

When I realised what I was really looking at I nearly fell and the sleigh driver had to grab me.

The entire palace was a fake.

It, too, was painted onto one brick wall.

The single wall that masqueraded as the great house was a truly huge construction. A hundred yards long and at least fifty feet high, it towered above us but was only one brick deep at some levels. In places it was cracked and vegetation now grew out between the sightless windows. When you were close by the hastily built wall you wondered why you had ever been fooled. I felt heartbroken.

At the back of the wall there was no pretence. The brick was not painted, nor were the wooden buttresses.

There were three log cabins, similar to those in St Petersburg that were said to be where Peter the Great had lived when he was building the city on a swamp. The snow around these three cabins was yellowish and smelled. Several pigs rummaged in the midden and there was the reek of boiling cabbage from a chimney. The waste from all three cabins froze before it drained into a nearby stream.

A man with round spectacles and furious dark eyes under a Jacobin hat limped quickly towards our halted sleigh. Behind him were two maids and a collection of serfs in white belted smocks that scurried and looked sideways with heads down as serfs do, except one had the face of a goblin and drew a finger across his throat and a very large man with a long white beard, who I took to be the family father, winked at me. The man with spectacles, whose whole body was twisted, spoke.

"Greetings, Alexei Nikolaevich,' he said, and I was surprised at the name. It was the name of the crown prince, the Tsarevich, the heir to the Imperial throne. I thought it must be a joke and we were playing games. "I am Monsieur Hippolyte," he continued. "I'm to be your tutor in Languages and Mathematics and all the usual subjects. I'm new here like you. Do not be offended by the stink, we'll do something about that."

It was at that point I heard the cry of a parrot in one of the huts.

"The bird has offended too," said M. Hippolyte. "He was saying subversive things in a café on Nevsky Prospect and like us was frogmarched here by the Okhrana, the secret police, who were at the Christmas ball. They thought I was your tutor in the Imperial Nursery. The parrot is fortunate not to have been sent to Siberia as are we all. We thank you."

The sleigh driver laughed and I thought it better not to say I wanted to go to Siberia one day.

I got down off the sleigh and walked towards my new tutor. He was restless as a river eel and had a small, trimmed beard. He put out his hand and I knew I should put out mine.

Then M. Hippolyte glanced slightly to his left with a weary frown, but it was too late.

I did not even hear the horse behind me as a strong arm scooped me up and I thundered away onto the steppe in the growing light. Whether I liked it or not I had to hold on to the rider and he to me.

A handsome face with a long moustache smiled down. He

49

had light curly hair and wide cheekbones and a very amused spark in his eye. I had seen him at the palace, one of the young men dancing with the blue-eyed princess. The horse was colossal and we were a long way from the ground, still galloping.

We headed straight for a group of serfs who gazed up from splitting logs and started to say their prayers.

At the last moment before he reached them the man drew his sword and plucked a scarf off a screaming woman's head.

With a flick of the wrist he then cut the scarf in two pieces and it fell to the snow. Then he screamed with pain and dropped the sword. "My back!"

He pulled the horse to a stop. He was wearing a cavalry jacket, a fur-lined pelisse, with one arm hanging fashionably loose over his left shoulder. At rest, his horse did not move an inch. Its nostrils sent up clouds of steam.

"Guess what I'm going to teach you?" he said with a laugh, but still in pain. And after a serf handed him the sword, which the man sheathed, we hurtled back to the huts. "Guess what's going to be more useful? Learnt any more French poems or other sedition?"

When he deposited me back at M. Hippolyte's feet the Frenchman was pretending a yawn. "That was Antov. He claims to be a Cossack. With a wounded back. How did he get that wound?"

I shook hands with M. Hippolyte. I had a fear of losing myself in other people, especially strangers. It scared me more than the horse ride, but afterwards I had not lost my soul, or whatever I imagined. There were orphans in the Imperial Nursery who feared they were losing themselves when they went to the toilet, especially the new flushing ones. I was glad the parrot was there but doubted if it was the right one. The young titled ladies who visited the nursery said the Okhrana always arrested the wrong people because SECRET policemen do not have to get things right.

"Get him inside," said Antov, worried. "He looks frozen." They hurried me into the largest of the huts and propped me against a massive blue and white, Dutch tiled stove, exactly like one in the kitchen at the Imperial Nursery. I took off my clothes and the two men helped me, all the time the blood returning to my extremities and an unbelievable pain gripped my hands and feet and in particular my ears in the warmth. A tear came to my eye, but because of the stove, not the pain. I was homesick for what was not even a home, the Imperial Nursery, as Antov bathed my fingers and toes with methylated spirits and I was given tea and a tiny glass of vodka that warmed my heart. I traced the story, the story of Peter the Great, the Shipwright of Saardam, depicted on the tiles on the stove with my fingers, as I had in the nursery kitchen. The two men frowned at the whiteness of my left big toe and Antov took out a knife. Then M. Hippolyte leant towards me and laughed: "Don't worry. We are not used to such cleanliness. It's not frostbite. We will not have to cut it off!"

The next twelve years of my life I spent with the two of them. They did not know how to bring up a child and M. Hippolyte sent away to St Petersburg for many books while I used to wake to see Antov staring down at me with what approached panic, like a new mother who finds herself rocking a cradle for the first time with a crazed monkey inside. It slowly dawned on me that they, too, were held responsible for the words on the piece of paper. LE TSAR DOIT MOURIR. They were as much prisoners of a whim of a weak man and his mad wife as I was, but they never bore me one moment's grudge.

At first, I made the mistake of thinking M. Hippolyte

was the less belligerent of my two tutors until, on the second night, an argument broke out. It was over nothing at all, like so many arguments. I was sitting on a bed in the main cabin and both men were smoking Turkish cheroots and drinking by the log fire, which scalded your front yet made your back seem more freezing, even when the stove was working. On the floor were oriental rugs with gorgeous curlicues and a miss-match of old, mainly red-upholstered gilded furniture that looked as if it had been looted from a palace. A narrow, polished-wood grandfather clock towered beside the fireplace. The hour and minute hands were stuck eternally at half-past-five on the brass clock face - tea time, said Antov - though the determined mechanism ticked loudly on and even played a little polka every hour. Antov further amused himself and me by making faces in a polished silver samovar by a huge tea pot with a tea cosy in the shape of a ship, a tall-masted clipper. There were old books everywhere that gave off a chocolate smell above the incense of cheroots and pinewood. The clock ticked and time hung as heavy as the snow on the trees. We all were quickly missing the life that we had thought stretched magnificently in front of us before we came to this Potemkin house. The construction was a lie, a fib, an illusion, explained M. Hippolyte, that got its name from the fake villages, often only made from cardboard, that Catherine the Great's lover, Grigory Potemkin, moved around by barge to impress and swindle her when he was governor of Crimea. The name M. Hippolyte called our home, 'Mikhailovskoye', was itself fake and ironic, and the name of the house near St Petersburg where the poet Pushkin was exiled for duelling. The argument on that night between M. Hippolyte and Antov was whether a blue flower the serfs had described in the summer meadows in front of the house was a forget-me-not or a damsel's eye.

"You are not used to the country. You know nothing of flowers. You have no estates," said Antov.

M. Hippolyte did not look up from his book.

"My estate is in the realm of learning."

"Are you calling me an ignoramus?"

"You came on the idea. Perhaps you are happy with it? If the cap fits."

"I am used to giving forget-me-nots to ladies. They would just want to forget looking at you."

"Oh, how witty," said M. Hippolyte, starting to colour.

"I don't suppose you've been with a woman since you were shot up in that duel. Were you hit in the balls? Did it matter?"

Then, without warning, Antov drew his sabre, which was by his chair, and swished it past M. Hippolyte's head, cutting off a small piece of his hat.

"Ha. You may start a new fashion!"

At this, M. Hippolyte leapt up. He drew a sword out of his stick like a wizard and, while Antov was laughing, marked his cheek with the épée. I then hid under the bed as they tried to kill each other, there was nothing fake about their battles, M. Hippolyte having the better of the fight until the housekeeper called the serfs who, after asking God and the Tsar's permission in a small prayer, pinned both men down.

Later, I asked M. Hippolyte about his former, near fatal, duel several times but then relented as I realised it was ill-mannered. I had learned about the poet Pushkin's death, defending the honour of his wife.

For the next decade and more, my childhood in many ways could not have been more idyllic. I loved M. Hippolyte and Antov.

I grew into a teenager galloping with Antov or sometimes with both of them because the Frenchman was a superb horseman, despite his injuries. I knew every animal and plant in the region and could name all the flowers. I even loved the fake palace. There was a growing, boundless joy in me. For a dare with one of the serf boys I climbed the fake palace wall and walked along the top. I adored the endless sea of grass in summer and each sunrise made me uncontrollably happy. I liked to walk through the fields of high grass, the heads seemingly too heavy for the stalks, marching towards the horizon in ranks of dark gold. When I strode through the stems now and again a doe would stick her head up and then bounce away, causing others to run too. Near to the cabins a weighted fragrance hung over the flowerbeds, moved constantly by an opera of large black bees. The half-naked serf boys took the horses down to the river for a bath, followed by the giggling serf girls, as golden orioles, a bird I knew from a book in the Imperial Nursery, made their liquid, three-noted calls in the trees. The Chinese thought of them as a bird of the best sort of heaven.

Then my body led me to seek another form of paradise.

The serf girls joined the boys in the stream, standing naked on the rocks in the middle, as the red sun went down.

I was restless, restless, restless. I went to the river every day.

One of the boys, Sasha, taught me to swim. He let me sit next to the tall girl, his sister, on the rock. I tried to talk to her but was so nervous the words did not come. But then, one day, the others left us and she kissed me on the lips. My breath deserted me. I was cross-eyed with surprise. I was turned to both stone and fire. At first it was only a polite kiss. The next moment her strong tongue was probing mine. "Come with me," she said. "I have something to show you."

We went into a bower where a robin played among the

fallen leaves and lay down together and she put her hands on what the ladies in the Imperial Nursery called my weenie and now was not weenie at all. In fact it was so hard, it seemed about to burst, and I cried out and she laughed.

She held me.

She took my hardness into her large mouth. She was not beautiful but I found my very soul flowing into her. I swallowed. Her breasts were quite perfect and her nipples erect. In between her legs was dark, mysterious, rasping, curly hair. She pulled me towards her with her rough hands and I was inside her. I was consumed by her fire and wanted to burn more.

"I love you. I will write you poetry," I said.

She smiled.

"I cannot read."

"I can read them! To tell you what I feel!"

"My father would rather you steal brandy and cigars and other luxuries from your teachers. We can be together every day. Let me show you another way."

She did and I became a thief for her. Her name was Masha.

I wondered if this was part of the world one made for oneself, by the river of dark fire.

When I was not with Masha, or Sasha, I watched the wind, like the hand of God, ripple the surface of the long grass in June and longed to be able to write about everything with intimacy like the poets I was reading. I often took the Pushkin poem out of the little silver elephant I wore around my neck and read it aloud, wondering what the word *Fumoo* engraved on the side meant. I had not really understood the word TOUT, everything, before I rode on those plains. I was beginning to belong.

Everything was crowding into my head at once, like

looking into the face of Attic Pan. Every tree and brook alive with power, with energy.

There was open woodland and pasture and then forest near the house, but to the south the steppe was unbounded and it was mine. Mine! I felt I was free. To me the land was an endless and precious domain that was all mine and equally belonged to everyone else. As I grew, I was up in the morning before the birds and riding out into the dawn. I delighted in the immensity of the horizons that scared others, in particular the serfs, who really feared one could disappear where the land met the sky in a hazy indistinction. It was in those border-lands monsters and witches lurked, but I did not care. I was in love with all my world, good and bad.

I galloped towards the morning star, my heart bursting and deer scattering ahead. To roam seemed to be in the nature of man and I did not have any real idea of Russia, except from my early schoolbooks. At times I got down from my horse and looked at it all. The vastness filled my head so completely it hurt.

There were other times I wept. I was sure I was different and that was why I had been sent away. I was as different as the Tsar's lion.

"You do see too much, my boy," said M. Hippolyte. "You must learn to filter it all through the prism of learning. But you must always be sincere."

Antov laughed: "Yes, once you can fake sincerity you will have all Russia at your feet. Personally, I think you are becoming a good Cossack."

M. Hippolyte shook his head. "You are just another bored and foppish nobleman, Antov. You were only put in charge of the Cossacks so they could blame someone when there was one massacre too many."

They then began to throw books at each other and made me laugh. I never quite knew when they were joking. Even when they talked about the faraway war in Europe.

Antov approved of my rides and encouraged me to go as far as I liked. Before my sixteenth birthday we went on a three-week expedition that actually took us into Siberia. We had to put our horses on a train and set off into the spring, Antov telling me all about the ladies of St Petersburg. We stopped at a place with thick forest and soon we had many deer, too many to take home. Antov even complimented me on my lack of emotion when taking my shots. This was quite at odds with what was going on inside me. I did not like to kill animals. I had to put myself apart. "Do not overdo such manly cold heartedness with the ladies. You are allowed to enjoy yourself sometimes," he laughed.

We had taken down our camp and were about to start for home when out of nowhere there was an orange flash and a huge tiger was on the back of Antov's horse before he was. It was more fury than creature. I had my rifle in my hands and the cat turned towards me and in his eyes and in his sheer rage I saw all that is the wilderness come together in the word TIGER. But I could not hide in the bright orange word as the reality snarled and spat. A shiver ran like lightning through me as the cat growled and all its face was creased into hatred. Every hair and whisker of it seemed to want to kill me and the spell was only broken when the horse screamed, the tiger's claws deep in its side. I was shaking, I tried to level my rifle. I saw Antov had the animal in his sights, he could not miss, but he turned his gun to the sky and pulled the trigger. The creature was gone. I was so relieved I burst into tears and hugged him.

"Why did you let the tiger go?" I asked Antov later as we travelled back to the railway.

"I do not know."

"I looked into the tiger's face. It was strange," I said. "It was realer than real. It was . . ."

"Yes, I know," said Antov, quickly. But there was a note in his voice that he did not want to know more.

We had left a deer for the cat so that she would not follow us. At least that was Antov's explanation. I think it was more in the way of an offering as in old religions. The serfs left flowers at brooks or tied things to trees in the same way.

Antov was silent for a long time, which was not usual. He had patched up the deep cuts on his horse and was walking by it. He was too proud to ride one of the mules we had hired. At last he said: "There is something holy about a creature who is so free, so beautiful, don't you think? The Cossacks say if you kill one you take its courage. I believe the opposite. I believe if you kill something like that you kill what is wild and vital in yourself. I think it is most unlucky. But, please, my friend, do not tell M. Hippolyte about this or I will be teased for all time for being a gentle Cossack."

When we stopped to camp by the railway line he gave me his precious Cossack dagger. "For being brave and being in awe. A brave man who does not know beauty is not a man at all, my little prince." I felt a connection with his ideas and knew the pity of it, because with Antov it would not last.

A library was established in one of the huts to start with and then three more huts were built and I read all the books in them, brimming with beautiful WORDS, and talked to M. Hippolyte and Antov about them. Antov maintained, whatever M. Hippolyte said, that he had been the Cossack leader of the Amur and Ussuri Cossack Host and he was capable of flying into a rage if anyone told him he was stupid. Though I was not sure if this was in defence of the fact he was not really a Cossack at all. He constantly sought to out-read and out-debate M. Hippolyte as he tried to outride, outshoot and out fence anyone. I loved them both. Yet I was aware of the often well-hidden frost in their hearts. When a serf killed one of Antov's fine horses by giving it too much cold water after a gallop, Antov beat him half-to-death with his whip made of a rope threaded through cherry-wood blocks. M. Hippolyte talked about it afterwards over a pipe and vodka.

"You are an animal, Antov."

"I know," said Antov.

The very next day I caught Antov painting a small watercolour for one of his girlfriends at a nearby estate. He wrote poetry too.

All the while, more books were being sent to me and I was cramming myself with knowledge and debating with the two of them. "Do you think Byron a better poet than Pushkin?" The strange voices of my dreams, which I shouted when awake, initially were beaten back by book learning, though I began to understand the things I said and not be afraid of them, or my ability to make sense of the world. One day a chessboard arrived and Antov taught me the moves and after a few weeks I could beat him. M. Hippolyte then condescended to play me and I finally beat him too, by which time they had both become less interested in the game. Mostly, while I read, they sat in front of the great fire drinking tea from the eternally refreshed samovar, their polished leather boots almost together, talking of how, perhaps, one of them might return to St Petersburg to plead the case for both of them, and me, as the grandfather clock TICKED time away, like a peasant hewing wood. They went through all the influential people that they knew and who was in and out of favour and who they should write to. "I served under Grigory Rementov, he will help me. All exiles think their condition temporary, a hiccup, a mistake, something that is going to be rectified, I suppose. But tomorrow we must do something." They poured themselves another vodka or French brandy. They never wrote a single letter or went up to St Petersburg because they knew it was futile and they accepted it like serfs, but there was no harm in dreaming in between working hard at what they were sent to do.

In the sitting room the clock TICKED louder. They somehow managed to purchase or find a billiard table and played billiards and the ivory balls clicked. They sat down again and re-read a month-old newspaper. The clock TICKED. The time was always half-past-five. Tea time!

And at each hour when it chimed its little polka it timed their boredom and their regret.

"Exile is a cold dish. It is a condition that is part of the Russian soul, internal and overseas," said M. Hippolyte one day, and they were both silent for a long time. It was made even worse after my sixteenth birthday by news from St Petersburg and Moscow as the world started to fall apart.

The serfs always seemed to know the latest news before we did and I liked going into the serfs' hut and asking them things. They knew I was of the Imperial Family, a prince perhaps, but they did not treat me differently and I loved talking to the parrot, whom they had named Lenin. I regarded them as servants who were friends, while Antov and M. Hippolyte thought of them as serfs, even though officially serfdom had been abolished.

Sometimes when I went into the serfs' hut the girls were dancing on the tables in their bare feet in red skirts while I fed the grey parrot apple and he shouted, "Workers of the world unite," and "The Tsar must die," in Russian. The serfs had taught him some very bad words too.

The girls were often dirty and the hut was a fantastic jumble with pigs and chickens and kittens inside despite M. Hippolyte's strict orders to them to wash their quarters and themselves. One girl gave me a kiss and another a drink of vodka that went up my nose and everyone laughed. Another girl gave me a kiss with vodka in her mouth and Masha hit her and swore. "He is my prince!" The man who looked like a goblin had a vodka still around the back that supplied Antov and M. Hippolyte, who never came into the serfs' hut. One wall was colourfully draped in fabric and another was hung with drying mushrooms and peppers. I had started to want to get closer to them.

At times, it seemed easier than with Antov and M. Hippolyte because they were so concerned about me.

The countryside became more dangerous after my sixteenth birthday, on the second of April, picked for me by the ladies at the Imperial Nursery because it was the holy day of St Titus the Wonderworker, who had been a child prodigy. You would have to be completely stupid not to see the sudden explosions of violence. I dreamed more than once of the dark river of fire, which seemed to be all around me and endless. It was so frightening I could not breath. INFINITY. I woke at night shouting, THE TSAR MUST DIE. Antov and Hippolyte must have heard, but they did not say a thing. One night I saw Rasputin standing at the end of my bed, although he was already dead. THERE ARE NO LIMITS TO HELL, were more words I shouted, and shouted. NOTHING

IS TRUE. EVERYTHING IS PERMITTED. I saw the poor German moral philosopher, said to be on the train with my parents, with his bushy moustache and his pearl-buttoned, grey silk double-breasted waistcoat, trying to make sense of the universe, as he was eaten alive by the singing wolves. I had thought such things might leave me. Despite everything, I had begun to accept our estate as my home. No calls to go back to St Petersburg or even Moscow had ever arrived. I had come to belong in the sweet sunshine on new leaves and light blue wood anemones.

Then, before Easter, M. Hippolyte and I went to a spring fair on an estate forty miles away and we rode there and our serfs followed on a large cart. I was glad Masha was able to come and snatched glances of her and her long bare legs. A manager of the Imperial Estates, a muddy-eyed man called Dimitri Saporov, organised the fair every year for his freed serfs and poor free tenants, although certain gentry came to share in the pickled tomatoes, little pies of cooked pike, vodka and foaming beer and see the peasant girls dance in bright red and black and green shawls with flowers in their hair.

Antov had been away in Perm, the nearest city, the only city, which he often said was the most boring place on earth, where people queue to watch paint dry or horses urinate, and we saw him pushing through the laughing, drinking crowd. Antov had a newly blacked left eye.

"I had unforeseen difficulties."

"With a woman?" said M. Hippolyte, chuckling in his wheezy way. They both went to Perm for women, as if to a bread shop. One mayor of that city had once built our Potemkin House, thinking Catherine the Great might pass by. She didn't.

"They set on me in an alley," said Antov, without explanation.

"I am sure you killed them all, you being a Cossack," said M. Hippolyte.

But Antov was shaking his head. He grabbed M. Hippolyte's hand.

"Listen, my friend. My black eye is nothing. But this is serious. Dimitri has gone mad and is to hang six serfs for stealing grain. By law he cannot do that." The smile went immediately from M. Hippolyte's face and Antov turned to me.

"You see those horses over there? Go and swap the saddles of those two and then tether them away from each other. It will cause a diversion. We can then, perhaps, stop this madness." I did as Antov said. I looked up from fastening the girth of the second horse as I heard shouting. At one end of the fair I saw what seemed at first like another stall but was a wooden platform under a strong branch of a tree. On the platform stood six men and six ropes hung down from a beam between two supports. A priest was there and retainers, private policemen, from Dimitri's estate. Nooses were being put around the men's necks. I knew that since Catherine's time serfs could not be hung by their owners or landlords.

Then there was a cry of "horse-thieves".

To steal a horse was worse than stealing a wife or a child to poor people. It took many years to earn a horse.

"The saddle of Dimitri is on my horse," came another shout. "He stole it. He is the guilty one. He is the guilty one that hangs our brothers!"

It was all that was needed. The spark on that warm afternoon. It went far past being a diversion. The crowd grabbed the manager of the Imperial Estates, who shouted it was a mistake, and rushed him to a little green by the side of the fair, beating him as they went with bits of wood and pitchforks. Dimitri screamed as a man from a butcher's stall cut off both of his hands with a cleaver and blood spurted. "My ring. My gold ring!" he wailed, as a nimble serf snatched it from the quivering middle finger of Dimitri's severed right hand. Others pulled down his trousers and the crowd, the whole crowd, laughed a low rumbling laugh as a man took down one of the sharpened pine tent poles, eight-foot long, made from the trunk of a Christmas tree, and I thought they were going to beat him with it and he shrieked louder as his hands were thrown to the dogs. But another man brought a hammer and they all laughed more as the pine pole was hammered up the manager of the Imperial Estates' anus and came out by his shoulder and they raised him up, wriggling, still alive. Another man was being beaten and I saw one of Dimitri's men push the serfs with ropes around their necks off the platform before he and the other estate retainers were brought down by the crowd. I saw our own head serf, Grigor, standing back with his arms folded. He caught my eye and nodded, as if giving permission, and Antov dragged me away as the whole village exploded in destructive fury.

"What . . . ?" I said.

"That is *samosud*," said Antov. "The people's judgement." He looked over his shoulder as we galloped away.

"I caused it. Switching saddles," I said. I was shaking with fear and sure damnation. "I caused it!"

"No," said M. Hippolyte, drawing his horse level. "That darkness is always there. It's just mostly we choose not to notice. Antov was only trying to cause a diversion, an argument, so Dimitri would go home."

"Are they dead, Antov? Surely they cannot be dead?" I said later that evening.

Twenty people, including a priest, had died at the spring fair and the militia had to be called in. Dimitri and two of his men had been impaled on poles. One man was still alive and the militia had cut his throat.

What followed was not a discussion about whether or not they were dead but whether they were in Hell. Antov said he did not believe in Hell.

"When I was at the academy one of the tutors, a German who had a bullet still in the side of his head they could not get out, said Hell was made up by the Etruscans because they were always getting beaten by Rome. If you think you're going to Heaven you do not try and fight the Roman invader, you just sit back and get killed. But if there is a hell, a hot place with demons and pitchforks and an eternal sea of fire you might be more inclined to put up a fight to avoid it. It used to make the German laugh until his face went all red around the bullet and he started hitting the table." M. Hippolyte shook his head. "Those six poor serfs being hung were already in Hell. They did not even own themselves. They were an entertainment at a country fair. The strange thing is that if there is an afterlife they all agreed, by stupidly and fatalistically pleading guilty, to the terms of their death even if hanging was proscribed under the law, so, I am quite sure they're all in Hell. I wonder which they'll prefer? After Russia, at least they'll find the realms of Satan to be warm. Many of us are in our own Hell, most often of our own making, and we accept it as quite normal." This made Antov slap his hip and for once they were almost in agreement.

"But are they really dead?" I whispered to myself.

I was hearing my own words. THERE ARE NO LIMITS TO HELL.

It was only the next warm month when a serf girl who served us - our serfs came back from the fair as if nothing had happened - who was no older than me, Masha's sister, the one who had given me a vodka kiss, died of the black typhus that beautiful spring with the fields full of flowers that I started to believe in the infinity of death. Masha ran to me and then on to the woods where she threw herself on the leaves and howled and howled with grief.

Nearly a whole, strangely tranquil year had passed, with occasional trips to the houses of the minor country aristocracy, to meet and dance with their spoilt daughters, when on one saint's day our serfs had a phonograph playing a jazz record that was meant for M. Hippolyte while the large bearded man, the head serf, Grigor, helped himself to some genuine French cognac. I never said a thing to my tutors, about the thefts, which they expected anyway, and in return the serfs taught me how to charm rabbits with cooing noises and find mushrooms with forked hazel rods held in both fists, and sometimes they said they had learned that such and such was happening in Moscow from "friends on the road".

"That's not a balalaika," said Antov, as we heard the music from the serfs' hut. It was The Original Dixieland Jazz Band playing 'Livery Stable Blues'.

He had seen a wire outside that he assumed was to hang things like mushrooms on to dry but went right up a tree. It did not make sense. "It is probably a superstition. These people are primitive," said Antov. I knew and liked the word PRIMITIVE. The serfs were not.

The music told its own story.

He burst in the door to find the phonograph playing. Two of the old serf women were praying to an icon in the corner. But then we saw the patriarch, Grigor, at the table, hunched over a tin can with a pair of earphones on his head. He was listening on a crystal set that I had seen described in a magazine.

"I'll give you a whipping for this," said Antov, not quite knowing what. But the dignified Grigor merely held up his hand for quiet.

"I am listening to a radio announcement in Moscow. The government is falling, again. This is a people's radio station from the Central Committee of the Revolution. The Tsar is finished. The revolution has started. People are not taking to the streets this time. They are taking the streets."

There was complete silence in the hut and for a second I feared the serfs might turn on us and spike us on Christmas trees, but they didn't. Instead, everyone seemed embarrassed. In the background the jazz played on. I liked to think it was because of the little bonds of friendship that had been built up. But probably it was that in a couple of sentences we, Antov, M. Hippolyte, the Tsar and I, had become irrelevant, perfect shadows on a sunshine day.

REVOLUTION is a powerful word, a turning-up-side-down word. You knew that to the base of your spine. When I said the word I saw the colour red.

"Forward comrades," screamed the parrot.

The next day all of the men except the goblin-like serf had left. They had taken the parrot and the prettiest of the girls with them. They had taken Masha and my indifferent though heartfelt poems.

The goblin-like serf had put on his best clothes and walked

around and laughed a lot. But then slowly things went back to normal and we were served our meals again.

"Storm in a teacup, you watch," said Antov. "You just see."

A week later, I was called into the main library hut.

"You have a little silver elephant, don't you?" said M. Hippolyte. "That was given to you by the Tsar? There are lines from a poem inside? Please say them."

I kept the little elephant around my neck at all times, even when swimming. The serfs had stared at it but did not try to steal it, possibly because they revered totem animals. I took a deep breath. The poem was by Pushkin whose poetry I loved and who had become a hero of mine because of the way he lived. He was a sensitive man but one who gave himself with complete passion to the world, not afraid to fight duels for love and honour. A tear stained the third line. I took a deep breath:

> "I loved you without hope, a mute offender;
> What jealous pangs, what shy despairs I knew!
> A love as deep as this, as true, as tender,
> God grant another may yet offer you."

The words MUTE OFFENDER had special meaning for me. It was not until I had finished that I realised there was another man in the room who did not look exhausted even though the mud and snow on his clothes showed he had ridden many miles. He had come from Perm.

"This is not the time for fucking poetry,' the man said. His body was young and strong but his face appeared old. He pulled off his boots and I noticed a small patch in his hair at the back, which was perfectly white, not grey but white.

Antov stuck out his chest.

"The poem shows he is who we say he is. We could be deceiving you. And we are pleased with our creation."

The man took out his handkerchief and sneezed quickly. He seemed impatient about everything.

"The Red Army is coming at you very fast. We must get him away from here."

M. Hippolyte blinked.

"How can they know about him?"

The man became angry.

"The Imperial Family are part of this secret so that means the Reds know. And your serfs know and if some have disappeared they have gone to join the local soviets."

The man cast another glance at me, shaking his head.

"We will send two riders for him tomorrow. Just him. You are both known and will be conspicuous if you go with him. Also, your exile is still not officially lifted. Put up a token fight and slip away when you can. Provide him with one servant, perhaps that idiot pacing about outside. Be ready," he said.

Later, M. Hippolyte and Antov smoked slow pipes by the large tiled stove in our hut. The grandfather clock TICKED as ever. Nothing seemed to have changed.

"We have things to tell you,' said M. Hippolyte, his face sad. "When you go from here you will speak to no one. You will pretend to be mute, like in the poem. You have done that before so it should not be too hard. Until you meet the man who will give you a word."

"What word?"

"The word is *Fumoo*," said Antov. For once he was not smiling or teasing. The way he first pronounced it, it sounded like FREE ME.

"What does it mean?"

FUMOO. The word was mysterious and squatted in my head like a green-eyed heathen idol. The word itself was not a surprise. It was faintly engraved on the side of the elephant.

"Perhaps you'll learn what it means one day. Perhaps not. But you are on a great mission. A great quest." Antov's hand was shaking.

"I will tell you what you have to say to the man who gives you that word," said M. Hippolyte. "You will be guided along your way, I am told. You are to say you are Alexei Nikolaevich. You have already set to memory all the lands the Tsaravitch will inherit."

"But that's not my name," I protested. M. Hippolyte had called me that when I first arrived but not afterwards. If I was called anything by them it was the usual *Mishka* or very rarely *Pasha*. The serfs had called me prince, but increasingly in a joking way and often with a breaking of wind and hilarity.

"It is now," said Antov, roughing up my hair. "You're to be taken to another place for final instructions."

Among their papers on a side table I saw a new letter bearing a coat of arms with an elephant. Beneath it was the word, *Fumoo*.

"Whose coat of arms are they?"

"You do not know? They are Pushkin's. I'll tell you all in the morning," said M. Hippolyte. It made me think of the Tsar and his elephants.

THE TSAR MUST DIE!

I went to bed both frightened and excited. I thought of what had happened at the fair. I then thought the world is turning. I closed my eyes and saw the river of dark fire. I did not sleep until dawn blew its cold air under my door.

EIGHT

NATASHA PUT DOWN the pages of the new packet that had arrived by post and wondered whether to make herself a cup of milky coffee. She had not had too many that day. She had gone into work only to find that the library had been temporarily closed while meetings were held to decide if it was open or not because of Covid. Natasha had been given the task of working out distancing in the student reading areas and the positioning of hand sanitizers, which were not going to be needed if the place was shut. She started thinking about the idea of the reverse flow of time. She wondered what it might be like to read Nabokov's *Lolita* backwards, to know at the very "beginning" of the back-to-front book that Dolores Haze dies in childbirth. To read the book in this way seemed to further enhance the character and the tyranny of Humbert Humbert's Faustian progress. That would fulfil Nabokov's desire for a novelist to be a teacher, but made it difficult to be a storyteller or enchanter, as all his tricks would be on show from the start. One would see behind the curtain of the Wizard of Oz. There could be precious little mystery, or suspense, or magic. Natasha felt that her own life had stopped or was slipping backwards after Paris. She felt completely adrift. So was the boy, who certainly was an enchanter. After the minute hand on the office clock moved to two, she was told to go home, hurrying, masked, down the subway in a shower of rain. She was glad to get back to the flat. What amazed her over again was that Alexei's time was so like her own, there was even a flu pandemic she had read an article on. And it may seem obvious to say it, but while he stood on the threshold of mass industrialisation and all its invention, which alienated man and came between peoples and states, and became an image which influenced all human behaviour, she stood at the doorway to the digital future, to the isolation of human beings; the further loss of true feeling. Natasha took out her mobile phone and hesitated on an email she had written earlier that day. It was a necessary reply to her friend at Harvard. It was the truth.

From: NatashaA@gmail.com
To: ChiChiChica Froment@fas.harvard.edu

ChiChiChica! It wasn't rape. I never said I was raped. I did not smash up the room. He did not smash up the room. Things just got broken in an argument. I am not a fucking victim, okay? What he did to me that day was worse than murder. It was soul murder. I was waiting for him in the room in Paris in the George V and he was late so I switched on the TV and there he was. There he was in French, in France, in a French-looking suit, speaking to a woman who looked like she was a model but was really a journalist. She had a perfect mouth and front teeth whiter than a bunny. He was telling her all about his new project. He was telling the Francophone world all about himself and his new project without an accent. He was smiling right out at me. He was smiling right out at me sitting there, dressed up, dressed up on the anniversary of the day we met. I was sitting on the bed. A table in the bridal suite was set for a candle lit dinner and he was talking to a media trolley dolly about how he was going to take confiscated heroin from the hands of Afghan warlords he had met when producing a movie there, and use it in Africa for pain relief in childbirth. We had never talked of this. The media trolley dolly looked as if she was going to cry and orgasm at the same time. I just wanted to cry. Hours later when he came to the room he explained why he was late because of his mother. It was true, he had taken her to the doctor's. But I had drunk most of the bottle of wine brought with dinner and I usually do not drink. The television spot had been recorded a month ago. He told me not to be such a spoilt paranoid American and the television that was in the way got smashed and I cried, Then we made love and it was violent. It was cathartic. Then we started to play games and there was a stupid, stupid accident and a lot of blood. He was very upset. Then I walked out, ChiChi. He never laid a finger on me that was not part of our love making or what came after. It was the man in Paris that got hurt most in the stupid, stupid accident. All the way back to my friend's apartment in the 6th arrondissemont I was certain he'd slept with the media trolley dolly and kept hearing him ask her in that soft way of his how and where she saw herself empowered in the future, the bunny-fucking bastard. We were angry with each other. That's all. But he hasn't rung. Doesn't Nietzsche say there has to be a little resistance on the path to happiness? There was blood on the silk curtains and I hope he was charged for them and the rest of the room. I am not a fucking victim! Yours, M'lady Marmalade.

Natasha then went back to the book and the boy.

NINE

A N EXPLODING SHELL woke me to the core of my
bones.

I threw the blankets away from my face. My other hand
was clenched around the silver elephant. For a second I wanted
it all to be a dream and that I could go back to exactly as it
was, the life with Antov and M. Hippolyte, where there was so
much talking but nothing ever happened and the clock ticked.
I then remembered my promise to the unholy Holy man to try
to discover if there is meaning in life. An alarm bell started
to ring outside the serfs' hut.

The word BELL spelt itself out in my mind.

Then there was the sound of rifle fire followed by the
whistle of another artillery shell and an explosion.

Before anyone stopped me I ran outside.

A third shell struck the façade of the fake palace, high up,
scattering rubble over our roof.

I went back inside and jumped into my clothes, button-
ing on my sabre harness when two cavalrymen came in and
grabbed me and I was put on a horse.

The goblin serf with darting eyes was with us. I think his
name was Oleg, which meant Holy, but no one ever called him
that. He had no saddle.

I looked down from the nervous horse and Antov and M. Hippolyte were gazing up at me.

"Use what we have taught you, my friend," said M. Hippolyte.

"Break hearts and heads that get in the way," said Antov, but not convincingly.

I reached out and touched both of them, despite myself. It was as if I was watching myself regretting not being CLOSER to them. Not telling them I loved them.

They both were looking at the ground and I saw they were most sad. I think Antov had tears in his eyes.

"Come with us. Please," I said. I felt a dull ache in my chest. It was sorrow. I was so sad. I felt in the damp air between us that both of them were really frightened.

M. Hippolyte shook his head.

"Perhaps we'll meet up later. But for the moment we have to remain here, according to our word. This may be our Thermopylae."

There was an awkward silence. I was so fond of them. I loved them. I wanted to tell them but the words stuck in my mouth.

Antov suddenly smiled: "Don't worry, I'll protect the venerable professor. If all else fails he can send them to sleep with a lecture." They then began to argue.

The escort and I galloped off into the pink steppe as more artillery shells fell, sending bricks flying and smashing off one end of the painted wall onto the huts behind.

I glimpsed cavalry and infantry heading for the Potemkin house, red banners streaming. There seemed to be thousands and more emerging from over a rise and out of the nearby forest. I had never seen so many people.

I wondered if any of the revolutionaries knew that they were attacking a carefully painted wall.

Our fake country house.

I saw one of our cavalrymen cross himself and mumble a prayer.

Two horsemen split away from the Reds and shot at us, but we were going too fast and they soon broke off and went back to join the attack.

When I looked back minutes later, our Mikhailovskoye, our little settlement, was burning. Tears were running down my face.

The library was burning. All those WORDS. I prayed for my friends who I was sure would not run. More WORDS. I quickened the horse. Again, I had a freedom.

On the evening of the fourth day, we came to a railway station between the towering pines, on the line that one of the cavalrymen said led to Siberia. It was snowing heavily and all the trees around were covered in a fairy-tale white and ice crystals.

First, I went into a room to take off my boots and another man was there. He spoke curtly to those with me, whom he told to wait outside. He handed me a glass of scalding tea and made way so I could warm myself by the stove. He was the man who had come to Mikhailovskoye, and I remembered him, I thought, from seeing him once at Selo. When he turned back to the samovar I saw the white patch in his hair. He refilled his glass and faced me again. His eyes were steady and fierce but cool. He looked me up and down as if I was a horse. He then handed me a bag that was full of sweets from his pocket. I took one of the large peppermints and it warmed my mouth. He snatched the bag back and took one too and crunched it down before saying in Russian:

"Very good things, Mint Imperials. Matters will become more difficult from here, my boy, mark my words. But do not worry. Your angels will be keeping watch. And there'll be others who'll try and kill you. Be on your guard as you make for Riga. What you're doing is of great importance and we will tell you everything by and by. Now you can go in and see the man we've brought you here to see. You must call him father. He is your father."

My astonishment must have shown. Who had they brought me to see?

The man laughed.

I sipped the scalding black tea but was as frightened of this quiet-voiced man as I would have been of the enemy. He had such a beseeching face, rosy cheeks and a well-tended moustache, but it was as if a cloak of dread trailed from his shoulders.

I was going to ask who exactly was in the other room but then I remembered M. Hippolyte said I should not speak. The man, who was selecting another enormous peppermint, seemed to be in control of things.

"Go in, go in. Pretty dirty work," the man said, in English, which I thought at the time was foolish and meant nothing. M. Hippolyte had taught me English very well. But I did not know English people then and how they often refer to things of great importance with a throwaway word or phrase.

I went into the waiting room and dropped my tea glass in astonishment and it smashed on the floor.

The Tsar was standing there and the rest of the Imperial Family were sitting, straight-backed on the wooden slat benches. It was so unexpected, I started to hiccup.

The Tsar clasped me by the hand and then hugged me, kissing me on the cheeks and I let him, still amazed. He was acting like a father, with all the affection of a father. He treated me like his son.

The rest of the family then stood and I went and kissed them. They embraced me warmly. The touching and the warmth made me short of breath. He was my father. I thought I was going to faint. I was trembling.

"You are cold, my son. Come to the fire and warm yourself," said the Tsar.

I was not cold so much as I could not seem to make my lungs work. Tears came to my eyes. It was as if on leaving my friends who were my family I suddenly had another family, a place in the world, a home. I warmed my hands next to his and listened to his advisors talking, as he smiled at me.

They had apparently been brought east by moderate elements in the government, but now only the Tsar himself appeared to trust in that illusion. He was running. There was hardly any luggage, any servants. M. Hippolyte had long since been quite open on how these matters were going to finish.

"Little one. Look at him, so strong," said the Tsarina. "He looks as if he could kill a bear."

I did not say a word, as I had promised. They gazed at me in the flares of smoky candlelight and I at them. The tallow fat had an animal smell. They were cheap candles in a cold place.

The Imperial Family did not cry or complain. It was too late for that. They talked of warm summers long past. I can recall the smell of lipstick and face powder from the sisters and the perfume of the Tsarina, and the sad eyes of the defeated Tsar, my father, under a defeated moon. DEFEATED was the word. For whatever reason, I accepted the fiction that they were my mother and father. That was my duty. The expression on the Tsar's face had made me angry and sorry for him for as long as I had been alive. But the family's emotion was not a charade. They all received me as if I was one of the FAMILY. I tried to smile.

"Why have you that smile on your face, even now?" he said, baffled.

I hiccupped again and they laughed politely.

They were like a hallucination. At first, I wanted to bow or kneel or abase myself in some way to affirm that this was the Tsar and they were the Imperial Family, but there was something about the ordinariness of the waiting room that prevented me. Or perhaps, now everything was finished, I was accepted as one of them too. The river of dark fire was coming for us all.

The dying boy, the other Alexei, now fully my little brother, had been carried in on a stretcher. I saw his face and he looked like me. Too much like me. He was the only one who was angry with me, angry with everything.

Angry as the TIGER.

His skin was the colour of wax and he hung there in space but not in time. I had the feeling that if I stared at him for too long I might stay with him, that we would become wordless friends together on the bloody canvas of the stretcher in that railway waiting room at the bounds of nowhere. His eyes were small and sunken.

Exhausted from my journey I found it hard to stand. Outside the wind howled.

I prayed the Tsar was not going to weep. I smiled at 'my' sisters who I knew from the Imperial Nursery, but I avoided the searing mad warmth of the Tsarina's tired eyes. She was my mother now.

"Do not say a word to anyone. Do not tell anyone who you are. Until someone uses the word that has been arranged. You will be directed to them. The most important of persons, but better not to know. The less that is known the better. That's what my advisors say," said the Tsar.

I bowed, slightly.

"What you are doing is of immense value even though you may not realise it." I was so tired and cold my part did not seem to matter in that deserted railway station that smelled of curing furs and pine resin. The Tsar stopped being the Tsar and became my father again. He put his hand on my shoulder and it was shaking. "Remember the elephant? Elephants never forget, you know. You still have the one I gave you? Remember the elephant. Remember me."

We stood, them saying goodbyes in the waiting room as if the express to St Petersburg or Moscow was about to arrive. Their plan was to slip away to the east. I was to go in the other direction. They said goodbye to me over and over. They were going into exile. Keeping to my promise I said nothing. I hiccupped. This was a great moment and all I could do was hiccup.

The spell was broken when the Englishman said the Red Army was near and the Tsar had to go. "You must leave immediately. For Riga. Your part in this is vital," he said to me. I liked the word VITAL. I caught the words of one of the advisors: "Let that little fox run. He will take the hounds off us for a while."

I then went outside and filled my lungs with freezing air as I stared at the trees. The word VITAL was in my numb fingertips. It was in my toes. The man's stupid words did not hurt me. I had a family. I had a purpose and a word. FUMOO.

I thought of it as FREE ME. It had been on the elephant all the time.

And of my promise to Rasputin, I made a bargain to learn what was true.

The snow swirled around the felt boots of the guard at the door and in the forest I did not look back. If I had I would have gone back to the small railway station where I saw them that last time. I remember many days like that as I led my horse with the two escorts and the serf.

My old, and splitting, riding boots trailed blood in the snow.

'You're not going to make it,' whispered the serf, frequently. He did not bow anymore. He did not address me as he should but bit into a raw onion as if it was an apple, spitting out the skin. The skin that I had used once to dye Easter eggs in the Imperial Nursery with those sisters I had just left. Onion skins turn them to gold.

I could not get out of my mind that the Tsar had asked to see me! That he had received me as his SON. Even if I was only to be a FOX. It made me giddy. There was a kind of glow around me like the halos of the saints in the icons in church. I thanked God. I longed for the icons and the incense and the droning of the papas.

The Englishman with his mints was obviously going to try to take the Tsar to freedom. To me the men guarding the family, from whatever provisional government, had a fatal, accepting look in their eyes, like wolves, like wolves when they have stopped their howling and growling and are silent, ready to attack, ready to be true wolves, acting as one indivisible and unlovable intelligence. I imagined those wolves might come after me but they did not, thinking I was not worth bothering with, I suppose. It is said that wolves only kill slow children and saints, but I knew better. According to the ladies in the Imperial Nursery, they ate my mother and father and many important people including a German moral philosopher. HELL HAS NO LIMITS. Yet the serfs say wolves are scared of human kind and wait for us to freeze before eating us. First they lick us until we bleed and then stand back and stare with those soulful wolf eyes, sorry for what they are about to do before, in a frenzy of small bites, they tear the corpse to pieces. That was among the cheerful stories the serf who travelled with us told me. He had not seen a child killed by a wolf but had seen a woman of the Old Believers killed instantly with one bite to the throat.

"They are good for taking witches too, little prince, and pretenders," he said laughing.

The serf kept saying that the distance we had to travel to be safe was impossible and before long he had me thinking that every time I got down from my horse to afford him a rest, the subtle give and crunch of the snow under my boots was going to end in silence. SILENCE for ever. I crossed myself frequently and asked my favourite saints to receive me as we rode into the uncertain night. I looked across at the serf hunched over his horse and he laughed at me.

From the railway station we headed north-west and after several days rode into a small town at first light and there was a screaming sound overhead and the brick walls either side collapsed in a wave of dust and snow. We went through the streets at a gallop.

I had seen my home shelled by the Red Army but nothing prepared me for the instant savagery of the artillery barrage from up-to-date guns.

The ground itself became elastic. I do not know whose side it was, but the town began to disintegrate, houses and gardens that people had tended for years and thought were permanent were blown to small pieces, as were those in them. The bricks and stones seemed to explode from within.

A horse and cart came swerving down the street towards me, its load of boxes spilling, and all that was left after another shell was smoke and the gentle rain of acrid horse blood. We came to a halt and I leaned down for a better look. In the boxes were books, a personal library a rich man was trying to save. There was Tolstoy and Dostoyevsky, Gogol and Pushkin, even Balzac and Dickens and, surprisingly, Mayakovsky. The peasants overwhelmed the leavings like ants, gathering the books.

"For firewood, master," sneered my serf. "Can all that learning boil a single kettle?"

Another shell whistled down and I was only conscious of seeing a wall come apart like a jigsaw I once swept off a table.

Metal shards flew towards me like swallows.

I knew that I must be bleeding somewhere and that this was the end. Yet the only trickle of blood came from my head, which spun, and I saw bees buzzing in fields of white daisies. I was buried under bricks and earth and gasping for breath. I thought I was dead but the small serf was pulling me out. I coughed and coughed, choking on the brick dust.

"You're not going to make it now, little prince. The two officers and all the horses are dead."

"I have to go to Riga."

He shook his sore-encrusted, moulting head. His hair was grey.

"Riga? That's a world away! Weeks and weeks. You will die. You will die." The little man was ecstatic in his pessimism. He was a thief. Antov had thrashed him many times for stealing things. Even things that were no use to him. Like papers he could not read. At other times he was thrashed for stealing things I had taken for the serfs. He was digging now and found a bottle of vodka in the rubble. His face lit up and he was literally dancing in his felt boots as if this was the best thing he could ever imagine happening to him in his life.

I longed to lie down and pull the soft snow about me like

a fur. I was no longer the person I thought I was. I dare not say my new name, even to myself. Yet, I was urged on by the serf, out of the shattered town over low hills until I was able to walk no more and as I looked up the clouds were smudged and darkened by another village burning. He pushed me on and cursed my blood.

"Where's your army? Where is your army, my little prince?"

He cursed me again and his eyes were like polished brass.

"None of your kind will survive," he said, happily. "Not even in a zoo." And from the things we saw on that road I had no doubt that he was right.

My head was spinning as I became weaker and staggered on. I felt the power of the river of dark fire and saw its INFINITY if I closed my eyes.

We passed a school playground full of dead children and two women huddling for warmth in the carcass of a plough horse, wearing its steaming intestines on their heads like hats. As the snow got worse the serf became more cheerful and that night we ate what was left of the rations and he drank the vodka and sang obscene songs. In the morning he was dead beside me with a smile on his face. There was snow on his hair and eyelashes and he had taken off his coat. The greasy bottle was by him. He had even taken my silver buttons though not the elephant that was around my neck, nor the dagger Antov had given me.

I hit him. I hit the dead serf again and again. I shook him. He felt insubstantial like a rag doll.

I hated the serf.

My teeth were clenched tight. I was angry with him, especially for dying but most of all for his easy fatalism. Tears came to my eyes. I made the sign of the Holy Cross over the man and left him propped against a wooden house with two of my buttons on each of his eyes. And despite all my modern education from M. Hippolyte, I prayed to Saint Michael and Saint Anna that someone might have the courage to bury him and then fled.

In the weeks that followed I lived in holes. I became a better thief. I became the ultimate THIEF.

I stole anything, just like the little serf. I ate dirt. I became so hungry, travelling on towards the north-west and where I thought Riga might be.

I stole clothes. I stole a papa's felt boots. I found a bible and stuffed the great pages between my undershirt and shirt as I had seen the serfs do. I bound my feet with women's silk scarves I found on the road.

In a small hotel in a town where all the wooden buildings were burned I discovered a small gong of the type used to call residents for dinner. It was about the only thing left. The word GONG seemed to leap in my mind. I banged and banged the gong. For even though the ruins were still smouldering, that day was a bright one. I then was frightened in case someone was going to come but no one did. I stole the socks off a dead man to put over my gloves as it was getting colder.

I slept that night under part of a fallen roof that rested against an old wall, listening to the wolves and wondering whether another rumbling in the distance was more guns or thunder. It was a moonless night and I felt the black-blue silence that seemed to walk around me. I said the Pushkin poem I had been given over and over, making a fortress of the gentle words.

The next morning I got up and my eyelashes were frozen together. I was in panic for a while that I was never going to open them again but they thawed and my body was pained with pins and needles as the circulation returned. I managed to get up and walk around and on the outskirts of the burned town I stopped still as I saw two small figures, women or children, hunched over something. They were eating. I was sure of it. I heard the noise. I hid behind a wall and banged my little GONG for all I was worth and they ran away back into the town. When I looked at what they were bent over it was a child's doll and tea set. The doll's eyes were open and staring at me.

Increasingly, the only times I saw the living they were running away or were an army that I had to hide from. I took bread from a dead soldier's pocket. I ransacked a church for the food the priests might have left and feasted on the holy wafers. I followed railway lines west and then north and my feet were bleeding.

On the outskirts of a town I saw a dead baby, grey in a pram full of broken glass.

At another village there had been a café. In it were card players still at their green baize table, all dead, not a mark on their bodies. I found some kasha behind the counter and stuffed it into my mouth.

One sunny day I had to dive into a snowdrift to avoid a patrol that had a prisoner on a cart.

The soldiers were talking of what they were going to do.

I saw the prisoner, a girl, a small, smiling girl swinging her legs on the back of the cart, as if on her way to a Sunday picnic, who was being led away to be burned as a witch by those who supported the new order. She was no more than twelve. That's what the soldiers were saying, and:

"She will need a bit of salt."

One of them went to the cart and felt the girl's thighs and arms and she let him. She was well fed and probably well born. There was an ecstatic expression on her face as if she were drugged or given vodka. I hoped she was drugged. She was saying a nursery rhyme but I did not bang my gong and try to help her. The word FUMOO was in my head. The words FREE ME were shouting inside me. I prayed for her but did not go to rescue her. I was taken with fear. Soon the soldiers' words were lost. She was gone.

Instead her little rhyme echoed in me.

"My love is like a daisy, a daisy, a daisy . . ."

The clouds were low and a slate grey and somewhere I let go of my gong. The temperature rose a degree or two and it then began to snow again, heavily.

I thought of no other word but DAISY, to the exclusion of everything around me.

It was a while later that I looked back and there was a single man on horseback, following me. He had seen me so there was no point in running and trying to hide. Was he hunting me as the FOX? He was wearing a black fur hat and a long black leather coat and had a rifle slung on his back and a sabre at his side. I wondered whether he was waiting for me to die of natural causes, though from what I had seen violent deaths were now natural deaths. In the evening he vanished and then when I looked again he was there in the dawn. When I stopped he stopped and when I set off he watched for a while and then followed. I could not make out his features because he was too far back, but the horse was well tended and he could have overtaken me in moments. Then I noticed something else. If I wandered too far to the left or the right he cantered through the snow and cut me off, forcing me ever towards the north, as if I was being shepherded. I tried going faster but I was faint from lack of food and one afternoon I was half-turning and staring back at the man when I fell down a bank and rolled until I hit the wooden sleeper of a railroad on which a train had stopped.

Up the line steam rose from the engine.

It was a massive black engine on a bend with a tall smoke stack and plough-shaped snow-catcher and a line of red and gold carriages, an exuberant and absurd assertion of civilisation in the wilderness. There were seven carriages in all with one behind the engine that was just a low steel platform, where two long-barrelled heavy artillery guns were mounted, surrounded by sandbags and soldiers with machine guns, which could destroy villages that never glimpsed the train. At the back stood a wood-clad guard's van and a door opened and a man with neatly combed grey hair and stern eyes stared down at me and smiled.

I looked back up the embankment and the rider was gone in the whiteness.

Exhausted, I climbed a small ladder into the guard's van and sat down on the wooden floor by a stove that seemed impossibly hot. The stove was in the middle of the floor and a black pipe led out through the roof. The man held out a loaf of bread for me and the train started to move. I had no idea who was in control of the train but was past caring. I grabbed the bread, listening to the sound of the iron wheels against the freezing metal track.

"My love is like a daisy, a daisy, a DAISY!"

The train made the sound DAISY every time the wheels went over the rail joints.

I do not know how long I slept but when I awoke the guard, I assumed he was the guard because he wore a brown uniform with a shirt that buttoned from the side at his neck, brought me a glass of sweet tea. I had had strange dreams of a white, wooden hotel in a faraway land on a windswept beach with crashing waves I had never been to, and a small, white light-house with a bell that went clank-clang, like the Kremlin bells, in the gale. I was worried for someone close to me and, breathless, I woke surprised and confused. St Petersburg is a seaport, but my dream was an alien land, another country, a different, thunderous sea. The guard half-opened the door and I breathed the freezing air in deep and stared out at the night and the moon over the snow-heavy forest. The train was rounding a bend and I had a clear view of the car at the front with the two great guns. I had no idea how far I had come or if I was travelling in the right direction for the coast. The motion of the train soothed and lulled me. The guard gave me another loaf and I ate it very quickly, keeping my eyes on him all the time as we thundered through the night. He did not seem surprised by my presence. Occasionally, when he smoked his pipe or drank his tea, he shook his head as if there was nothing to be done. He left me once to go forward in the train and then we speeded up and I peered out of a tiny window and saw mountains and a town burning. When he did not come back I went to the door into the next car-riage and through the glass saw him talking to a man with a wispy beard and glasses who looked very serious. There was a corridor in the next carriage as in a proper train. The guard then returned. There was not much in the guard's van except a little table at one side and a desk at the other.

After a week the guard allowed me to sit at the table. He was a strict man.

He wrote things down in a book and, at times, stood up and closed the book with a bang.

On the cover of the book were the words in gold letters, Trans Siberian Railway.

One day, I saw the guard's revolver on his pad of blotting paper. I was able to make out the name, L. Nagant, below the hammer. Antov had one. The man stared at me and blew smoke from his pipe. He did not look like a train guard.

Periodically, we went out onto a platform at the back of the train where he had to check that a brake mechanism, with a wheel like a car's steering wheel, was working. We were flying along in between the dark forest and as I stood there, my breath smoky in the freezing air, it was as if all my past was rushing into night and infinity. All of the pretty ladies, all the fine gentlemen of the cavalry at the Christmas Ball at Selo were whirling into the flurries of snow and into oblivion as if they never existed. The Tsar's yellowish face looked on as we crashed forward into the night, bewildered and indistinct. The guard put his hand momentarily on my shoulder as if he knew what I was thinking. FREE ME.

Three days later, I heard the sound of artillery in the distance and I wondered if he was taking me to the army for whatever side. The train slowed.

The guard took out a metal pocket watch and in the yellow lamplight looked at a map of the line pinned to a board. There was a string of amber beads on his desk. He must be from St Petersburg where everyone had them. He must be important. He must be with the Reds, or both sides. The sound of firing came again.

He went over to the door and opened it, much further this time and he had to break a film of ice that had formed. He smashed it with the back of a shovel.

"This is where you must get down," he said. These were

his only words to me ever and he had an educated accent. He pointed to the snow beside the track. He then gave me a small paper parcel. The train slowed slightly as we rounded a bend.

All Russia seemed beneath me as I looked down at the snow and the steep embankment and the guard pushed me hard from behind.

I fell over and over and stood up to see the locomotive disappearing into the night.

There was the sound of guns up the line and I moved quickly into the dark of the forest. There was a flash of fire above the trees and a crash like thunder as the guns on the train opened up. I found myself with the absurd hope the Soviet train made it through and prayed to the Saints and to the Holy Mother.

The night closed around me completely but I was relieved to be alone again. My hand was still clutching the little parcel the guard had given me. I should have been scared but I was not.

I undid one end and felt inside. It was full of sweets. I had hoped for a second that they were Mint Imperials and that the Englishman had arranged all this. But they were cheap sugar sweets like the serfs made.

With my back against a tree I put one in my mouth. It tasted of rose-water and mastic. Away in the distance a wolf began its mournful song and was answered by others. Then even though I was alone, I howled too. I knew the language of the FOREST. I knew the reality of the dark RIVER, and that helped me too.

TEN

NATASHA PUT DOWN the boy's story. It would terrify her to be lost in a forest at night. With wolves. This made her think of the man in Paris. Then she could not stop thinking of the man in Paris. She could not stop thinking of their dangerous passion. The trouble was she did not know how seriously she had injured him.

It was difficult to revisit such a thing, let alone say or write. After the television had been smashed, after their love making, he had kissed her pubic hair, which she had partially shaved but he said it would look better completely gone. She was still in another place and then he was back from the bathroom with a cut-throat razor and was scraping away her remaining pubic hairs. It made her think of a Warhol film with the voiceover of an underage girl protesting about her pubic hair being shaved and handed to her before giving birth. The man in Paris had nicked Natasha with the razor. The crimson blood was on the cool, impossibly white, sheet. "This blood seals our bargain," he said, licking the blood as he continued. His erection, still hard, rested at the top of her thigh and was getting harder again and then she felt affronted by the whole situation and hemmed in and put her hand out for him to stop, but knocked the blade, which was so sharp he had said it could cut silk, in the direction of his penis and there was an explosion of warm blood. There was no other word for it, an explosion. He cried out and there was pushing and shoving.

It was the first time the man in Paris had had an expression of complete panic on his face and she was grabbing his mobile phone to ring for help and he grabbed it back and then there was another argument and partly she started to leave and partly he began to throw her out, while holding a hotel pillow to himself, and she screamed at him when she discovered she had also been cut on the hip. There was blood everywhere. She snatched up her dress and shoes, ran out to the corridor, and put them on in the elevator and went to the nearby apartment of a good friend in the 6th arrondissement, who had told her the key was under the hall carpet if she needed a room. She had then burned her bloody clothes. It was not rape, but she could not tell ChiChi what it was. She was still mad with the man in Paris. He had been acting as if he owned her. He did not own her. But his silence drove her insane.

It was all as absurd as the young man who on the same day discovered himself to be part of the Imperial Family only to be lost in the war and the snow. Another packet had arrived.

ELEVEN

THE UNEXPECTED MANUSCRIPT: PACKET VI

L OST. I WAS LOST again. It seemed the natural condi-tion in the forest. Yet, strangely, it made me happy.

After an hour of pushing through the heavy snow and close trees I was back at the same, lightning-split tree I had started out from.

EVERYTHING REPEATS EVERYTHING.

The phrase came from my dreams.

There is only our own representation of reality. I had heard that too. Yet other people's words and ideas surfaced in those dreams. The forest had the fatal quality of a dream.

Maybe my home, my true place of dwelling, was in the lab-yrinth of the forest, not in a palace or even in the world. It was not a good thought but perhaps I had imagined everything since being rescued as an infant. Perhaps I was still in the East, fleeing from the burning train and the wolves. I pictured the princess who had helped me, to get rid of the thought. I hoped she had escaped. I hoped the dancer had escaped too.

For a few miles I escaped into the words SUGAR PLUM FAIRY.

I tried to steer by the sun and the position of the north star, like Antov had taught me, when I could see through the low, dark clouds. I had gone at right angles from the line for

I assumed the guard had pushed me out into the night for a reason. But I did not know. He may have been trying to save me from an attack on the train or kill me. He may just have been tired of my company as we crossed a changing, burning land. All that was in front of me now were snowfields and forest. I walked slowly for day after day and each day it became harder as my feet swelled and were more and more painful. It seemed I had left the world of people behind forever except what was in my head, my words. I had the remains of a brass compass from one of the cavalrymen, but the glass had been smashed and the needle did not move. It was always going the right and the wrong way. The snow was blowing from the side and I walked for days, sleeping in the lee of trees and drinking snow melted through a woollen hat I had found. The nursery rhyme of a doomed girl on a cart followed me.

"My love is like a daisy, a daisy, a DAISY."

The forest became thicker but then I arrived at a clearing. I took a step into the clearing that was about a mile wide and stretched as far as the horizon in one direction and I slipped immediately.

I stopped myself crying out.

It was ice. It creaked slightly to the touch of my boot. I was on a frozen lake and then I saw something that made me jump half out of my boots and made the hairs at the back of my neck stand on end. What I saw was an icon of my predicament and all Russia's and more. I felt the eyes of the Holy Man burning through me and remembered my easy promise to seek meaning.

Under the clear ice, in the shallows at one end of the lake where the snow had blown away in the blizzard, were hundreds of bodies of girls in white blouses with black office skirts. The skirts were long and the white collars starched and very proper. They had been brought a huge distance from the nearest modern city to end their life here under the ice for a reason of state they most probably did not know and which I could only imagine. There was no visible sign of harm or violence or how they all died in this lonely place. Their blouses were still buttoned. Whoever had them killed was totally in control of who did the killing.

The bodies were perfectly preserved and I had the small and nagging thought that they were librarians.

They looked like librarians I had seen in a town near the Potemkin house. Perhaps their crime was to know of books probably now forbidden, like those blown into the street by the artillery barrage. M. Hippolyte had once told me that when Julius Caesar had burned down the Great Library of Alexandria he killed all the librarians and all their families and fed their bodies to the jackals and the crocodiles in the river, so no one would even know about the civilisation and learning that had been lost, all because it was not specifically Roman.

I stared down and I wanted to feel more for them than I did. I wanted to cry, just as I wanted to when I left the railway station. I wanted to be troubled, not fascinated, with the dreamy beauty of the floating girls and wondered if this was my curse, like the bleeding of my dying 'brother'. I wanted at least to feel anger and not be frozen, too. I stepped out onto the ice in my felt boots and looked down at one of the girls in the enfolding silence of the snow and forest. I glanced around at the dark pines that fringed the lake and nothing moved, so I knelt down on one knee and took off my glove and gently touched the ice. It was so cold my hand started to stick there as if this was a fairy tale and I was to be imprisoned as well. Never take your gloves off young man, my tutor, M. Hippolyte, used to tell me when we went walking. I presumed that he was now dead. He had many dreams, mainly of going back to Paris to save all the books in the libraries that he feared the Kaiser was going to burn. The Kaiser had kept himself warm as a student by burning an entire poetry library in a house he was staying in one winter. He was a man of few WORDS.

KAISER means the same as TSAR but did not have any magic. I wished I had a magic charm to send away the ice and make the girls' hearts beat again. To make them laugh. To give them lilacs.

M. Hippolyte often wore a lilac flower in his buttonhole in the spring to mark a lost love, possibly the lady he fought the duel for, who had made his heart melt.

The ice groaned as I shifted my weight. The girl below me did not look dead. Her eyes were the complicated, variegated blue of certain cornflowers and her hair a light blonde and her curls billowed out in the water. Somehow, between life and death, the ballet bun that held her properness in place had become unfastened. Her eyes were playful. She seemed eternally on the verge of a wonderful smile, the sort that poets write about. Her lips were coloured with a subdued rouge, suitable for librarians. Her shoes were missing as if she had kicked them off to run to her love. She was older than me but not much. She was hypnotic, entrancing and around her hundreds of other young bodies bumped and floated serenely under the ice.

There was then a cracking sound and a flight of grey-blue pigeons left the pines.

I kept very still and felt as if I could not breathe. I heard a human cry and got to my feet in too much of a rush and fell, headlong. I picked myself up and ran across the transparent ice above the upturned doll eyes of all of the librarians and dived into a snowdrift. I tugged on my glove and pulled the new snow around me like a blanket. I was shaking as much from fear as from cold when I saw a line of men on horseback coming slowly along the shore of the lake in single file and starting out across the ice.

The men then stopped.

They did not seem in any way interested or surprised by the girls under the hooves of their horses. There was no way they could not see them. The horsemen were bound up against the cold in coats and furs and every man had a rifle and ammunition belts. A mule following the horses carried a small canon with the wheels hung from its saddle bags. It was impossible to tell what side they were on as both Red and White had stopped carrying flags and banners or wearing anything like a uniform, but their furtive yet confident manner proclaimed they were dangerous.

Dangerous like wolves.

I tried not to shiver.

I knew if I gave my position away I was going to die.

On the command of an officer the soldiers cantered across the frozen lake and disappeared into the thick forest and shadows at the other side.

I stayed where I was with the snow feeling red hot against my cheeks. I thought of the girl under the ice.

When I was sure the horsemen were gone I stood up, trembling.

Before I left the lake I went and kissed the ice over the girl.

For a moment my lips stuck as if she were holding me there.

I pulled my head up, then stood, and walked quickly off the creaking ice.

The tears in my eyes froze to my face.

I set off away from the lake in a different, more northerly, direction. Antov told me moss grew on the north side of trees. I did not know what else to do. I did not know where the enemy was. I did not have a clue where I was going. I was frightened one minute, smiling my frozen face into happiness the next. I yearned for the little serf's insults, for anyone, but there was nothing but snow and forest for mile after mile.

I saw deer and stopped stock-still once when a bear crossed the track, slowly, dragging its bulk through the snow. I sucked on the bitter seeds of pinecones and gorged on rotten puffball mushrooms under the snow. But soon I was sick to my stomach with hunger again.

The whiteness of the snow became the gaps in my existence that was falling apart. I wanted to lie down and sleep. I wanted to draw up the blanket of snow and dance with the blue-eyed librarian under the ice. I then shook myself and hit myself on the head as M. Hippolyte would have done:

"That is extremely immature thinking, young man."

IMMATURE is a word not unlike rotten puffball mushrooms.

I almost said my new name out loud. I then went on and on, hungry through the bone-aching cold like any other Russian, bent like a peasant. I was probably going around in circles again and I began to question what all this was for. I prayed. There was the long howl of a wolf and I quickened my pace.

I did not think of giving up and snuggling down in the inviting snow.

Then, on the seventh day there was a different scent.

I smelled the STEW.

Like a wolf, I smelt the stew from two miles away, and I do not exaggerate. It stung my nose and lips like a bee amid the scent of pine and more snow on the wind. The smell was a velvet brown and set to a waltz. I began to drool like a dog. Then I slowed, fearful of another mounted patrol.

The word STEW haunted me as well as the scent. In any language that I knew it was possessed of a most wonderful poetry. I tried to make do with the word inside my head.

But it was no good. I was beginning to feel dizzy and stagger. It was as if there was a wild animal in me and I was prepared to kill for that food, whatever it was. Oh, dear God, I am sorry in advance for my sins, I thought as my hand went to my knife, Antov's Cossack dagger. My hand was shaking but more from fear than anticipation.

Ahead of me the trees thinned.

There were three wagons, like little houses, with stove chimneys and men dressed in sheepskin coats sat on the wooden steps, drinking vodka. I was astonished by the sudden sound of laughter. Then, out of the biggest waggon, like a dasha, decorated with painted board work, folk-art depicting simple religious dramas and the harvest – I had seen the same on the estate I had been brought up on – came a woman with bread and a large plate of pickled cucumbers and tomatoes. Over to the right of the men were a string of horses and several mules. These were not poor animals but alert and well fed. Directly in front of me was a metal tripod and a black cooking pot in which bubbled the stew and around which sat twenty strong looking men, mostly armed. To their left were more caravans. Two young girls came shouting out of one and began to fight over a scarf. A man sang and another played on a whistle. Steam and contentment rose from the small camp and I smiled at one of the girls.

There was a shout and I was grabbed from behind, my arms pinned to my sides, unable to draw my knife.

"Look, my brothers. Look what I have got for our pot."

I struggled and the men laughed. My knife was taken from me and passed around as they talked away, some in Zingari, a gypsy language I did not understand. They laughed and howled and I felt my knees go from under me as they carried me towards the bubbling pot.

"You'll not deny us fresh meat, little boy?"

I struggled more. I was seventeen but tall and managed to kick one.

"Stop this foolishness," said an aristocratic, educated voice behind me, and all did. Several looked scared as they edged away from the stew and the fire. The man who had grabbed me put me down and dusted my clothes. Slowly, I turned to face the steady blue eyes of a broad-shouldered, severe-faced woman. One large, long-fingered hand rested on a revolver in a sash around her waist, the other on her bony hip. She was tall with delicate cheekbones and was obviously not part of the rest. She smiled.

"Who are you and where do you come from?"

Her deep voice was calm and melodious and kind now, like a schoolteacher. Still, I did not answer. My tutor, M. Hippolyte, had told me to speak only under certain conditions and to one person. I realised now to do otherwise was risking sharing my identity, especially my assumed identity, and that would be as much suicide as a little serf drinking vodka without a coat. And after meeting the Tsar, my father, I was determined to carry out my mission. I did not speak even though I liked the grand lady who seemed to me like a duchess. Yet there was something odd about her.

"Has the forest run away with your tongue? Or perhaps the fairies? The fairies can do that. Do you like my fairies? For no good reason these men look to me as a leader."

One of the men plucked up his courage and came back towards me.

"We should search him. He may be a runner for the Reds."

The woman shook her head and the thought seemed to amuse her.

"This one is of noble birth. I can see it in his face and bearing, I can. And in those soft hands. He will tell us who he is by and by. The Whites are in retreat and do not threaten us. I feel a sadness on him. The sadness of all Russia. And yet, there is a rebel spirit there too. So, you thieves and murderers and sons and daughters of Scythian dogs, give him some stew and do not tell him what is in it. Give him back his knife. If he had anything valuable he would have been dead a thousand leagues ago. Look at his eyes. He has seen too much."

So I ate and ate with them and was sick and they laughed and I ate again. They said I was a wolf. The stew was good and later they told me it was made from deer they caught in nets, having driven them with arrows they threw with the aid of a leather cord, wrapped around a notch below the flights. I had been worried the meat was that of corpses frozen in the snow. Or those cooked fresh on a fire.

"My love is like a daisy, a daisy, a DAISY."

"Eat up, little one."

As we set off at dawn through the forest I realised we were not alone. There was an endless throng of people. One second I was looking at the grey and ochre forest floor and the next it was moving, a sea of blankets and old coats and pots and pans. Heading away from conflict and towards the sea. Every now and again a man or a woman or a child fell and was left in the mud and the snow and at night the wolves howled. There was no need for the Reds or the Whites anymore. The forest and the cold and hunger did the killing. But we rolled on, vigilant.

The journey up to Riga, crossing the Moscow road, was a long one but we lacked for nothing. The band I had joined was like a wild animal which ate everything along its route, but somehow they parted on good terms with those from whom they bought, begged, stole, conjured, and cajoled and for whom they performed magic tricks with a drum roll and a magnesium flash and a pretty girl.

"Did you plan to run away to join the circus?" said one gypsy girl, who I longed to have a conversation with. Increasingly, seeing the state of my stolen felt boots, the old woman let me ride in her wagon. When I was dozing she pulled on the red ribbon around my neck and looked at the silver elephant but just smiled and put it back with a finger to her lips. One day she pulled on her clay pipe and said, "Fetch that pot over by the wagon wheel?" in English. I did, and realised too late my mistake. She answered in English.

"Good God! I hardly believe this. You are meant to be dead. They have patrols out looking for you. Tipped off by the Tsar. You must keep close to me at all times. They say you are a deaf-mute, but I can see that you understand. You must also understand, I know who you are, my "mute offender". I'll steer you in the right direction at the docks. Have no fear. I will say you are an idiot we are training as a clown. You see, I do know, little prince."

For a moment it was if my heart had stopped.

What the woman said about the Tsar was not true.

Who was she?

I was glad, relieved, but I kept silent.

When we got to Riga, a pretty town of soaring church towers and domed palaces, it was full to bursting with those trying to escape to the sea. Indeed, those in the town set up barbed wire and barricades to keep refugees out. Troops fired in the air at a crowd in front of us when we attempted to drive into the centre. This was Latvia and they flew their own flag. We joined up with a more extensive circus of fire-eaters and tight-rope walkers and trained animals and fought our way through the blizzard and the starving crowd to the docks. There were sea-going barges over a hundred feet long to take the tents and seating and the cages and the animal acts for those lucky enough to be selected. And every few hours a panic seized the great rivers of people that a bombardment was about to begin from the Red or the White army, or even the German fleet, sailing in to rescue the German Tsarina. Men were offering up all their family jewellery, or even their wives, "she is twenty, with good teeth,' for the boat ride across the North Sea to England, or to Sweden or the Netherlands or France. The more loved and prized and attractive the wife, the quicker she became a ticket. There were little knots of Cheka, the new Russian revolutionary government secret police in their long leather coats, flicking amber beads on strings, looking on amused and unchallenged.

"There is no bread," came a shout. There was no food for anyone and then the crowd would suddenly rush back to the church towers of the city on the news that potatoes were being given out or papers guaranteeing a passage by a wealthy merchant.

Rumours raged around the dock like a swarm of angry bees.

Old women and children were trampled in the chaos. I saw one boy, face down in an ice puddle, one hand still holding onto a school geography book, the other to a toy rabbit.

The noise was tremendous and I heard two words repeated again and again, BOAT and PASSAGE. Respectable men and women howled and fought like animals. The noise and the smell grew of human beings trapped there like cattle. The rumours were shouted from man to man and the story often changed as it went. The Whites attacking the town became the Reds in the shouts of twenty men and women.

One thing that could not be denied, as I threaded my way down narrow cobbled streets to the dockside, was that the sea was freezing. I did not think that salt water could freeze.

Close into shore it was already a churning, pebbly mass that only needed the temperature to drop a couple more degrees to become solid.

If it did so, everyone was going to be trapped. There was a special darkness to the clouds as the shivering crowd watched the water.

I was exhausted after I wrestled my way back to the circus people I had been travelling with. Even they were scared and had to ration food and a gypsy girl and I huddled together under a blanket to eat.

The next morning the air was clear and I got up in the warehouse where we all were sleeping. I stepped over the woman leader and went out into the dawn. There had been talk last night that there could be no place on the circus barges for anyone without skills or performing talents and an old babushka had said she was going to give her place to me, even though if she were left here she was surely going to die.

Picking my way back to the wharfs, I saw one of the docks had been cleared and a group of important men, one in a white cowboy hat, was already watching people doing tricks on horses. They were hiring for a circus in England and that meant a free passage on a barge. Antov had taught me to ride well, though not at first. Then he told me that horses do not like to be touched let alone have a man on their back. Once you understand that, you begin to ride. I made friends with all horses after that. I hurried around to where the queue was.

Two men began to fight for the next place at the head of a queue of twenty, but I ran up and jumped on the waiting horse and galloped along the dock, threw down my hat, turned the horse around and picked the hat up on the way back.

I charged the group of men and made the horse rear and then step back. The only trouble was that, overconfident, I miscalculated and the horse and I nearly fell into the freezing dock. I managed to get control, embarrassed, and then I heard a voice cry out in English.

"Hire that one. Hire that lanky young fucker. He takes risks."

I saw the woman I had travelled with on the other dock and she was smiling. I did not want to leave the friends I had made, but she nodded her head and held up her hand in goodbye. Then she was gone into the crowd.

But I had made enemies too among the other boys and men waiting for a ride.

'We'll show that gypsy Cossack filth. We will feed him to the monster. We'll watch. We will feed him to the monster." My mind focussed on the word MONSTER.

That was a word I had been called in the Imperial Nursery. The word filled my head and took me away from the cold and the shouting. MONSTER. It took me too far back to the warmer world of a ballroom and white satin dresses.

I had rounded a rotting wooden shack when I was struck on the head and knew only darkness.

When I came round in the pitch black I was winded and my shoulder and back hurt and I felt myself all over for broken bones as Antov had taught me after a fall from a horse. I must have fallen on one of the hay bales near me for I was unharmed. I took a deep breath. There was a faint light seeping through a hatch cover above me and I concluded that I was in one of the sea barges waiting to take the circus across the North Sea. The hold was cold and vast and smelt of tar and salt and decaying wood below a strong odour of animal.

The word MONSTER came back into my head. There was a movement at the other end of the hold among the straw. I swallowed. I began to shake from fear as much as the cold.

I backed away from the noise and came to a stop against iron bars, the bars of a cage. My knife was useless against a MONSTER.

My shoulders were against the cage, the open top of which I could just see because of the holes between the planking. A gap of three feet between the top of the bars and the hatch indicated that the animal, whatever was moving ahead of me, was very large.

Yet however much I closed my eyes hoping that when I opened them I could see better, I could not penetrate the darkness of the hold.

There was a rustling in front of me and then the whole boat listed in the calm water of the dock.

Whatever the cage was for moved again and the boat listed the other way.

There was a thick covering of straw in the hold but the planks still shuddered with each movement. The creature was immense. It was truly a MONSTER.

Shivering, I tried to tell myself this was nonsense. M. Hippolyte had said human understanding is often the result of shouted assertions, whether internal or external, like the shrieking in a monkey house. These cloud our perception to such an extent at times it can be impossible for us to DENY that there is a PANTHER in our BED. Antov had yawned and actually quoted a French aristocrat called Montaigne who said there was nothing to fear but fear itself.

"I think you understand Montaigne more from your insufferable arrogance than any logic, Antov," said M. Hippolyte.

The creature, or creatures, moved again.

Then I had the thought that it might be a lion and remembered a print in one of M. Hippolyte's Latin books of Christians being fed to lions. I was not quite sure how big lions grew. My head hurt and so did my shoulder.

There was a large bump on my scalp that the matrons at the Imperial Nursery would have smeared with butter.

A shaft of light came from above as the tarpaulin was pulled back an inch. It was the youths I had heard talking on the dock.

"I don't believe he don't speak," one of the boys said above me. "I was talking to one of his gypo friends. He listens to everything that's said. He's a phoney or an aristo or a spy. He don't speak but he will now . . . It's going to get him. The monster is going to get him, ha, ha!" The light then vanished.

They were waiting for me to scream and cry out.

Then there was the movement again of a creature so large it made the barge actually tip forward.

I was breathing very fast now and was convinced I was in the cage with the lions. Or even a TIGER. I pictured the snarling, spitting bright orange cat that had attacked Antov's horse. My hand went to the dagger he had given me.

I waited, tense for the attack. Was the cat going to kill me with one blow or would it eat me alive? I heard my own heart beating.

I stood on tiptoe waiting for the roar, waiting for whatever it was to spring. A bright blue scream formed inside me, yet I was determined not to cry out. That was the sacred promise I had made. I felt there was a presence in the darkness watching me and I heard colossal breathing like a summer wind on the steppes. It smelled almost sweet, like roses and crushed marigolds.

My mind wandered to the stories of strange creatures not known to science that the serfs used to talk about around the fire in winter. They spoke of things they had never seen with the fanatic conviction of travelling preachers.

Perhaps it was a *vodionoy*, a water spirit that could grow as big as a house and was waiting because they only ever ate at midnight.

Frantically, I found a door in the cage behind me and tried to open it. I shook and shook the door and it made a clanging noise. On some of the animal cages down by the dock the doors were only tied with rope or chain. But here there were several chains and four smooth padlocks that I counted. I rattled the chains again just the same.

There was laughter above me.

Then I heard the beast, whatever it was at the other end of the hold, move again. There was a great and heavy sound of a foot fall. A cat did not have a tread that was so heavy. Perhaps it was a bear? I had heard my serf tell stories of how bears are such gluttons they start to eat you as soon as they catch hold of you. There was a river smell and I thought of the *vodionoy* again.

My legs were trembling but I drew myself up to my full height.

The innocent arrogance of Antov succeeded over the reasoning of M. Hippolyte. Perhaps there was nothing there at all but my fear? And if I was already as good as dead, what did it matter, what could this nameless threat lurking there in the darkness do to me that had not already been done? Except eat me, M. Hippolyte might say. It may have been simple hysteria, but Antov won.

I took a deep breath and edged forward and as if by a miracle my foot moved and then I moved the other, still more scared than I had been of anything in my life.

I approached the creature at the other end of the darkness and held out one hand, expecting any moment to hear a growl and a deafening roar. Why did I not hear a growl? I could not remember what sound water spirits made.

I then jumped out of my very soul as I felt something warm and a little wet touch my hand and in a moment was gone.

The *vodionoy*!

I crossed myself repeatedly and silently said a prayer to all the Saints and to the Holy Mother.

The fleeting contact made me stand as still as a statue and I felt fear beyond words.

Had I put my fingers in the mouth of the creature?

It knew where I was and saw in the darkness better than I did. Any moment the mouth might come back. The water spirits had been known to eat whole families.

I remained still, except for the occasional trembling.

I felt a light expiration of breath on my face and I was being touched by whatever it was, gently, on my head. It did not make sense.

It seemed to be hovering above me like something diabolical. I silently said another prayer I had learned in the Imperial Nursery.

I reached up slowly to touch again whatever it was that seemed to be sniffing me. Could it only be a giant horse? I had seen huge carthorses being worked in the fields at the Potemkin house. Blinking in the darkness I had the impression that the creature moved backwards onto a thicker bed of straw. I heard the straw crushed under the heavy footfall.

Any second it could rush and crush me against the bars. I saw a bull crush a farmer's arm on a nearby estate and later he had died of blood poisoning. It had waited and waited until it had the right moment.

My legs were still shaking but the worst thing was to show fear. I walked forward and held out my hand again and then I went cold.

My hands touched a tepid, living skin harder than anything I had ever touched. It had ridges like a mountain range or the surface of the moon.

The surface was indented and hairy in places. The beast did not pull away. It let me put my hands on its huge body. It was like nothing I even could imagine. I ran my hands up and down immense and heavy legs of which there seemed to be three in the front. What animal has three legs? Or six? Or five? Did the *vodionoy* have three legs? It was like a riddle. I stood back and doubted my own senses.

I felt very weary and slowly I sat down in the straw, straight into a pile of dung.

As I did so the animal touched me again. The touch was gentle and soft and warm.

With great difficulty I held my face steady.

This time it very distinctly stroked my face. The animal was stroking my cheek.

When I got control of my breathing I told myself there was a keen intelligence out there in the darkness.

Was the monster trying to comfort me?

It was a revelation that left me in wonder. The stroking stopped and we remained there in silence, each peering into the darkness.

I heard a sniggering from the hatch above.

"It's killed him. It's a killer. It killed a man. It's true."

Perhaps whatever it was intended to tease me, like a cat does a mouse. I began to breath very rapidly indeed.

"Getaway you scum," a man yelled above. "Cast off forward. Cast off aft. She's tied on."

The boys ran away along the planking above and the barge began to move, slowly at first.

I had never been at sea and after a few minutes we began to feel the undulations of the waves. The whole motion of the sea was strange to me as if there were nothing solid and true anymore.

For nearly a day, the waves were small and lapping the side of the boat. The creature did not move. But then we started to pitch and corkscrew through the swell.

The barge had begun to head out into the open sea before its timbers could be hemmed in and broken by the already forming ice. I experienced a moment of true panic. I had learned to swim in a creek near my house but not very far and I knew I would last only minutes in the icy water if somehow I was to get out of the hold. The *vodionoy* would be in its element.

The soft mouth-like parts touched me again and were gone.

I looked around me but saw nothing.

The boat rocked more and my head started to spin. I did not know up from down.

The creature touched my head and this time remained there, examining my hair.

I closed my eyes and put my hand onto the thing.

Whatever it was that the creature had touched me with I held onto hard this time.

A wave hit the side of the barge and there was a sound like an explosion.

We both were frightened, I felt, as the flat-bottomed barge rolled and pitched more. The animal began to make little noises of alarm and I stroked its ridged skin.

I gave the creature an apple I had saved in my pocket.

The soft, mouth-like parts gripped it and I heard the sound of eating, but further away. I had no idea what the creature was. Another mouth was somewhere else. Perhaps it had many heads and many mouths. M. Hippolyte had told me of the Scylla in Homer, a beautiful nymph that turned into a monster with many mouths. And then there was the Hydra.

Outside I heard the wind was getting up and I wondered whether I could squint through the crack in the hatch cover.

I patted the mouth parts that were near me again and climbed up the bars and tried to peer out through the crack. I endeavoured to make a spy hole larger with my knife, but it was no use. The wood was too thick. I could only see a little.

In the distance the sky was light but had gone a strange greenish, grey colour.

Above, the clouds were jet black and I could feel the strength of the wind through the aperture.

Snow and hail were being blown ahead of the wind.

The sea stretched away and away into nothing like the steppe and the waves broke on themselves in foaming torrents.

I watched fascinated as the waves rose, much higher than the boat, as high as a small tree, and when one had hit us another followed. The wind blew harder. In the distance I could see the lights of another boat signalling. The day itself was becoming darker, dark as night with only a yellow-white band on the far horizon. The storm was growing and I had to hold fast to maintain my position at the top of the bars. The waves then began hitting the side of the barge with a bang like a cannon and suddenly water was in my eye and I fell.

Another wave sent water splashing down on me and onto the creature.

I went back to climb but with an extended curling limb the creature drew me down to the hold floor.

More waves rocked us and we pitched so violently that I thought we must go over and I began to pray again to the Saints and to the Holy Mother. I prayed for the monster as well. It, too, was dwarfed by the storm.

The creature stood.

It had drawn back into the darkness and was swinging from side to side and making the movement of the boat much worse. I heard shouts from above but they were lost in the screaming wind. I had begun to feel very sick but having not eaten for a while was not able to bring anything back. The creature was making an anguished noise and I stepped forward again and the strange, bendy limb sent me flying.

The animal was bashing itself against one side of the boat and then the other. The timbers of the barge smelt like field mushrooms with rot and I wondered how much they might stand. I was convinced we were going to go down, if the monster did not kill me first. It had occurred to me that its present comradeship might only have been brought about by the strangeness of our situation

I went forward again and, guessing right between rolls of the barge, took hold of one of the huge legs. I reached up and grabbed the bendy limb and pulled as hard as I was able. The limb wrapped itself around me like a snake but the creature began to kneel and I had to move to one side as solid horns which came from its head region were against the deck. Was it a demon? The animal then lay down and I remained still. If I tried to move it became agitated again as the storm screamed and whistled through the hatch cover overhead. There was a flash of lightning visible above through the small hole and a detonation of thunder followed and the creature gripped me tighter.

After a while the storm seemed to lessen in its fury but then began to build again and was so much more savage than before.

I heard rats squeaking in the timbers above us and was convinced we were at an end. I had read that rats tried to leave a sinking ship when all hope was gone. All my knowledge of the sea was from books and I had not even been on the river in St Petersburg. I nuzzled my head into the ridged grey skin.

The word IDIOT entered my mind to the exclusion of the monster and the storm.

My promise to the Holy Man, Rasputin, was over.

A low, insistent sound then filled the space of the hold. It was not coming from the deck above, but from the creature. It was as if I was not being rocked by the sea anymore but by a cradle of infinite and subtle sound. With the strange and almost silent musical vibration, the monster told me not to be afraid. It was a note that made my whole body tingle like a tuning fork. A bright, sunlit, singing sound deep inside my chest. It was a sound that calmed both the monster and me. It was as soothing as a mother's lullaby that I had heard in the serfs' hut, but at the same time made one lucid and gave a space to think. Not merely think, to hide in a word like IDIOT or MONSTER, but to go out into the world.

That sound seemed to place all I had seen, all the horrors

that I had experienced, in a new context. In the song of the monster I glimpsed the absurdity of the world I had been travelling through and what we could all be, even the most vicious and stupid.

Eventually, after many more hours, the motions stopped and I must have passed out.

Above me there was a commotion and I heard the shout of the American, the ringmaster, who had hired me.

"If they've been messing with . . ."

The hatch was thrown open and I blinked at the light and the unmistakable shape of the man who was dressed as a cowboy. He had long blond hair under a large wide-brimmed hat. At his waist was a gun belt with two pearl-handled pistols. He was more than a little overweight.

"This I don't believe," said the American.

I turned round and looked into the eye of the creature for the first time. It was an elephant. It was not a tiger or a lion or a *vodionoy*. I had crossed the sea in the darkness with an elephant and cursed my stupidity for not realising that the middle leg was a trunk. The animal was the size of a small mountain crag.

There in broad daylight it was the most obvious of truths and I was angry with myself for being a simpleton.

The elephant had an intelligent and kindly gaze, both wise and playful, the eyes a very pale blue, and I knew instinctively, without looking further, that the creature was female. It was an elephant! I felt for the silver one with the word *Fumoo* written on its side around my neck to show her. An African elephant. I had seen elephants in books of course and at the Selo palace zoo on that winter's day with the Tsar and at the circus in Moscow. But I had never been so close and unprotected. The beast put her heavy trunk around my body and gently hugged me to her. I thought of the elephants on the Pushkin coat of arms in M. Hippolyte's study, the poet proud his family came from Africa. Had the little silver elephant belonged to Pushkin? The word filled my head again, ELEPHANT, SION, but I left it there and turned back to the creature.

'Looks like our killer pachyderm has found a friend,' said the American in the cowboy hat.

I noticed the chains on the animal's back legs.

The American took a step nearer and the holster belt he wore creaked.

The elephant then lifted its trunk from me and let out an ear-splitting sound in contrast to the gentle one that had calmed me.

The American backed away but smiled.

"Come see me when you have finished with your new friend, my boy, when we land. I have a job for you." The American held up a hand and waggled his finger. "This is my circus. We are anchored off Denmark. We have dropped the Skagerrak pilot and are waiting for one for the Humber and England. We lost one boat but it's going to be plain sailing now. Maybe another week."

One of the sailors then threw down some ship's biscuits, which I could not eat, and hay for the elephant that she ignored. The American was still there.

"I'm going to have such a spectacle in England. A real show. I'm going to hang this murderess from a crane by a chain. That's going to be her fate for tearing one of my best animal men in half. In half! Even a man like myself who has seen what Indians do, did not think that possible. In half! Now she has to face the music. They already did it by crane in Erwin, Tennessee and electrocuted one in New York. We could, of course, combine the two with the proper safety measures. They shot a lion in Norwich, or some such town, and drew a crowd of a thousand people, all paying good money. In Erwin they drew a crowd of two thousand five hundred people. It was a wonder. They burned a negro for abducting a white woman the same day and no one much came. The public demand new things. It will be the greatest show on earth. In a world in chaos we have to show the beast who's boss, don't we, boy? I remember you. You're the rider. I think you have a great future but don't get too fond of that critter. She tore my man apart when we took her calf. It was sent to a White general for a banquet. We can't train an African elephant. They're vicious. Like an Apache Indian. Jump you when your back is turned, although this one didn't wait for the man to turn his back. They don't forget and nor do I. It's two weeks from today and we're gonna paint her red to make her look even more bad. Oh, yes. She's gonna die ugly."

Yet for all his vicious words when he had gone the elephant relaxed and again her trunk rested gently on my chest. For the first time in a long time, perhaps the whole of my life, I strangely felt truly at HOME with her. I had begun making plans to escape when we got to land, even though it was absurd for me to travel with such a beast. I already loved her, completely. She rested her trunk against my hand. The end of an elephant's trunk is like a hand and she tickled the centre of my palm as if she was trying to cheer me up. She was not asking me for anything with her big eyes that seemed to absorb and forgive all the hatred and badness in the world.

That was precisely why I had to help her. She was the most intelligent being I had met in my walk across an insane and broken world.

TWELVE

NATASHA WAS SITTING at her desk in the empty library, eating a chicken sandwich on rye that she was not meant to bring in. The acting chief librarian had the sort of eyes that could locate a breadcrumb at thirty paces, or spot if someone was doing a little writing on the side. One girl had been let go, but Natasha had assured the woman in charge she was not writing, however she could see from the librarian's suspicious smile that she did not believe this was true. Natasha ate the sandwich quickly and immediately wanted another. She wondered, in anticipation of her meeting with the mysterious Russian woman, Nadya, how much of the story was actually true, how much fiction. She drank a mouthful of coffee that was equally illegal and then took out her phone. That was forbidden too. There was the slamming of a door in the library building that echoed through the entire place and she was reminded of her dream and expected to see butterflies. She looked down at the phone and saw an email she had received earlier that had made her mad.

From ChiChiChica Froment@fas.harvard.edu
To NatashaA@gmail.com

You told me that you were covered in blood when you left the hotel. You were covered in blood, your white blouse was red when you went to your friend's flat. You got rid of all your fancy clothes. All the clothes that he had bought you. Forgive me for stating the obvious but that does sound like rape to me and not rough sex. More than that, and you know this to be true, the man is making a fool of you. He has got you in his power. He is stealing the Natasha I remember. He is stealing your identity. He is still inside you, fucking with your plans. That is also rape. He only wants to destroy and maybe he can turn that passion in you his way. Don't let him. He wants to control you. He wants to hog-tie your intellect and lead you by the cunt. It is the only way men like him deal with intelligent women.

Please, let's see each other?x ChiChi

Natasha wished she had not told her former professor anything. She certainly knew where to hit. Even though she was a size taller than other girls, Natasha had always been frightened that she was in danger of disappearing, like the orphans in the Imperial Nursery on the toilet. In her first memories it was into the landscape, into a tree or rock and then into another person. But she could remember her mother had once embarrassingly remarked in front of friends that Natasha avoided sitting on her potty for a while, because she thought she was losing part of herself in the act of defecation. Later, when she found she could disappear into a book like 101 *Dalmations*, she worried she was in danger of being trapped in there too. It got worse as the books became better. She felt she was inside the Russian book now and it was not totally a good thing. She wanted to appreciate the Elephant, the calming figure at the centre of the storm, in her own life. She wanted the strange creature and its song to help her let go of the man in Paris.

She turned to the book's next packet that had arrived in the mail. Natasha also pressed the elephant app on her phone and listened to the strange, singing sound again. She was sure it was meant, however imperfectly, to be the sound of the elephant.

THIRTEEN

THE UNEXPECTED MANUSCRIPT: PACKET VII

"YOU STILL ALIVE down there, boy? Welcome to England."

The American was an unusual man, even in Europe and by the standards of the time. He was very tall but quite fat and went under the name of Mr Masterson and wore red, lizard skin high-heeled cowboy boots to his white suit, which had a three-quarter-length jacket and a white waistcoat. He did not have a necktie but a cord threaded through a piece of turquoise and gold that was his lucky charm and that he had stolen from an Indian burial ground forbidden to all on penalty of an eternal curse.

I learned later, too, that he had won the circus in a card game.

He had bright, laughing blue eyes, like the turquoise he wore at his throat and just as opaque and unreadable, and the impish face of a child that made his age hard to tell. The one thing that was impossible to deny was his enthusiasm with which he approached whatever scheme, good or bad. If he knew about the dark river of fire it did not worry him.

The hatch covers had been rolled back and it was a cold, sunny morning. Potatoes were thrown down for the elephant and bread for me. I had to force myself to eat the damp, mouldy loaf as I still felt sick. We had juddered to a halt an hour before and now made our way very slowly as we docked. Was England where I was meant to go? Orders were shouted. "Tie up forward." There was a bump. "Tie up, aft." And we were still. I thanked the Holy Virgin and all the Saints.

I went over and hugged the trunk of the elephant. ELEPHANT. That was all I ever called her. To call her a girl's name or any human name did not seem at all right. She was a wild thing with a different frame of reference to our own and as I had no birth name we were brother and sister in anonymity. She lifted her trunk gently and fondled my ear. I knelt down and looked at the brass shackles that had a heavy padlock. At least, they had not been welded.

I sighed.

She was such a beautiful creature, magnificent, but at the same time intelligent and endearing. Her ears were great curtains when she set them apart from her massive head and when she took the slightest step towards me the barge shuddered. She towered to the top of the roof, as high as a tree. In my mind I shouted out I was going to free her and almost at once I felt the vibration, the note I had felt before, something that sounded a happy chord within me and shone a different light on everything. She reached out her trunk and put it gently on my head.

There was a noise from above and the vibration stopped. The American was back.

"I want that beast blood red, do you hear? I want her drenched in BLOOD. She tore one of my best men apart and I want it to show. We can parade her through the streets to the Big Top." I smelt the scent of rich cigar smoke as the American peered down into the hold.

"Do we do the boy too?"

The American thought for a moment.

"The boy! The boy! What a stroke of genius! Oh, yes. He can be the son of the trainer that was torn apart. And he does seem to have a rapport with the animal. We can parade them through the streets with that boy on her head. Yeah, drench the boy too. We'll say it is his father's life blood. That will draw them in. After all that blood in the trenches the public demand a real spectacle, a thrill. That'll draw them in from as far away as London."

He said those words and then red dye splashed down on us. My fists clenched by themselves and I very nearly shouted up through the hatch at the absurdity and idiocy of it all and then I remembered that benign note, that wonderful vibration, the humming, singing sound that cracked apart the mundane of a moment ago and went over and sat between the elephant's legs and gripped one of them hard. She did not move but took the splashing with the dye as if it were a bath.

When it was over we both looked as if we had stepped out of a slaughterhouse.

I stood up and gazed back at her and the colour made her strange and fierce. They had turned her into the monster that the show required. I went back and held her legs in protest again as above I could hear the American. "Get your tickets for your first glimpse of the killer monster, soon to be scientifically executed." I heard children scream in mock fear on the dockside.

A stone was thrown down into the hold and hit her trunk and bounced off. I threw it back and was glad when I heard a shout of pain. The American's voice boomed out.

"There's a boy down there, folks. Have a care! A boy who has lost his father torn apart by the jungle beast you see before you covered from head to toe, from trunk to tail, in the man's red blood. The poor child is covered in that blood as well and that's why he threw the stone back again, sir. He devoted himself to the care of this beast as did his father and wishes to continue to do so, even after such a crime against himself and his poor mother who died of shock reciting the Twenty-Third Psalm. She was a good person who did not deserve this. Move away now, ladies and gentlemen, so planks can be put down and everyone in the good city of Hull will be able to see the beast before she is sent to the hot place of eternal torment. But let us have a hand of applause for this brave boy who honours his father in what he does. In a moment you will see his parent's blood spattered on his clothes and tears still in his eyes . . ."

It was not anger I experienced at the American's words, more surprise. I sensed that the elephant felt that too. In Russia I thought that I had experienced every sort of lie: a house being a lie, a bridge being a lie, a Tsar, a revolution. (I, and most people, educated and non-educated, rich and poor, agreed with the shining ideas and ideals of the REVOLUTION constructed in brilliant thought, in a library with the very best intentions, even Antov and M. Hippolyte, but not what happened to those fragile ideas when they were carried off in real life's RIVER of dark fire, which had swept my Russia, and its laudable revolutionary dreams, completely away.) Indeed, in many ways, I was somewhat short of the whole truth myself. Yet nothing quite prepared me for the man in the white cowboy hat. He altered the world as he spoke to the way it pleased him, not with shame but with an exuberance and complete relish as if he were eating a fabulous meal.

The talent had its roots in what M. Hippolyte called a paradox. "If a Cretan tells you all Cretans are liars, how can he be speaking the truth?" At this, Antov had grinned. "What we Russians bring to the debate is to accept there are as many different versions of the truth as blades of grass on the steppe. If we think a thing is true it is so. We are a generous people, unlike these cretins you refer to." The American was generous. He solved the paradox by building a new Crete, a new world, from lies.

Planks were put down into the hold so the elephant might walk out. There was talk of a crane if not and the creature nudged me as if she wanted to comply. She brushed me with her trunk towards her left leg and then held that leg up. With the help of her trunk I climbed up until I was out of the hatch, with my legs across her neck and my knees behind her ears.

Slowly, and with baby steps, she edged her way up the thick oak gangplanks that began to bend. I rubbed her ear to reassure her. I gulped in the salty, smoky air of the dockside, glad to be heading for dry land. She inched forward and then with a supreme effort emerged into the sunshine. There was a cheer and she paused, blinking.

A crowd had gathered along the dock and at the dock gates. It was not only those from the docks that had gazed down at us in the hold for a few pennies, but the whole of the city seemed to have turned out. There was even a fire engine with its ladder partially extended and soldiers from a local military establishment in dull, brown battledress with their rifles at the ready. There were hurdy-gurdy men and their monkeys and candyfloss sellers and standing by the American in his white suit with his six-guns at his side on a raised dais was probably the mayor of the city, who had a chain of office that glinted in the winter sunshine. There was a cold wind blowing from the sea and a light covering of snow had settled. A short way up the road a bareheaded preacher was declaiming from a pulpit on how it was a mortal sin to be beastly and to eat certain beasts was forbidden.

"The Lord of Hosts states in Leviticus that no one shall eat ravens, red kites, geckos or chameleons. Neither shall you eat any kind of owls or cats. You must only eat creatures with divided hoofs and therefore shall you not eat elephants . . ."

The crowd laughed.

The elephant then walked forward along the dock and there was a hush so you could almost imagine that you could hear the ticking of the aldermen's watches or the clock in the great clock tower.

"There she is, my lords, ladies and gentlemen," said the American. "The murdering monster that I promised you, covered in the blood of her victim and ridden fearlessly by the boy who saw his father ripped apart. Such a brave, brave boy. We know the whole country, the whole world, owes a lot to such brave, brave boys from every family in the land. And don't worry, ladies and gentlemen, no expense has been spared to secure your safety as this monster is taken for safe incarceration near my Big Top, so that she can be dispatched in a week's time."

I do not know, I still do not know, if the elephant understood every word or indeed any word said. She certainly understood the tone of what was being expressed but, as she walked up to the city fathers, what she did next was more out of playfulness than anger.

She raised her magnificent head and trumpeted.

The sound was so loud that children and women ran and one of the soldiers cocked his rifle.

She then stepped forward and put her trunk into a large bowl of lemonade of one of the street vendors, sucked up the contents and turned and sprayed the dignitaries, missing the

American, who was no doubt her real target, by a few inches.

There was a cheer from the crowd.

"She's got the right idea. Let her go," shouted a woman.

A photographer dashed in front of us and there was a flash as he took a picture. I thought the elephant was about to bolt. She did not. It was only when she stepped forward again that I realised that the pictures were going to be in the local newspapers and probably national newspapers. It added to my need to escape. ESCAPE is a good word.

"That was an endearing trick with the lemonade, but this is a wild animal," said Mr Masterson. "The African elephant is untameable. Untameable. Gaze at her enormity. She is four yards tall at least, and ten trunk tip to tail hair. She weighs six tons, which is more than any automobile, and those tusks are two yards long. She is a jungle killing machine. A monster from the darkness of all our pasts. She has to be executed. That is what the law demands. But in the same civilised way as you all decided to go to a just war in this greatest of all democracies, I'm going to let you choose whether we shoot her, hang her from a crane or electrocute her. I'm for the latter as it is the most scientific method, recommended by the finest minds and appropriate for this new visionary age of ours. We'll circulate cards and in a week's time when you all come to the show you, the people, will decide on how the monster will meet her end."

At that, a band began to play and we followed it through the town.

For the most part, the crowd was in awe and the only other rock thrown hit the euphonium player. It was a curious feeling being perched up so high above the crowd and a spectacle for everyone to see when I had been trying to hide everything about myself. I wondered if, by now, the revolutionaries had a picture of me. There was no Russian photograph I knew of that was recent. I was then overcome by a wave of sadness that I did not have a picture of M. Hippolyte and Antov. They had been so brave in remaining behind. I had been wrong to think of them as idle strollers at times.

What struck me too was that the people here seemed so much better clothed and fed than ordinary people in St Petersburg. A sailor with a bottle suddenly capered in front of us and the elephant trumpeted again. We then turned down a road to an open area where the Big Top tent was being erected and behind it was a huge metal cage with a sleeping area. I got down from the elephant and was about to follow her inside when I was grabbed by the American who pulled me back. He was surprisingly strong.

"You and I are going to have a little talk, my boy. You seem to be the star of the show, my show. I want you to understand what this is all about. I have taken a shine to you. A definite shine!"

Most of the circus were in caravans on one side of the Big Top and the animal cages were on the other. A high fence had been erected and was already being painted with an elephant trampling men and impaling a child on its tusks by a talented local artist who, working fast, still had many more panels to do. There was the sharp smell of dung from the camels and horses and a roaring from the lions and tigers. My hands shaking, I helped put the elephant in the cage and held tight to her trunk, pledging silently I was going to be back later and we were going to escape. She looked at me and blinked. Her eyes had long lashes.

"Don't worry, boy. You can come and go as you please. He can come and go as he pleases, okay?" said the American, to a small crowd of circus people who had followed us. "Anything he wants within human reason. Give to him like yesterday. Or you will have to answer to Sam Masterson."

Sam Masterson had his own house that was on this piece of wasteland.

It had belonged to a railway manager and the American had persuaded the manager to rent it before going to Riga to add to his circus. The manager was currently with his wife's family in the Lake District, a part of England that sounded very agreeable, the home of many poets, doubtless congratulating himself at the stroke of luck of meeting Mr Masterson.

The American took me across to the house and ushered me indoors, which was a surprise. Except for toilet facilities the house was now one large room and very expensively furnished, with a pretty showgirl sitting on the settee who jumped up when we entered and took Mr Masterson's white hat.

"I hate these teeny-weeny British houses where there is no room to breathe. I'm an outdoor man. Born on the range. So I had the floors torn out. I think it is an improvement. You were great with that elephant, son. You sure have an intelligent civilised look about you for one of these Russian circus horse riders. Are you sure you are a deaf mute? Convenient that you are, as you cannot tell anyone that you are not who I say you are. You'll have to get used to my theatrical whimsies and terminological inexactitudes. Now, Miss Emily, run this man a bath. He looks like he needs to soak a thousand miles of steppe out of his hide."

Miss Emily, who had a delightful smile, ran me a bath. I could not stop looking at her. It was a long copper bath with a patent water heater beside it that delivered scalding hot water at the turn of a tap. I blinked. Miss Emily had red hair that was in curls close to her head. She had delicate features except for a definite, slightly turned-up nose and very large sky-blue eyes, reminding me a little of the princess at the Christmas Ball in St Petersburg. She was wearing a frilled bodice or basque of a silky material and dark tights, which must have been her costume for the show. My mouth fell open. I had seen lady tightrope walkers and trapeze artists in similar things, but nothing like Miss Emily. She smelled of that delicate though powerful French perfume used by the ladies at the balls in Selo palace. I wondered if she was going to give me a bath like the specially licensed servants did in the Imperial Nursery: ordinary people, let alone serfs, were not allowed to touch the Imperial Family. I could feel my body was hoping for this too fervently, I wanted her most visibly, and tried to think of one of the longest and most boring sermons the Papas used to give us, especially one on how penitence and suffering itself can become a dangerous indulgence. Even this was no good and instead I began to think again of Mr Masterson's easy ability with the truth. I recalled one day at Mikhailovskoye, when the snow prevented any of us from going far on foot outside, I had simply said: "The river will be covered over in ice for the rest of the winter." It made it possible to get around the estate on horseback. M. Hippolyte, had put down his long, clay pipe and raised his eyebrows.

"So that's the truth?"

"Yes," I said. I knew he was going to ask me a school-work question but expected one on physical geography or the Russian winter.

"How do you know something is the truth?"

I thought we were back on the questions of how we see the world.

"From observation?"

He nodded and took another puff of his pipe.

"Good answer. What if you look, though, and things seem to be one thing and really are another? This building looks like a great mansion from afar. It is not until you get close that you can see the reality. You can look down at a pile of leaves that is in reality a viper. Or think there is a viper when there is a pile of leaves. How do we know the river is there at all?"

I laughed.

"I do. I swam in it."

"How do you know the river was not a dream? How do you know you are not now dreaming?"

He was smiling his impish little smile and curling his small moustache. Yet I felt a chill.

"How do you know you exist at all?"

The philosophy lesson was interrupted at that point when Antov shoved his dagger through the cords of the chair my tutor was sitting on and pricked M. Hippolyte in the bottom. The Frenchman jumped up.

"Because one is bored . . . ?" said Antov. "Don't weigh the poor boy down with *Cogito ergo sum*, I think, therefore I am. We should not start out from first principles. We are in Russia. We are either bored, drunk or completely confused by the fairy stories we tell ourselves. The only way we know a river is a river is when we jump in drunk and drown. A dagger in the bottom conquers doubt." Already M. Hippolyte had picked up two chairs and thrown them at Antov before looking round for his swordstick. However, it was a revelation to me that all my book learning might be for nothing and laid down a basis for doubt and that I must question all things. Thinking about it and my missing friends distracted me only a little from Miss Emily and her black-bordered corset.

"Miss Emily, you go and get us some victuals and let this hero have a bath and wash the blood off. Like Homer's heroes washed themselves in the pools of Attica in the rosy-fingered dawn."

Mr Masterson was now standing behind his desk and he took off his gun belt with the pearl-handled pistols and for a moment I was worried that he was going to get in with me, which would have meant all the water would have been displaced. To my relief he sat down at his desk and began to sift through papers. I had taken my clothes off down to my combination underpants, which had been supplied by St Petersburg and were of the expensive kind. I was embarrassed but had often washed in front of the gypsies and so took off my combinations and eased myself into the blissful water while Mr Masterson looked at photographic images through a magnifying glass on his desk. I lay down under the water in complete joy and washed my hair twice. When I came up for the second time I heard Mr Masterson say.

"You have mighty smooth skin for a gypsy or a Cossack. I make no observation in that. True, you is sunburned on your hands and face but the rest of you is pretty damn soft. My, if you could talk I bet there is a story there to tell. I used to live in the West, on the frontier, where you have to be able to sum up the other fella real fast or he may kill you. That even goes for boys like you. I knew Billy the Kid when he was a young man. I rode with him when robbing banks seemed the best way of making money. He had a sunrise smile just like you do. It was usually the very last thing most people who opposed him saw on this earth."

He paused and rocked back in his chair.

"What if I were to say to you that your mother was a no-good, syphilitic whore too bad to live in a pig sty, who fucked more men than religion?"

I continued to stare at him. I knew there was no way he

could possibly know my mother. I didn't. I gave him my wide smile and splashed down in the water again and he appeared content. I had got all the red dye off me now and in some ways felt I was betraying the elephant. Yet if I was to help her I had to get into the confidence of Mr Masterson, who appeared to like children, or at least the young, because I sensed he was a child deep down.

Then the door burst open.

"This is going to go wrong! I can feel it. It is going to go very wrong!" said a dark, middle-aged man I had seen organising the animal cages. "We are new here and we make the big trouble for ourselves, you see. One of the animal trainers left already. Elephants never forget," he said. "Elephants never forgetting. If they don't get back at you in this life they will get you in the next. Where your six-guns then, Mr Masterson?"

The American lay back in his chair and calmly lit another cigar.

"Now calm down, Roberto. I love you so much I am going to let you make an announcement to the entire troupe. To the entire troupe. Even the tigers and lions if you want, that everyone is going to get paid. Did you hear the ringing magic of that little word? Everyone is going to get paid with the advance money that we have got in so far and that is not counting today or selling on those barges and boats we came across in. You'll get your pay too, Roberto."

The man seemed stopped in his tracks and momentarily looked to me for help.

"We're going to get paid?"

"Today, if you want."

"But you should have sent back those boats, Mr Masterson. The poor refugees will now starve without those boats. They will starve and the Reds will sweep down on them."

Masterson sighed and took out one of his pistols and spun the chamber.

"Well, that was taken out of these blameless hands, you can tell everyone that. I had to sell them to the government here for a military scheme that I am not meant to divulge but is of national and I mean national importance and will endear us to the good folk here about. I feel for those poor souls, I really do. I have myself journeyed West without hope and only the Lord God to pray to and he not out of bed on account the morning was too damn cold. Do you think you can go and get this trainer back? The elephant might not forget but the elephant ain't paying him. Anyways, the boy is better by far at looking after the creature. Did you see the way that this hero rode him through town? I'd like to see you do that. He deserves the Victoria Cross. He deserves the Medal of Honour."

Roberto wrung his hands. I was not clear whether it was at the prospect of money or what had happened to those we left behind on the dock in Riga.

But at that moment Miss Emily came back through the door with a flourish and two plates in her hands. The steaks weighed down heavy on the plates and I felt my mouth begin to salivate, just like in the forest when I had smelled the stew from two miles away. I again thought about those on the dock at Riga.

"Now who's for steak and fried onions? They are fresh from the market. Can I get you one too, Mr D'Annunzio? Roberto?"

While Miss Emily was getting another steak I slipped out of the bath and dressed before she came back. I was fed and Mr Masterson looked at me rather suspiciously again as I used my knife and fork to eat the steak and in particular forgot to use the fork as a shovel for the onions and other vegetables. The steak was huge and so good it made me feel a little sick so I did not eat it all which was just as well as it was followed by vanilla ice cream with what was called raspberry vinegar and a cup of wonderful coffee, which I sipped and savoured. Mr Masterson had a relationship with a hotel owner in the town who had a brilliant chef who had escaped the war by lying about his eyesight. Mr Masterson had his meals cooked because he had promised to direct the world's press to the hotel when the elephant was executed. I looked at the blood on the steak plate in front of me and did not finish my ice cream either.

"My, what a delicate little heathen we have amongst us . . . Now, go to your quarters and lie down, my boy. This lady and I have important matters of the sawdust strewn ring to discuss. And then a little sleep. Come back in a few hours."

Miss Emily raised her eyebrows and Mr Masterson rang a huge hand bell he kept on his desk. A man came to the door.

I was shown my own quarters in a hut at the back of the house. We passed a pile of homely things I took to be the railway manager's belongings. I stood in front of them for a moment. There were dolls and teddy bears and a colouring book of the type of ordinary childhood I never had and at that moment truly missed. There were wedding photographs and cheap furniture and a sign which said Home Sweet Home that had been embroidered and a half-submerged silver cup for learning to swim that even the gypsies did not want under one of the heavy beams that Mr Masterson had had taken out. I cursed myself not just at enjoying the steak so much but relaxing with Mr Masterson and Miss Emily as if they were friends and not the enemy of all I had recently discovered. My hut was warm due to an iron stove and had its own water cistern and tin bath. Mr Masterson had said he was in need of a "little sleep" after his steak and several glasses of American whiskey and I wondered if the red-headed Miss Emily stayed to have a "little sleep" with him. I lay there clean and felt like a traitor to the elephant after all she had taught me. I tried to remember the sound and the vibration that showed me the world anew. Tears ran down my cheeks as I thought of the elephant and what was planned. I had been so easily won over but what could I do? I had been bought with some half-cooked cow and frozen milk.

I did sleep for a while and when I awoke it was much later in the afternoon and the light had started to go and a cold wind had got up. I went straight up to see the elephant and the painted stockade around her cage was nearly finished. The artist was still busy on the last picture, of an elephant tearing apart a Kindergarten and children running in all directions while the beast lifted one up with its bloody trunk. The artist was painting quickly and complaining to the man called Roberto.

"I have more or less run out of red."

Roberto nodded.

"It good picture. Mr Masterson will be pleased. We get you more red if you want. Mr Masterson say lots of red. Lotta bloodiness."

The artist went on painting and then Roberto noticed me.

"You cannot come in here now. Go away."

I stood there and stared at him. He knew what Mr Masterson had said. He raised his hand to me but I did not move. Over his shoulder, through the last gap in the boards, I was able to see the elephant. Roberto turned and looked at her as suddenly the inch-thick bars of the cage appeared fragile if she became angry.

"I let you in for ten minuti, ten minuti. I not let you in for a second longer. And I no have key so you just go up to the bars. You go to the bars, that is all. And no tricks and monkey business. I know when people making the monkey business."

I stared at him and he got out of my way.

"That boy have witchcraft in him," said Roberto.

"Then get him to get me some more red,' said the artist. "It can't be bloody if I do not have fucking red."

I went to the bars and the elephant put her trunk up to my hand and I knew she felt my sorrow and confusion but it was all right. The bars were quite wide, about a foot apart, and though I had eaten better since I travelled with the circus band in Russia my weight had gone down and down. I easily squeezed though the bars. I put my arms around one of her legs and hugged her tight. I said a silent prayer to all the saints, big and small, and to the horizon that I was going to free her and we were going to walk out of this place and I was going to take her home. I thought of the word on the silver elephant, FUMOO, and how Antov pronounced it FREE ME. At first I had the notion that somehow 'home' was going to be Russia, but then I realised that probably could never happen and anyway it should be her proper home in Africa. I had a clear vision inside my head of her running through the jungle with delight. It was an endless jungle by a great, happy river under a vast pearl grey sky and the land there was nobody's and everybody's: it was all in a state of Grace before men thought of such limiting things. As these pictures came to me the vibration, the low sound, emanated from the elephant again and suffused me with light and hope. The poet Pushkin would approve, I was certain. The elephant played with my hair with her trunk and I did not know why all men and women did not think as I did. It was so simple.

I heard a movement behind me. The elephant's song ceased.

"Look at him, he is on his knees before her. He prays to the elephant like a God," said the artist. "Such innocence and courage. Perhaps they are the only innocents left in Europe. I'd love to paint the boy. Before he's corrupted. Do you think it takes longer to corrupt a deaf mute?"

Roberto, the animal trainer, was not listening to the artist.

"I donta like any of this thing. It'sa all the monkey business."

"Didn't one Pope have monkey saints in the Vatican?" said the artist. Then there was a commotion behind him and a white-faced boy with a damaged eye threw a stone at the elephant that hit her on the trunk. I nearly cried out. The elephant reached and grabbed me with her trunk but I slipped away running after the boy, angry.

When I got outside there was a trumpeting cry.

It was not my friend. It was another elephant.

I ran quicker after the boy. He was running towards the sounds of the baleful trumpeting. An animal was crying out in pain and fear for help. I heard my own elephant friend answer with her cry of defiance. I felt the wave of her presence hit my back.

The boy looked behind and grinned and then dived into a small tent. He did not seem frightened of me and I followed him. In the tent was a big man who had a long, stout stick in his hand topped by a sharpened, three-inch piece of metal. Before him was a small Indian elephant that he was trying to make stand on a stool. Two clowns were watching, each with white faces and giant shoes.

"Stand," said the man. "Stupid girl."

The elephant swung her trunk, confused and frightened and trumpeted again. When she did so the man stepped forward and stabbed the metal into the back of the animal's knee. She then picked up her leg and held it above the stool. Her two front legs and her trunk were slashed and ulcerated from her 'training' in the past. There were tears in her eyes.

I threw myself at the man, who was much bigger than me. I had, of course, lost my temper in the past but usually with myself. I was so used to M. Hippolyte and Antov fighting each other that I did not have time for it. In the journey here I had avoided trouble. But what I saw made me so angry. I had no plan but sought to knock the man down, which I did but he was soon back on his feet and holding the blade on a stick in front of him. He stank of drink and his eyes were wild.

"So this is the boy raised in the forest by wolves who has come to take our jobs? The one who can calm the mad elephant by his touch?"

He slashed at me with the blade and I had to dodge back.

Then a man kicked me from behind and I went down but jumped up again.

"So you're quick are you? We'll see how you feel with your guts on the floor."

He slashed again and cut the front of my jacket. The blade was very sharp. The boy I had been chasing, threw a stone that glanced off my head.

"Kill him, father."

The trainer advanced. He was a black-haired, black-bearded man, bare-chested and with red pantaloons. My head was spinning and he came for me again and I reached for my knife.

"Got a knife have you, my little wolf? Well, I have something better."

He reached under his waistcoat and took out a pistol. All the trainers had them.

"Let's see if you can dance."

He fired a bullet near my feet and I did not move. He fired another and I did not move. It was not that I was not terrified. I do not know what it was but my hatred for him froze my brain into a coldness. I stared at him. He fired a third bullet. There was a shrill trumpeting.

The small Indian elephant then knocked him over and ran out of the tent.

There were shouts outside. I hoped the poor creature had finished the man, I know you are not meant to think such things but I did, only then he stood up and this time I saw he meant to kill me.

There were two shots from behind me.

One of them hit the man in the shoulder and caused him to drop his pistol.

Blood spurted all over his shirt.

The second caught him in the foot and he fell to the floor.

"If there is one thing I hate it is being disturbed during my afternoon nap which is essential for my constitution and digestion," said Mr Masterson. "Grab that junior version of this piece of shit. My God, is this an apple I find in my pocket? Let's have some real fun now. Put this on the boy's head."

The clowns, who had not come to my help, grabbed the white-faced boy and stood him by his father. One of them caught the apple, thrown by Mr Masterson, and placed it on the terrified boy's head. It fell off once but the clown hit him and told him to stay still. The American, who had put his pistols away, then reached inside his voluminous jacket and took out a smaller version. He came over to me and handed me the gun after spinning the chamber.

"Now, I am sure a boy like you has learned to shoot some in his adventures. You must know the story of William Tell. This man was set to kill you and to spoil the biggest show I ever had in all my born days. A show that will get me known all over the world. I want you to shoot this apple off this boy's head to indicate to all, including yourself, that the show comes first. You were chasing him, fit to kill him and now you can. The catch is, if you do, you get handed over to the authorities and hang. So what is it you want to do, boy?"

I was trembling. I felt if I backed down I would have no influence with a man like the American or any hope of freeing the elephant or of carrying on my mission. I held the gun at my side. I had been schooled in shooting by Antov but more in the use of the hunting rifle than the pistol, although he had showed me tricks. He was quite able to shoot a rouble out of the air with his pistol while M. Hippolyte sneered. What Antov told me was always to look at the target and trust your body to place the shot, never to squint down the sights. I sighed. The boy in front of me was shaking with fear and all of this had started from a stone that had been thrown at the elephant, who had been showing me through her supernatural means of communication how I and others should behave. I could not fire at the poor boy. He was no more than ten. Tears were running down his cheeks like those of the little elephant and all around me were silent. I was not going to fire. I was not going to risk his life.

I raised the gun and fired.

The apple fell and split in two just like in the story.

I glimpsed Miss Emily a way to the side of me.

The boy fainted and at first his father was in hysterics, thinking he was dead.

"I am going to have the constables on you Masterson," he wailed from the floor.

The American blew a ring of smoke.

"Go straight to the chief constable. He's a friend of mine and I sent him a case of Scotch only this morning. I'm sure he'll be on your side and not throw you in jail for self-mutilation, child-molestation and cruelty to animals. In this country they really come down hard on the latter.

The American then took the pistol from my hand.

The two clowns were already dragging the animal trainer and his son outside.

"You are a wonder, my boy. A true wonder and I want you to be part of my plans. We are partners now." The American then led me out of the tent. "That was good shooting. I have never tried that myself. In all my years I never, ever tried that. Shooting an apple off a boy's head. That's the stuff of stories, boy. That's the stuff of stories. You are a regular Billy the Kid. I must tell you of the time when Billy was in this house that was molested by rabid cats underneath and he just came over all silent like you did and shot those cats through the floor. Shot them through the floor. Bang! Bang! Bang! Bang! He knew where they were by a kind of sixth sense. He could sense the very life force in something before he killed it. I like you my boy and I trust you to do the right thing. When I handed you the pistol you might have shot me and cut and run but you did not. You know that I have to execute that elephant you seem fond of but recognise I have saved your precious life. That truly speaks of breeding and fine morals and I want to let you into my plans."

I did not sleep much that night. When I found myself dropping off, I imagined I had an apple on my head and the person who was going to shoot it off was me. The next day Mr Masterson knocked on the door of my room and gave me a warmer coat he had just bought. I had been lying on the bed speculating how far I might have got if I had tried to hold everyone up and take the elephant with me. It was exactly the sort of thing that Antov and M. Hippolyte might have found very funny. The coat was a fine one, on the lines of a reefer jacket that sailors wear but made from the richest cashmere by a London tailor. The closer Mr Masterson presumed on my friendship, the stranger it felt. We then went for a ride in his new motor car, which, of course, turned out to be a Rolls Royce. It was either his, or he had borrowed it from someone. He was a little disappointed by my indifference. I had seen and been driven in such automobiles often in my early years.

"You must have ridden in a lot of these in your village," he said, and lit another cigar. The day was windy and he was wearing a huge fur coat over his suit. He had left Miss Emily at home.

We were taken to an immense dark building down by the docks. It was a warehouse and many of the windows were smashed. There was a dock to one side that was full of barges like the ones we had come across on. We knocked at a door and were immediately let in and inside it was a different story, a hive of activity and boxes or crates were piled high, right up to the ceiling in several places. There was a strange smell of disinfectant, church incense and an odour like fruit when it has gone bad. Mr Masterson inhaled and beamed.

"That's the smell of money, my boy. That's the smell of money."

I wondered what exactly was in the boxes. He read my mind.

"Bodies, boy. Bodies from the front. Brave boys that have

been shipped home. There was a charity that raised money to get them here and I took over the concession. This is a money maker, a money maker, what ever way you look at it."

It then struck me, like a blow to the chest, what the boxes were. Piled high in a simple network of wooden bays, because they were in many cases unable to support themselves, were simple pine coffins. I had come through dreadful places on my journey and had seen many dead people, I thought of the amused face of the serf or the girl under the ice with the other primly dressed librarians. But it was the sheer scale of what had been happening in the war that I found hard to comprehend. M. Hippolyte had taught me much about the campaigns of the past, especially those of Napoleon and his march into Russia that had led to the death of so many. He and Antov spoke late at night after too many drinks of the campaigns they had engaged in, M. Hippolyte in the Moorish part of Africa, Antov in the Far East, where Russia becomes China. At these times they did not brag or shout as when they were fighting each other and I had come to know why. The warehouse was beyond even this quiet sadness and realisation. This was no war of Cossacks or duellists but one of the age of the machine gun and armoured car. I had seen them in the newspapers and been under an artillery barrage. The wooden bays went all the way to the roof and where full had thirty coffins reaching to the dirty skylight. Here and there the boxes had rotted and an arm hung out of one. In another, part of a skull was clearly visible.

A SKULL. White as a dawn mushroom.

My fists were clenched in my warm new coat to stop my hands shaking and I nearly started to speak, to ask how, if man is so clever, as M. Hippolyte taught me, can he possibly kill so many of his finest young men?

The American put his hand on my shoulder and spoke very quietly.

"We are partners you and I, that's how I see it. In some ways you are the perfect partner, one who can keep secrets and will not tell and I don't mean that in no cruel way. What I've learned in life is that you have got to accentuate the positive. Go for the opportunities that the Lord God puts in your way. Doesn't He say in the bible not to bury your talents, which were a measure of a whole lot of money, but make them work for you? That's what I have always done ever since I quit my shit hole of a town and set off in search of better things that at the start had me running round with a bunch of outlaws. I then gets into the circus business accidently and found I was better at it than that old soak Buffalo Bill, but everything is changing and I need a waggon load of money for a new venture. That is why I need your help with the elephant, but I will tell you more later."

Our footsteps echoed as we went to the end of the warehouse where a group of men were working furiously. They had rags tied around their faces and were opening coffins and removing the bodies to a central table where certain of the bodies were chosen to be put into much more expensive coffins. The smell here made me almost retch but I did not want to show anything in front of the American. There was a team of older men and one woman who were adding bits of uniform or part of a disintegrating hat to one body. The dead man's face was white and purple but he had been handsome. The woman checked all was well and then, with a huge smile, picked up a large wooden mallet and beat the dead man about the face.

A clerk came running up. He had glasses and a shade for his eyes attached round his bald head.

"We have at least five hundred orders to be returned from the officers missing list. At least five hundred! A few have asked for an open coffin but we have advised against it. We have done all the necessary in case the coffin gets damaged accidently. When Mavis has finished with them even their own mothers won't recognise them. All at fifty guineas a time!"

The man was so happy he did a little DANCE. I wondered what was the new business the American was getting into that he needed all this and the death of the elephant. The American took me over to the officers missing list that covered a large table and said:

"We select an officer, no one high-ranking, who is listed as missing in action, or killed, place of burial unknown, and write a long letter to the mother about her son's bravery saying that acting on behalf of a field hospital charity we have the body. We can have it buried or send it to her for burial. But she must realise that her boy was so brave at the end and suffered such terrible wounds that the face is unrecognisable. Most go for it although, and even I could not credit this, one Duchess wrote back that her son was never any good, she did not believe he was ever brave and we could throw his remains on a manure heap for all she cared. But there is no underestimating the sentimentality of the upper-middle class. They would have their paladins stuffed and mounted on the mantelshelf if they could, to reflect their own glory."

All the time the American had the broadest of smiles.

I wondered what happened to the bodies of the ordinary private soldiers, who were too obviously not officer class even after Mavis' mallet. Their fate was made clear.

"Good thing you freed up those barges and stopped them going back to Russia," said the clerk. "We tried ploughing the unwanted bodies into a friendly farmer's field to add to his soil after they had been read over. But there was no breaking them up. Tough little buggers and hard as leather the British Tommy, even in death. So we dump 'em out at sea. If they come up from Davy Jones's Locker on our shores, then most likely the government will think it has made a cock-up, lost a ship somewhere and declare the matter secret. If we get them far enough out they will drift to Norway. No one is going to make a fuss in Norway. He's a tough little trooper your new friend, Mr Masterson. Doesn't bat an eyelid at all this. Isn't he the boy that had his dad killed by the elephant and then rode it through the town? A credit to you, boss."

Mr Masterson looked pleased and proud. He liked the word BOSS.

The clerk smiled at me but I must have been staring back without expression because he looked away, turned back, scratched his head, then looked away again, nervously. I sensed he wanted to shake my hand but I could not bear to be touched by such a creature. After the loss of my friends M. Hippolyte and Antov, I much preferred the company of BEASTS.

We then got into the car and drove back to the circus and on the way Mr Masterson had the chauffeur get out and buy us all an ice cream. We sat eating them in the warm car watching much poorer people dodge snowflakes in the chilly wind outside. I could not imagine the Tsar, or especially the Tsarina, stopping the state coach or automobile to buy an ice cream, eating one themselves and certainly not getting one for the chauffeur. The American was a thoroughly modern man. He finished his ice cream before I did. Some of it had melted onto his hand.

"I never quite had the time to settle down. I never had the

time to have a boy," he said in a curious moment of reflection before we drove off.

I went and saw the elephant every day and no one stopped me. I had thought at first that she was to be executed by the end of the week but there were problems in getting a license, written permission from Hull council and something called The Ministry of Works to do such a dreadful thing. In the meantime, I went and did my best to communicate and console her that I was on her side and I felt that she understood me. I felt too that she was concerned that I was involved with a man like Mr Masterson. The strange vibrations from her occurred more often, which no one else appeared to experience, though I saw that Roberto was, at times, agitated near her, and this further confirmed the view she had implanted in me, that the world as it had become was absurd, the work of a committee of madmen, a confederacy of FOOLS.

I had large ideas and strange dreams of what I must replace it with but first I had to get her away. From the present river of dark fire.

Mr Masterson became increasingly friendly and fatherly towards me.

The Big Top was up and twice a day there were shows which included animal acts, trapeze artists, tight-rope walkers, clowns and trick riders like myself which was combined with Mr Masterson's story telling of the Old West and shooting pots thrown into the air filled with sweets for the kids. He had the gypsy women make up a suit for me which was just like his and got hold of a holster and two small but real pistols. Together, one night, we routed a group of gypsy riders dressed as Red Indians and I did tricks like getting out of the saddle and bouncing back into it. Antov would have approved. I cannot deny that I loved the applause that came afterwards from the crowd who seemed beside themselves and gave us a standing ovation. The tent was full every night and people came from as far as Manchester, which I was told was a large city a hundred miles away, to see the show.

Yet with every ticket Mr Masterson gave away a leaflet advertising the dread but inevitable once-in-a-lifetime event of "the new century."

THE NECESSARY DEATH OF THE MURDERING, UNTAMEABLE AFRICAN ELEPHANT BY MEANS OF SHOOTING, ELECTROCUTION OR HANGING FROM A CRANE.

There was an accompanying picture of an elephant that had been hung in Erwin, Tennessee, from a railroad crane and I had to go to my room and lie on the bed and breathe deeply to control myself when I saw it for the first time. There was also a voting form and a pre-paid envelope.

About two weeks after we had visited the warehouse I had just left the elephant and given her a kiss on the trunk when Mr Masterson sent for me.

He was behind his desk smoking a cigar and arguing with Roberto on exactly how the execution might be staged. Miss Emily was there and gave me a big smile so I gave her one back. I had a feeling that like myself she was somewhat a prisoner of circumstance rather than a willing conspirator. She was dressed as for her act today in a light blue costume with black stockings and laughed when she saw me staring. She held up an admonitory finger and then smiled like a summer field of flowers.

I blushed and she giggled.

I had seen her skip into the ring, climb the rope ladder and do a few swings but she did none of the complicated tricks performed by an Italian gypsy family, who in no way opposed her as she guaranteed them a high place on the bill. For some reason a group of carpenters were in the house and engaged in building an oversize swing in the area of the bed. I had so long since stopped wondering about the motives of Mr Masterson that I did not find it in any way odd. There was a very large gun on the desk that was either painted gold, covered in gold leaf, or, again I put nothing past Mr Masterson, gold-plated or solid gold.

"There he is, my partner. How are you doing little man? Miss Emily has sent out for some hot chocolate so you can have some too. There is hot chocolate and biscuits. Come and look at this weapon that I got sent up this morning from Holland and Holland. I bet you have never seen anything like this. It is almost an artillery piece."

My gaze went over his shoulder to the open gun cabinet, secreted behind a bookshelf, stocked full of hunting rifles and Winchesters but also bunches of keys, including those for the elephant's stockade which had a blue ticket attached. I knew the keys for the gun cabinet were kept on his person though I had seen him search in a box with a tiger on the front on his desk for a duplicate. If only I could get that key. I tried not to show anything in my face or my eyes. A man came in with a tray of hot chocolate and Miss Emily handed me a cup with two biscuits on the saucer and, smiling, mussed up my hair with her other, long-fingered hand.

". . . I probably do not need to tell a performer like yourself,' Mr Masterson said to me, "That this is an elephant gun. I can see you are not going to get sentimental on me. Lately, I have been thinking that this might well be the best way of all. A scene where the elephant is menacing, say Miss Emily here, clutching a child. We can get a baby from somewhere can't we, honey pie?"

Roberto was shaking his head.

"They not allow you to do that in Big Top."

Miss Emily, who had gone back to sit on the bed with her legs crossed, said: "Why do you have to kill poor elephant, anyway? Could you just pretend? Like you pretend everything else and it happens? Like pretend to be big cowboy?" Miss Emily's voice was very musical but she affected a foreign accent that was not quite correct. It was said she was Russian but she did not look, feel or act so.

Mr Masterson made a yelping noise.

"Not you too, sweet Emily. You gotta understand."

The carpenters who were putting up the swing stopped hammering.

An awkward silence came over the room. We could all hear the shouts of the gypsies outside and the occasional roar of the lion. Miss Emily was not smiling anymore and Roberto began to take a step towards the door.

Mr Masterson drew a pistol and pointed it at one of the carpenters. They did not need a verbal order. They ran from the house.

"Not you, Roberto," said Mr Masterson, as he lay the pistol down on the desk. He then took off his gun belt and went over and opened the door that I knew concealed the water closet. He dropped his trousers and sat on the wooden seat of the pot, which was a highly decorated patent blue and white design by Thomas Crapper that Mr Masterson had let me use. There were similar ones in the Winter Palace.

"You enjoying your cocoa, my boy? Miss Emily, you enjoying yours? Roberto don't get none because Roberto is having one of his negative days. You must think positive, Roberto.

Things do not stay the same for the flick of a horse's tail, no sir. And I am not a fake cowboy, madam, I have driven beef to market with the saddle scars to prove it, but no more. And after my time with the regulators and with the Hole in the Wall gang, I rode with Pancho Villa. He is a good man betrayed by people who said they were his friends. He has a vision. Why are we having the elephant show? We are having the elephant show because it is the future. Not just my future, partners, but all our futures! Pass me some paper, Roberto, and quit this defeatist talk. Pass me the fucking paper, Roberto."

After he had cleaned himself Mr Masterson came back to the desk. He reached down and took a contraption out of a box and assembled it on the desk where it was pointed at one of the builder's sheets stretched out and nailed to a wall. It had a lens like a camera and a six-inch wheel above and below. He connected the contraption to the electric current and light shone from the lens and vague pictures appeared on the sheet. There was a picture house in Perm but I had never been.

"Emily, close the curtains. I want all the curtains closed. Close the curtains. This, this is why I need the money, boy. This is why we need the big one, Roberto."

On the screen flashed a moving picture sequence of the image on the leaflet I had already seen of the elephant being hung. The next one was of an elephant in New York being electrocuted and smoke coming from the contacts before the terrified creature fell to the floor. Then there was, inexplicably: a shot of the Russian revolution and Lenin and next troops going over the top in France and Queen Victoria wobbling and hitting a fence on a bicycle, only to be comforted and got to her feet by her small daughter, and then two lovers kissing under a full moon. I was astonished that intimate memories could be bought and sold to a man like Mr Masterson and projected onto a sheet. Somewhere they might have film of the Tsar and his family and even of me when I was younger. It seemed strange that the flickering sequences of youthful conscripts getting killed in the trenches were going to live on, to be truly eternal, while their bodies rotted in the ground. I thought of the ICONS and the incense in St Basil's, whose builders were blinded so they could not replicate its beauty, and wondered if that was all religion was, vague, faded pictures for us to mumble over when any original emotion or truth had been forgotten.

Mr Masterson opened the curtains. The daylight rushed back into the room and the sunshine fell across the table where Miss Emily had filled a vase with chrysanthemum flowers given to her by an admirer in the town. The American then jumped up on a wooden chair. Mr Masterson was a very nimble man for all his bulk.

"These moving pictures are the future. The future, I say! I knew when to get out of being an outlaw and start running a circus. But I can make more money selling my far superior motion pictures of the killer elephant around the world. That is only the start. The start! That's why I have got you the swing, honey pie. There is a whole motion picture business in the States and this elephant can be the start of it. I wanted to photograph you on a swing covered in flowers. I thought I can set a whole story around that. A whole story. There is an even bigger market for love! What do you think of that, Roberto, with your Fifth Column ideas? It seems a pretty good plan to me! Am I the only optimist on this God's earth? Let's do it, I say. What possible argument can you have against being rich?"

serving the Church through my work at the ITI, first as nsel, and then since the beginning of 2014 as President ful students from all over the world. I came to witness are really formed here.

achieve much through the grace of God and by working erous benefactors and the many friends of the ITI. Some : new campus in Trumau, the start of our *Studium Generale* l as the very many inspiring people I have had the great years. I have learned so very much and I am profoundly

and our oldest son has already left for university, whilst ed it was time to hand over to the next generation of

GOD IS NOT REAL... AND NEITHER ARE JEHOVAH NOR JESUS NOR ALLAH... RELIGIONS POISON THE MIND AND KILL HUMAN LOGIC.

FOURTEEN

NATASHA SAT BOLT upright on a stool in the Korean deli across the road from her apartment on 20th. She had had a pre-recorded call this morning saying that she should not come into the library. It was strange that the call was pre-recorded as there were only four people in all working in the library and she had expected the carefully modulated voice of the acting head librarian. The university had obviously thought it necessary to install an automatic digital switch-board that the acting head librarian was able to access, with a pre-logged voice code, to send out the message. The voice was alert and zippy and male and a little New England and could have been one of the more educated Kennedys. What bothered Natasha about the call was what bothered her about the story of the boy and the elephant. It messed around with authorship and time. She was reading and experiencing the boy's narrative without knowing who wrote the story, or when, or exactly why. With the call this morning the non-personal message, pre-recorded in the past, had now been triggered, possibly by an algorithm, to affect Natasha's future. There were shouts outside and she looked up and two men, crack dealers, one in a navy coat, one in a combat jacket, were fighting over a place in a newly refurbished doorway to sell drugs to clients who were getting fewer. The person on her right looked up from his Latte and shrugged:

"I wish all of those junkies would fucking kill each other.

I hope the Covid gets them. I hope they choke good."

When she glanced away the person on her left still was asleep, his forehead resting against the counter. He was probably one of those on furlough who travelled into the city, even though they did not need to, impelled by a Kafkaesque force. One of those who feared losing his shared identity with the strange future past that is Gotham. Above her was a camera, recording the passing of events. Out in front of the shop there was another, recording the fight of the two dealers. Somebody would be watching a screen and a camera would be watching them watching the screen. That mattered in a strange way that related to her dreams and the boy's. She rubbed her index finger of her right hand down the spine of the book in front of her. It was *An Experiment with Time*, written by the philosopher, aviator and fly-fisherman, J.W. Dunne, whose work on dreams that come true had so influenced Nabokov. The waiter poured her another coffee and brought the pot down with a crash in front of the man sleeping, with no effect. No one was wearing a mask today. The scent of fried eggs and hash browns was making Natasha hungry. She caught her own smile in the mirror and sent an email she had written carefully in the apartment, striking out and re-writing several times, a little bit of then that was to become now in an instant up at Harvard.

From: NatashaA@gmail.com
To: ChiChiChica Forment@fas.harvard.edu

There is a lot in what you say about me. A lot of what you say is true. Yet, the intellect does not drive everything. The world would not be as it is if it did. I did not expect loving you, did I? There are unexplainable moments and objects where we least expect them. The stars emerge to wink at us and confront our unambitious ideas of space and time and being. And we need the darkness to see them. All I can say, all I can confess, is that with him, the man in Paris, love ran to the dark. I would give everything to have one minute of it again, though, unlike Pushkin, I can never bear to think of him happy with another. I want him now. I am part of generation P. I needed to restore PASSION. But that is not possible anymore. I have to look to other things. I have to care for my mother, but in earning money on the other side of the country I will hardly see her. I have to put the dreams and the poetry and the mad love on hold.

Here is another chunk of the Russian book. I have to meet the Russians soon who sent it to me. Do not worry. I have not got in touch with the man in Paris. X

Natasha sent the email and then sat staring into her coffee. The waiter came and stood in front of her, filling her cup, and hung there in his silent way, in his red apron, his spiky, thick hair seeming to stand on end, to interest her in ordering, but she did not reply. His appearance was always the same and always with an aura of being out of time, as if the place was a portal to every other Korean deli. When she thought of the man in Paris she thought of his words before she thought of his appearance, although she found him very attractive. He was much better at telling stories than her mostly loving father, who had wanted to tell you everything at once. Sentences came slowly out of the man in Paris, like carved granite. From him Natasha knew Heidegger said that BEING consists mainly in dwelling. Paradoxically, the man in Paris did not dwell anywhere for very long. After she had met him at the gallery party in New York, the next time was three months later when he was back from Kinshasa. He said he was from England but did not have an accent. He was a film producer and had been working on a story for a film in the north of England but roamed all over the world. He never talked to her about his family or his parents, just his plans. She wanted to believe him. She wanted to believe in him, even though she knew, deep down, somewhere in the buried common sense of her mother, that she should not trust him. She loved his smile. She hated him for Paris, where he claimed to be most of the time, and she wanted to kill him for not phoning her. He was never content. She knew he was not content with her. Other men paid her compliments. He itemised the blemishes, seemingly not in a cruel way, but like the SERPENT running down the GARDEN OF EDEN to Eve. The boy did not give the elephant a name, and Natasha did the same with the man in Paris. He was beyond her experience. She did not need to fill in all his details or his description to herself constantly, as with other men. Natasha stirred her coffee. The man in Paris was part of her, he was inside her head. He seemed to have taken her over. He appeared to have the trick of living outside of time, in different dimensions. She opened the book by the aviator Dunne, the man who had made the first fighter aircraft, for whom the dimension of time was the next challenge. She had brought it with her to try and understand her present, and how the boy's story of the past was flowing into her future.

Dunne had started out with dreams and realised that now and again he was able to see the future and there was no past, or present or future. That was how we perceived time. Natasha thought of being the butterfly in her dream, always in the present. The trouble was in order to talk about time you had to talk about the 'now' and you could only see that from outside, like a painter painting a picture of a painter painting a picture of a painter. (She thought of the artist in her building who had cut off his hands). The idea of fixing a "now" point in time and space, which has already gone and become something else as soon as you try and fix it, had fascinated Einstein and Dunne's work broadly fitted in both with Einstein's theory of relativity and the contradictory theory of quantum mechanics. It was the kind of logical, illogical hall of mirrors that had sent her lovely father mad even when he tried to remain grounded between the pages and the seedy reality of *Cannery Row* in his flophouse. Dunne dreamt of a serial regression of observers and dimensions ending in the supreme ultimate observer, or God.

The first half of the book described dreams predicting events such as volcanic eruptions. Dunne thought only in dreams does the wakeful attention that prevents us from seeing beyond the present moment fade and allows fragments of the future and the past to appear. To Natasha, reading was a certain sort of dreaming. As a child she had slipped out of time into *101 Dalmations* to avoid the pain of the present.

Natasha took a sip of coffee. She was about to go when the waiter, unsmiling as ever, brought a plate of unordered eggs and hash browns. She looked at the whites and the yellows and the golds as he stared at her and everything was recorded by the camera. The eggs and hash browns only moved their "now" forwards by being in the sight of many observers, so Dunne would say, but they tasted amazing.

On her phone calendar Natasha saw the meeting with the Russians was the day after tomorrow.

When she got back to her apartment door there was a package outside. It was another photocopied instalment of the actual manuscript. But how, as there was no one else in the building, had the postman got in? The delivery unsettled Natasha but she was hungry to read on.

FIFTEEN

T HAT NIGHT, AT the circus, when I was with the elephant, I said a PRAYER for the American.

I was able to see that in his own way he was trying to be a good man even if by conventional standards he was blind to any Christian morality, though I had heard him pay lip service to such when I accompanied him and Miss Emily to a grim church in the centre of the small and dirty city called Hull to be seen amongst the city fathers who were delighted at the prosperity he had brought. He had prayed with them for the boys of the town lost in the naval battle off Jutland, where everyone had expected an easy victory because that was the way it had always been with the English and the sea before warfare had become industrial. He joined in the prayers for an end to war and the godless revolution in Russia, even though every day he made money from those two things. I recalled M. Hippolyte telling me of examples of men from history like Napoleon and Caesar, for whom POWER itself was, perhaps, the only morality. Even with such men there were cracks, weaknesses, where the light might get in and revelations of the kind I had experienced with the elephant changed them too. I prayed to the Saints and to the Holy Mother to intercede for me. I even thought of trying to get Mr

Masterson to come and see the elephant and for him to feel the hopeful message, the song, she gave off and change his dreadful ways and figure out how he might use his tremendous energy for good. The only trouble was, I reasoned, that I had to speak to him to explain my own revelation and therefore break my word, give my identity away and spoil my mission. Then there was the danger that Mr Masterson might use the elephant's mesmeric power for his own monetary ends. The other consideration was how the elephant herself, good as she was, might, finally, react to Mr Masterson about the matter of her beloved calf being seethed in her own milk and fed to local party officials. There was no denying another, much smaller elephant had ripped apart my elephant's keeper and stamped on the remains, according to the gypsies. But my elephant was completely innocent of the crime for which she was going to be executed. So I left the matter among the imagined incense and icons, and in the representations of the pure hands of the Saints, in particular St Michael, and, of course, the Holy Virgin.

It was as I made plans for Mr Masterson's soul that life was making them for me.

I came back one bright, windy afternoon to Mr Masterson's house, where he now insisted I live. He had had a gap knocked in one wall and the shed I was in moved up against it and plastered round so, although I still had my own entrance, I could come out of my quarters into his. The plank wall of the shed was thin and there was a knot hole an inch wide in the door to the American's quarters. I was able to hear Mr Masterson's loud voice at times and, if I put my eyes to the hole, could see what was happening in the room. I did this on certain occasions to check that there were none of Mr Masterson's private business meetings going off before I went in, but then, that afternoon, I happened to see Miss Emily in the polished copper bath.

NAKED.

I should have stopped looking but I did not.

I do not know if she was able to see me but I was certain she knew I was there. She conducted the whole affair in a dream-like way, with the sun streaming in through the net curtains on her white bosom and thighs and her long and perfectly muscled legs. She reminded me of a wood nymph in a print in Antov's bedroom that managed to be both classically beautiful and beautifully arousing. If I were an artist I could not think of a way of making Miss Emily more affecting.

She smiled in my direction, showing a dimple to the right of her mouth and a slight gap between her front teeth and stood up in the bath and did a full, slow turn, so I was able to see all over her. Her breasts stuck out, large and unsupported and her nipples were red. Her bottom was a dazzling white, like the finest satin, her belly flat. I realised though, without her circus make-up, that she was a little older than I thought, with the trace of lines at the corner of her eyes, though I could not say how old. It somehow made the secret even more special. More naked. I stood gazing at her, in particular at the dark, reddish forest between her legs.

I became hot and almost beside myself. I wanted her.

Miss Emily, the trapeze artist, was the most attractive woman I had seen since I had been exiled from St Petersburg, or probably ever. In the end, she nodded ever so slightly in my direction and stepped out of the bath and wrapped herself tight in a fluffy white towel as there was a knock at the door. I hardly slept that night.

The next day, I spent all morning with the elephant but when

I came back to my room I heard movement on the other side of the door to Mr Masterson's quarters and I imperfectly hoped it was Miss Emily in the copper bath again. It made me aroused to think that I had been naked in the self same bath. I had even tried to tell the elephant about the matter in my thoughts but she had hit me playfully on the head with her trunk. I also had sought to reassure her about getting away and that I had seen the keys.

But it was not Miss Emily.

Instead, I saw Mr Masterson and three thin, severe looking men, one of whom had a beard. They were young and two wore long leather coats and flicked around with little strings of amber beads. This was the plain clothes uniform of the Cheka, the new secret police of the revolution. I had seen them at Riga. The third wore an army greatcoat. They spoke English with a Russian accent. I was sure they were Russian.

"It is told to us you have young boy who bleeds. It is of great importance we see him."

Mr Masterson was giving them a look across the table that was impossible to figure out and I never wanted to play cards with him.

"Bleeds, you say? You're the fourth party to come here this morning asking such questions. Bleeds? A boy rode an elephant that I covered in fake blood and he got covered too. Maybe that's what you mean?"

The man in charge of the small party looked a little angry with Mr Masterson's casual manner and the strangeness of the house. The other two were looking at Miss Emily who stood behind Mr Masterson's chair and was in her costume, smiling modestly.

"No, it is not what I mean. The boy we want has bleeding disease. It is called haemophilia. Who were other people?"

Mr Masterson took a drink of his American whiskey and then blew a smoke ring that hung over the desk, a satisfied smile on his face.

"We do not employ cripples or the infirm. Perhaps you should ask at the hospital?"

The man in charge was not to be deflected.

"The boy riding the elephant. He comes from Russia?"

Mr Masterson shook his head as if that was an impossible question.

"Like the United States of America, I do not ask where people come from. All I want is talent and hard work. But if folk come in here and ask me questions about my acts I want to know who I am talking to. I have a man from *The Times* in London coming to see me later. Which side of the Ruskie civil war are you on? I have had one very strange woman ask me questions, then a bunch of aristos in comic opera uniform, then a man pretending to be a priest and now you."

The leader looked at his two fellows.

"We are from new democratic citizens' republic of Russia," said the man proudly. "We must see boy. We have heard of incident where a man was shot and injured. We must take boy into custody for questioning."

Mr Masterson laughed.

"I have had dealings with you people. So you're the new Red Army? Well, you are all as Kentucky cuckoo bad as each other as far as I am concerned. All as bad as each other. I have no boy of that description and even if I had I would not hand him over to any Joe who comes in here off the street and tells me any sort of fairy story. What is it he is meant to have done? This boy? What are you trying to imply one of my blameless boys has done?"

The man who was the leader looked at his two companions

and they nodded. For a moment I thought they were going to attack Mr Masterson, which might have been silly as his guns were on the table in front of him.

The leader then reached into his inside coat pocket and brought out an awkward wad of money. It was all in large, British five-pound notes.

"I authorised to give you sum of money to help us take this boy back to Russia."

Mr Masterson sighed.

"Why do you want to do that? What crime has such a boy committed?'

"It is who he is that is crime."

Mr Masterson laughed.

"So what is so bad about the boy you want? Are you chasing around like those Frenchies with their guillotine? That didn't end well and I think you've maybe got confused."

Then one of the other men said: "You going to kill an elephant in a week's time. It says so on posters. There's no difference. This boy is an enemy of state."

"And what makes him so?" asked Mr Masterson.

"We believe that he is part of Imperial Family and must be brought back to Russia for trial. If you have him we are authorised to give you money."

Mr Masterson stared at the money. There was a considerable amount, perhaps thousands of pounds. A smile crossed the face of the leader, who had turned to the others, and it was not a pleasant one, like the moon catching a muddy puddle of water.

Mr Masterson leaned back in his chair, took Miss Emily's hand and laughed out loud.

"So you think you can buy Sam Masterson, do you, boys? I rode with the best there is and I don't do no-one's dirty work. You walked through my circus on the way here and I think you may have got a glimpse of what perhaps are the most talented group of showmen and women, high-wire artists and horse experts ever assembled and we may never see their like again. They have, to a man and woman, emerged from the gutters of the world to such starry heights of modern show business. If you want to find kings and princes don't come looking in my sawdust ring. Or we may have to set you on as clowns. Now get out and don't come around here no more or I'll shoot you right between the eyes. Question one of my boys and girls? Over my dead body."

After they had gone I went and hid in the elephant enclosure. Even if they did not frighten Mr Masterson they frightened me. In Riga they said the Cheka stopped at nothing. They would shoot their own mothers if ordered, or even if not, to try out their new pistols.

I stroked the elephant's trunk, asking her what I should do and she nuzzled close.

It was about half-an-hour later that I heard the shooting.

There must have been about ten shots and it seemed to go on for a long time although I knew it was over in seconds, that's how real gunfights are.

Then there was a cry.

"Get the doctor! Mr Masterson's been shot! Get the doctor, get the car! We got to get him to the hospital! We got to get him to the hospital! He's bleeding!"

I then heard Miss Emily screaming and crying but I stayed where I was.

"Please, please don't be dying, Sam!" she said.

I had heard her cry out the same way when Mr Masterson saved her from pretend savages in the circus ring. This time her voice sounded genuine. It is hard to tell with actors and actresses.

But I did not go out to her. I knew I must stay with the elephant, no matter what. She was my future. I had to use the confusion to get her away.

When it was dark I slipped between the bars and looked up at the moon and stars and shivered, even though I had my warm second-best jacket on. I went straight to my quarters and gathered a few things up in a large red, white-spotted kerchief I used in the show when I played a bandit. I took all the money I had but left the guns that Mr Masterson had given me. I did not want to provoke anyone into shooting at me, or the elephant as the Reds and the militia would be after us anyway. I then stood in front of the mirror and combed my hair. Antov had said it was important always to look one's best when things are at their worst. I put sweets from one of the gypsy women in my pocket and went into the big room with the projector and the swing covered in paper flowers.

The moon shone through the muslin drapes.

I went to the desk and located the box with the tiger on the top. I moved the bookshelves back; they were on a hinge and perfectly balanced and so swung out easily. I put the key in the lock and in a few seconds I had the keys to the elephant's cage and shackles in my hands.

Breathing hard, I listened to every movement of the night.

I closed the gun locker and bookshelves. I did not take one of the rifles for the same reason I did not take my pistols. I had been going to open all the other animal cages to help my getaway but concluded that the poor things would all be shot and mounted on a municipal wall. I paused at the desk where there was a piece of writing paper and a fountain pen.

I felt there was a message I must communicate and I probably owed Mr Masterson money for the clothes he had bought me, though most of them I did not take. In the end I left ten shillings. I opened a safe in the desk with one of the keys and took twelve gold pieces I might need for the challenges of the open road and put them in a pouch on my belt. I did this in lieu of wages as Mr Masterson only gave me what he called 'pocket money'.

Dear Mr Samuel Masterson,

I leave this money to pay for any clothes I am taking away with me and towards your treatment for the gunshots. I have taken a number of gold pieces in lieu of wages but which I will return to you in full. Thank you for not giving me away. You kept your sacred bargain to a partner. I have learned much from you. I must also thank you properly for saving my life. Now I must keep a bargain to an animal I cannot let you kill. Please do not follow me. Alive, the elephant has much to teach us.

Then I put the words the princess had heard at the ball. My misquoting of the French poet: "TOUT EST MOI ET JE SUIS TOUT" The American was impressed with any sort of French. The idea that we are everything and everything is the whole of humanity was what the deep sound the elephant made communicated to me.

I puzzled over signing the letter, I couldn't give away my identity.

So I signed the letter, Elephant and I.

The effect that Mr Masterson had on me was so strange I almost regretted not going to the hospital to see him.

Then I turned to face a small, silver double-barrelled pistol and Miss Emily, spectral white in the moonlight. She looked down at what I had written.

"Didn't think you were deaf and dumb," she said.

I pointed at the picture of Mr Masterson on the desk and raised my eyebrows.

"Yes, I think so," she said. "I think he'll be alright. They got him in the shoulder and hit an artery in his leg. But they've stopped the bleed."

I made an inquisitive gesture with my hand towards her. She smiled.

"That doesn't matter. It might take too long to explain."

Her accent was now not Eastern European or a clumsy imitation of American but that of the British upper classes.

I looked at her pleadingly and pointed at the door.

She thought for a moment and what she said surprised me.

"I know . . . Fear not, I know exactly who you are. Sam killed one Russian agent and wounded another but with that lot there are always more. And there are others after you, the Whites, whose motives are not pure and who may want to harm you. They've got their own princelings. Don't trust a soul. Make inland for the town of Goole and then towards Rotherham and Sheffield. Another guardian angel will catch up with you by then and instruct you. I'll say that you probably went north heading towards the Northumbrian ports but do not know where you are going as you are a stupid deaf mute. Be careful and speak to no one. You really love that creature, don't you, my little prince? True love is a rare and precious thing."

Her smile was wistful.

I didn't answer and then she laughed.

It was a perfect little laugh and she kissed me on the cheek just at the side of my lips. I felt the blink of her eyelashes on my cheek. I wanted to kiss her but left quickly and took deep breaths when I got into the cold air.

When I recovered myself, I started to wonder who exactly

Miss Emily was and who she was working for. There were many questions in my head, but no time and I could not break my vow of silence.

I went straight to the cage of the elephant, who was ready and waiting and seemed to understand.

First, I removed the hated shackles and then I opened the cage door and with me leading her and her leading me we tried to tip-toe, as much as one can tip-toe with an elephant, to the back entrance of the circus.

We slipped between the cages of the lions and tigers and as we did so I felt the vibration and there was no noise from any of the big cats or the horses. The moon came dramatically from behind a cloud over the sea as we almost got to the entrance and we stopped.

Before us was a line of gypsies, men and women, who did not impede us but threw paper flowers and chanted things in their own language, incantations to keep the traveller safe. Someone must have seen me go to the elephant cage.

One handed me a basket of food.

It was the tradition the gypsies had for any fellow per-former leaving the circus that they considered a friend and proper human being, a *djinni mengro*. I was touched and the elephant stopped and brushed the hand of an old woman at the gate with her trunk.

"You do good," was all she said, and then the elephant and I were on the road.

We walked out of the city following the great river inland.

Despite Mr Masterson being significantly wounded, I had no doubt that as soon as he left hospital he was going to be after me, as was half the disappointed city and the men who had shot the American, not to mention the White factions.

The night was freezing and both my breath and that of

the elephant showed in the moonlight. It was not cold like the cold in Russia that you can feel all through you but is dry. It was a wet cold and when it became day we would need shelter. Everyone needs shelter.

The black houses of Hull seemed to go on forever. We were near to the docks and they were poor, two-storey houses and already deadly quiet because work started before dawn. Here and there a dog barked inquisitively in a back garden and stopped, unsure of the heavy steps that passed in the night and shook its kennel. The streetlights were out and there was only the moon and stars to guide us and they scuttled behind clouds at times.

Every so often a light or a candle or an oil lamp would be lighted at a window, or on one occasion a window was drawn up and a man actually shouted out in surprise as the elephant's head passed just below his sill and the rest of her obscured the gleaming cobbles in the moonlight.

"An elephant, a bloody elephant, I've seen an elephant!"

"And I bet it's bloody pink. You should stay out of that boozer. Close window and get back to bed."

We crossed railway tracks and then on the outskirts of town a lorry and a horse and cart had been stopped by a group of policemen with lanterns. There was a school and a large clump of trees and I left the elephant in the blackness, stroking her trunk and willing her to stay there and I crept a little nearer. It was too early for a police search. I smelt the tea the policemen were brewing on the brazier and overheard what they were saying to the man on the cart.

"Why are you being inconvenienced in peddling your black market rabbits, sir? Don't worry, we don't have time for you. We're here freezing our knackers off trying to catch a bunch of Russian anarchists who shot the cowboy at the circus.

Terrible people they is. Eat their own children. They say the white-hatted cowboy's going to die. But we'll get them. What the bleeding hell is that? The fucking night moved."

I jumped as something touched the top of my head. I felt the elephant's enormous presence behind me and she ruffled my hair with her trunk. She had been growing in excitement since I had taken off her shackles and let her out of the stockade.

Luckily, the moon went behind a cloud at that moment and the policemen's lamp did not reach into the shadows.

I grabbed the elephant's ear and pulled her round and back into the dark playground of the school. She was like a child who was out of lessons. She kept on ruffling my hair and shoving me about with her trunk.

"Maybe it was one of your bomb-throwing Russians," said the man in the cart.

"Piss off,' said the policeman. "But first give us one of them fat rabbits."

We circled back a few streets and over a railway line and then found a path that ran near the river, which once might have been an historic road but was abandoned now and overgrown, except for the occasional milepost or flat stones underneath that were built to last longer than the new tar highway out of town. I was walking beside the elephant.

Out in the River Humber we saw the light of several boats and a colder wind blew in from the east with the first glimmer of dawn. It was a pink dawn, the kind of dawn that the serfs feared brings bad weather. The sky behind then turned an infernal, glowing crimson, as if all the devils in Hell, all the demons and sprites, were about to rush down and devour us. Yet to the elephant and I, the day was in carnival colours at the reality of our freedom. Inside I was dancing and so was the elephant. I have never seen a beast so happy.

The sky grew lighter and there was the occasional snow-flake as we made our way along a line of birch and ash and I whirled around and around in sheer joy. It settled here and there and made things instantly beautiful. It hid the mud of the paths transforming the world completely, though it did not snow hard. Then, to my amazement, the elephant stopped too and did a stamping from foot to foot that shook the flat stones and produced a minor quaking of the earth. This seemed to please her greatly and if it were not for my vow I might have started to sing. Instead, I tried to do a Cossack dance that Antov had attempted to teach me. The elephant's trunk went up, and for an awful second I thought she was going to start trumpeting. I supressed a laugh. Here I was in the middle of a foreign county, trying to escape men who wanted nothing more than to kill me, with an enormous African elephant, painted red, who was sentenced to death too. Yet we were happier than we had ever been in our lives because of one simple thing. In that dawn, we were free.

It was good to smell the earth and feel the world around me again.

She seemed to know instinctively and trust me that we must move along before the world was up and about and we went more quickly.

I held onto her ear and then, when she felt I was tiring, she raised one front leg and with the aid of her trunk I climbed onto her neck and we went so much faster along the old road with only my thoughts for reins but none were needed. I stroked the smooth flat top of her head and she flapped her great ears in delight and a pheasant took off ahead of us with its alarm call. Then out of sheer happiness and with no one to see us she broke first into a trot and then a run that had me hanging on with my legs to the sides of her neck and with my hands to her huge ears.

I had never seen an elephant run, let alone been riding on one which was doing so.

The earth seemed to cleave in front of us and no obstacle appeared too great for her to overcome. She left her prints in the patches of snow. Then, so as not to scare me, or the morning, she slowed her pace to walking again, her trunk up, thoroughly pleased with herself.

The red clouds behind us faded and became dark as did the sky above and it started to snow fitfully again. It was not the blanket of heavy falling snow that I knew from home that silences everything, disguises everything. It was more an intimation of snow, fading at times into cold rain which made the elephant's neck slippery and began to wash off a little of the red dye from her head. She was, truly, becoming a pink elephant.

Out of devilry I tried to stand on her back, as I did shakily on a horse, but slipped and had to grab onto her ears.

It was a much longer way to fall than from a horse and she made a snorting noise to chide me like a child. I stroked her head again.

That morning I did not only feel free, I felt everything was real. Beyond real. Every colour new, every sound hypnotic, every scent irresistible and sweet. I felt they all merged together and I could hear colours and see sounds in a cornucopia of everything, though it was more subtle than that. "Tout est moi!"

I had my sacred mission, I knew. But that did not feel as real as my friend under me. She was more than a friend. I remembered the Imperial Nursery when the pretty ladies came to visit, and sometimes take away children, and no one came and visited me. When I looked sad, the question being in my eyes if not on my lips, one of the matrons looked at me and said it was because I was INSANE. "But even the peculiar are of service to God," she added.

In the distance on the tarmac road to the right of us was a cart. We needed to hide. With my knees I encouraged the elephant to move quicker, it was fully light now. In a field just ahead I saw a tumble-down barn, and we made for that. It was large and dry inside and a farmer had left several bundles of hay there and two barrels of potatoes that the elephant ate. They had not been feeding her enough at the circus in case she became too strong and broke out of the stockade. I had seen her taking a trunk full of sparse grass and weeds along the way. Now, she feasted and afterwards she lay down and rolled on the straw and I laughed at her as she put her legs in the air. I had never seen her do that. She had never dropped her guard for a moment in the stockade.

She looked at me and blinked and then I half-felt, half-heard the mesmeric vibration, the very low, rasping, singing note that went deep inside me and converted all my thoughts to good and allowed me to see the world for what it was.

I lay on the straw, my head against her side, and listened to her enormous, slow beating heart.

She trusted me enough to go to sleep, and soon I would have to if we were going to make progress the next night. The last thing I remember was putting my head against the rough warm skin of the elephant's echoing chest.

⁂

When I woke, the elephant was standing over me and pushing me with her trunk. She was propelling me onto my feet.

It was evening and not quite dark and I heard the sound of motor vehicles and went carefully outside and saw brown tented lorries moving slowly down the road and troops singing and heading for Hull and a boat to the fatal battles in France. I thought of the coffins in the warehouse Mr Masterson had showed me and I wanted to run across the frost-covered fields in between and shout at them to stop, to be sane and serious about the world and not go another step. I heard the sound of the mallet on the young, dead faces.

The elephant lay her trunk gently on my shoulder.

When they were gone and quite out of sight I mounted onto the elephant's back and we slowly walked on. There were blood red berries on the holly and hawthorn.

The river narrowed further and we got near the lights of the town I took to be Goole.

There was a modern iron bridge and soldiers everywhere and more lorries and marching men singing "It's a Long, Long Way to Tipperary." I wondered where Tipperary was and if elephants and exiles were safe there.

We skirted around the town and took a lane between fields that had been left to go to weeds and managed to dig up some turnips and I fed the elephant the apples from the basket the gypsy gave me.

She loved them. They were sweet apples. When we set out again she had a spring in her step. I ate a sandwich of spiced sausage but did not drink the little flask of vodka, or whatever the white spirit was. I left it in the field for an English serf to find and hopefully to drink in the warmth of his own house.

Further on, perhaps an hour, there was an old stone bridge across the river that was not guarded, and a great nest of locks, rising one above the other and some at angles, where several rivers joined a number of canals.

There was a large, neat, red-painted hut by the river with a dim oil lamp near the window but no one came out and, occasionally, there was shouting and fiddle music. The keeper of the locks had finished for the night and was having drinks with his friends.

I was walking by the elephant as we headed for the stone bridge.

There was something I did not like about the deserted towpaths and the empty bridge.

My hand tightened on the elephant's huge ears.

In the distance, miles away, a dog barked.

I patted the elephant's side.

At that moment, several men came out of the hut and when I turned there were two others blocking the path behind me.

"It's bloody them. Sithee! We've caught them. Them Russian spies."

The accent was so thick and violent that at first I did not understand. These men from the hut were ruddy-faced with drink.

One of them laughed.

"Fucking elephant ain't a Russian spy."

"It's red."

"It's probably pink after what we've been drinking. It is fucking pink. I've been drinking too much, I have."

Another man held up a stave.

"We're most likes in for a dirty great reward. This animal killed a man and t' boy's mixed up in a shooting wi' a man in hospital fighting for his life. He looks a cruel young cunt. Is tha' going to give up peaceable, or shall we rough tha' up a bit?" he said, loudly, in the way I had found lower-class

English people talk to any foreigner. The group of men were ten feet away.

The man with the stave was strongly built with a powerful jaw.

I did not answer him, I only stared back with no expression.

"We'd best go for one of Home Guard patrols," said a nervous voice.

This did not go down well with the other men.

"They're all tied up with convoy movements. They don't want no bothering by us. We're about our patriotic business, we is. We're elephant hunting."

They all laughed.

"And they'd get their grubby fingers on our reward if they help."

"But they've rifles."

"What do we need with rifles? said the first man. I had often seen the vodka talking with Antov and M. Hippolyte, not to mention many other of my countrymen, in particular the serfs, and the blood that results. The elephant that towered above them on the lock side like a house must have shrunk in size after what they had drunk and they then added in the fabled size of the reward.

"I say we rush 'em," said the first man.

They looked at each other. Several with staves raised.

With her trunk the elephant made it possible for me to climb up on her neck and grip securely behind her ears with my legs. The men were screaming and yelling as they came along the towpath towards us.

She then, swinging her heavy trunk, knocked the five men in front down like ninepins, trumpeting as she did so.

It was as simple as that.

I recalled that M. Hippolyte had told me how advantageous

the war elephants of the African general Hannibal were in defeating the Roman army, although he did also stress that victory was mainly due to the tactics of the general. The men facing us had no tactics at all.

It was time for us to make our escape.

We turned for the bridge, but then one of the two behind us lit a torch, a clumsy, spitting thing of pitch on the end of wood. I felt a charge of fear go through me from the elephant below. She was terrified.

"Don't fucking like that, does tha'?"

She backed away and they all got up and started taunting her and another torch was lit and then another. They picked up loose cobbles from the path by the lock and hurled them at her. The men were smiling again and laughing. We crossed one huge lock on the river that was like a bridge with the men after us and then confronted another full lock almost at right angles to the first channel. The slippery path along the side of this lock became too narrow for the elephant.

"We got you now. We got you now, an elephant and a Red spy. That's what they said. That's what they bloody said. We're going to be rich, mark me bloody words. First pint's on me."

"That'll be t' day."

Then one of them got carried away and threw a blazing torch and it struck the elephant on the head, just missing her eye and burning my arm in a shower of sparks. Another torch then followed it and overshot but the elephant had backed too far. I saw the black depths below us and we appeared to hang there and then, to the cheers of the lock men, we toppled over into the lock, throwing up a mountain of water.

It was freezing and took all my breath away and I gasped to the surface and the elephant was nowhere at all in the darkness. It was the dark, uncaring river of my prophetic dreams.

We were going to die.

I slid down under the water again as waves broke and broke again inside the lock.

The cold hit my face as if I had been kicked and my hands and my feet were already numb and hurting. I fought back to the surface but not before breathing water and went down again and thought I was going to pass out.

All around me was cold and BLACKNESS.

I had always thought of Hell as hot and I like the cold and snow of winter, but this was the worst place I had ever been. And I was so tired and a voice in my ear said do not fight, go to sleep, you do not need to fight, and I realised it was the DEVIL himself in me, and I fought again for the surface.

I swam with difficulty in my heavy clothes, gasping for breath. I snatched at the side but it was smooth as a plastered wall and still I did not see the elephant.

A current like an underwater hand was pulling at me and I had started to sink again when I found a wooden post with a foot of rope attached to it and clung to that like a rat. I heard people shouting above me and saw a torch reflected in the water.

"They're both done for. That's deepest fucking cut. They're both done for. We'll say they fell in. I can't see nothing. I can't see nothing."

I felt a tear hot on my cheeks. This was my stupid fault for trying to go too far too fast.

I had been arrogant and reckless again and the elephant had suffered.

Then I saw a movement at the other end of the lock.

It was just for an instant and it was gone when I looked again.

There was then a huge banging sound and a wave moved

up and down the lock and nearly had me away from the wooden post and the piece of rope. I hung on.

"What were that?" said one of the men on the bank.

"Maybe lock gate moved. We're expecting a barge. A big munitions barge, iron wheels, shells and the like. That's t' canal into River Don. I didn't want it to take time if it came. Safety's off. Lock's not likely to open on its own. We've done that loads of times and it's too heavy and then there's water on t' other side. But if it did come open it'd flood bloody steelworks to Sheffield and Rotherham. Germans'd love that."

There was another huge bang and the lock gates ahead of me seemed to open a fraction and the head of water rush through for a second and close.

I then saw the elephant's delicate trunk end above the water.

She was breathing through it even though her feet must have been on the bottom of the lock.

She intended to smash her way out.

"Fuck me," said the voice above. "The elephant. It's on t' lock bed ramming gate. Under-bloody-water. If she splinters gate we'll not be able to use river for months. It's a strategic waterway. They'll fucking shoot us."

There was a silence above as men fought for sobriety.

"Open bloody gates."

"But anyone in there'll be swept down and killed?"

"We've no choice. We're at war. That elephant is a proven killer and t' bloody boy is a Russian spy. If we find bodies afterwards they might still give us t' reward."

There was the sound of feet running on the bank as the elephant hit the lock again.

"I don't want any part in t' killing," said a voice.

"Then you won't get part of share out."

I looked up and saw men pushing the white-painted arm of the lock and another unwinding what seemed to be a screw, and there was a sudden and terrifying pull from below and then another as the black water in the lock around me began to boil.

With a hollow booming sound the elephant rammed the lock gate again and the men fell off the white lock arm.

I was dragged down.

The next thing I knew I was being hurtled through the lock gates on top of a huge wave.

I had lost track of the elephant.

There was a terrible crashing as the lock behind me disintegrated and the wave I was on broke and boiled.

The incredible force of the water turned me over and over and again I was going down.

Where was the elephant? Where was she?

I came up again and had a vague impression of a tree over the water and then another wave broke on me and it was as if all the rivers and all the seas had hit me and there was nothing.

The sun was up and the day was fully light when I came round and the first thing that greeted me was the end of a warm, inquisitive trunk and her hot breath on my face. The elephant was standing guard over me on the riverbank with her trunk in front of my head as they probably do with their young when the little ones are sleeping. My head ached. I was so cold I could hardly move but grasped hold of the trunk and kissed it many times. I tried to see where the lock was and picked it out way in the distance next to a small tower.

I shivered so hard my teeth chattered and I heard the elephant cough, but her eyes were bright.

Everywhere around us on the riverbank was wreckage

from the lock and upturned barges and uprooted willow trees. Shards of wood and planking had been thrown up into the fields where cows now grazed on the hard, frosted grass. My hand shot to the silver elephant around my neck that miraculously had survived, as had the pouch with the gold pieces on my belt. The large red, white-spotted kerchief, which I had stuffed inside my shirt, was several yards away.

Then, twenty yards upstream I saw a body. It was one of the men who had attacked us. It was the large man with dark hair and a big jaw. I could tell who he was from his blue coat, a sailor's pea jacket. I had no doubt at all we were in even more trouble. He was curled up, knees to his chin, like a baby.

The elephant then did a most peculiar thing.

She lowered her body onto me as if she were going to crush me into the mud.

I made to move but then I felt the warmth of her underside. There was liquid coming from a protuberance and I realised that she was still making milk for her baby. Her body was super warm and I felt a rush of heat back to my fingers and toes and was able to move them again. I coughed up lock water. I then drank the thick, creamy milk by putting my open mouth under the dribbling teat. Her milk tasted of black treacle though it was quite white and my drinking it pleased her because the singing vibration started which made me feel so much better.

We needed to build a bonfire to warm her and to dry my clothes but the day looked a fair one and we had to keep going. I walked beside her holding hard onto her ear. She rubbed her trunk against me to reassure me. I looked into her eye and saw both sadness and kindness. She had saved my LIFE.

ॐ

We stopped still near the man who had his face down in the grey mud. It was as if the SILT were sucking him into the ground. His dark hair curled and was neatly cut. He might well have been the lock keeper. I thought about taking his warm blue coat but left it there. I did not want to roll him over and see his eyes.

I fixed on the word SILT and that mercifully blurred the event.

There was nothing whatsoever we could do for him but I said a prayer and made the sign of the Holy Cross that he should be forgiven for his disgusting drunkenness and ill-considered moment of murderous greed, barbaric cruelty and complete stupidity. Antov had once said that acts done in drunkenness should always be forgiven, which provoked ironic laughter from M. Hippolyte. "So if my mother was raped by a drunken Prussian, I should forgive him and invite him for a hand of cards? This sort of barrack-room wisdom is beyond the ridiculous. I suppose the Cossacks are always drunk when they start to massacre the Jews. If they finish bashing the last baby's brains out before they sober up that is quite all right then?" That was not the first time I heard the word JEW, I had heard it on the Tsarina's lips, but the first I heard the word linked to Cossacks and massacre.

The dead man with his face in the SILT had hated me in those minutes on the lock side and been prepared to kill me partly because I was a spy but mostly because I was a Russian and even more that he wanted a reward. On my journey to Riga I had frequently heard former serfs denounced as Jews so that others might take their property. It seemed that anyone whose property one coveted might be called a Jew. When I asked a priest in the local church why people hated them he said it was because they killed Jesus Christ. I said it was the

Romans who killed Jesus, but the papa began to fiddle with an incense burner and said if I wanted to keep the money I had in my pockets I had better keep away from Jews. I told him I had never had any money in my pockets and he became quite angry. He became even more angry when I pointed out that it was the other way around and people were always taking things from Jews. The Tsar's estate manager, Dimitri, who was pierced with the Christmas tree, was said to be a JEW. I brought the matter up with M. Hippolyte and Antov and in the end Antov said quietly: "It is fear and ignorant men that make these labels of race and nations. There are only people, wherever you go. There are only people." M. Hippolyte nodded and lit his pipe. I was about to ask if either of them was Jewish but thought it better not to. It did seem strange, in the presence of the elephant and her gift, that anyone should want to kill another man just because they were from another piece of earth or had a different hair colour.

A way down the river a barge loaded with hay and animal feed had been upset, though there was not the destruction and flooding beside the river the men at the lock had forecast. The elephant spent time eating as much as she could. I noticed then there were cuts on her flanks and feet where she had been swept through the lock and every now and again she coughed. I was torn between joy that we were alive and frightened for her. I tried to light a fire but the matches in my pocket were wet and the lighter given to me by a gypsy who tried to introduce me to smoking had run out of tar spirits. But on the horizon I saw chimneys and black smoke and presumed these were the towns we were meant to head for.

I could taste the iron and steel in my mouth and feel the soot in my nose, but the journey took a great deal longer than I thought and in the end the elephant was limping more.

I made her stop and gentled her whenever it was safe.

The cold wormed its way into us. I began to shiver uncontrollably and felt I was going to faint.

The elephant's eyes were streaming and I saw her stumble. We took the chance of going on the towpath as there was no one about. But then in the distance we heard shouts and had to hide in the outhouses of a red brick bakery. I smelt the bread and stole some loaves for the elephant from a delivery cart but she was too troubled and lame and in pain to eat them. I ate a few mouthfuls of the hot, doughy bread. It burned my tongue. We had to find warmth and safety

We became more and more tired and then stopped in a quarry that was about fifty yards from a long black building which was belching smoke and a red glow came from inside and flames from a smaller chimney.

I felt the heat from where I stood. I warmed myself on the colour red.

It was like being very hungry and looking in the window of one of the cake shops on Nevsky Prospect at all the full plates and the smiling faces and the waitresses in their uniforms of black and white, flitting from table to table, from countess to merchant's wife. I was so cold, my head was spinning and for a moment I was back in the ballroom at the Selo palace with the ladies' ball gowns swishing into my face writing LE TSAR DOIT MOURIR.

I jumped at a noise behind us. I expected a patrol. We were both too exhausted to run.

I blinked.

There was one man in dirty blue overalls that were too big for him. He had the questing look of a small animal. He had a thin-lipped smile of uneven teeth. He pushed what remained of his hair across his bald head.

"By Jove's Heavens, that's an elephant. I prayed to God this morning for help and here it is. I prayed to God this morning and he has been so good as to send this sinner an elephant. Thank you, God. Thank you."

But he was not looking at the elephant he was smiling at me. "Don't be suspicious. You don't have to say anything. Perhaps you are unable to, my friend."

He had such kind eyes and saintly demeanour that I knew he was not going to turn us in for reward or notoriety. I wondered what he had prayed for that involved an elephant, but most of me was too tired to care. If only we could get into that factory with the furnace then we might both became warm again and I feared for my friend's health and life and my own.

"My name is the Reverend Charles Hunt from the Parish of Masbro'. I run Park Gate Forge now all the poor lads are away fighting that useless war and most have been killed that I know. They made the steel that kills them. In my Satanic Mill! What good is that? How does that honour the Almighty? Stay here now and hold out until dark. I'll fetch you some food and clean clothes in the meantime. It's not often you pray and a boy and an elephant come along."

His voice had a soothing musical quality that the best priests have or develop.

He then disappeared in the direction of the factory and we spent tense minutes huddled together.

But the man was as good as his word and brought me black tea in a large enamelled cup about a foot tall, with a small one on top. He called the whole thing a mashing can or Dudley. I drank from the small cup.

There were also two pieces of bread covered in beef

dripping. The taste of the fat on the rough loaf was like a banquet.

For the elephant the Reverend Charles brought a bag of apples and potatoes.

He gave me a suit of blue overalls similar to the ones he wore, a sweater and a red woollen cap and I was soon out of my old damp clothes and into them. I felt like crying with gratitude and the elephant reached out her trunk to him.

"It's just like the Almighty to send me a pink elephant and a silent boy," he said. "I suppose that's the only way he can bear to put up with man and this war. He has a sense of humour, has God."

That night the Reverend Charles came back and led us into the factory. It was a good thing he did because we could see from the quarry that a military roadblock was being set up on the road at the side of which we had just walked.

The small man did not seem to care. He went on his way across the cobbles whistling and then opened a huge door and inside everything glowed red and we stepped forward and into the building, luxuriating in the warmth. The Reverend Charles smiled:

"I used to think Hell was like this but since I have been working here for the war effort it is total heaven. We have three open-hearth furnaces and a bright bar mill. The steel from the furnaces goes to make munitions and tanks and that from the bar mill often goes, among other things, to make metal crutches. Strange that. Perhaps it would be better not to make the first so as not to have to make the second. Sorry, I went to Oxford, you know. Balliol as an undergraduate. You probably don't know what that means. Too much intellectual enthusiasm even for God and he sends me an elephant. A pink elephant!"

He stared for a moment into the glow. The warmth was coming back into my body and I felt pins and needles in my face. The elephant did her little dance of happiness and the Reverend Charles laughed:

"The elephant likes my dragons and they like her. That's what they are to me. If you treat them like living things, and they are living, they treat you well too. Since I started thinking like that we never had any accidents here, even though they took every horse we had for the war. Every horse. We had lovely horses. But now I only have my dragons. And this elephant! God has sent me this wonderful elephant to help. Rejoice!"

Within hours, however, this was impossible, as the elephant took with a fever and I thought she was going to die.

The Reverend Charles did too, I saw it in his eyes and heard it in his voice. He kept talking to me even though I did not reply or even looked as if I understood because I am sure he knew deep down that I did understand. We were put in an area called the Metal Bank by one of the furnaces, which was an immense space lit only from above by dusty skylights, but whose front opened onto the even bigger space where the three furnaces were on top of steel gantries. These were kept going around the clock, heated by a gas jet from coking ovens. I never gave a thought to the pursuit going on outside.

"I think her wounds, on her feet and her chest, may have become infected and I will make some poultices to fetch any pus or infection out. I fear, too, that she may have an infection on her chest from getting so wet and so cold. She is a long way from home. You do not seem to have suffered from the same malady, my boy." The Reverend Charles smiled as he listened to her heart and she let him. "Good, good," was all he said. He then knelt down and intoned a little prayer and I knelt and prayed with him, which seemed to please him greatly.

"I'm a bit of an imposter, you know. I'm actually a Catholic priest but because of an administrative War Office mistake they call me Reverend and presented me with a large vicarage, which is now given over to orphans. I was with a Catholic charity in the trenches, by God, and was hit by shrapnel and sent home. There was no one to run this works and one old man to teach me how, so instead of saying Mass and all the other stuff I do my work here. It seems better that way, although I suppose I should not be making steel to turn into bullets. Anyone who has seen that slaughterhouse prays that one side wins and quick, it probably does not matter which one. Even the devil can do good. Don't listen to my sedition. Or my blasphemy. I do go on. One day they will come and arrest me. I can tell from your eyes you have seen the terrifying limits of man's abominations, my child."

I looked up from my prayer but did not nod or smile.

"It is unforgivable that one so young and innocent has experienced such horror. Horror. No doubt that is how you lost your voice. I do not care what you have done and I do not ask. I do not judge anymore. I leave that to poor old God. You are safe here with me. No one comes on my domain."

With that we both went back to the elephant and a compress was put on her head to bring down the fever. I stayed by her day and night for two days and when he was not working the Reverend Charles came in to see her. He even brought ice to put on her head to try and bring down the temperature, but it did not work.

On the third day he stood up from dressing a wound on the elephant's chest and said: "I have an idea. I have an idea," and rushed as fast as he could from the room. He did not return for hours and when he did it was with various buckets and a suction pump. He attached the suction pump to one of the teats I had drunk the elephant's sweet milk from.

"She is lactating, producing milk. I wager that she has lost her calf in childbirth or soon after. The production of milk increases the body temperature and if we can draw enough off we may go some way to breaking her fever. I am not a medical man but it is worth a try. I have had a word with a vet that I trust and a herbalist. They have indicated other things I can give her and the vet is coming to see her. He works at a great house nearby."

It must have been hope that let a tear run down my face but when he reached out to put a hand upon my shoulder I pulled away.

"My, you are a strange one," he said, going about the business of connecting the pump and drawing off her milk and becoming more and more excited. In the end he filled five buckets with the thick liquid.

"I will let it down with water and give it to the orphans. They do not get fresh milk all the time and there is a dreadful problem with rickets. Dreadful. All this wealth being dug out of the ground and turned into machines and we still have medieval diseases. The orphans will be grateful to your African friend here. Just think of that."

But the fever did not abate and on about the ninth day, I had not been out of the Metal Bank and away from the elephant except to empty the toilet bucket that the Reverend Charles had given me. I knew from the softness and the kindness of his voice he was preparing me for very bad news. I had watched other children receive such news in the Imperial Nursery and knew the change in the voices of the ushers and the la-dies-in-waiting and the nuns. I tried to will the GOOD.

HAPPY is a word you can hide inside even when you are not.

The vet came and shook his head and I thought it was for the worst but it was because he had not been so close to an elephant before. I was with him all the time and I saw from her eye that she would let him examine her. In the end he gave her several large pills and a preparation of herbs that the herbalist had given to the Reverend Charles.

"I have seen this do the trick in horses but never anything bigger. The herbs can do no harm. You will know in a day and a night if the fever's going to break. She will not have a chance after that, I am afraid. Don't worry, my boy. I know where she is from and what they were going to do to her and you'll have my complete and utter silence on the matter. Charles here is a good and special friend."

That day and that night I did not leave her for a moment.

I talked to her in my head of how much she meant to me, that she was a mother to me and one day I was going to take her back to Africa and away from all the stupid wars and circuses. She made noises to me and I think that meant she understood. I so did not want her to die. I knew how easy it is for things to DIE.

When night came I had my head on her trunk and my arms fiercely around it and I was praying and demanding of all the Saints and the Holy Virgin that the elephant get well.

She uttered her small noises again but did not have the energy left to make that low vibration that had so changed the way I now looked at things. I prayed for her not to leave me and in my exhaustion and emotion was overcome with sleep.

When I awoke she was standing above me and raised her trunk.

I sat there open-mouthed.

Then I jumped up and buried my head in her trunk, showering her with kisses. I was so pleased.

I thanked all the Saints and the Holy Virgin, even though I knew they had no hand in things, that that was just flowers and mirrors by the dark river in my dreams. It was comforting all the same.

She pushed me away slightly and then roughed up my hair.

The Reverend Charles was watching us from the doorway. He had a sack of food in each hand.

"It is good that you show your joy, my dear boy. Now let your friend rest and eat. The worst is past. But she needs to get her strength up or we will have a relapse. Come here and help me with these bags. I wonder how old she is? The vet was telling me that the big females are often past sixty years old and live well beyond that. He thought she might be in her twenties, so a strong young thing. And I have a special present for her that you may give her."

The Reverend Charles put his hand inside his overalls and took out a pineapple. The orange fruit looked even more exotic in the strange light. I had seen them at the refreshment tables at the balls long ago. I remembered liking them a lot.

PINEAPPLE is a word you can enjoy.

"You give it to her. It is your love that has brought her back from the edge, you know. The vet was given it at the great house where he works, the Woodhouse we call it. It is the biggest house in England. Queen Victoria thought it far too big with its three hundred and sixty-five rooms, one for every day of the year. Far too big. Then there's what we call the castle wall, built with the stones from an old abbey a few

194

villages away. But the family always say that wall was a castle. They grow the pineapples in the horse droppings and straw of the stables. I do hope she likes it."

I took the nobbled fruit from him and presented it to the elephant and she approached it with great solemnity; perhaps it was a link back to an Africa she had never seen.

She gripped the fruit gently with her trunk and then put it in her mouth.

I saw her eyes light up as she chewed on it and kept every drop of juice in her mouth for as long as she was able. She even lifted her trunk and trumpeted weakly.

I hugged her more and when I turned the Reverend Charles was gone.

SIXTEEN

NATASHA WAS SCARED. She was worried she would be tongue-tied. She was about to meet the Russians and in the elevator had been marvelling that the boy, Alexei, had taken a vow of silence on his near impossible journey to add to his other problems. He had always to be on his toes, a child of the moment, not an imagined future, to survive. Yet the boy was intensely spiritual to live within himself. He was not a slave to time. Natasha was not expecting the elevator doors to open straight into the apartment itself in the art deco block on the Upper East Side and nearly dropped the cakes she had brought to the tea party. It was like an entrance in an old film with an audience of well-dressed people in front of her who had nothing pressing to do at four in the afternoon. What struck her first was the smell of incense in the room and a large icon of Tsar Nicholas II, who looked, in primary colours, Christ-like to the point of idiocy. He had been placed under other more traditional icons in a corner of the room where glass doors led out onto a wide balcony that looked down onto the autumnal trees of Central Park.

Natasha was wearing a smart lemon-yellow suit and silk blouse that she reserved for formal occasions, and high heels that nearly caught between the lift door and the marble of the entrance stairs. It was a classic Chanel suit with the heavy, little gold metal chain in the back of the jacket so it hung correctly, the slave irony of which was not lost on Natasha.

She had bought the suit on the trip to see the man in Paris when she had burned all the clothes she was wearing that night. Including the blood-stained, white Versace blouse. All of them. She could still smell the acrid smoke in her friend's apartment on the rue du Cherche-Midi and see the astonished and sympathetic faces of the *sapeurs pompiers* when they found her naked and weeping in a corner. She persuaded them not to call the police. These carefully turned-out Russian émigrés would not guess that about a librarian.

Paris had been a try at breaking free, like the butterflies in her dream.

The Chanel suit, bought next day, was part of her new armour.

There were seven people in the room, all of whom looked at her in a stern mixture of amazement, suspicion and wonder.

One of them was an Orthodox priest who elaborately crossed himself every time he passed the picture of the Tsar.

The room was decorated in a warm red with ancestor portraits, leather sofas and a white fluffy carpet covered in Middle Eastern rugs. Underneath the incense there was a smell of Turkish coffee and toasted tobacco and the scent from vases of pink roses and a sense of intricately wasted time.

She noticed a postcard of Putin on a white marble mantelpiece packed with invitations.

A tall, dark woman, who once would have been a great beauty, opened her arms to Natasha and smiled. The woman moved stiffly and her hair and make-up looked to have taken hours.

"Little one! You cannot imagine how good it is to have you amongst us at last! I knew you would come. I told you all she would come."

She kissed Natasha on the hand and curtsied and then

three times on the cheek. Covid was probably an ugly rumour to them. The woman then turned to the large icon of the Tsar and crossed herself with two fingers extended. She genuflected. Natasha was unsure what to do but the rest of the room followed and did the same thing. It was as if the revolution had never happened. Time seemed to have stopped around 1906 and a banshee police siren somewhere in the park was a welcoming fix on reality.

"We are so happy you are here," continued the elegant woman. "And you are beautiful. Beautiful! Little one . . ."

Natasha was trying to think of a reply when a small red-haired man threw himself at her feet and began to kiss her hand and would not let go. He held her hand very tight and the kiss had become a slobber. She felt his tongue on her knuckles. Natasha was still uncertain what any of this was about and she smiled down at him and pulled her hand away sharply, at which he appeared to be grateful and had to go and sit down.

On the way in the subway she had played the elephant app over and over. It was an innocuous, low frequency, part higher-pitched singing sound that reminded her of whale music and was obviously meant to be like that in the boy's story, except it had no effect on her whatsoever. The red-haired man was now crying. The dark-haired woman steered Natasha to an old leather armchair.

"My name is Nadya and these are my friends. This is my sister, Sophia, and that is Jelena and this is Father Grigory who is going back to Russia soon now that the church is respected properly once more. And this is Sergei and his little friend."

A severe man who was holding a whippet with one hand under its front paws, almost by its throat, and was wearing a medal on a long ribbon round his neck came towards her. He had anarchic grey hair and enormous staring eyes. He sniffed at Natasha, as if making sure she was real. He seemed suddenly angry and his dog appeared angry too and barked.

"Sit down, Sergei, and have some cake," said Nadya. "You do not know how much excitement you have caused, little one. Natasha! It is so wonderful to find you. You must have cake and there is Turkish coffee unless, of course, you would prefer tea. Or there is caviar. Jelena is the one who can make the Turkish coffee so well. I make it too, but you have to get the timing right. Come, Sergei, and sit down and introduce Natasha to your lovely dog later."

These people did nothing. She could feel their inertia.

The priest moved close to her and began to recite prayers faster and faster and she had to stop him anointing her with a strange, scented oil. Another man produced several bottles of vodka. There was then a pop of a champagne cork. Two unsmiling maids brought glasses and trays of caviar and blinis.

'We have champagne. Crimean champagne. We will taste Russia! The earth! The sky! We must drink a toast to our new arrival," said Jelena. They all toasted her and Natasha toasted back and half-expected them to throw their glasses into the fireplace.

"This is so exciting for us," shouted the red-haired man. "You have no idea what this means."

Natasha nodded. She had no idea.

The champagne sat by her on a polished wood table. She slowly drank the Turkish coffee and ate small, honeyed almond cakes as an avalanche of Russian conversation exploded around her like firecrackers. The man who had delivered her parcel tied up with hairy string came into the room and even before he greeted Nadya, he crossed himself in front of the icon of the Tsar.

"We are so pleased he is now a saint," said Jelena. "He was made a saint for all the suffering he had gone through. May the Tsars be restored one day! Such suffering. He is now Saint Nicholas the Passion Bearer. You must know that, of course. Of course you do, little one. You are so clever."

"No," said Natasha and there was silence for a second and then the conversation rolled and rattled on.

"Ah!" said Sophia. "It is only clever people who say that!"

Her sister Nadya sighed contentedly and said that their family had a factory in Moscow that made marzipan for the Tsars from a recipe an ancestor was given by the French writer Balzac and that her grandchildren were thinking of going back and re-starting the family business. It did not only make marzipan but also chocolate and every sort of sweet for the Imperial households. They had been minor nobility, but rich. One uncle, when the snow did not come, had his servants put sugar down in his drive for his sleigh. Her great-grandfather had refused to hand over his factory to the Bolsheviks. "You cannot imagine, little one. He was shot and his body was thrown into a vat of boiling sugar. That is not proper for such an important man, to end his life like a *marron glacé*. The factory is much the same today as it ever was." Natasha heard snatches of stories of family and homeland and loss in English. There was a fierce edge to the homesickness.

She cleared her throat. She was wired from the very strong, very sweet coffee and her mouth was dry from too many cakes.

"What I wanted to ask was . . ." They all looked at her and she faltered. "I suppose you want my opinion on the part of the boy's manuscript you sent me. I must thank you all and say that it's . . . most amazing. Where did it come from . . . Who . . . ?"

The powdered blonde woman called Jelena held up her hand.

"Please do not trouble yourself at the moment, my dear. Not here. Not now. We know you are very learned and are brilliant. We would like you to get to know us first, if that is not impertinent. There is nothing we would like more than to hear your views, it will be an honour and a privilege, my darling."

Natasha nodded.

"Little one . . . !" Nadya clapped her hands.

Natasha saw everyone was looking at her as they were eating and drinking. It was as if they were devouring her.

"I will try and do my best. It . . . It is a most moving and astounding story and echoes ideas in Nabokov's work."

Everyone was leaning forwards and hanging on Natasha's every word.

Then an argument broke out at the other side of the room, she thought, at first, about Nabokov. The man with the whippet came striding up and thrust an invitation into Natasha's hand. His face had contorted into a snarl.

"I have not been consulted in this. Not properly consulted at all. I am insulted. So you are the Natasha? You will please come to the wedding of my granddaughter, please. It will be out in the Berkshires. I'd be most honoured, princess." He bowed deeply and kissed Natasha's hand.

He then left with his dog, arguing with the red-haired man as he got into the lift.

The whole room seemed to go quiet as Natasha realised what the man had said.

He had called her princess. PRINCESS! She felt like

the countess Natasha in *War and Peace*. She must tell ChiChiChica!

When Natasha left she walked away from the park. She did not know this ritzy part of town well and turned down a street off Park Avenue. There was not a soul: there were no cars and no pedestrians. Natasha had dreams like that more and more often. Dreams of emptiness. Heart-aching loneliness in the centre of deserted cities. She hoped it was not the future. Why were these Russians so in love with the past when the future was dissolving? That's what buildings did in Natasha's dreams, dissolve. There was no one on the street ahead. She could walk in the middle of the road if she wanted to. She started to run, even in those stupid heels. She started to run and did not stop until she got back to the park and saw a yellow cab. She was at the start of something and she did not exactly know what. People always had these feelings and dreams on the cusp of a great change. The vertiginous NEW. The boy was the same. He was her brother in anxiety. She saw on her phone that a new part of the manuscript had arrived. She wanted to get home and immerse herself in the boy's WORDS.

SEVENTEEN

THE UNEXPECTED MANUSCRIPT: PACKET IX

"WE ARE AT the mercy of dark forces! They have abducted my sweet, defenceless Miss Emily, my lady on the flying trapeze, my love, my dear one, from right under the noses of the police after I, Samuel Masterson, was shot down like a dog and put into the hospital. My elephant has been stolen too that was to be the star of my coming show, the greatest one night only extravaganza there has ever been in the history of the circus or even show business. That show must go on and I will pursue these rattlesnakes, these Gila monsters, this so-called nest of Russian spies, whoever they are, to the ends of the earth to get my sweet Miss Emily back. She's the sweetest and most beautiful creature alive and I fear for her safety in all senses both physical and moral."

The report in *The Times* newspaper, which the Reverend Charles handed to me, showed a picture of Mr Masterson with his arm in a sling and on crutches.

I did not fear for Miss Emily. I did not think she would wait around to be abducted.

If anyone could look after herself, she could, whatever she was up to, and to describe her as sweet and "defenceless" was dangerously misplaced, although she sent a shiver through me, especially when I thought of her, deceptively soft and lily-skinned, in the polished copper bath. Like a woman in one of Antov's Sherlock Holmes stories, she was a combination of heart-bending beauty and charm, and a cool independence and intelligence absent in most men.

However, I was worried that Mr Masterson might track us here and because he did not mention me.

I was pleased to see that later on in the article it said that the doctors had noted Mr Masterson was going to have to stay in a sanatorium for several months due to one of the bullets piercing his lungs. But I was sure this was not going to stop him for long. Elsewhere, there was an article questioning whether Mr Masterson had ever been a cowboy at all and saying that he had an incredible likeness to a man wanted for multiple marriage fraud in upper New York State.

The circus had now moved on without him as there was a dispute about tickets bought for THE EXECUTION OF THE KILLER ELEPHANT FAMILY SHOW.

There had also been a sudden and unstoppable fire in a warehouse down by the docks that had been left to burn out by the Fire Brigade and was said to contain lumber and barrels of salt pork. Police were investigating. A picture showed one English bobby looking in the other direction.

The Reverend Charles had watched me for a few moments as I read and I realised I had revealed to him I was not only able to read, but also read in English. When I glanced up he was not there, leaving only my own shadow flickering on the wall.

There was no mention in *The Times* whatsoever of the incident at the lock, which I found puzzling, though there were several cartoons of drunken men seeing pink elephants rampaging through the countryside. There was another, smaller story referring to Mr Masterson far down the page that noted how one Russian diplomat of the revolutionary government had been killed and another wounded in the unexplained shooting incident involving Mr Masterson. This was thought to be an accident, said the account, and rumours that a member of the Imperial Russian household was in the country had been discounted. The Tsar and his immediate family were under house imprisonment by the Russians in conditions that had been internationally witnessed as humane. They were being moved to other accommodation in the Urals. The piece talked of 'the former Tsar' and the abdicated Nicholas II and there was a picture of him in happier times with his cousin, George, Prince of Wales, to whom he was almost identical. They had been photographed together in Germany, dressed in German navy uniforms, to please their cousin, the Kaiser.

In the end, *The Times* article said, all the Russian regiments had mutinied including the Imperial Guard founded by Peter the Great of my beloved tiled stove. He was a clever Tsar who had the story put around that he was able to crush a rouble in his fist and was a giant, when in fact the opposite was true. Peter amused M. Hippolyte, who told me he beat the army of Old Believers by waiting for them to pray, as was the custom with Russian armies, before opening fire. M. Hippolyte had been trying to educate me in the ideas of Niccolò Machiavelli and how they influenced present day German and British Foreign policy, but not Russia, he said, which preferred astrological fatalism and holy men like Rasputin, who Antov would impersonate and try to turn water into vodka, especially after the man I made a bargain with was murdered and pushed through the ice.

The article talked of Nicholas as "Bloody Nicholas" who killed so many of his own people, who let his elite cavalry charge on women and children, and I thought of the tall, nervous, awkward man tickling the ear of the lion.

In the large, very clear newspaper photograph, just behind Mr Masterson was a tall woman with broad shoulders staring directly and threateningly at the camera. I was astonished. She was the woman who had rescued me in the forest and with whom I had travelled to Riga. The woman had a very square and heavy jaw and was talking to a man in an astrakhan coat. He had his back to the camera. There was patch of white in his hair. I knew very well who that man was and smelt the Mint Imperials.

I was not sure whether to be pleased, or very, very frightened.

Mr Masterson who, if he had any sense, which over Miss Emily he did not, should walk to the nearest large port and take the first boat back to America and rejoin the desperate outlaw gangs he claimed to have ridden with. I had a feeling it would be a good deal safer.

I am sure Mr Masterson loved Miss Emily, though, even if he did not know quite who or what he was loving when he had his 'little sleeps'.

I nursed the elephant for the next seven days and most of the nights to be sure of no relapse and then fell into an exhausted unconsciousness, which the Reverend Charles said lasted two days and nights, and woke refreshed.

My prayers had been answered and it was to my complete delight that when I got to my feet and stretched, the elephant stood up too.

She then came straight to me and tickled my hair and face in a thank you before sitting down again and making short little grunting noises. She was happy and later that morning she ate a huge amount of potatoes and apples and sugar beet. Her head no longer felt hot to the touch. I knelt down and prayed to God and all his Saints and Angels.

"She does seem to be getting stronger, doesn't she?" said the Reverend Charles. "Now I have a favour to ask you. Come on with me."

I left the elephant in the Metal Bank and followed him out into the area below the three furnaces, his dragons. Two men were at work putting something into one of the furnaces.

There was a flash of white light as the furnace door opened and then closed again, a kind of light that I had never seen, it made me blink and see a forest of blue after-images.

"We will go and see the furnaces presently. What I want to show you is over here," said the Reverend Charles.

We followed railway tracks that were in the building to an old steam engine. It had a very narrow chimney at the front and its boiler of water appeared to be held together with leather belts.

"Behold, the future. I call her Martha and she's a very old lady. There are parts of her that are forty years old and although she could never be as dear to me as your living elephant, I don't want her to fall suddenly into a million pieces. All she does is drag the scrap and the pig iron ingots to under the furnace stage, to whichever furnace needs to be stoked. Then we send it up on a hoist. That's all she does, but it is vital. If she were to fail, the furnaces would have to be shut down and relined with bricks and clay. It's a long process that demands a lot of labour we don't have."

He went over and patted the aged machine, which did, I must admit, look very friendly.

"What I was wondering, if you will excuse my temerity, young man, is if your elephant might stand in for Martha, while I and one of our furnace men replace a couple of her parts. Then she'll be the future again. One day such machines will do everything for us and we will have to re-think our worn out morality about work and social class. Even the revolutionaries will, especially the revolutionaries. All I need her to do is to pull a couple of these cars loaded with scrap. An elephant did in one of the works before, I don't know what happened to her but there are photographs. It will keep her occupied."

I didn't even nod. I just stared at him without smiling.

"Of course, we'll have to allow another two weeks at least to get her fully better. Perhaps a little longer. Just imagine a future without work, without the need for a working class or servants? It is coming, one day."

This was something I had discussed with M. Hippolyte after we had been doing Latin, it may have been the Annals of Tacitus, but the matter of the slaves' rebellion and the figure of Spartacus came up. It was a thrilling story, though not from the Latin I had to translate, but told by M. Hippolyte with the slave hero beating legion after legion until he finally was defeated by the patrician, Crassus. "All revolts are about trying to remove the chains of slavery," said M. Hippolyte. "The trouble is that, as the philosopher Marx said, the oppressed people quickly take on the characteristics of the oppressor." Antov yawned at this. "But if there were no serfs who still act like serfs, even when freed, who would wash my socks? Who would wash your appalling socks? I bet the slave revolt was over Spartacus having to wash a really nasty pair of socks." But M. Hippolyte did not rise to the bait. "Each day science discovers new ways of making our lives easier. Soon there will be no need to work. There might be no need for a state, fancy that? Everybody paid for doing nothing." Antov gave a cheeky little smile. "Everybody a member of the Imperial Family, eh?" They both laughed, but I knew that in our exile both of them were fascinated with pictures of new trains, flying machines and automobiles.

The Reverend Charles reluctantly left his beloved engine and looked up at the furnaces. They were like three houses of the kind built by peasants in the Mexican desert I had seen in a book in M. Hippolyte's library. They did not look in any way modern. They did not look in any way safe or even capable of holding molten chocolate. Instead of a normal door, in the front of the building was a yard-square hatch that was raised by a chain.

"Come, I will show you my dragons."

I followed the Reverend Charles up a ladder that was almost too hot to hold onto. Once on the metal stage I could discern the heat through the soles of my shoes. One of the men was about to open the door. The Reverend Charles handed me a pair of blue-tinted glasses. I put them on.

"Step nearer,' he said.

For a moment I did not move. It had occurred to me that these three men might easily make an end to me by throwing my body into the furnace like Samuel in the bible. I hesitated.

"Don't be frightened," said the Reverend Charles, and went to take my hand but I snatched it away and stepped nearer as the furnace door was pulled up. I possibly stepped too far as the heat hit me like a punch in the stomach. But it was much more than that. It was so hot it felt cold and I shivered. I closed my mouth as I felt all the teeth in my head as if I was eating ice cream or drinking iced water. The glasses let me look into the furnace at the magma of metal inside, lurking there like a sentient, living being. I understood why the Reverend Charles referred to the furnaces as dragons.

A man stepped past me and flung a shovel full of white stones into the furnace.

"She needs lime. So we put in limestone. In an hour or two we'll tap the metal. There are forty tons of steel in there. Forty tons of special steel for aircraft and car engines," said the Reverend Charles.

The worker who had been loading the furnace grinned at me, showing a mouth that had lost many teeth and tossed the shovel towards me and I stepped out of the way.

The Reverend Charles smiled and picked it up.

"I think Ernest here was wondering if you want to have a go?"

I blinked. I had never knowingly worked in my life and had not known anyone intimately that had. I certainly did not regard riding in the circus as actually working.

I picked up the shovel, the blade had been cut in half to make it easier to throw limestone chips or ore or sand through the door.

I filled it with the limestone and stepped nearer and felt the heat draw a radium picture through my body. I nearly dropped the shovel and my teeth felt raw to the nerves again. The limestone clattered around the door and none of it went in. Not one piece. The men just smiled and patted me on the shoulder.

"Work is often harder than it looks, young man," said the Reverend Charles. "We will be tapping the furnace soon and you can help us then. Do not take it as work exactly, more of an adventure. I can see you are new to labour."

The next day the Reverend Charles came and roused me. Close up, his features were sharp and his eyes determined and close together. In my dream Miss Emily had her hand on my thigh. The Reverend's mouth curled into a smile and his hand may have been on my leg for a time before his shaking brought me round. The elephant's trunk then separated us gently but with maternal firmness. The Reverend Charles folded his arms in front of him and said: "I was only trying to wake our little man . . . Damn. Wrong choice of words. We're tapping on number one. It's quite a sight. Why don't you come and help me, my boy? I did not mean any harm. I did not." He then rushed off and I glanced at the elephant who was pleased at his departure. I jumped into my overalls and did not see what the fuss was about.

The process of tapping was a mystery that happened around the back of the brick-built furnace building. Somewhat below the furnace and a chute leading from it was a giant ladle on a railway bogie, a platform on four iron wheels. Underneath the bogie in a long pit were moulds into which the molten metal was poured when the bogie was dragged along.

The Reverend Charles explained this to me in a hushed voice as if it was the secret of all secrets.

"It's a process not without fatal danger," he said, putting his arm around my shoulders and then, seeing that I did not approve, taking it away again. "If there was one single drop of water in the ladle there'd be a hell of a bang. If I was to throw in a treacle tin full of water there'd be a crater where this furnace once stood. We'd all be angels on clouds, dear boy. Or, when the clay bung that holds the steel inside the furnace is burned away, it can spurt out too quickly and those who have released the dragon's secret are vaporized!"

The Reverend Charles was quite breathless when he said this.

"I hope you won't be offended but I've drawn a poor pencil sketch of you and you must permit me to show it to you. I took a drawing-from-life course at the Ruskin while up in Oxford, to repent my aesthetic sins and to provide a corporal foil for my metaphysical studies. They used to send models up from London and then bus the girls out again in case they corrupted our undergraduate flesh. It so helps to look on naked flesh once in a while to get perspective when one has been contemplating Transubstantiation. We must snatch Beauty when we can, we who toil in the furnaces of Hell. Now, when I shout I want you to shovel, not throw, those bits of manganese ore down that chute into the ladle. Do not touch them as they are hot, heated in that small furnace there, and poisonous as an adder. Then we will see a real firework show!"

I went over to where he suggested and saw a pile of small, dark rocks. I still was not sure of participating in work, but I did very much want to see the fireworks. And I was not at all sure what he meant by telling me about his drawing hobby.

The Reverend Charles provided the fireworks sooner than I thought.

He and two men were at the other side of the metal chute that pointed down into the ladle. One of them lit the end of a metal tube connected to an oxygen gas hose and there were sparks and a fierce glow. There were even more sparks as the Reverend Charles applied the lance to a clay bung that I deduced held back the furnace's white hot steel. He lit the fiery lance a second time after it went out and there was a breaking sound and then a shout and they dived away and a river of white hot metal leapt from the furnace into the ladle and illuminated the whole dark space as if it were a cathedral. For a second everything was in microscopic detail in a way I had never seen before. I then felt a wave of heat and there was a shout from the Reverend Charles and I began to shovel my hot rocks, shaking as I did, and then, as he had promised, a fountain of stars and fire flies and phosphorescent snakes exploded into the air and up to the black roof, which were exactly like the fireworks I had seen at Selo after a ball for the Tsar's birthday. I nearly cried out with sheer wonder and then I slipped and it was all I could do to stop myself sliding down the chute into the ladle. The sparks cascaded down on me and burned in places through my overalls, but I was laughing with delight. A place that looked like Hell was transformed into Heaven.

After the "tapping" we had breakfast of bacon and eggs fried in a frying pan on the furnace door, bread and dripping and many mashing cans full of sweet, milky tea. I was introduced to the two other men who worked the furnace. At first I thought they must be from the lunatic asylum, the Reverend Charles had told me he had at times employed those unfortunate to be in such a place and on one occasion was working with three child murderers and a depressive. It was only the depressive's humming that was a problem, the others, he said, had worked very well. In fact, the men who I had tapped with were skilled and had come from a works in Sheffield. It was just their rangy gate and thick accent that made them sound odd. One of them was so used to working on the furnace stage he was able to do cartwheels in his clogs across it for a dare.

"We've to recruit where we can in these times. A group of boys from a borstal are coming by and by. I'm promised they'll work well or they will be disciplined. Most who experience this place do tend to like working here. It only looks like the infernal place. Actually, it's very nice."

If it looked like Hell in the factory at least it was safe and I quickly got into the routine of tapping and then helping pull on ropes that often caught pungently on fire to drag the little chariot on which the ladle rolled, filling each of the moulds. One had to be careful as a man in another works had stepped into a mould full of white-hot steel. It had spoiled the steel, laughed one of the men, and now the ingot was at the works' gate and men spat on it for luck.

The elephant had grown fully well now and enjoyed her work although she did not seem exactly to like the Reverend Charles. She pulled the heavy scrap waggons as if they were full of hay.

At night I joyed to hear her heart beat and the strange vibration that spoke of new and better worlds.

The Reverend Charles used to sketch me after the shift and took a long time rearranging my arms. One day he asked me to take my shirt off and was not able to stop touching my skin. I did not like that. But he would tell me of the beautiful things he had seen in Italy and that he was a disciple of Michelangelo and Bellini.

"I think beauty in the world is what foreshadows the life beyond death. Especially a beauty like yours,' he whispered one evening, and seemed so overcome he went away to where he slept and I did not see him again for a day.

It was, I think in July, that he put his hand on my shoulder and almost had his cheek against mine. I pulled back.

I stared at him.

Perhaps it was my lack of speech and expression that made me special to him, like the pictures in a museum. I was not as real as the men and boys who worked on his furnaces. I appeared on a mythical beast and every day he seemed more taken up with me. There was an engine inside him that I did not care to discover more about.

At night I thought of Miss Emily.

The Reverend Charles was shaking his head.

He was very upset and not with me.

"Please, my dear boy, please don't worry. I don't want you . . . to do anything. I just thought I'd tell you. I come bearing ill-tidings. Very bad news and I pray you do not slay this messenger. I thought I'd tell you as I flatter myself that we have become friends. It's none of my business, of course, who you are or why you are in this country. I think I should tell you though, that the Tsar Nicholas and all the Imperial Family, his wife and his daughters and son, Alexei, are all dead. Shot to death by the Bolsheviks who have announced it today in the newspapers. I'll not comment but leave you with the newspaper."

It is hard to explain the great void that I felt from the news.

A bell had begun to toll deep inside me and far, far below. It was as if everything had been lost, all light extinguished and the winter winds come forever. This may seem far-fetched in that I was told he was my father after he had sent me into exile, but I am not talking of the personal man. Every single Russian felt as I did, I wager. The Tsar was a religion about a state: not a state religion. It was as if the sky had turned yellow and the sea red, horses had started to bark like dogs and cats discuss Chekov.

Then, in a moment, I was angry with the stupid man who had lost the war with Japan. With Japan!

It was so cruel, so very cruel and ordinary and grubby and unthinking. The Imperial Family had been put up against a basement storeroom wall in the town of Ekaterinburg in Siberia, at what was called the House of Special Purpose, belonging to a merchant named Ipetiev. It happened at two in the morning and the Tsar, the Tsarina, the Tsaravitch Alexei, the four daughters, who I knew and played with as an infant, Olga, Tatiana, Marie and Anastasia, the maid, the doctor, the cook and the footman . . . They were all shot with Nagant revolvers by eleven men and not one of the family or servants made a sound. I thought of the revolver on the desk of the train guard.

I thought of the cries of The Tsar Must Die in my infant dreams.

The order was given to a commander, Jacob Yurovsky, by the Urals Soviet as the White Army guns were heard in the distance. The bodies were then burned and dissolved in acid. A tear ran down my cheek.

No wolf in the forest was ever as cruel.

I got up and walked out of the little cabin, next to that of the workmen, where the Reverend Charles did his drawing and went to the elephant.

She knew, without any WORDS, what I was feeling. It was too enormous like the dark, unfeeling river of my dreams. The paradoxical, inspiring force, where all ideas come from. I had seen The End in the Tsar's defeated face at that tiny railway station. They were all dead and I was ALIVE. I was the next in line.

The earth rolled under my feet.

I stared into the pale blue eyes of the elephant.

They were going to come for us now. It was hard to hide in WORDS anymore.

I was in a daze that grew until winter started to come back. I toiled and sweated in the furnaces and even let the Reverend Charles draw me again, though he did not touch me. He must have sensed a change in me after the news about the Tsar and the Imperial Family or the daily news that there was going to be an armistice or ceasefire. It was then that the boys from the borstal arrived and were being shown how to operate the Bright Bar Mill whose steel was, among other things, used to make the supports for crutches. One day I came down the ladder to find four youths about my own age catching the red-hot bars as they came out of one of the machines with a pair of tongs and then threading them through again. It was a process even the older men tried to avoid as one mistake could send the bar through an ankle.

"Hold up, 'ere comes t' Rev's mental bum boy."

"Tha' can do me if tha' wants, only don't tell."

At this they all laughed.

I began walking back towards the Metal Bank when the elephant, hearing the laughter, came out on her own. I held up my hands to send her back but then a piece of limestone thrown by one of the boys hit her on the head. I turned around.

"Shall we see how long it takes to burn a hole through to her insides?" said the bigger boy. "My brother is in t' Greys and he did it once wi' a German horse. Just to see. They heated this iron up and burnt it through to t' guts. Then they shot it. I'd like an elephant on me wall."

The boy was as tall as me but far broader with a wide face and black hair. He stood straight and confident, yet his mouth was twisted.

"So tha' going to stop me are tha', dumb boy? Mental boy?"

"Rev must love this one. He can't tell tales. After he takes it up t' bum"

Another said:

"He probably don't know about t' lockout."

"How folk who worked here was locked out one day so t'

217

works might be run on conscript labour,' said the biggest boy. "One man died o' pneumonia after walking home. Coughed his guts up. Another two are still poorly. But he can't hear that, being deaf as well as dumb. Me uncle worked here."

A skinny one with pimples on his cheeks then said: "And I bet yon Reverend did not say that his family owns this bloody works for all he claims to help t' poor. He's helping himself, that vicar. He probably helps himself to t' orphans too."

I stood where I was, not expressing emotion. I did not like what I heard but I was grateful to the Reverend Charles for shelter and warmth, whatever his other agendas. One of the boys threw another chunk of limestone at the elephant which missed.

The biggest boy then grabbed a piece of metal that had been heating in the brazier, probably to be beaten into a different shape. It was not always clear what the metal turned into. These might be a support for something. In the boy's hands it became a sword with a red-hot end. Taking up a fencing pose he touched me on the arm and I jumped as the metal burned my flesh. The smell of scorched overalls filled the air.

He came at me again and this time I dodged back and was round him.

"That's all tha's good for, running?"

One of the other boys pushed me from behind.

The boy touched me with the red-hot metal on the other arm and the elephant trumpeted but I held up my hands to her.

"Gi' him a rod and then us can kill him, no comebacks. We'll say he went mad and turned on us. We're only witnesses. Unless they ask t' elephant."

They all laughed again and one of them handed me a much

thinner piece of metal with a glowing end. The metal was hot in my hand.

The boy came at me, lunging for my stomach but I was able to parry the blow and send his bar in a high arc and it landed with a clatter by the door.

I held the bar up to my face, as I would have a sword in fencing lessons, and then away at an angle and smiled my brightest smile.

The boy ran for his bar in a fury. He came back whirling it around his head like a windmill.

I let him pass, dodged and burnt him on the backside. He screamed.

He repeated the process three times, not learning, and each time I made him scream louder.

"Tha's fuckin' dead!" he said.

This time I disarmed him. He toppled backwards onto the ground and I held the steel above his eyeball. I wanted to kill him.

"Don't! Stop him!"

I touched him on the side of the cheek and he howled. The howl echoed in the roof spaces. I then walked away, feeling ashamed almost immediately.

I went to the elephant and led her back into the Metal Bank. For a long time she turned her back on me, disapproving of what I had done and, most of all, that I had enjoyed it. Only when I was nearly falling asleep did she come and ruffle up my hair. The next morning, from one of the men tapping Furnace Three, I heard the borstal boys had escaped and had been picked up by a military unit on picket duty.

EIGHTEEN

NATASHA ARRIVED PROMPTLY, as always, for the wedding of Sergei's granddaughter on a freezing day in the Berkshires.

It had taken her three and a half hours to drive from New York in a rented car to near the town of Arrowhead, where she knew Herman Melville had written *Moby Dick*. She did not like weddings. The man in Paris had said he wanted to marry her more than anything in the world and she had believed him. Natasha had worshipped the ground he walked on. Yet there was a time early on in New York when he rang and said he had gone to a friend's gallery. He then phoned her and said he was going to be late and had forgotten to switch off his phone. He had a stupid little clip on his belt where he put it. Her phone was on loudspeaker. Natasha had just opened a magazine when she heard him speaking to another woman in French. Natasha's French was not perfect but as the man constantly hinted about showing her Paris she had got A's in every extra class going and was pretty fluent. The woman was talking about Natasha. The woman laughed about *l'américaine* and said something about Natasha's dress sense. There was more laughter, static and then nothing. When the man in Paris came back to the apartment Natasha asked who the woman was and he shrugged and said 'a friend'. He did not seem bothered. She did not persist and then they made love. That was a long time before going to Paris where it all went bad.

He did not rape her. The man in Paris. He did not rape her. Nor had she tried to kill him. She was sure. She was. Was that what he thought? Was that why he had not rung her?

It was more complicated, idiotic and human than that.

Today, she had borrowed an outfit from her friend who owned the apartment on 20th. It was a formal suit in a reddish-orange and she wore her hair up. In the mirror she had looked the unfriendly side of severe.

Most of all she did not want to look like a princess.

"Little one, you look so wonderful! You look just like a princess!" said Nadya, who met her in the drive of the small estate and hugged her and kissed her cheeks three times. There was a large but not ostentatious house built in the French neo-classical style, without columns but with sweeping stairs at both sides up to a double front door. It was a grand country house in miniature. Her car was parked for her and she looked at the forested grounds that led down to a lake, the other side of which was an ancient Greek temple. What surprised her more, to the point of being open-mouthed, was the matt-blue onion dome of an orthodox church that was peeping through the reds and greens of the oaks and maples. There were gold stars on the ultramarine blue.

Next, she was being kissed by Jelena.

"Little one! There is such drama. Drama! The nanny of the bride hates the boy so much she has thrown all the family silver into the lake and they are going to get divers to go down while we are in the service. Sergei's wife is in hysterics and a psychiatrist has been sent for along with the divers. They will share the same taxi."

Natasha then saw Sergei approach and let him kiss her three times like the others. It was a mistake. He was immediately angry with her.

"I've met people like you before and think you are digging the gold," said Sergei. Both he and his dog were staring hard at her. Natasha was caught off guard.

"The expression is gold-digger. I'm a librarian. I'm somewhat puzzled why you should think I'm interested in money," said Natasha.

Sergei laughed. His grey hair shook.

"Everyone is interested in money! Everyone interested in Romanov money! Before revolution Tsar's personal wealth, much outside Russia, is nine thousand million dollars. Now that is sixty billions. That is apart from real estate, diamonds and land stolen in Russia. Christ Jesus is interested in such money!"

He then stamped off through a path in the wood in the direction of the blue onion dome. Natasha swallowed. No one had ever called her a gold-digger. She took a deep breath and smoothed her hair.

Nadya came over and put her arm around Natasha's shoulders. She wished she had worn a coat.

"Little one. Do not worry. Sergei all his life is convinced that he is the Tsar. His mother tell him so. All he is Tsar of is a very successful kitchen worktop company. He is a nice man really. You will see. Come, let us go to the service."

Jelena and others huddled close around her and nodded. A priest arrived and blessed her. A little girl was holding an icon of Tsar Nicholas.

The church inside was cold and thick with incense and the altar covered in precious icons. "Sergei built this himself, you know, with his own hands. It is a copy of a chapel on his grandmother's family estate."

Natasha lost herself in the chanting and the singing. The bride and groom were very young and impossibly beautiful.

Several men had brought their whippets into church and were holding them just like Sergei. Every inch of the church that had been bare stone was now covered in white flowers.

All the people in the church but her seemed to belong. It was a place to dwell from Pushkin. Natasha had had the feeling that she did not really know who she was anymore since Paris. She tried to rationalize it as the usual identity crisis when a person tries to go out into the world and fails. Natasha identified so very strongly with the driven, precocious boy in the story. A friend had called her borderline Asperger's when it came to her work obsessions, not content with anything short of a hundred per cent and Harvard. Another had said she was borderline personality disorder, which meant dangerous crazy, after a rival was spiked on the home straight in a four hundred metres final and as the winner, Natasha got the blame.

A few days before, Nadya had sent her what purported to be Natasha's family tree, linking her to the boy. It seemed ridiculous. Her grandparents were English. Yet of her great-grandfather there were no photographs at all. She looked closer at the wonderful hand-drawn tree in different coloured inks and gold leaf. She was a bud at the end of one line, the Princess Natasha Alexandrova. She was descended from several generations of buds only indicated with a gold crown. She could not stop shaking her head. A princess! She clapped her hands. That was what princesses do!

She smiled. Any uncertainty, especially as to her own identity, left her troubled. But then, belonging or not belonging scared everyone to the point of panic these days where society, family, religion, art, true love, all that was stable or at least manageable once, was becoming the blank of Mr Melville's great white whale, the white screen of death on the all-consuming computers, the great digital cut off. Facebook access denied.

A princess? The man in Paris had called her that.

Deep down she wished she had Antov and M. Hippolyte to help her. Antov reminded her of a Red Setter she knew as a child.

Without warning she began to weep. She never wept. Everyone around her seemed to approve. Many of the older women were weeping too. Once she had wanted a wedding like this, before Paris. The service droned on in prayer after prayer, opaque ritual after opaque ritual. Towards the end the priest got up into a pulpit and addressed the congregation.

"It makes me proud to be an American, to see such a gathering for this lovely wedding . . ." This came as a surprise as nearly everyone invited, except herself, was pointedly Russian.

The mood which had been tense in the church, lightened immediately the Wedding March was played and everyone emerged into the sunshine. Natasha felt the warmth on her forehead. She walked back to the house with a feeling of expectation. That was one of the things wrong with weddings: apart from being about romance and religion and death and property rights, they built up an ache of expectation in the guests. Who will I meet at the wedding feast? It was the same with the story. It was impossible for these people to see the boy, the little prince, as he really was. There are always disappointments when expectations have been built.

There was a small lawn at the back of the house and a marquee where the old men paraded with their whippets and their decorations, some obviously of their great-grandfathers. Just inside the house was an orangery and a small library with a day bed for reading, full of imported antique furniture, all in exquisite taste. When Natasha looked around at the guests there was none of the coarseness usually associated with the newer Russian community.

Natasha helped herself to a glass of champagne, even though she was not going to take a second sip, when Sergei was in front of her again.

"Excuse me for my words before. But it is tense time for me. Did you enjoy the service?"

She nodded.

"I didn't understand all of it, but very much."

He smiled a wistful smile.

"Come with me. I show you something precious."

He led her into the library and went to a corner and unlocked a gleaming rosewood desk. He took out a box and set it upon a table. He motioned for Natasha to open it. She did and inside was sheet after sheet of blue paper with the occasional white sheet in between and more at the end.

"This is the original? All the manuscript?" she asked, and Sergei nodded

"We want to know all about the Prince and the elephant. That is what we must know. We want you to have access to these original papers if it is useful and see what you think. They will be in New York. We will send the rest in photocopies. Go to where he went in England. Go to Russia even. We want truth. The truth, I should say. Please excuse me for my bad manners earlier, princess. It is your field to go through the information and see what you think. Please come to another meeting when it is done at Jelena's summer house on Long Island. We want to know what you think. If it is a true story or fiction. How we came by the story I am not allowed to say. You are the boy's descendent, we are sure. Now, I have to get back to my guests."

"Before you go. Did you send me the emails of typed manuscript?"

He shook his head.

"No, I was not involved in that. Or those stupid elephant noises."

He left her, startled, with one fresh photocopied packet of the story in her hands, tied up with thin pink ribbon like a lawyer's evidence in a trial. She then examined the original. The paper smelled old. Of chocolate, like the boy's books. She put it back into the box with some reverence. It was thrilling to touch the actual paper the story was written on after all these years. She had no doubt, this wasn't a fake. There was something real and true here. Natasha was going to find out just how much. She closed the box and went outside.

Natasha next walked round the back of the house to find an orchestra playing and it seemed that everyone had begun to eat and drink more quickly. By the lake she saw that the young couple were still having pictures taken. Then she noticed a rotund woman with a stick run up to the bridegroom and start to beat him. Sergei and others, possibly with the psychiatrist, were hurrying over to stop her. Whippets were barking. The group of divers looked on.

Obviously, the handsome, rich, well-connected young man did not live up to the nanny's expectations. He was not a prince in her eyes. Natasha laughed. She wanted to get back in touch with the boy in the book.

Even though she was very tired after the drive back to New York through rain, she read the beginning of the next packet. That night she dreamed she was married to a gingerbread Tzar whom the people ate, and her father played guitar, a Neil Young song about a gambler, on a sun-baked jetty where the tar ran and there was the smell of salt water and diesel. On the horizon everything was burning. Her father had looked up at her and smiled: "No one ever dies,' he said.

NINETEEN

THE UNEXPECTED MANUSCRIPT: PACKET X

I SAT ON the warm neck of the elephant, heading away from the Rev. Charles' works, in the fog-hung light of a November dawn, my head level with the upstairs windows of the terraced houses, and I saw a man in his combinations, washing at a bowl, and in another the naked back of a young woman brushing her long hair on a wooden stool. There was no one on the streets and I had to get to farmers' fields and a quarry on the edge of town before this place of heavy industry woke. I had a cough.

The Reverend Charles, our benefactor, expected that the military was coming to seize the elephant even though the war was said to be all but over, and had told us to prepare to leave in a hurry. There was a fuel shortage and a need for heavy horses to pull large loads. But he did not expect what happened.

Before dawn, as one of the furnaces was being made ready to tap, four policemen with a senior detective burst in through the main doors of the factory and went straight to the Reverend Charles. He was in his little office and I, being part of the team ready to tap the furnace, was round the corner. I heard them "charge" him.

"Charles Hunt, you are hereby charged with gross

indecency and illegal sexual acts with young and innocent persons below the age of consent and of the same sex and committing buggery. You may be charged with other matters in the future. Anything you say will be taken down in evidence and used against you in a court of law. Have you anything to say?"

The Reverend Charles then laughed.

"All I have sought to do is help young people. Who are you going to charge with the war? Or is the war an act of decency?"

I held the word DECENCY in my mind. But it was not good. I had to face what was happening.

The constables set on him and gave him a kicking before dragging him out to a waiting horse-drawn cart. That was the same as in Russia.

I went straight to the elephant, changed from my wooden furnace clogs to my boots and got my few things together.

The elephant was standing up and waiting for me. She had already sensed the danger that lay behind DECENCY.

My only thought was to try to get to the great house, the Wentworth Woodhouse estate where the veterinarian worked. The unfortunate Reverend had talked of my hiding in a barn there only the day before. He had been going to tell me more of a plan.

When I turned to lead the elephant out, one of the furnace men, Ernest, was standing in my way.

But his face creased into a smile.

"Don't tha' bloody worry. I'm not going to dob you in. This is good news for us. The Fitzwilliams who own mines will like as not tek this forge over and we'll get proper workers again. Not that I'm saying you and that great lady haven't done a fair job. But you'd best leave now before t' military come and take that elephant away for war work or whatever. Mark my words. Get shut of this town. There's been a riot between Russian royalists and Bolshies right in t' town centre. They've put 'em all in jail. But listen, sithee, a tall woman came and gave me a pound note. A pound note yesterday, and tells me to tell you today to make for quarry on t' road out of here at back. She had scary eyes. Look sharp, I can tell you what road to take. Don't worry too much about the Reverend Charles. He's been steering too close to t' wind for a long time. And there's been an explosion at Thorpe Hesley pit, so no bobbies about. Shame though, I'm sure t' borstal boys lied but there's no smoke wi'out fire, I say. And I've got no money to pay you with, t' wife took quid, so here are a few cheese sandwiches wife made."

The last house had passed behind us as I ate the crust of the final sandwich, having fed three to the elephant.

I had not wanted to be paid for my work and had got exactly what I wished for.

But astride the elephant on that foggy morning we had escaped.

We were FREE again.

The fog hung in the hollows and in places was lower than the elephant while a splendid sun came out above and warmed us.

I turned around and saw the town stretching away with furnace after furnace, factory after factory to the next-door city, the smokestacks and pipes burning off flares of surplus gas protruding above the fog, much more numerous than the occasional church steeple. It was sad that the people there were only defined in terms of what they made, their faces beaten into ploughshares and frying pans, and that was a prison and a crime.

Then rising out of the mist I saw a sandstone quarry ahead and tightened my grip with my legs and we stopped. We turned towards it down a lane.

There was something tomb-like about the dark, dripping ledges of rock that hung from above that scared me to the pit of my stomach. In the distance a bell was ringing, an alarm bell, and I saw and smelt a motor ambulance with a red cross pass us on the main road.

I hesitated and got down.

Still I did not approach the quarry.

There was the sound of another ambulance bell approaching. I walked the elephant forward and felt she, too, was reluctant. The bottom of the quarry was a well of fog out of which stepped a tall figure I was familiar with.

It was the woman with very blue eyes that I had met in the forest with the gypsies and circus people. Like many in the circus, she did not have a name.

"So, it's good that you are still alive," she said in Russian. "How very clever of you in the circumstances to travel with a large African elephant."

There was a half-smile at the corner of the woman's mouth. It was a cold morning but she only wore a thin cardigan over her blue dress, which, as she moved, revealed the large pistol she carried in her belt. The woman was looking at me in a strange way and it seemed at any moment as if she were going to reach for the pistol.

Where we stood in the quarry, among the swirls of mist, there was no one to see and perhaps no one to hear, with the occasional sound of the bells ringing and ringing on the ambulances.

I was not sure whose side exactly the woman was on, but if she tried to kill me the elephant would not take kindly to that.

I sensed a mixture of fear and distrust in the elephant. The bullets in the revolver might hurt her, might even cause her to pause as one would for a wasp sting, but they would not penetrate far into her thick hide and she would trample the woman into the mists and the floor of the quarry, however quick she was.

A third ambulance passed on the road, the bell ringing out. The woman's hand moved from the revolver. The sound of the bell died away in the fog.

"The bells of Hell go ting-a-ling-a-ling for you if not for me," she said, wistfully in English, and then smiled.

She switched back into Russian.

"The jails in town are full of White and Red supporters looking for you, little prince, and the cowboy ringmaster has put his white hat on again and is on your trail. It is said that children have been going to have a peep at the elephant. I need not tell you that with the deaths in Russia your position is even more dangerous, some might say hopeless. You're now the only heir. That places a great weight on your young shoulders and what I say to you now is good advice. It is time to abandon this elephant here and either let her go back to the factory to help with needed munitions work, or to the circus with the American, who may have changed his mind about killing her because she is such an attraction. Being of noble birth, you will take a decision that puts the continuation of the Imperial Family before sentiment."

I stared at the woman and she saw from my face and the way the elephant began to swing her trunk that this was not a possibility.

The woman sighed. She then spoke in English.

"Well, I had to fucking try. Now, listen to me very

carefully. There may be a way out of all this, but you must follow what I say to the letter, is that clear?"

Again, I stared back at the woman without expression.

"You'll follow this path out of town until you come to a small lake, a dam, the other side of a village. The village will all be at the pit disaster. You go past the lake into an estate deer park and then turn to your right. In front of you on a hill you will see a mausoleum of complete neo-classical ugliness. Past this is another even stranger building, Hoober Stand, also a mausoleum or folly. No one lives there. It is shaped like the things workmen make their tea in here. Dudleys, I think they call them. There is a barn by this structure where you will find food for the elephant and for yourself and you're to spend the night there. The next evening, as it gets dark, you are to go to the great house, which you should see straight in front of you to the west. You'll see the lights. You'll be expected and taken into the house where you will meet the man in authority who will say a word to you. You know the word. When you are given that word then you will immediately say who you are with all of your titles. If you cannot remember them all I have written them down on a paper with your food. Only speak to the man who says the word to you, no other. I'm sure you understand. The word written on the little silver elephant around your neck."

A fourth ambulance passed.

"God speed," the woman said.

I had turned in the direction of the sound.

When I looked back the tall woman with blue eyes had vanished into the mist. She had spoken of the word on the silver elephant and there were a million questions in my head.

There was the sound of another ambulance far away on the road and I wondered how many men had died and that made me realise how much danger the elephant and I were in. She was looking into the grimy, pearlescent distance too.

She raised her front right leg and I climbed back onto her neck. I turned her around and after a few nervous minutes on the main road we branched off into the lane that the woman had suggested.

Then the full fear caught me that the Russian government were not now hunting Tsar Nicholas any more, they were hunting me and I started to tremble so much the elephant stopped and reached up with her trunk and messed with my hair and stroked my hand. I was breathing faster and faster, and coughing, so that I could not take a proper breath and she realised this and arranged her trunk in such a way as I was able to climb down and walk around. I was so completely annoyed with myself, for although I was beginning to look like a man, I was behaving like a child and to cap it all, I burst into floods of tears, for the Tsar, for my mother country, for everything and all the time the elephant stood by and comforted me, rubbing my back with her trunk.

She waited for me to get hold of myself again.

We were in a lane next to a cornfield and I tried to focus on the simple things around me to stop my thoughts. I wiped my hand on my overalls that had picked up black, greasy dirt from the fog and then I noticed something strange about the cornfield. It was November but the field had not been harvested and, when I approached, I saw the ears of corn were still there but mired in black from the chimneys down the valley. I thought the smell of burning and melting steel would go when I got outside the town but there was the reek of burning everywhere, as if the world were catching fire. I coughed again. There was an absence of the beauty of nature I had taken for granted. There was no bird song. Even in the snowy forest when I was crossing my country there was always the song of the birds.

I touched a bush and more soot came off on my hands.

And there was the smell of sulphur behind the soot and several of the chimneys in the valley were spewing yellow trails into the sky.

The thought of the untouched steppe I could never go back to brought further tears and complications. It was like a parlour game, like the charades that were played by the ladies-in-waiting in the Imperial Nursery to amuse the children. I was told to say I was the Tsaravitch but I plainly was not that. Was I now the next in line to the Russian throne or merely a lowly decoy, an illegitimate and mad child that no one wanted?

Who was I?

The elephant's gentle trunk on my shoulder only made things worse.

She was the only MOTHER I had now.

I fell on my knees and hugged her.

Then the sound of marching feet to the south of us snapped me out of my indulgent grief.

I got back on the elephant and saw a company of soldiers appear and then disappear into the fog. It was not a small party and there were about a hundred of them, I estimated. They had their rifles on their shoulders and were seven abreast and keeping exact time. They were not the straggling conscripts we had seen before, they were professionals. "Left, right, left, right, left . . ." shouted their sergeant.

The fog then became thick between us and I only heard the purposeful sound of marching feet. If I was right, they were going in the direction of the great house, the Woodhouse, the one with three hundred and sixty-five rooms that Queen Victoria found too large.

The elephant and I continued along the lane.

We came to the village that, as the woman had said, was empty, the cobbles shiny with the mist, the houses at some points no more than grey slate roofs in the fog.

In no time at all we were heading out towards the lake.

It was only by luck that I was able to see the troops that had passed us had set up a roadblock into the Wentworth estate where the small lake was. We stood very still as twenty men argued about where to put a sign. We then took another lane to a farmer's gate and, opening it, were able to skirt the lake on the other side and come upon a path as the woman had described. First there was the domed mausoleum. Then ahead of us, sticking out of the fog, was a black building that indeed looked exactly like one of the mashing cans the workmen used. I hurried the elephant on.

When we got to the building there was a barn beside it, again as the woman promised.

There was the silence of the fog all around.

A pheasant then flew shrieking up and I jumped and so did the elephant and we saw a group of deer, a stag and several hinds in the entrance to the barn, eating a sack of potatoes that had been left for the elephant.

They sped off into the mist.

I was glad to see the deer and above me, fluttering higher and higher with its song, a lone skylark ascended into the grey sky.

Inside the park there was the music of birds.

The building, another mausoleum or folly, had sloping sides made of sandstone and ended in a little turret and on top a small dome.

I left the elephant munching on the potatoes and went through iron gates to stand looking straight up at the tower. The door, to my surprise, was open and I walked inside, expecting to find tombs and ancestral sarcophagi, but there was nothing except a spiral staircase that led to the roof and I climbed up, through another small door, and looked out over the parapet, well above the grey blanket of fog.

There was a breath of wind and in the distance the fog cleared for a second and I glimpsed, it was only a glimpse, the biggest house I had ever seen. There were stone columns and staircases and even a castle wall of a much earlier age at one end. It was far bigger than Selo and larger even than the Winter Palace.

I swallowed. That was where I had to take the elephant.

I walked down the metal stairs again and had a thought about the absence of tombs. Perhaps the family was new to the place. Perhaps no one had died yet. Or perhaps they had built a mausoleum because this is what they thought incredibly old families did, proving they were not so old.

I went back to the elephant and in the night we heard the sound of the ambulance bells again many times.

To soothe me, the elephant made that strange, singing sound that allowed me to see the world anew, calmly and in such a different way. I knew I was taking a risk for both of us if I did what the woman in the blue dress had told me to do, but I saw no other way out. The only safety for me, or for the elephant, was to declare myself, say what I had been told to say, hope they would believe me, and with that thought I fell peacefully asleep in the crook of the elephant's trunk.

The next morning I opened my eyes and stood. I was in the barn by the Hoober Stand folly and there was a basket of fragrant apples and potatoes and nothing left of the tinned meat sandwiches. There were hay bales but no elephant.

The elephant was gone. I began to cough and panic.

Pulling on my coat I ran out of the door in my bare feet.

There was fog all around, choking and yellow from the factory smoke in the valley.

Then below me I saw her.

She was rubbing herself against a tall horse-chestnut tree, making the branches shake. It was a large spreading tree but the branches moved as they might have in a high wind, and she was scattering on herself autumn's un-fallen nuts and bits of twig. I laughed, but there were tears in my eyes. I took hold of her ear and led her back into the barn. She was the most important part of my life now. She was my good and positive passion. For me she embodied innocence and grace and what was decent and right in a world thoroughly broken and left a WASTELAND. She was the gentle spirit that turned away from war. I loved her and in turn that made it possible to love myself and the world and to turn back the river of dark fire. But she was more than that in a curious way I did not fully understand. She was everything. I stroked her rough, indented grey skin and kissed her on the trunk.

⁂

When the light was safely starting to go I climbed the tower again and turned the brass handle of the door at the top. The fog was still there, but on the lawn in front of the house there were burning torches that one minute I saw and then not.

I thought I saw men on this vast lawn, but it must have been a trick of the fog because they quickly disappeared again.

The house itself was lit.

It looked like Selo viewed from the lake but many, many times bigger and there was a sparkle inside from great chandeliers. The lights went on and on and the front of the house was at least half a mile long. It was exactly like one of those immense new ocean liners that I had seen in the newspapers, floating above the grime and poison of the fog.

It was time to go.

I went down the spiral staircase and stood in front of the elephant for a moment and prayed, even though I knew it didn't work, to Christ and the Saints and the Holy Virgin that we would succeed and heaven would receive us if they shot us. I stressed I hoped that human decency and civility was going to be shown to us. I felt the calming vibrations through the elephant's trunk.

She winked a blue eye. I hoped she was praying to her gods too.

"What do you do when you are frightened, so frightened you cannot move, cannot talk?" I asked Antov one day, who tried to claim at first no such thing had happened to him. M. Hippolyte looked up from his book and said, "However much you are frightened, however much you let yourself experience fear, that focus can only have a bad result on the outcome. If I am going to shoot Antov here and am so terrified of him my hand is shaking like a reed then I will miss and he will kill me, possibly steal my precious books and say awful untruths about me to ruin my reputation. Once you have decided on a course of action, do it quickly. Quick as mustard!"

I mounted the elephant and taking careful note of the direction of the house went down through the fog. Here and there deer ran from us and in one place a fox until we were on the flat again and walking towards the mansion.

In my breast pocket I had the note that had been left for me, giving me final instructions. There was an empty feeling in my stomach, but I was resolved.

We walked forward towards the creamy light.

Then out of the fog at either side emerged other figures, who were also going towards the house. At first I wondered if they were guests or the military, but I soon saw they were miners and ordinary people from the town.

"It is . . . It bloody is. It's a bloody great hefalump. Come on, lads. We're going to win wi' an elephant on us side. We are going to win like bloody Hannibal."

"It's a bit pink."

"Tha's been drinking."

"Well done for bringing her, lad. Hang on tight. It might get well nasty. We've come to burn house down."

There were men too with miners' lamps and helmets and I began to realise that the demonstration of what had seemed hundreds was of thousands of men and very serious. There were red flags and elaborate banners.

The crowd of miners was so great it was not possible to get any further and they formed a ring around us and did nothing that might upset the elephant, even though they were all very curious. If they had come to burn the house down it was strange as many of the miners were in their Sunday best with waistcoats and collars and ties, topped off with flat caps. The faces of young men were deeply lined and old, like sliced grey putty by the torchlight, as were those of the boys who worked in the pits. One, who plucked up courage to stand alone right before the elephant, still had coal dust on his face as he had come straight from underground. He had no cap on his head and it took all his courage not to run as the elephant reached out and ruffled his dust-caked hair. He then laughed and smiled such a smile as might light up the deepest hole in Hell and everyone around us laughed and from that moment we could do no wrong.

"He don't talk, that one riding. He worked at Parkgate wi' elephant. He's alright."

Those around us said a fence had been erected ahead and for the moment we were not going to get any further but numbers were growing all the time. The boy was called Albert and he worked down one of the Fitzwilliam pits. He was in charge of a pit pony called Lily that dragged the coal carts underground. The ponies only came up out of the blackness for two weeks a year.

"But when they do you should see her. You should see our Lily dance and kick her heels. They can find their way down t' pit when all lights go out. Lily saved me life when there were a roof fall. Pulled me back. Lad next to us got squished with half o' Yorkshire on top of him. She's lucky, she is. That's why I wanted to meet your hefalump. They say she's lucky too."

All around me men and boys were coming forward and touching the elephant and moving quickly away.

"They like her," said the boy. "They think she'll take any bad away. Tha' believes in luck down pit. I lost me brother to an explosion like they had yesterday. It's not meant bad them touching t' elephant for luck. It's like they'd touch a saint or a wishing well."

One man stroked the elephant's trunk.

"I bet your mam don't let you keep this one in a cage in t' bedroom."

A woman by him passed me a bag of sweets and a group of men began to sing a music hall song. There was a carnival atmosphere at times but there was no doubting the purpose underneath and the anger. It was said that sixty men had been killed in the explosion and the men and women had come to the great house for justice. There were suddenly more miners from a pit called Danby, under different ownership, who had all been sacked and were dressed in rags and charity clothes. These men had stares that went over the horizon and into tomorrow.

More joined all the time. There were thousands.

"There'll be no justice 'til we tek that house and all like it down brick by brick. There's blood on their coal money. Fitzbilly may be a good owner but he is an owner. We own t' land. It's ours."

Another man emerged from the crowd. He was tall and better dressed and wore a bowler hat. He was from the union, the boy said. He stood on a box and spoke. "If we stay together fuck all can stop us. We are like this elephant. We can go through anything. Three cheers for t' elephant!"

They cheered us three times and the elephant seemed very pleased.

The union man then continued:

". . . They've known that coal dust in the air can explode in a moment. All you need's a light and a bit of gas but it's not just a normal explosion. Gobfires tha' calls them. It's like being on the Somme and one of those mines being put under your trench. Whole bloody pit goes up. They've known about this and now there's another sixty got killed. Got bloody killed. Blown to fuck and buried. And what do they do? What do their Lordships do? They have a bloody ball. We must tear t' place down. Tear it down, stone be stone. It's built with us blood. Burn t' bloody thing. Blow it to kingdom come."

Another voice spoke up nearby.

"It's said troops have been brought up because t' Prime

Minister and Royalty is there. T'King. There's a meeting going on."

"Well, we got an elephant. It's on us side," a man laughed. "It's not pink, it's as Red as we are. It's on us side, lads."

Before we knew much more we were at the head of a party of miners and steelworkers ready to push towards the lawn with their red banners. I wondered if the troops were there and if they would shoot and what I might do if they did. To my right I heard a preacher.

"'Yeah, though I walk in t' valley of t' shadow of death, I fear no evil, thy rod and thy staff they comfort me . . . Thou has preparest a table before me in t' presence of mine enemies . . . My cup runneth over . . .' We are marching with t' Lord, brethren! We will call on Him for justice in this matter. We will let His still small voice thunder in t' presence of those who' d murder for mere gold trinkets and t' false trappings of this world . . ."

Around me I heard cries of Amen. This was different from my country. I must admit I never really did understand completely the strange relationship the British worker has with its aristocracy and those with a great deal of money, which are almost never the same thing. There is also a middle class, or there is said to be a middle class, that people with fake modesty or foolish bragging claim to be a member of, but no one I met ever fell comfortably into this category.

Those next to me were all workers and very nice and I was offered and took a sausage sandwich and a drink of strange, thick beer. Before long I was clapping my hands to their chanting for safety, freedom and better wages, which as the true Tsar, was a strange position to find myself in.

They were not at all like our serfs with their superstitions, glorious idleness if left unattended and endless fatalism. I thought of the little serf who helped me but then drank the vodka and died, willingly, joyfully drank the vodka to release himself. I had once made Antov fall off his chair by asking, "Why do we have serfs? I know they are meant to be free but shouldn't we free them more?" I had been doing the French revolution with M. Hippolyte, a period which he seemed to relish, especially in his present exile. Antov, not citing his smelly socks this time, had argued that morally reprehensible as slavery was in the modern world, Russia would fall apart without "freed" serfs to make up for the idiocy of the aristocrats running the country and the estates. The serfs had become accustomed to privation and the knout, the rawhide whip with metal hooks, and were the true saints of the state, rescuing the public peace when their masters squandered, drank or gambled away their earnings. In a way they were Russia. M. Hippolyte had laughed at him. "Please make sure to explain this to them, when they come for us, my friend. I'm sure they'll listen to your moving sophistication and justification of their plight. Before they roast you on a slow grass fire, that is."

The fence that was ahead was broken down and we surged forward. We had now reached the fringes of the lawn and the men continued to march, they were coming from all directions, there was no move whatsoever to stop them. "We did this once before," someone was saying. "Company bobbies, t' mine police, came for us day after and smashed ganger's leg so he couldn't work again."

"We'll smash them tonight. All bloody lot," said another.

The first line of torches, which were ornamental not defensive, had been reached when all of the miners stopped.

It was not by any command.

I then detected the strange, almost inaudible singing

sound, more a bending of the air and time, coming from the elephant. Those nearest turned towards her smiling. She lifted her trunk. The small sound grew louder.

We stood then for perhaps half an hour in silence as indoors an orchestra began to play and the ball was underway. In time, a footman came out, followed by another.

"He who is in charge will approach the house."

"No one's in charge. We're fucking communists," shouted a wit, and many laughed. The mood had lightened. Everyone seemed to be looking at the elephant.

The second footman then whispered in the ear of the first.

"Don't worry, lad, there's still time to leg it," shouted a miner.

The first footman cleared his throat again.

"The party inside bids that the elephant approach."

There was a cry of "no", but the elephant seemed to understand the matter and almost trotted forward over the damp lawn, sinking in slightly as she went. A contradictory cheer then went up behind us and doors directly in front of the house and beneath the staircase were thrown open and a bright white light shone out onto the foggy evening.

The entrance was six yards high and suddenly I was in a ball of light and surrounded by ladies in gowns on staircases with men in full evening dress. It was one of those rooms that a mounted hunt could go into to receive their morning drink before setting out and when coming back with their hounds. I glanced up as we walked forward. We were before the main staircase of the house itself where there was a group of men, including one with a red sash who was smoking a large cigar and who appeared very like Tsar Nicholas, so much so I hardly believed what I was seeing. On his right was a tall military man and on his left a smiling diminutive individual who, from his constantly trying to reassure the ladies around him, I took to be a politician.

"Who is this?" said the man with the red sash. "Who is this that comes to my ball mounted on an elephant?"

The military man peered down at me.

"Be careful, sir, he could well be concealing a Mills bomb or a revolver."

"But not an elephant," said the man with the cigar, and everyone laughed, absolutely everyone and did not seem to want to stop. He laughed too. He was obviously not used to making jokes.

"Pray silence for the King,' shouted another footman.

No one was in any hurry to be quiet.

I stared up at the unsure, timorous face with whiskers and a beard and was convinced I was looking at the man who hailed me as a son, Tsar Nicholas, the man I had left in the railway station waiting room. I could hardly catch my breath. There was the same straightening of the back and attempt at authority. I thought I could see the panic in his eyes, as when he took me to the zoo waiting for more bad news about Japan.

The shabby, disappointing King wore a dinner jacket that made him look like one of the waiters. He was not at all the best-dressed waiter in the room. The suit was somewhat old and, on the red sash that announced his rank, there was a stain. He wore a red cummerbund and had a gardenia in the buttonhole of his dinner jacket.

I knew it was a gardenia because Antov had showed me a picture of one and had said they had a magical scent when it came to seducing women. M. Hippolyte had scoffed that unless a woman seduces herself one could put the gardens of Versailles on one's head and have no chance. Just behind the King was a younger man. He seemed to be trying to advise the King who kept wafting him away like a fly. The younger man was in military uniform with a great deal of medals I bet he had not earned.

Even without military uniform the King so completely resembled Tsar Nicholas that I wondered if this was an elaborate trick that had made me journey many thousands of miles, a further punishment for what I had written at the Christmas Ball in St Petersburg. What I had dreamed about his future.

"Now, my boy, do not be frightened. Do not be frightened at all, either of those in here or the men outside. I want you to tell me your name. Please tell me your name?"

I stared at him and remained silent.

I was not frightened of him. No one was.

The elephant shifted under me from side to side.

"You are commanded to tell the King your name. You are in the presence of the King of England. Tell him your name, why don't you?" said the politician, who had a strange whining accent. He had dark hair that fell across his forehead. No Tsar, not even Nicholas, would allow an interruption like that.

There was a rustling of dresses and shifting of feet around me but still I said nothing. The orchestra had stopped and people had left the dance floor to crane their heads over the balconies.

Outside on the cold lawns there had been singing of worker's songs and hymns but now there was silence too.

It was as if everyone had stopped. As if the clocks in the ballroom were stopped. Like the grandfather clock in the main cabin behind the Potemkin House. The whole world had come to a halt save a poor waiter who dropped a tray of glasses and the clashing silver tray on marble made a noise like cymbals that went all the way up to the painted, moulded ceiling. Then there was breath-holding silence again. The chandeliers

247

sparkled and the sequins on the gowns glittered as everyone was captivated with the creature below them and me astride her neck. The elephant remained calm and hardly moved. She seemed quite at home at the ball.

There was no fear or alarm, apart from the tall military man, only a frantic interest. A few voices began to chatter away and I heard some say it was a stunt dreamed up by the mine workers' union, others that it had been arranged by a man they called Fitzbilly, or King Billy, who owned the house, and pretended to like the miners.

I was staring at the man who they called the King, if that is what he was, when a note was passed to the politician who whispered in the King's ear. The King seemed confused. The politician handed him the note and the King squinted at it and put on a pair of glasses. The politician nodded. The King then spoke, his voice shaky:

"I'm told there is a magic word that will loosen your lips."

Everyone on the staircases clapped when he said this. It appeared to be part of a game.

"I am told that magic word is *Fumoo*, in a pagan language long lost, much like your Welsh, David. I say again to you, *Fumoo*. What does it mean, David? What does such a name mean? I love parlour games though. I say again to you, lad, *Fumoo*."

Still, I remained silent. I wanted to speak but it was as if I had lost the mechanics of having a voice.

"Please tell us your name," added the King.

I took a deep breath. I had memorised exactly what M. Hippolyte had told me to say, in English, plus additions of my own.

There was quiet again and then I spoke. I drew myself up, straight-backed on the elephant. I did not want to fumble my

248

words like the man they called the King. My voice rang out loud and clear.

"My name is Alexei Nicolaivitch, previously Tsaravitch, now following recent events we are Tsar of all the Russias . . . By the Grace of God, we are Alexei, Emperor and Autocrat of All the Russias, of Moscow, Kiev, Vladimir, Novgorod; Tsar of Kazan, Tsar of Astrakhan, Tsar of Poland, Tsar of Siberia, Tsar of Tauric Chersonesus, Lord of Pskov, and Grand Prince of Smolensk, Lithuania, Volhynia, Podolia, and Finland; Prince of Estonia, Livonia, Courland and Semigalia, Samogitia, Bielostok, Karelia, Tver, Yugor, Perm, Vyatka, Bogar and others; Sovereign and Grand Prince of Nizhni Novgorod, Chernigov, Ryazan, Polotsk, Rostov, Jaroslavl, Beloozero, Udoria, Obdoria, Kondia, Vitebsk, Mstislav, and Ruler of all the Severian country; Sovereign and Lord of Iveria, Kartalinia, the Kabardian lands and Armenian province; hereditary Sovereign and Possessor of the Circassian and Mountain Princes and of others; Sovereign of Turkestan, Heir of Norway, Duke of Schleswig-Holstein, Stormarn, Dithmarschen, and Oldenburg. We are head of the Orthodox church of all the Russias, holder of the orders of St Anna and St Vladimir. I am the Count of Hesse and Lower Saxony and a cousin of your esteemed Royal House. I am the true commander of the Imperial armies and the Imperial fleet. Our father and his wife and son and daughters have been murdered on the orders of the Ural's Soviet and we come seeking your love, understanding and your gentle protection." I paused.

There was complete silence. No one was smiling now.

"And this is my good friend, the elephant!"

What immediately followed was that complete, internal, painful absence of sound that follows an artillery barrage.

There was a ringing in my ears and intense shock for perhaps a whole minute in which everyone looked at each other and thought this was part of an elaborate joke, but the reaction from the Royal Party was enough to tell everyone it was not.

TSAR was the word filling my head. It was not a word I could hide in. I was not a Tsar. I prayed my performance would protect the elephant.

I repeated what I had just said in French and was going to do so again in Russian when the King held up his hand, dumbfounded and astonished. Advisors were whispering in his ears but eventually he said: "Welcome, er, Alexei . . . The ball will continue. See that this splendid elephant is watered and fed and send that young man . . . His . . . Imperial Highness . . . to me immediately he's refreshed and dressed. I came here for vital talks and the next thing I know there's an elephant. An elephant, by God. I don't know what the Queen will make of all this. I really don't. She'll say I've been drinking."

And that was it, for the moment. It was a relief to be a sideshow, a circus act again.

With that he turned and was gone, shepherded by his advisors, leaving the party still on the balcony arguing, and the orchestra struck up again, a waltz, while a hushed order went around the staircases and the corridors that no one was to leave until further notice, for their own safety, because of the demonstrations outside. I was sure that was not the real reason. I was also not certain how my announcement had been received. The ladies and gentlemen started to move up and down the staircases in their fine clothes, gazing at the elephant, who was no longer making the hypnotic sound. I did not know what the ball marked, but it was a very important occasion and just like in the Selo palace, the men were very handsome and the women beautiful and then I saw a face I recognised, a raising of the brow into a half-smile, a prominent nose and deceptively dreamy eyes and red, curly hair. I blinked. The lady was in an immaculate white dress with a diamond tiara on her head and a diamond clasp at her throat. What was she doing here? I was fearful. She put a long finger to her rouged lips and then was gone into the crowd and I was staring at a group of military men who stared distrustfully back.

A small party of solemn retainers carried a ladder to the side of the elephant, but I shook my head.

"If you can help us take the elephant to the stables, sir, we would be most grateful," said one of the footmen, who was obviously not yet convinced of my pedigree. "It's a very large establishment and she'll be most comfortable."

Ahead of me, massive doors were opened and there was applause when I did not get down but rode the elephant through a dark passage into a courtyard. The cold struck me in the face and if they did not believe me and intended to shoot me this was an opportunity. But a party of footmen followed and a crowd of grooms had the doors of the stables' hay barn open and ready.

There was a huge space inside, warm and fringed by rows and rows of fine-looking horses. The servants fussed with the wooden ladder again, but the elephant held up her leg and I was able to scramble down to the floor. I looked up into her face and hugged her trunk and kissed her, which produced a series of gasps from the footmen.

"I'm going to have to leave you here, but only for a while. I have to arrange for us to be safe. I have to do that," I said, out loud, but the elephant already knew and she made one of her grunting noises, but then came the long, low vibration that I felt to my toe bones. And then the sound was gone.

I turned to the man who appeared to be the most senior groom.

"Please can you lay straw down for her and she likes potatoes and apples? And if you have it, give her a pineapple as a treat. Do not restrain her. You may find it fatal. If she is anxious in any way at all, I am to be roused, day or night. Do not stand on ceremony. Please come to the house and straight to me. What's your name?"

The man looked at me amazed but very interested.

"Patrick."

"Well, Patrick, if you can do this for me I will be forever in your debt. We both will. Please come to me if there is the slightest problem."

But I stood there for a long time. It was not possible for me to leave her just like that, I lingered. She was my real home. My Sion. My Jerusalem. We had been part of each other's lives for so many months now and I loved her more than I loved my own life. I wouldn't have got to this strange place without her but, after being with her, after hearing the poetry of her song, I cared more for her individual safety than any narrow nationalism or the absurd idea that I was now Tsar of all the Russias.

In the end the groom, Patrick, said: "Do not worry, sir, for a moment. We have elephants in here all the time, sure we do, and quite often hunt with them and play polo with them out on the lawn. She'll be safe with us and I'll send someone to get a pineapple for you to feed her when you look in next."

So I patted the elephant on the trunk and went back into the great house where the orchestra was playing a quickstep. I was missing her already.

I did not go back towards the ballroom but up another staircase, every bit as grand, hung with fine paintings and lit by chandeliers. There was thick carpet underfoot and I was very aware of my contrast to my surroundings in my simple blue overalls, but every time I stopped so did the party of servants and footmen and maids following me. Eventually, we got to my rooms, decorated in panels of Chinese silk with strange birds, dragons and flowers. There was a large bedroom, with a four-poster bed, that looked out onto the lawn, where I saw the miners still gathered in the shifting, brownish fog. They stood like a ghostly army.

There was a sitting room and a dressing room, all decorated in white and gold, and a room with a huge enamel bath where the water had been run. A maid, a small, dark, joyful and pretty wisp, dashed out of the bathroom and that was when I saw her for the first time, her eyes wide in a panic, but when she saw me, her large, rouged mouth arced into a nervous smile. Her skin was shining and luminous, like in a Leonardo painting, her hair dark brown, as were her eyes. And there was a loveliness about her manner as well as her perfect, if, when startled, slightly sad gaze. I guessed she had seen horrors. I felt for her and sensed she did for me and I knew she was going to be my friend. More than friends. I immediately yearned for her. She reminded me of someone. It was as if I knew her very soul already.

"Anna, you're meant to have been out of here by now," scolded the head footman and she vanished, but I ached at her departure and wanted to see her again.

The other footmen bowed and departed too, leaving me with a tall and angular man who wore evening dress.

"My name is Ibbotson, Your Highness. I am to be your butler and dresser while you are here. This is the Bedlam Suite for bachelors like yourself. First, I must introduce you to one of the foibles of the house. Here is our little silver casket containing confetti, sir. It is made with large, dried violet flowers for this room. Different rooms have different colours and flowers. The house is so big, sir, that if you go out and about on your own you must scatter some as you go so you can find your way back. We throw this stuff at weddings, in this country, we do. Many of our guests think it a charming custom, but they still get lost. We had the Kaiser here once before the dust up with Germany. He was always getting lost, which just goes to show. Listen to me talking nine to the dozen when your bath water is getting cold. Do excuse the fact that I am not like other gentlemen's gentlemen. I talk. I chatter. I offer an opinion, a joke or even a racing tip. People like it, or they don't. But the world is changing, as I'm sure you know better than most."

In the corner of the room there was a desk with a pen and sheets of blue writing paper. My life had become so full that I intended at the first occasion to set it on paper before I went to bed each night. And I wanted my story to be known if the very worst was to happen.

I started to undress.

His eyebrows were raised a little when he saw the Cossack dagger that Antov had given me.

"I very much like your manner," I said.

Ibbotson looked pleased.

"It's on account of my being in Vaudeville, sir. But I then went to the wars and got my foot shot up, which is not good for a song and dance man. Then I had to go down the pit to make ends meet and blow me I bring the house down on my

254

bad foot. So I am out of work yet again and was offered a job back here at Wentworth Woodhouse, where I started as firelighter, aged twelve. I don't talk like I'm from round here because of the touring. I even played the London Hippodrome as a comedian. We need more comedians. Where did you get those scars, sir? You've been in the wars too, if you don't mind me saying."

I was not fully listening to him as I got into the blissfully warm water, I had only had cold baths under a hose at the factory. I was thinking of the maid called Anna and how her short, dark hair curled across her cheek in the new fashion. She was so completely pretty. There was something about her of a girl, Sophia, I played with in the Imperial Nursery, whose hair came to the sides of her angel face from a central parting. We played waltzing together, taught by the ladies-in-waiting who laughed at how serious we were, how I held the little girl's hand high. We had cuddled in her bed in winter! I loved her. I had expected to see her again but I never, ever, did. I do not mean I did not like other girls like Masha and the other serf girls, and in particular seeing Miss Emily in the bath, especially when she stood up. But this was different. What passed between us was silent and far beyond anything to do with our bodies. And now my thoughts were full of Anna.

I had not expected such a delightful complication when I came into this great house.

"Now we will have to get you dressed very quickly, after a shave and a trim of the hair," said Ibbotson. "You will notice two thick, grey woollen-tweed jackets with crested silver buttons on your bed, sir? These are Spencers, made special for Wentworth. The house can still get painful cold and some guests wear them under their apparel. I expect you are used to the cold though, being from Russia. There's still a bear keeper on the staff but not a bear. Will you be requiring a uniform, sir? I do not know if we have Russian ones, but we do have white jackets . . ."

I stopped him.

"Why do I want a uniform? I have just escaped a war? Do you like uniforms, Ibbotson?"

He was silent for a moment.

"It's not of course my place to say, but no, sir. A hair shirt with fancy buttons, if you ask me. Soldiering is uncomfortable enough without uniforms. I'll see if we have a nice dinner suit. I'm sure we can find one. The finest tailoring, sir. We would in normal circumstances have one made up, but the King requires you very quickly. And, if I may be so bold, I wouldn't take that dagger with you. It'll spoil the hang of the suit."

I was then shaved and my hair cut by the Woodhouse barber before Ibbotson brought in a suit with another footman who had been a tailor and it fitted perfectly across the shoulders although was very loose at the waist.

"We'll have to feed you up, sir. I'll send down for the senior maid to serve you with a little biting on, food that is, before you go to the King. He may want to talk to you for a long time, I don't know. I'll send for the senior maid."

I stared hard at him.

"I would be very pleased indeed to have the new maid serve me. The one who was in here? The one called Anna? Please can you have her serve me, Ibbotson? I'd very much welcome that."

I then went over to a bundle of clothes and my kerchief that lay by my overalls and the dagger at the end of the bed. I reached for one of the gold pieces I had taken from Mr Masterson's safe. They were in a small leather pouch on my belt with other precious things like a carved wooden flower from a gypsy girl. The silver elephant was always around my neck.

"Please, Ibbotson, accept this as a gift for our future friendship and in no way a payment. My father, the late Tsar, made many mistakes, in particular not making friends, and you have already made me feel I have achieved some sanctuary. However, there are those who would do me harm and I will want to know if any shadows are looming my way. I am sure you know what I mean."

I in no way meant the money as a bribe as it would have been in Russia. But Ibbotson looked dumfounded.

"It's not necessary, sir."

"It will please me."

He took the gold coin and looked at it closely.

Then, spontaneously, he went into a music hall song and dance act: "Oh, your baby has gone down the plughole, your baby has gone down the plug. The poor little thing was so skinny and thin he should have been washed in a jug, in a jug . . ."

When I stopped laughing, he said: "I'll take my payment for the song, sir, if that is all the same with you, and thank you very much. My cousin is one of those outside who'll not work for a while. I'm sure they appreciated your elephant. I thought it was going to go bad for a moment. Better the money is for my song and dance. That sits better with me. Now, I'll go and gee-up Anna. She's a pretty little thing all of fourteen or it may be thirteen. She's a refuge seeker too, sir. A Hebrew, I am told. She has no one. Enough. I chatter. I talk. I exit. On my way I goes, sir!"

Anna came in ten minutes later with a trolley laden with all sorts of wonderful food. It was the menu from the ball and read like a fantasy to one grown accustomed to simple fare. *Caviar Frais, Consommé Froid Madrilène, Saumon Truite et Mayonaise, Fillet de Boef Poéle, Poularde aux Perles Noires du Périgord, Timbale d' Homard Royale, Neige au Cliquot, Cailles aux Raisins* . . . I must have eaten but I do not remember a morsel. Everything was about Anna. I kept looking at her exquisite mouth. I wanted to kiss those lips. And the dimple on her right cheek. She laid out the gold-bordered plates in front of me and served me a selection of *hors d'oevres*. She could not seem to look at me this time and then I caught sight of myself in one of the mirrors. In my black suit and starched collar I was every inch the gentleman. They had given me a light blue sash and cummerbund, to denote my origin, I suppose. On a table were various orders which I held available for me to wear. I ignored them.

"Do you think my clothes are better now than when I came in, or do you not think clothes matter?"

She kept looking down at the floor.

"You'll get me into trouble and you too," she said abruptly.

"Where have you come from?"

She didn't answer.

"You may sit down. Please sit down by me at this table."

She shook her head and looked even prettier.

"I can't. I can't."

"Why?"

She looked as if she were not trying to offend me and angry with me at the same time.

"I know who you say you are. I know what happens to those like me in your country. I know what happens to girls here. This is not Russia. Now I am here and in service and there are rules . . . I did not mean that . . . You have an elephant . . ." she said, faltering. "That is impossible."

258

I smiled at her.

"She will vouch for me. She will vouch that I am not a monster."

"Even with a dagger like that one?"

"That was given to me."

"You should throw it away. Into a sewer."

She seemed about to run from the room. Her eyes were wide with fear but fierce.

"Would you like to come and see my elephant with me?" I said. "She's a most wonderful creature. She is an African elephant and they say they are untameable. Are you untameable, Anna? What is it you want to become? I love your name and all about you. I will write poems for you. They will always fail to express the wonder you are. But I'll carpet your way with them. I will carpet the world with them."

Her eyes widened more as I said this and I stood up and I think I might even have kissed her then, so overcome was I by those brown eyes and her ethereal sadness that my family had probably been instrumental in causing, if Ibbotson and two footmen had not come in and said: "His Majesty requires your presence immediately, sir."

TWENTY

NATASHA WAS IN New York comparing sections of the handwritten manuscript when the home in Sacramento where her mother was called and said there was nothing to worry about, but she should maybe fly and see her mom soon. There was a careful, resigned note in the voice of the usually bubbly and optimistic black female manager of the home that Natasha was suspicious of, but further questions had yielded nothing. "I think she needs your visit soon, my love," was the manager's non-accusatory parting shot. She had said there was nothing obviously medically wrong but that her mother was talking a lot and even shouting and doing little dances and then talking about scientific things they did not understand and that did not make sense. The phone call had come just as Natasha had also re-read part of the boy's story about how the elephant had been treated and how she was going to be executed. It was not like Natasha, but she had burst into tears and could not stop crying. She must have showed it in her voice when talking to the manager of the home. How the elephant was to be killed FOR PLEASURE had not hit her so hard before. It was all so unfair.

She had immediately booked the next flight.

Natasha had a row of seats to herself and took out her phone to make sure she had had no more messages and noticed she had an email from ChiChi. She had wondered after her last email if the woman had given up on her. She did not want anyone knowing what had happened when she pushed away that straight blade razor in a Paris hotel room. The man in Paris had called it a cut-throat razor. The razor had a handle made from mother-of-pearl.

From ChiChiChica Froment@fas.harvard.edu
To NatashaA@gmail.com

Generation P? P for Passion? I'd say Generation A is more about anger. But it is always hidden. How was the new meeting with the Russians? Are they like the old Russians in the story? I love the way the boy announces himself as the ultimate Russian geography lesson. Cool. I want to be in his story with the elephant. Are you sure you did not write this? You are a good writer and should not have given it up. You will start again. You don't want all that energy coming out in other ways. Except with me. When am I going to see you, Natasha? Don't you think at times that the boy and his elephant are becoming a fucking obsession? That said it is MUY COOL. I want to be in this story with the elephant. If only life was so simple as saving a fucking elephant who is trying to save the universe. She should only save women. Serve no man, Natasha. That's what ChiChiChica says. But tell me, are you in trouble? I got a call from the NYPD the other day and then from a policeman in France. They wanted to talk to you. They wouldn't tell me what it is about. Call me, Natasha. I need the full story.x

Natasha put her phone away and did not reply and tried to sleep but tended to breathe too deep if she had a mask on, like now. The plane landed at Sacramento International and she took her time getting her things together and descending the steps from the aircraft. The Sacramento airport trademark of a Jack Rabbit always amused her. It was a slow town and she much preferred it when her family lived near the coast. The airport, like the plane, was more or less empty and she took a cab immediately to the home. She could have taken buses, but she had to know what the problem really was.

When she pushed her way through the heavy glass doors of the home, the managed smell of urine hit her, even through her mask. It was not that the place was not a good one, a very good one, thanks to what her father had left and his military Medicare package (his later work was for the government), which included his wife, but did not quite include everything that she needed to the same extent, which was why Natasha had to work. Or that was what she told herself. The manager took Natasha straight to her office.

"Your mother's dementia has developed in a surprising way. Several doctors have been to see her and recommended a brain scan because we were worried and which you won't have to pay extra for. You mother has early onset dementia but she also has an inoperable brain tumour . . . I am so sorry to tell you this, but she does not have long to live. Perhaps weeks. But it may be days. She does not know any of this and I would not tell her, or try to tell her. She thinks your father is coming to play her a song he has written about their visit to the Sierras and she is very excited about the scientific problem he is working on, about cats being dead and alive at the same time and protons disappearing in perfect vacuums and then reappearing again. I do not understand a single word."

Natasha nodded but did not attempt to explain. She should cry at this, not the elephant.

When she went to her mother's room she expected to find her in bed, but she was standing in the middle of the room and had one of her "character" skirts on from her ballet days. She had a lovely open face and dreamy eyes.

"Is your dad parking the car? He's not so good at that, is he? I hope you two have not had an argument again."

Her mother whirled around the room. She was so light on her feet. Natasha had never felt that light, even when running in the Nationals.

After a while she asked: "What have you been telling the nurses, Mom? About Dad's work?" Her mother stopped dancing.

"He's told me what he is working on and how the government is out to get him. He says he knows how to make the same energy appear at exactly the same time in two different places. It's to do with Schrödinger's Cat that was both alive and dead at the same time. They want to make a weapon. To do with natural disasters. They are either going to give him a medal or kill him, or both."

Natasha's mother danced around the room again and Natasha began to cry.

Her mother and her father had been in love all their lives and some stupid line of a math equation that he had not realised the significance of, had driven him mad and killed him.

"Don't cry, my darling. You never cry. Shall we send out for some ice cream? I'd like that. What's that book you have got under your arm? You've always got a book."

The next day her mother, Cecilia, had what the manager called an "earthquake" of a stroke and was sedated in bed.

Natasha read the next packet of the boy's story that she had brought with her in a chair in the corner of the bright room as she waited for the end. She had always objected to the absurd brightness of California in dark times.

TWENTY-ONE

THE UNEXPECTED MANUSCRIPT: PACKET XI

I WAS TAKEN to a dark, wood-panelled room with a roaring fire by which the King stood with a cigar and a glass of brandy in his hand. At one end of the room there was a portrait of a beautiful brown horse. There were three other people in the room, looking out of the window into the fog. One was the military man in his uniform, the other the politician and the third a handsome younger man with a fine moustache and an amused twinkle in his eyes, who I had not seen before. I planned to grow a moustache one day.

"I'll not order the army in against those who have served in the trenches and many out there have," said the military man. "I know the papers are crying for blood and a firm hand, the fucking *Daily Mail* as usual, but I'll have none of it. There are five thousand out there, outside our window, and that's about what the Yorks and Lancs lost in Normandy."

It was very moving to see the man I had thought a typical soldier before now on the verge of tears.

The three at the window saw me and before any further introduction, the King turned to me, nodding slightly and rolling the cigar around his wet lips. "What do you advise?"

They were all looking at me and I felt I had to answer.

"This is not my country and I only know a little of this

dispute, but I have had contact with the workers hereabouts and know they are good-hearted men. Agree to their demands on safety. I think the general is right. If you try to put down this peaceful demonstration by force it will grow into something much worse. I do know that with a heavy heart from my own country. It seems a problem of safety, not public safety. Do not make it political. I was in that crowd and that is what a tiny number of them want. If you meet them with an army there is a danger you will turn them into an army and there are far more of them potentially and you will lose."

The handsome younger man came over and shook my hand hard.

"Well said, Your Highness."

"Those are fine words, sir," said the military man.

"You put it so eloquently," said the politician.

The King beamed all over his face.

"A very good answer indeed and we will see it is done, we will see it is done presently. Only one thing gives me a little unease. It's too damn clever for one of my family!" The Tsar, I remember, said more or less the same thing.

He looked at me sternly and the smile had turned to a frown.

The others were staring at me.

But then the King laughed and came and patted me on the back and everyone else laughed too.

"Only having a bit of fun," said the King. It was not at all what I was used to from the Tsar. "This man here's General Haig, head of our armed forces, this is David Lloyd-George the prime minister and your host, here, is Earl Fitzwilliam but we call him Billy."

They came to me and shook hands. The King, who sat

down, then continued. I saw there was an oxygen bottle tucked away next to him.

"We don't go in for any of this bowing and scraping here, things are far too fucking serious. Sit down. I like you my boy, though naturally I have questions. Now, if these gentlemen will allow me, I want to hear your entire story in private. We can bring them in later, when we'll discuss the matter with the security services. In the meantime, Billy, why don't you try to meet these pit leaders and see what their demands are about these gobfires? I thought they were going to turn nasty, my boy. The servants say your elephant saved us, you know. Some sort of song. Do elephants sing? We'll discuss the miners tomorrow too. We don't want to find ourselves murdered in our beds. This was meant to be a ball to celebrate the beginning of the end of the fucking war, not the start of another revolution. The old Queen would never forgive me if I were assassinated. She'd call it carelessness. Do excuse our British humour, young man. No disrespect to your father who I liked and loved like a brother. Now, all the rest, be off with you and leave me with my latest problem."

They laughed and left and when they had gone he said: "Take no notice of my manner. I want you to go back to the very beginning and tell me the complete truth. I do not want to be told what you have been told to say. Or if you have I want to know that too. Believe it or not, we have already learned of one plot to murder you since you arrived, my boy." He saw me looking at the oxygen cylinder. "They forgot to tell a horse I was king. It rolled on me. *Nil desperandum*. Death is the Almighty's way of telling us to stop worrying."

He flicked his cigar ash into the fire and coughed occasionally, as I sat at the other side of the fireplace. He was trying to effect the air of a loved and favourite relative. It worked better than it would have with his cousin, my father, the Tsar. I coughed and he looked at me in a worried way.

"Will you promise me one thing, your Majesty?"

"Please call me Uncle George. I'd like that. Even if I find later it ain't true."

I smiled.

He was staring at the little silver elephant around my neck.

"May I see that?"

I handed it to him.

"This says *Fumoo* too?"

I nodded and showed him how the poem came out.

"How ingenious."

"I think it belonged to the poet Pushkin."

"Who obviously used it to pass messages to young ladies," he said, beaming. He handed me back the elephant and I sat down.

"Will you promise me one thing, sir? That whatever happens you will save the elephant? She is very dear to me. She is also very important. She calmed the mob last night. She has a gift."

He looked at me without expression at first but then nodded his balding head again.

"I will."

They had obviously already discussed what to do with us.

I then took a deep breath and told him my story right from the beginning, leaving nothing significant out. He was my only hope and I sensed that he would know if I was lying. People must lie to him all the time. I did not even leave out how the vibrations the elephant made had changed my way of looking at things. I started with my early life in the Imperial Nursery and he laughed when I told him of the ball at Selo and what I had dreamt and written about the Tsar and his death. I told him of M. Hippolyte and Antov and all of my journey, of the librarians in the frozen lake . . . The only thing I did not mention was meeting Anna but that in itself made me want to have this amiable, out-of-his-depth middle-aged man on my side. I also omitted who had told me to say what and when. I had come to realise on my journey that the absolute truth is a very rare animal, constantly facing extinction even in those who would be good. In the end the King was silent for a long time. I was conscious of the ticking of a clock again as I stopped talking, a big grandfather clock at the side of the fireplace that struck midnight. I coughed. I had been talking for three hours non-stop and it was a new experience, the words had flooded out of me and he had held up his hand when at times I wandered off into Russian though not when I used the occasional French phrase. All of the time we were not attended by footmen or maids and he lit and smoked half of several cigars and replenished his own brandy glass while I drank only iced water.

He then looked at me with a very serious expression deepening the lines on his face and I expected the worst.

"Well, dear boy, I believe you and you have come through such a lot with flying colours. The trouble is having you here does put me in a pickle. There are things here that are very different. I am the head of state but I have very little power. The lowliest worker outside down in the fog has more power than me. The only time I have power is when people think I haven't and then everyone conspires in the law courts to surprise me. But it is all on behalf of a mythic, unwritten constitution, never real. I am like the charlatans in the music halls who do magic tricks. When all of the audience agrees there is a mass illusion. Good thing I like magic tricks, eh?"

He threw the end of his cigar into the fire and took a sip

of his cognac. I had a drink of my water, which Ibbotson had told me came from the high moors because everything in the vicinity tasted of the coal that made the fortune that built the house.

The clock chimed and for many more minutes afterwards we both sat there, staring into the coal fire until, quite suddenly, a large piece of coal shifted.

"I do not know if I want to be the Tsar," I said.

He smiled broadly.

"I still don't know if I want to be King. Fun, isn't it? Now, I've to go down to this eternal ball. They always seem to mark another cycle of slaughter, these balls. Haven't you noticed? Of course you have. I have put you on a table and we'll talk tomorrow."

He then reached for his oxygen cylinder and a nurse appeared from behind a screen and I saw a secretary had been taking notes. The King then noticed me looking at the portrait of the horse.

"That is the famous Whistlejacket racehorse painted by Stubbs. Legend has it that the horse accidently saw the picture and tried to destroy it, thinking it was another stallion. Or perhaps he thought the other identical horse threatened his own reality. We must all be careful of destroying ourselves like that, or even our image, mustn't we?"

My table at the ball was near the King's and a waiter brought me a glass of champagne, which I tasted and the bubbles went up my nose, but which I did not drink. I wanted to keep my wits about me, but they were already bewitched and seduced by the ball under the huge crystal chandeliers. The King was greeting a number of men in uniform and others with orders around their necks I took to be allies and diplomats for the great game of the coming peace. I wondered if in my dinner suit I was invisible, but that was not the case. A number of couples came to my table and bowed and offered their condolences for my father. One man had to be led away weeping. Then a bright-faced girl came over and said: "I don't suppose you really know anyone here, so would you care to dance, Your Highness? I've been put up to this, but would you dance all the same?" I hesitated but the orchestra was playing a waltz I knew well and I had been taught to dance in the Imperial Nursery, then by Antov with M. Hippolyte playing the piano, next with serf and peasant girls and finally with the often tubby daughters of the local aristocracy. This girl was not tubby and I nodded and we stepped out onto the floor. She was wearing a white ball gown with her hair up in a bun and ringlets and she had a mischievous smile. I thought of that time when I was very young on the floor of the ballroom at the palace of Selo with the ladies' dresses buffeting me in the face like so many waves at sea. Now I was dancing myself with one of those ladies and from a shaky start my confidence grew and the girl laughed as I whirled her around and around. I felt like when I was on a horse and I was galloping full tilt across the steppe towards the red line of a dawn. It was beyond happiness. I was shaking with delight.

We both became aware that we were attracting attention and when the music stopped there was applause.

"Perhaps you will permit me the next dance?' said a familiar voice behind me, and the first girl curtsied and then moved off, disappointed.

I turned around and looked into the face of the woman I knew as Miss Emily from the circus of Mr Masterson.

"I am the Marchioness of Headfort, Your Imperial Highness. Do, please, call me Rosie. Do excuse the temerity of my introducing myself but I want no accidents later when we meet with the King. Now, let us dance. There may be also something about to happen that will amuse you. A little cabaret."

She was a completely expert dancer and again I felt myself carried away on the music. I looked down at her beautiful face that was smiling up into mine and thought of the time I had seen her naked and she had stood up in the bath in Mr Masterson's quarters. She gripped my hand a little tighter.

"This house is . . . ?"

"Is mine? Up to a point. Golly, it's so nice to talk, to be able to talk with you. You kept your vow of silence, which is why I trust you. I'm not the Countess. That's Maudie over there with that nice young guards officer. I'm Billy's friend. No, that's not quite the truth. I can see from your expression that you are growing up. I'm his companion, his mistress. There's a lot of that goes on here. That's what all the rooms are for, I suppose. Do you like the house? Or do you think it vulgar?"

"But . . . The circus and Mr Masterson?"

She drew very close.

"Perhaps it's best not to ask too much too soon. This place is a circus too with its share of lions and tigers. Billy is the biggest beast. He's the richest man in the world, the newspapers say. Much more a king than a king. Everyone is a little frightened of Billy who's much richer since the war. He went and fought early on but was terribly shell shocked and does not talk as much now. He was a nicer man before he went. He's like a man possessed at times. You're a very good dancer, you know. It's splendid to hear you speak. People do not actually speak to each other enough. The history of the British Empire is mostly one of ambiguous silences."

At this, she whirled me around and the music quickened. Her hair hung down in little ringlets and the diamonds sparkled under the light. Yet, even here, there was a hardness about her, her hands, her body, her eyes when I looked closely, and I thought of the softness of Anna and felt I was betraying her. It was only for a moment, because then the Marchioness whispered close in my ear in a way that both tickled and made me feel giddy and weak.

"Do you really own all those strange places? I did like your entrance on the elephant."

I nodded. "Well, I think others lay claim to them now."

"Goodness, how sad," she said, and I blushed as I realised I was being teased. She laughed.

"I am sure there is a way of getting them back. I am sure Billy can fix it if anyone can. Don't pay any attention to the King. He's useless."

It was then there was a commotion by the King's table and we both looked across and saw a man on crutches in a white cowboy hat. It was Mr Masterson. He was being restrained and so were two sour-faced men he brought with him.

The Marchioness stopped dancing and led me nearer.

Mr Masterson was shouting above the music.

"I heard that an elephant that's part of my circus show and one that's being tracked by me has been brought here to this very house. The animal is my property, Your Regal Highness, and all I ask is that you hand the creature over to me. I have the bill of sale and these Pinkerton men with me have taken witnessed affidavits. That she elephant is a very dangerous animal when roused. She tore her devoted keeper in two pieces and more. I have been shot and put in the hospital when it was thought that I was protecting a child who turns out to be a spy or a Russian nobleman. He is certainly the criminal who stole the creature. The elephant is quite clearly my property and here, in my hand, is the bill of sale."

The orchestra had stopped and there was the sound of hissing and booing.

The King looked at Mr Masterson, disbelieving and slightly afraid. The space between the King's mouth and chin quivered.

"Do unhand this man," he said to the footmen. "It seems we've heard something of your circus. But bills of sale can be forged. If the animal is yours perhaps we had better take you to her and see if she comes to you and greets you like the benefactor you claim to be. We are sure she'll come and welcome you."

There was a hush of expectation around the room.

Mr Masterson stopped and drew a deep breath.

"Well, Your Highness, I don't think that's a good idea . . ."

The King nodded and grinned and puffed on his cigar.

There was more hissing and boos and laughter from the audience directed at Mr Masterson after this judgement of Solomon and he turned and saw the Marchioness and myself: "There she is, my little Miss Emily! Miss Emily the trapeze artist from my circus! Emily, please come to me, honey pie. I've missed you so and our afternoons together."

Even the King looked surprised at this point.

"That's my good friend, Rosemary, the Marchioness of Headfort," said Earl Fitzwilliam, coldly. "Your words have ceased to be amusing, sir."

It was instantly obvious who was really in charge. Who everyone was scared of. A few of the couples backed away.

Without any more ado, half-a-dozen footmen restrained Mr Masterson again.

". . . I still have the swing, honey-pie! Our flower-decked, love swing!"

There was nervous laughter at this. Mr Masterson's face was red and anguished.

"I still have all the motion pictures I took of you. You can be a big star. That's the future, my dove. I don't know what you are doing here with all these stuffed shirts. You can be a big star if I can just get the money. Don't trust that boy. He's a Russian spy. He's one of those Reds. I don't believe for one moment he's of the aristocracy, taking my money like that. Gold pieces given to me by Pancho Villa himself. You come away with me to California, to a little place called Hollywood, and I'll make you a big star. I promise, my little kitten honey pie."

Everyone was laughing now and several thought Mr Masterson was part of the entertainment.

At this point, there was the sound of a heavy blow from a footman's truncheon and no more was heard from Mr Masterson, who was dragged off for a "little sleep" without Miss Emily.

"Goodness, how sad," said Rosie, with a wink. "What a silly man. That's how unpredictable this world can be, I suppose." I looked into her determined eyes and said absolutely nothing about the gold pieces and then we danced again and again, observed in a suspicious way by the shabby King.

The Marchioness, because in every inch that is what she now was, kissed me warmly on the cheek and finally went off to dance with her husband who had been entertaining a "second cousin" and the ball was still not drawing to a close. "We'll see each other tomorrow," Rosie whispered and was gone and I watched her laughing as she waltzed. Billy Fitzwilliam, the man who owned the house, looked on and after the dance she went over to his table. He was tall and so very handsome and there was always a half-smile on his face that never really changed and complimented the twinkle in his eye and impression of boundless, charming, effortless energy. He was immaculately dressed and held himself very straight. Yet, if you looked closely, in the instant when he turned away from the person he was talking to and before he greeted the next, his grey-blue eyes were steady and chilling, like a cat. There was perhaps also a yearning for a dream he could not quite create out of all the grime and smoke. He was the focus of the room. The servants around him did his bidding without being asked and those at his table who were meant to be his friends had a worried expression. I had no doubt he was as clever and ambitious as he was cold, but there were the remnants of an innocence there too that made men like him even more dangerous. No one seemed to mind Rosie going to him except me, who felt a slight pang, not of jealousy exactly, but of regret at having to give up such a beautiful companion. I then asked a footman to show me the way down to the stables and went to see the elephant, who I felt I had neglected.

A door was opened and she got up immediately out of the clean straw and shook herself. There was a light on and a stable boy in attendance, sitting on a stool, reading an illustrated book. The barn was warm from a big stove and the elephant came forward, towering over me.

She was so pleased to see me she did her little dance.

"I'll be in the stable office, Your Highness," said the boy. "She is a magnificent creature and has been no trouble." He then left with his book through a side door by the stove, which he left open.

The elephant went back slowly and carefully to her straw

bed and lay down and I lay on her chest, in my fine, new dinner suit, listening to her heartbeat, and then to the wonderful, singing vibration that turned all the intrigue of what had just passed with Rosie and the King and Mr Masterson into moonbeams and primroses. Perhaps it had even averted revolution and the burning down of the house with the King inside. All such things were absurd and did not matter. I saw the world again as it should be.

"It was very bright and cheerful up there, but I would rather be down here with you," I said.

The elephant pushed me with her trunk and I was conscious of another presence.

"Do you really mean that? That you would rather be with the elephant than all the money upstairs?"

I turned to see Anna. She had come through the door by the stove and was still in her black and white maid's uniform. At the other side of the barn through an arch there were two lines of wrought iron horse stalls.

"The elephant can tell you. Can you hear that low sound? Can you feel that sound? Inside you?"

Anna looked puzzled and so vulnerable standing there.

"Come closer, she'll not hurt you. I promise she will not hurt you. Put your hand on her chest. Please . . ."

Anna was wearing a grey cape over her uniform. I marvelled at her long eyelashes.

"I'm not meant to be here."

"Nor am I."

We both laughed.

"If you are not meant to be here then why are you? In the middle of the night?" I said.

She came closer to the elephant. She still was not sure.

"I wanted to see your elephant. That's my trouble, I always

276

want to see the elephant. I always want much more than has been given me."

There was a silence.

"Then come and see her. Feel her heartbeat. I know she likes you. I can feel she likes you."

She came a little closer, put out her hand and then backed away again, angry with herself.

"The other servants said she killed a man. She killed a man and the circus man has come to take her for dog meat but the King won't let him. They've put the circus man in a cell in the ice house at the other end of the stable block and he's going to be sent back to America on a boat for the police there to deal with. The cook says the American should be put in the electric chair for being bad mannered to the King. She said the American wanted to do that to the elephant for killing the man."

I held out my hand.

"They took her child and sold it to a man who killed it and ate it. But she did not kill her keeper. Another elephant did. The gypsies told me. And that she was stolen from a zoo. She is just bigger than any elephant at any circus. They want to kill her for the spectacle. To sell tickets."

"People are always killing children."

She looked around in the barn, terrified at creation. Her delicate wax-white features and serious eyes frozen into a frown. I feared if she ran now she would not come back. The elephant turned and fixed the girl in her calm gaze.

"I got her away," I said.

"I know . . . Oh, why did you have to come here . . . This is not a good place. This is probably the worst place in the world."

Anna was trembling as she approached but she stuck out

her elfin chin and put one foot in front of the other until I took her hand. A change then occurred in her and she was no longer shy of me or frightened. She touched the elephant's trunk briefly as we stretched out our hands. She laughed and stepped back and I did too.

Her hand was cold and I rubbed it.

I wanted the touch of her skin against mine. She laughed and, it was forward of me I know, but I kissed her on the cheek and then we were kissing each other.

Anna gazed at me bewildered and even prettier.

"You danced with those beautiful ladies. There are countesses and queens out there." Her tone was accusing.

"And I'm here with you."

That was how it began.

The elephant stood up and walked to the front of the barn guarding us as we climbed onto the hay bales at the back. We then fell into each other's arms and kissed like innocent children.

We listened to the horses kick and whinny in their stalls and somewhere far away the orchestra played and we gave ourselves up to love.

꙳

At breakfast the next morning only a few hours later, I fed Anna with bread and dark, almost black, honey, honey as I had never tasted, all the way from Greece and a present from the King of that country, who I think was in exile too and somewhere in the house trailing dried floral confetti. He was one of those who greeted me at the ball and I heard he had been found lost on the roof several times, looking over the edge.

He was a monarch but all he had left were several stone jars of honey.

Anna pushed my hand away and I was overwhelmed by her kisses.

"I thought you wouldn't see me this morning."

I laughed.

"That I'd send you away like the tyrant I am? The elephant would never forgive me. And you're not going to get rid of me that easily. Not every girl wants to take on an elephant and an exiled Tsar from a lunatic family who've gone mad trying to rule an impossible country."

Her lips were shaking. I recited a poem to her. I told her it was by Pushkin, like the one in the elephant.

> "Love's sweet elephant, more than animal,
> Thunders amok through our life's brief dark space,
> Trailing wild flowers, infinite for all,
> Because he has drunk of heaven's grace."

"Your elephant is a lady elephant."

"The poet is writing about himself. About his pure love. His passion. The poetry in everything."

When I told her, between more honeyed kisses, about my upbringing she was more than surprised. But I dropped the piece of bread and honey when she said she had arrived at a nearby railway station, covered in the white clouds of shunting engine steam, crying, without a soul in the world. Her family, she said, had all been killed in Russia, or in Germany, or the war. She had travelled across the channel to London with a man who tried to molest her and she had jumped on a train without a ticket. She got off here thinking there might be Russians because there was a River Don and Russians are sentimental.

She had been born in Rostov-on-Don and her parents had been well-to-do merchants. But she hardly spoke any Russian now.

"I remember a café that served hot chocolate."

"Well, we'll have chocolate for breakfast in future."

She looked at me sadly.

"I just want you. That's all I want of the world now."

We had agreed to meet again that night at ten when I went down to see the elephant and then there was a knock at the door. Anna jumped up and brushed the crumbs from her dress and stood, her eyes looking down and hands in front of her.

"I hope you enjoyed your breakfast, sir," said Ibbotson. "The King wants to see you urgently in the same room as before. You're to dine in that room later but may I suggest blazer and whites for lunch and the initial meeting? I've already laid them out in the dressing room and perhaps a sporting club tie? We must introduce you to cricket now that you are here. The Earl has been going on about it. If you ever understand it you may well get to understand our country's little ways."

When I was shown into the room I had been in so intimately the previous night there were many more people, including two women taking notes at the dining table. The King smiled and nodded at me.

"Take a seat, my boy. We don't stand on ceremony. Don't for God's sake take that down." The secretaries stopped, unsure. "And please come away from the bloody window," the King snapped at the general, who was looking out into the fog at the working men who still were on the front lawn. I had seen them from my own window and there appeared to be more of them now, not less. *The Times*, which had been brought to me at breakfast, was full of stories estimating the true casualties of the war from the British point of view, especially in relation to battles begun early on, such as one in a district of northern France called The Somme, where twenty thousand were killed on the first morning. I was sure that the general must have seen this too. He was constantly wiping his eyes and said: "I do wish . . . I do wish I could do something for them." The prime minister, David Lloyd-George, then went over and said: "You have, you have," in a friendly voice I did not trust. He had the sincerity of an undertaker.

In the room also were the Earl and several others who looked like politicians and then the door opened again and in walked the woman with sharp blue eyes I had travelled with in Russia. She wore, as was her wont, a long blue dress but today there was no pistol or thick leather belt. With her was the man who had taken me to meet the Tsar, the man with the curious patch of white hair at the back of his head. He had similar penetrating eyes to the woman and was wearing the astrakhan coat I had seen before, which he removed and handed to a servant. Even more to my surprise, Rosie, the Marchioness, came into the room and everyone stood. She tucked herself away by the prime minister, who could not take his gaze from her, nor could the King.

The prime minister stood up again and coughed.

"I need not mention the secrecy of these proceedings. I have been touching on the business surrounding the Russian holy man Rasputin this morning with the King and our involvement. Perhaps the two gentlemen who came in late, due to their duties, might introduce themselves. I think they are already known to certain of us here. They are from our most secret intelligence services."

There was a sigh from the King. "Get on with it."

The man who had taken me to see the Tsar stood up briskly.

"I'm pleased to see that there is one of our successes in this very room," he said, nodding at me and the King fidgeted again. "Please allow me to introduce myself. My name is Weston St John Paget-Brown and this person, in the rather fetching blue dress, is my brother, Cleethorpes. Luckily, my mother went to Weston before it became known as Weston-super-Mare. She was a fan of English seaside resorts. Our brothers, Brighton and Frinton, both distinguished themselves at Ypres and received posthumous gallantry decorations. I tell you these details because you must understand we are human beings as well as operatives of the most powerful security apparatus of the most powerful empire there has ever been on earth. I'm the head of the now combined Secret Intelligence Services and after his adventures in Russia my brother here is the new head of domestic counter espionage and has special interest in Russian and Irish anarchism and what the newspapers fancifully call terrorism."

The general coughed. "Why's he in a dress? Captain Cleethorpes or whatever his name is? If that is his name, which I doubt."

The man who had called himself Weston sighed. "The dress is a needed disguise, sir, that he used in Russia to help bring the young man you see before you out and that operation is far from over, as you will realise."

"We should have thought of that at The Somme. Sent them all over in can-can dresses," said the general, gloomily.

"Very witty, General Haig," said the prime minister. Even the secretaries stopped writing as the comment hung awkwardly in the air.

The King blew on his cigar that had gone out and the Marchioness gave a little cough and an ironic clapping which was most appreciated. But the general was annoyed and his eyes were still watering.

"Wouldn't have made a blind bit of difference to those poor men,' he said.

"Should this boy be present? There might be things he does not want to hear. There may be things he should not hear," said one of the politicians.

Weston gave a wry smile. "He will hear them sooner or later."

There was an awkward silence.

"Let's please get on," said the King. "Rasputin?"

The man who had called himself Weston nodded to his brother Cleethorpes who took up the narrative. I thought of my promise to the Holy Man. To find the truth.

"Yes, Rasputin . . . Our people in Moscow were approached by acolytes of the man called Rasputin, who, among other things, promised influence with Germany because of his hold over the Tsarina, the countess of Hesse, who in turn was your cousin, sir. At first, we took notice but then we heard of some of the things he got up to, orgies in graveyards and the like, even in deepest winter and it can be perishing cold there, so we dropped the idea. We wrongly concluded he was off his head. Then, as the war started, it became clear that we had to do something about him because he was supporting a separate peace with Germany. We befriended him through the embassy and it was thought we were getting a long way to changing his mind on Germany and the war, but history had even outpaced him. Behind all that religious tosh he was a very clever operator. He was cleverer than the whole Russian government put together and wanted a draconian clamp-down on the revolutionaries from the start. But it was all too late and when Nicholas acted it only inflamed the situation. A course had been set for destruction as early as the failed revolution in 1905. The conditions among the poor in Russia, mixed with a simplified version of Marxism, were dynamite. Rasputin became the symbol with the Tsarina of dangerous repression and it was agreed that he should be removed. We had to try and stop the rot. We established a new Russian network under the title of Motherland that we hoped would be mistaken for a far-right Old Believers organisation if discovered. The protocol of the British government at the time was that we, the field operatives, had *carte blanche* to take whatever action we deemed necessary to protect our own country and to harm Bolshevism in whatever way possible . . ."

The head of the Secret Intelligence Services, Weston, then stood up. "What my twin brother is trying to say is that this was the start of a train of operations and events, rather than the removal of one man. Cleethorpes is a Cambridge man resplendent in his modern languages, while I'm Oxford and get to the nub. He is Blues and Royals and I'm Lifeguards."

The King made a wheezing noise and said, "So you killed this turbulent priest?"

The twins both spoke at once and then Weston vacated the floor to Cleethorpes. "Perhaps that's putting it a little too simple-Simon, sir. A bit too easy-peasy. Let me explain. I managed to convince Rasputin and his close followers that I was a transvestite deserted from the Tsar's cavalry."

Mr Lloyd-George laughed: "There's difficult for you."

The woman taking notes looked up confused. Cleethorpes continued: "There was a plot to kill Rasputin at a party led by a group of idiots who could not by themselves kill mice, Prince Yusopov and a few other hysterical homosexuals who

284

never got around to anything but being aristocratic and sentimentalising their own stupidities. It was easy for me on the night in question to get everyone at Yusopov's party drunk on a mixture of cherry juice, vodka and laudanum so that they were in happy slumber with their teddy bears. Rasputin, of course, was not so affected and wanted me to dance again. I had been doing a fairly good rendition of a much-practiced Anatolian belly-dance. I said no. He told me he could hypnotise me to dance or bark like a dog or be taken by him as a woman, which I was going to like. He said life was all about power, convincing people about things, and everything else was sleight of hand and moonbeams. I said I agreed wholeheartedly, gave him my sweetest, blushing smile, and shot him once between the eyes. He looked surprised and a little hurt. I put poisoned wine and cake about the place and poured cyanide down his throat. I then put him through a hole in the ice in the river, which was bloody hard because he weighed a ton and I nearly froze to the chains I weighted him with and went down with him. Not a happy prospect. Later, when the sleeping princes woke, I told them how brave they had been to shoot the madman and they believed me and went about telling everyone else. The trouble was that was only the start of our problems. Everything unravelled after that, so in retrospect the mad monk almost seemed a stabilising influence. The Tsar dithered one moment and then massacred women and children and banned alcohol the next. Can you imagine the asinine stupidity of banning vodka in a Russian winter?"

Around the room heads nodded in general agreement, though some of the civil servants and the stenographers were trying to look shocked. It was the King himself that I thought looked most alarmed. I felt COLD in that warm, wood-panelled room.

I thought again of Rasputin staring at me with those incredible, luminous eyes and smelling of cloves and chocolate and pine mastic. How he was interested in the strange and prophetic things I had said to the ladies at the Imperial Nursery after waking from my dreams.

The Rasputin I knew was very tall. He seemed kind. I did not think he could die. He understood exactly the relationship between the raw power of nature and our ideas. He understood that however pure an idea, that idea has to live in the world and survive that world's turbulent power as it would a river of dark fire.

That there is a constant interchange between the light and the dark.

"Kiss me, Pasha," he said, and I had let him.

He was murdered, would I be next?

"If I may interrupt my brother for a moment," said Weston. "To frame what my brother is about to tell us there are two contextual matters that I hope will not bore you. Russia was and is increasingly hard to work in, even for fluent Russian speakers like my brother and I. Firstly, the order to do away with Rasputin was taken under Secret Protocol 127, as my brother says. Secondly, it was also decided early on by the British Ambassador to Moscow, Sir George Buchanan and the King's secretary, Arthur Bigge, that it might inflame the British worker and damage the war effort if Nicholas was to come here."

The King made a snorting noise and took a drink of water. "He used to call my father Uncle Bertie. Nicholas made a pass at my sainted grandmother, Victoria. We used to dress up in each other's uniforms to confuse the fucking Kaiser." The King appeared very sad at that moment and very like his cousin, the Tsar.

"Isn't there a picture of you both in German military uniform in Berlin in 1913?" said Mr Lloyd-George, raising his eyebrows. The King chose to ignore him.

"My wife did not like him, though. Hands all over the place, Nicholas. Apologies, my boy, but the truth. Thank God my wife's not here for all of this. She did not like the man but this skulduggery over not saving the poor Tsar would shock her. Shock her profoundly."

The various politicians and the two intelligence brothers glanced at each other. General Haig merely remained watery-eyed. Weston continued: "It became clear to us when the Kerensky government fell and the Bolshevik lot took over that we had to act. At a conference in Oxford the position had been advanced that it was probably better for the revolution to succeed because in a basically feudal country like Russia, amid the post-war chaos, it was most likely to fail after a few years. That would serve as a minatory example to the would-be revolutionaries around the globe. At this very moment *The Times* correspondent estimates that a thousand people die from hunger in St Petersburg, now called Petrograd, every single day. After Rasputin's death we learned of secret talks between the Romanovs and the German government at a time of great hardship for our brave troops. And we had to look to the future. The contagion of Bolshevism could not and cannot be allowed to spread like the influenza. But it was better to let the Reds make a mess and fall out in their own country. The Kaiser has now abdicated and there is chaos on the streets of Berlin, the government in Bulgaria has fallen. Perhaps my brother will continue."

Cleethorpes gave a little cough.

"As I said, none of this was easy-peasy. We bribed members of the Urals Soviet with gold pieces to move the Imperial

Family to Ekaterinberg in Siberia. This was because there was a plan by Maria Rasputin, the monk's daughter, among others and a White detachment to free the Imperial Family. I passed on details of the plan to the Soviet saying that I was worried that, by the logic of the Revolution, the only possible solution was the death of the Tsar. I had no view, of course. The Soviet members were five fat, untidy men and they all smiled and nodded and took their hats off. They tested the gold coins by biting them. Events took their course and afterwards we removed these untidy men of the Soviet that had participated, permanently. So justice was served."

The King blinked: "You mean, I murdered my own cousin, my own flesh and blood? People used to say we were like twins! You cannot go around murdering people like this!"

General Haig sighed: "We've all murdered many millions more than that recently. I have."

Rosie, several of the politicians and Cleethorpes were looking at me.

The King stood and so did everyone else: "You murdered the Tsar . . ." he said, angrily. "You'll be arrested. You and any of your accomplices. I won't have people like you turning up in dresses and swanning around murdering members of my family. He was a very kind and nice man to me."

Weston nodded his head and Cleethorpes smiled penitently.

But in the silence that followed it was the King who looked awkward and unsure. He reminded me again of the late Tsar. The King and everyone but the two spies sat down again. I had not moved from my chair.

Weston then spoke and all the friendliness had gone out of his voice and he was again the fearsome, abrupt man with the Mint Imperials at the railways station the last time I saw my father, the Tsar. "We have explained to you, sir, that this was a secret protocol, backed by an order in council, which you signed in defence of the realm giving us freedom to act."

'What do you mean?" said the King.

"He means you signed the order," said Mr Lloyd-George carefully, but with half a smile.

"I signed the order that the Tsar and his family, that poor boy and those lovely girls be shot to death in some freezing hell hole?" said the King. "And to put a bunch of ragged-arsed revolutionaries in the Winter Palace?"

There was a long silence and then the King rushed out of the room followed by the prime minister and Sir Arthur Bigge. Rosie came over and put her hand on my arm and then left the room with Earl Fitzwilliam, who also looked most concerned.

"Damned good show to take it so well," I heard him say.

It was decided at that point to break for lunch and Ibbotson came and took me back to my rooms. If I closed my eyes all I saw was the face of the Tsar at the railway station, already a man of no importance alive. In death he had roused a certain sympathy. I lay on the bed looking at the ornate carvings on the four poster and thinking how I only wanted to get out of all this with Anna and the elephant. I knew, beneath all the British humour and kind words, that the victory parades were perhaps a week away, so the servants said, and then I would be even more a loose end that had to be tied back forever. They did not fear what I would say or they would not have described their part in the death of the Tsar so casually. I was nothing. It was so like the Tsar's own arrogance. Most of all, events had passed my country by. I was like a lost shadow from those sunshine afternoons at Selo, chasing grasshoppers.

When we resumed, the King was in better spirits. There was news of the German surrender and everyone clapped politely and then sat down. Strangely, to me, that was all. No one did a dance or looked over pleased. The man known as Cleethorpes was still in his dress, I had the feeling he had not left the room. The King spoke: "Now, I want to know what you have to say about this boy and who he is and what he is. I suppose him saving the elephant was your idea before it even crossed his mind?"

Cleethorpes shook his head: "No, sir, that was a complete accident. I was getting a lot of people out of Russia that we needed, bankers and the like. I paid minor aristos to say they were part of the Imperial Family so we could deny this down the line and discredit the Whites who we did not want to support on account of their being mad and boring and useless. But we aided Alexei here, off and on. One of our Bolshevik friends pushed him from a train and we thought we had done for him but he turned up in my camp like a hungry wolf cub. He's a tough one. We were jolly surprised he survived. I helped him along the way because his position was different and, we strongly believed, he was directly related to the Tsar, even though the Tsar and Tsaravitch had not yet perished in Ekaterinburg. In time we thought the boy might be easier to deal with than the Tsar or anyone else in the Imperial Family. This was because the boy was better educated, more intelligent and splendidly open to modern ideas. He was a favoured alternative. As you have heard, sir, this boy has had a different upbringing, suggested, I was told, by Rasputin to the Tsarina when he was small. She was only too anxious to put him as far away as possible."

The King looked impatient. "But if he's not of the immediate Imperial Family what use is he?"

Cleethorpes nodded and fiddled with a glass on the table in front of him and his brother held up his hand for a pause. But eventually the man in the blue dress spoke: "The boy Alexei, sitting with us here, is the natural and legal successor to the Imperial Throne of Russia. I believe this. He is the result of a liaison between the Tsar and a dancer at the St Petersburg ballet called Mathilde Kschessinskaya, a descendent of the poet Pushkin. He was always told his mother and father were eaten by wolves."

"Who?" said the King. "A dancer? Wolves?"

The name was repeated slowly.

"The Tsar signed a decree back in 1905 that in the event of a tragedy, they foresaw a bomb, there had been a lot of assassination attempts, Alexei here, could carry the Romanov blood line on."

I sat up very straight in my chair.

Up until now I had remained silent even though I felt very angry about the shabby way the Tsar had died. I did not like what they were saying or the easy way they had in saying it. I was breathless. I interrupted.

"I had to memorize a poem by Pushkin that was in the silver elephant given me by the Tsar. The word *Fumoo* I had to say to the king was on the elephant's side. I saw elephants and the same word on a crest on a letter M. Hippolyte had."

The secret agent in the blue dress brightened at this.

"Well, you do seem to have a fondness for elephants, Your Highness. There is an explanation. Peter the Great was given an African slave as a gift and called him Gannibal. Peter was not the kindest of men at times but hated the old order and the feudalism and serfdom that went with it. So he educated

Gannibal to become a gentleman and a general and a politician who married into the Royal Family. Pushkin, Russia's finest poet, is a descendent of Gannibal. His crest contained the elephant and the word *Fumoo*, which means freedom or homeland in a Cameroon dialect. It is my information that this dancer is a descendent of Pushkin by one of his many love affairs that Russian schoolchildren are brought up on. Like your elephant, you can trace your lineage back to Africa. We probably all can."

I took a deep breath. Perhaps the dancer, the SUGAR PLUM FAIRY gave the silver elephant to the Tsar. Perhaps the tear on the poem was hers.

The strange thought came into my head that the elephant, the real elephant, had been trying to find me all this time.

But what they said also hurt. Physically hurt. Like a knife between the ribs.

The faces in the room were turned towards me. My mouth was open.

"What is my mother like? Do you have a photograph of her?" I said at last.

"Is she black?" asked one of the politicians. There was supressed laughter.

"Pushkin was not fucking black," said General Haig.

Weston shook his head too. "Quite so. A dark man by all accounts but not black. As to a photograph of the lady, no, but I am sure one can be found by the end of the day." He gave me a winning smile that made me hate him and his kind all the more.

"I saw her dance," said the Marchioness, looking directly at me. "I saw her dance in London and in Paris. She was very beautiful indeed. She could hold an audience in the palm of her little hand and make military men weep. She was beauty.

They probably took you as a child from her because of who your father was. There was nothing she could do. A friend said she danced at the Christmas balls in Russia and was a principal dancer in St Petersburg. The last I heard was that she was resting after an accident on her ankle. That was years ago."

I nodded. "Thank you. Does anyone know . . . ?" My voice faltered. "Does anyone else know what happened to her?"

Cleethorpes shrugged. "We think she is on the Riviera at the moment. Quite a character, she once let live chickens on stage to upset a rival. As I said, we only think she was your mother. There was also a Danish dancer who the Tsar was friendly with. It does not really matter from a lineage point of view, but I will jolly well do my best to find out who really is your mother. I do like puzzles," he said.

"They said my mother and father died on a train . . . I remember . . ." I began.

"Looking at this dear boy's face, I'd say it was Kschessinskaya," said the Marchioness. "I do not know why you have to be so cruel. And we all must appear so insincere."

Cleethorpes nodded. "Unfortunately, only savages and animals have the luxury of sincerity. At times I envy the elephant."

"At least that beast is not a savage," said Rosie, tapping her fan. "The little silver elephant around the boy's neck is a love token." I could see there was something between them that I did not understand. She, too, was obviously connected with the secret service.

"I wish to ask another question," I said.

"Ask away," said the King. "Not that it seems to do much good."

"What happened to M. Hippolyte and Antov who were

exiled with me? I saw you Mr Weston, if I may call you that, immediately before I left the Potemkin house. Do you know what happened to them?"

The man in the dress spoke, despite a shake of the head from his brother. "They sadly vanished in the tides of revolution. From what we know they died defending the serf women against the Reds and very bravely. They were quite a pair. M. Hippolyte was a younger son of the Count of Orleans. He did well at the École Normale Supérieure and the Académie Française hailed him as one of the finest young minds of his day. He was wounded in his first duel in Paris when he decided to delope, to fire into the ground, against a jealous husband the wife still loved. The man then shot and stabbed him. The wife then stabbed her husband and was guillotined. That's the French for you and how he became a tutor in St Petersburg. He blotted his copybook with a few more duels before being exiled to educate you because of a general clean-out of French tutors after the 1905 revolution. Antov Parlovich was a distant and dashing relation of the Imperial Family. He was for a time in charge of the Amur and Ussuri Cossack Host in between bedding every woman in sight. He was a superb horseman but he killed one of his officers who was about to roast an old Jewess over a fire to find where she had hidden her gold. One of the other officers then shot Antov in the back. He was exiled to teach you to ride and such. I am so sorry."

It was the "I am so sorry" I could not swallow. The fake words stuck in my throat like witches' bread.

I was on my feet in a moment and, snatching a pair of gloves from the day-dreaming General Haig, I slapped them across the man in the woman's dress's face in the way Antov had taught me. I then slapped him again for good measure.

I remembered how the Tsar had slapped me and wanted to do better.

The room and the King were aghast.

"You are a liar," I said quietly, but I was trembling with rage. "I challenge you to a duel. Pistols or swords, I do not care. You killed those good friends of mine as surely as you killed the Tsar. They would have been skewered on larch poles. I can accept that grief. I have seen much grief. But do not expect me to be a fool. Now I will kill you."

The man in the blue dress shook himself and smiled. "You are certainly Pushkin's descendent, by God," he said, before his brother Weston dragged him physically from the room. I stood there with the gloves in my hand that the Marchioness gently took from me and passed back to General Haig who was looking more cheerful. I was doubly angry for a moment because I felt I was being treated like a child. The two secretaries had long stopped taking notes and then we heard shouts from the lawn outside. Someone opened a window.

"Is the workers' demonstration back? Are we to be cut down?" asked the King.

I went with the Marchioness to the window to look. The rest of the room joined us.

On the main lawn Weston and Cleethorpes were having a row that had escalated into pushing and shoving.

"We work in intelligence. We are not dons. We do not have to explain everything. We certainly do not have to tell the naked fucking truth to children," said Weston, pushing Cleethorpes into the mud.

The man, seemingly unencumbered by his long dress sprang back up again, fists raised. "Mother always favoured you and you're still bossing me about as head of this intelligence service. I did exactly what was needed and what was agreed. I got hundreds of people out of Russia and if we can't tell the fucking truth to our own King who can we tell it to?"

"You are so naive."

The man in the blue dress then hit his brother a series of fast, hard blows any one of which might have felled a horse. Weston did not get up.

At that moment the miners appeared out of the mist again and one man laughed and shouted.

"Well done, lass, but don't thy hit him again. He'll be back at coalface soon. Bloody war's o'er and t' pit has settled. God Save The King! Come and have a beer wi' us."

Then, inexplicably, both spies were carried off on the miners' shoulders.

"That's the sort of England we've all been fighting for," said General Haig, finally in tears. "Makes you proud."

TWENTY-TWO

NATASHA READ THE revelations of the intelligence agents about the dancer and the Tsar over and over and wondered what deep psychological effect finding who his parents really were had on the boy in such a cold, public way. She admired his anger. She read the story until it became a dream she was part of, like when her grandmother had died and she had read 101 *Dalmations*. A horn honked outside the building and then she was back in the chair in the corner of her dying mother's room. She so now wished they had spent more time together in the last few years. Her mother had always been fun. Now and again Natasha went to the bed and stroked her mother's chestnut hair. It was not blonde like her own. That came from her father. On the seventh day, the doctors had thought her mother was coming round but she began to breath harder and harder. It was not Covid, they said, but even then Natasha did not realise it was the end. The doctors had to remove her hand from her mother's an hour after she died. Natasha did not cry. She was frozen there. She had never felt so alone.

Her mother was buried next to her father.

The very next day after the funeral Natasha fled from her relatives and went back to New York. She had meant to ask about any family Russian connections, but it had gone completely from her mind among the tears and sandwiches and glasses of whiskey at the wake. Two weeks later she was in St Petersburg; the Russians had given her a lot of money to do research and the library had allowed her time off and had arranged a special exchange visa. She had the last three packets of the boy's story on her computer. In a gallery, the Hermitage, she sent an email to ChiChi.

From: NatashaA@gmail.com
To: ChiChiChica Froment@fas.harvard.edu

I will come and see you. I will. But not yet. I still have not finished with my story and things are not as bad as you are thinking. We are all thinking, thinking, thinking all the time. Critical cholesterol, as Sontag said. We don't look properly at the world. Experience its raw power. I am here now in St Petersburg in the Hermitage café. I walked up the wrong steps, thinking of the man in Paris. I must still be angry as the guards saluted crisply. People in charge scowl at each other here, and it works. Also, I was not wearing my mask, which is another thing the elite never do. The queue was down steps at the other side and must have been two miles long and had its own weather. I am excited at seeing where the boy is from. Everything is different here and I feel as high as a kite. I did not tell you my mother died. I never realised death was so difficult until she passed. That it is such an infinity. Even after my father died. With him the craziness of it took the pain away a little. I will come and see you. The police are probably just following up on when I burned all my clothes and accidently set fire to the apartment of my friend. The firemen thought I'd been assaulted. Don't listen to what anyone says to you about me. I will come and see you but not yet.x

Natasha pressed SEND. She then spent three hours walking around and lingering in front of the Cranachs and going back to a room full of Van Goghs, including one he had painted of a vineyard with blood reds. When she got back to her hotel there was a note from an old girlfriend, saying she would meet Natasha tomorrow and a ticket to go round Tsarskoye Selo, where the boy had described the Christmas Ball. Natasha jumped into a taxi.

It was a longer drive than she thought.

When she arrived a tiny woman who spoke faltering English showed her to the ballroom and left her there. Natasha was entranced. Somehow the friend had got her in after hours and there was no one. The parquet floor shone and the floor-to-ceiling mirrors were as the boy had described. There was a view through windows at the other side of the room to the lake. The great chandeliers were preserved. She could imagine the couples waltzing around and the small boy under the Christmas tree with his silver elephant and his rebel thoughts and drawings and the dresses catching his face. Slap-one-two-three. Slap-one-two-three. Natasha began to dance around the room with a transported smile. She would have loved to be at that ball. She pictured the Christmas tree. She could see the dark green and smell the pine needles. She got to the centre of the room and then saw the small woman smiling at her. Natasha did not want to leave. There was an excitement about the ballroom that matched her own and also a sadness. She also believed in the story of the boy so much more. The small woman waved her to come and disappeared through a door. Natasha followed.

She was led through a series of rooms full of paintings.

In the last of them, the woman stopped.

"Here is the Amber Room," said the small woman. "I

am sure you know the story. Up there is the picture that Catherine the Great hung upside down." They both laughed. The woman left her and Natasha stayed in the room for a while, wondering where the Tsar had stood and the Tsarina sat, smoking. Wondering exactly where the boy had been.

When she asked about the elephants on the way out the woman shook her head.

"They are not here anymore," she said.

The next day Natasha met the Swedish friend who she had been at Harvard with and who worked for her embassy. They walked along by the windy river that was brown and fast towards the Peter and Paul Fortress that Natasha wanted to see because Dostoyevsky had been imprisoned there. The friend, Åsa, had read the manuscript.

They stopped and watched a boat pushing hard against the tide. Seagulls screamed overhead. "There were a lot of these deceiving accounts at the time written by people on both sides. There has never been total proof of what happened to poor Alexei. The one who was sick. There have been claims of finding his bones or generic Romanov DNA, but nothing conclusive. Even the church has never been convinced as the debate is all too political. The boy, as you say, does not claim to be Alexei. But would you, if you were Alexei? I think there is a keen intelligence at work here and we are not being told the whole truth."

Her friend took her into the Peter and Paul Fortress, which was neither large nor impressive, and the cell that had housed the writer of *Crime and Punishment* seemed luxurious by modern standards. The cell had a view of the Neva River. Natasha could not imagine the writer who was put, trembling, blindfolded before a fake firing squad, ever being there. And she had no sense of the Imperial Family either among the white marble tombs when they went into the small Cathedral, with its high spire and crowning golden angel. A party of Chinese tourists was clustered around the resting place of Peter the Great, the man who educated the African slave Gannibal and received the first elephants for the zoological gardens. There was a smell of cheap cleaning fluid, not incense. It was much more than not feeling her parents were in the small cemetery where they were buried. If there was any emotional reality to Russian history, the Imperial Family were meant to be here. Her Swedish friend sensed her disappointment.

"It doesn't feel like they are here, does it? Everyone says so. There is still a disagreement about releasing what little the city council have of Alexei's alleged bones for burial. Officially there is no trace of the Tsar's family remains so there are no forms to cover the burial of bones that do not exist. It is a little heart-breaking, don't you think? Like Kafka. People have so much violence in them. Even those who have lived dull lives. Come on, you must move out of that hotel and stay with us for a few days. Then visit Moscow. You must visit Moscow. That's the fun place. Here is a bit like Venice. Even the ghosts are dead."

TWENTY-THREE

THE UNEXPECTED MANUSCRIPT: PACKET XII

THAT NIGHT I was not able to stop coughing and in the end got up out of the bed and put on my shirt and trousers, shoes and socks and leant against the wall. I felt my chest was congested, blocked as if with mud, and it was easier to breath that way. I had a fever. The sweat was dripping down my face and into my eyes. I went to the window and the sky was dark outside and the old clock on the mantelpiece showed it was twenty past two in the morning. I coughed some more and choked and felt a panic that I was going to die alone in this enormous house and thought about going down to see the elephant but I did not want to wake her and upset her. I should not be so selfish. She had been through far more than I. So I took the little casket of perfumed violet petals I had been given to find my way back and quietly opened the door of my room and started to wander along the corridors. I could breathe better standing up. There were other trails of different blossoms and petals, rose and jasmine, lavender and a yellow flower that criss-crossed the uniform green of the carpet. Occasionally, I heard laughter behind a door, or a shout of pleasure and behind one on the top floor there was an argument going on in French about the possibility of coal production in Ethiopia. On the second floor there was a party and a girl in a very short, white, Grecian-style silk nightdress lounged outside, smoking a cigarette in a long holder. She beckoned me. I smiled but did not go inside; there was a tyranny that angered me in how the questing trails of blossom were serviced by the sleepy-eyed girl. Her white stockings had a ladder on her left leg just below the knee. I wondered if she was a maid by daylight. She was very young and very slim and attractive with her jet-black hair cut short in the modern style and curled in line with her cheekbones, like Anna. She put her leg up on a little gilt chair by a small table. Then we both jumped as a black musician playing the trumpet ran down the corridor and went into the party room, followed by a naked, middle-aged lady. Another couple came towards us and offered the sleepy-eyed girl a small silver box, from which she took a white spoon and sniffed white powder. She offered it to me but I shook my head and the couple went inside. With my unsteady walk, corpse-white skin and staring, feverish eyes I must have seemed drunk or doped. There was a shout and more trumpet playing from the room and the girl smiled and opened the door wider and held it there. I saw a tide of flesh, heaving like the sea, on the confetti-strewn carpet and the immense four-poster bed. I glimpsed one of the politicians and the honey-rich, poor Greek king. The room had a red glow and was obviously a garden of all delights. Something Anna said came into my fevered head. "This is the worst place." I then heard the words of another girl: "My love is like a daisy, a daisy . . ."

"No," I said to the sleepy-eyed girl at the door of the party room, and walked on. I walked my fever walk for several hours before getting lost trying to find my way back. I felt a little better.

Then I took a broader corridor and on his own, in the

middle of the passage, I saw King Billy. He was immaculate, dressed for dinner. There was not a hair of his head or line of his jacket out of place. He stared straight through me. There was not even a suggestion of a smile on his face. But it was as if a strange light shone from him to illuminate the universe he was the centre of, even in the night hours, among his lost guests' trails of confetti.

I could not continue to look into those eyes. I turned and managed to retrace my steps to my rooms.

I then climbed back into bed in a state between waking and dreaming.

I was conscious much later of a knock at the door, but even though it was now light outside and the sun streaming through between the curtains, I was not fully awake. In a dream, in that nether land between sleep and waking, the little serf who had died from drinking vodka was laughing at me. How did I know all this was real, he was saying. How did I know the King was the King and the man I had met at the railway station was the Tsar? How did I know anyone was who he said he was in this great sad house of adulteries and prostitutes? What is King Billy going to do to you? Do you think your elephant can make all of them better? Is this your kingdom, Tsar? You are only an orphan without a name . . . An unwanted child . . . Do you think your mother wants you now taking tea and cakes on the Riviera where she has a son already? You were never wanted . . . !" Then wolves were chasing me to eat me with the German moral philosopher who knew my parents, in that distant, polite way one pretends to know people one meets on a long train journey.

The knock came again and I was fully awake now and the air was cold and there were the delicate leaf patterns of frost on the windows where the curtains had not been fully drawn and a pale yellow sunshine was trying to get into the room. I did not answer the door, knowing it was not the time for Anna to bring in the breakfast or for Ibbotson to dress me. I wondered if it was one of King Billy's midnight confetti girls. The previous evening I had been down to see the elephant and had expected to see Anna but she had not arrived and I assumed that she had been caught up in the preparations for the King to go back to London to celebrate the end of the war. Peace had taken everyone by surprise. Then I had begun to worry and wondered whether there were other explanations. That's the trouble with explanations, they multiply.

I had hugged the elephant very close.

It was strange, contradictory almost, but I seemed to love Anna more now I knew I maybe had a mother. I think the elephant understood. I wanted to share my news with Anna and what I had done and said in the meeting, which I was sure would have repercussions. But the knock might also be my enemies. I drew back the curtain and saw the fields were now perfectly visible and covered in white frost that made me think of home. I then went to the drawer and took out the Cossack dagger that Antov had given me. I unsheathed the knife.

I approached the door in my dressing gown.

"Who is there, please?"

"Probably someone you do not wish to see."

I recognised the voice of Cleethorpes.

Slowly, I opened the door. He brushed past me taking the knife from me and putting it back in the sheath on the table where I was due to have my breakfast. It was like one of Ibbotson's magic tricks. I did not see how he did it.

"Word of advice, old chum. Never show a knife to someone you intend to stick it in. I remember when it was taken off you the first time we met. You were half-starved. A young wolf at my door. I'm sorry about yesterday. Damned hard cheese. And I don't want you to think that your very existence led to the death of your father. But the Tsar was quite prepared to let you play the decoy. I should have put it better. One tends to think of problems as fixed, unchanging, intellectual puzzles and that's probably why the whole world has gone to Hell on a handcart. But there was more than your situation to consider."

I stared at him. His dress discarded, he was now a square-jawed man in his thirties with those piercing blue eyes and rich academic's voice. His long, curly hair that was part of his disguise had been cut short in a military fashion. He wore a khaki army uniform today with a Sam Browne belt. The uniform had the rank of colonel.

"Have you come to fight our duel?" I asked. "You killed my friends and the Imperial Family." I had no doubt he was my better, my superior, in every martial way, but it changed nothing.

"No. As I said, I apologise. I will roll over on my back in a position of submission with my arms and legs in the air, if you like. Anyway, you might even win. No, I have come to give you something that I think you will want. I went scouting around in the library here, I adore libraries and have been away from them so long, and they have got every programme from every play every member of the family has been to. Including the ballets at home and abroad. Here is the lady most likely to be your dear mother. Pretty as a picture."

He knew exactly what he was doing. He handed me a red government file box he had obviously borrowed that, when I opened it, was full of ballet programmes. One showed a woman dancing the 'Dance of the Sugar Plum Fairy' and I remembered the dancer at the last ball I went to. I was sure it was her. I held up the programme with trembling hands. She was far more beautiful in the photographs than I remembered her that night, even though the thought kept running though my brain: "My father and mother were eaten by wolves on a train in Siberia." She was small with a girlish figure and elfin eyes and broad lips which curved into a smile. I saw also a sadness and fragility which I am sure I was not imagining that made her even more lovely. I flicked through them and she was a considerable dancer, perhaps the best of her generation.

"Thank you," I said.

"We've asked the embassy in Monaco to look for her, very discreetly."

"What you did in Russia is still wrong."

He half-smiled.

"Of course, that depends how you look at it. Wrongness, and all that. But I understand what you say."

"The Tsar?"

He paused.

"I've been talking to the King. I have been listening to some of the things that you told him. We made a recording. It's going to be big in our business. What you told him about your elephant and it changing the way you looked at everything. You were very convincing. By that I do not mean you are telling lies. The King has been to see her and was most impressed at the effect she had on that angry crowd of workers. He has come under her spell. Would you take me to see her? I would very much like that. We will do whatever we can to protect you and I will also continue to look for your friends, Antov and M. Hippolyte. I, personally, did not orchestrate that Red attack and I was told your friends were dead, but there is always a chance. There are millions of people who have died and millions more on the move all around Europe and the world. But I'm an optimist, unlike my brother. Now, please, do stop glancing towards that bloody dagger and I'll leave you to have your breakfast. I recommend the porridge and the kippers and toast and raspberry jam. Damned good to be on friendly terms again."

I sat on the bed for some time looking down at my slippers and then, hating myself for what I had become a part of, noticed there was pink confetti on the floor from another room. Dried cherry blossom. I was sure Cleethorpes had not dropped it. The confetti led from near the door to beside my bed and then to the fireplace and stopped. An intruder had been into my room during the night and left it there. I would most surely have noticed even though I was very tired when I went to bed. Was it meant to make me more scared? There was another knock at the door and Anna brought in my breakfast. She closed the door behind her.

We embraced immediately.

I kissed her and she kissed back passionately and I managed not to cough, but then she pointed to the door. "Sorry, I couldn't come before because we were in such a flap. There are soldiers outside your door and in the passage. They're all over the house. Most of the guests have left and everyone has been told that all the business about you and the elephant was a Royal joke, the King being so witty. There is going to be a big ball down in London. The Earl and Lady Maud and the rest of the family and the Marchioness are due to follow, though they seem to be dashing off for days on their own a lot. Most of the servants have been given time off for the celebrations and street parties but a good few have run off, hoping for better, after seeing your elephant and hearing how she charmed that crowd that were going to attack the house. She has become a symbol for them. Of hope. The place is getting pretty empty,

308

except for the soldiers, two guests poorly with the Spanish Flu and the locals from the hunt. The servants are being told the soldiers are because there might be another demonstration. No one believes that. I'm frightened."

She was trembling and the more I tried to calm her down the worse it became. She began to tell me of running down a street as a child where even the air seemed to be burning and wanting to go back for a doll. Her mother had gone back and she had never seen her again. She told me that after being discovered crying on the railway station here a family had taken her in. Taken her in as their own, without a word. They were poor people and could not afford another mouth but saw she was in need. They did not care what country she came from or race she belonged to. They had fed her rice pudding with raisins in a little house where the trains rattled past.

I showed her the red file full of pictures.

"They think this is my real mother," I said.

"She is beautiful. I like to dance."

We then kissed again and arranged to try and see each other later with the elephant. We agreed that it might not be possible. We sat there in each other's arms not wanting to waste a minute. Time threatened love's infinity. I played with a lock of her hair, trying not to cough.

"If I had to leave suddenly with the elephant, in extremis, will you come if I send for you? Oh, please say you will. Then we might go on our way together."

She drew her arms passionately closer around me and kissed me.

"To the ends of the earth. To the ends of the earth."

I did not eat anything of my breakfast but when there was a further knock at the door and Ibbotson entered I was sitting in front of my bacon and egg and Anna was across the room. He looked at both of us and then went over to Anna and produced an egg from her ear. He tapped on the egg and to both of our surprise there was a bright yellow chick.

"You can go, Anna. There is much to do now we are short-staffed."

She nodded and smiled at me.

When we were alone Ibbotson followed the trail of confetti to the chimney.

"Been having visitors, sir?" he said. "I do like magic tricks. I like those where the escape artists get out of impossible situations, don't you? I wouldn't be surprised if there was a staircase to the roof in that chimney. Best not have a fire in there."

He put the warm chick in my hands.

"I went for a walk early in the fields up to the mausoleum, Hoober Stand. The troops was already engaged there digging a big hole. They were not happy, having drunk a lot of free beer last night on account of the good news. When I asked what the hole was for the sergeant came up and said he was looking into it, it was his hole and I was to make myself scarce. All I know, sir, and I do not mean to cause any alarm, is that it is an elephant-sized hole and they had a small field gun up there that the yeomanry use on exercises and a case of dynamite. I do not think they were digging the hole to fill it in again, but you never know with the army. I see you have been at your writings again, sir."

He nodded at the blue pages on my desk.

He paused for a moment as I looked down at my toast.

"Now, we will have to move along. The Marchioness has requested your company. She intends to show you the house and the ruin. You might even go for a ride, so I will lay out a tweed hacking jacket and jodhpurs. There have been all sorts of men in comic opera uniforms coming up to the gates hearing rumours but they have been turned away. May I urge caution in every direction, sir? There are guards at your door, sir, as Anna has probably told you. Do not leave any writings about the place. You appear all in, sir. Have you got a fever? They heard you cough in the night."

I looked up at his long, worn face.

"Thank you," I said. "I am really quite fine. I have a head-ache but it will go.' I said it even though I was in a sweat and felt a bit of a shiver.

We went to the stables first and I was able to see the elephant for a few minutes. The Marchioness, Rosie, stood at the door. I kissed the elephant on the trunk as I left.

"I hope you are as attentive to your lovers as you are to that elephant," she said.

We mounted our horses, she was on a grey and I was on a powerful black stallion, an oddity in a stable of hunters, but then we were cantering to the gallop across the deer park. In the fresh air I began to feel better.

I heard her laugh behind me when I cried out for sheer joy as I rode the beautiful horse at full tilt towards the horizon, the way I used to in Russia.

Eventually, I reached a fence and saw across a piece of cleared land there was a pit wheel and men with coal-blackened faces going into a hut. They stared at us, not with resentment but with resignation. There was something in the slope of their shoulders that showed the misery, the weight of their lot, to earn money for those on the other side of the fence.

The deer park was entirely surrounded by the mines and the factories, in sight and sound of the cruel material world while it pretended a classical beauty. It sickened me like the soot on the air. A stream nearby ran pus yellow and was totally dead. I waited until the Marchioness was next to me. She was beautiful too, really beautiful. She was gazing at the smoke belching out of two impossibly high chimneys.

"*Les fleurs du mal*," she said.

"Baudelaire."

She looked surprised and smiled.

"You have read him?"

"Yes, I have. I had good tutors."

She walked around me slowly, examining me.

"You ride without a single care. If I were in your shoes I'd be scared and the horse would know. That horse can be difficult."

I shrugged. A difficult Russian anything was capable of being more difficult than the same creature in England.

"Is that why I was put on him?"

"Not by me. I know you can ride." She gave me a smile that went beyond the playful. "And you know everything about me. Few men have seen me in my bath. I knew you were watching me. You're growing up fast. As fast as you can ride. Thank you for not giving me away, I'm most grateful. If you were still a boy you might have blurted it all out to that idiot, the King."

What she said next made me sit straighter in the saddle. "I did see your mother dance and she is quite lovely. I once thought of going into the ballet myself but do not have the iron will and the stamina. I hope you find her. I started out as a dancer and an actress and then assumed a role and a part in this house's doomed family. I did all my dancing with large fans of ostrich feathers. Goodness, how brave! I was humble Rosie Boot, the Variety Girl. Maudie, Billy's wife, is not the dancing sort. The only trouble is that someone like me gets bored. Steer very clear of new women like me, dear Alexei. Some suffragette ladies and I once blew up that Lloyd George's summerhouse to wake up his conscience about women and the vote. He'll talk himself to death one day. I thought you were so sweet challenging that monster Cleethorpes to a duel. He was so insensitive. I could have killed him. I might."

She was wearing a tailored riding jacket in dark green with a yellow and black silk scarf at her neck. She rested a riding crop against her jodhpurs. Her curls hung loose in the slight wind.

"Let us ride to where I have ordered a little picnic. It's such a nice day. Try not to kill yourself and therefore please most of the King's advisors."

We rode all around the deer park, sending a herd of spotted deer running and watching two stags fighting for the hinds. The house was splendid from the little rise of hills and I marvelled again on how extensive it was. I am no expert on architecture, but the massive front of the house was in a classical style with its Greek columns and staircases, faced in a honeyed stone. At the very end of this terrace of accommodation and pleasure was an old wall constructed out of greyer stone that looked like the ruins of a castle, but I knew from the Reverend Charles it was fake. We stopped on one of the hills where two servants had brought a hunt-style picnic. There seemed to be a servant behind every tree.

A hamper was spread out on a picnic blanket and they gave us a little bow and hurried off down the hill. I dismounted and Rosie said: "Help me down, will you?"

I did so, without thought, and she grabbed my shoulders and kissed me on the mouth. It was not a short kiss but the French way. I tasted her lipstick and peppermint toothpaste and did not resist. Even though I loved Anna, I wanted Miss

Emily, as Rosie had been. I understood more about the Tsar and his interest in ballet.

"Yes, you are growing up. Now I can tell my grandchildren that I've kissed a Tsar. You don't trust me, do you?"

I smiled.

"You let me go from the circus with the elephant. Mr Masterson was going to electrocute, shoot or hang her. Why should I not trust you?"

She passed me a glass of wine. "That man who trusted me is imprisoned in the ice house."

I shrugged, trying to seem relaxed. "I think he should be very glad of the time he was able to spend with such a beautiful woman."

She hit me playfully with the riding crop. "Have they talked to you about money yet? You must get your hands on the Tsar's investments in English banks and be paid an allowance in the mean time. You have to take it while you can. Billy says the banks made a fortune out of the war and even your revolution. Look down at the house, it's the most splendid in the country and Billy has two million a year personal allowance. This house sits slap bang on the Yorkshire coal and iron fields. He makes his money from the soot and toil that encircles us, and from the bloody war, much more than Masterson, though Billy's business friends tell me it will crash before long. But Billy will already have moved on. He has big dreams, dark political dreams behind all that politesse and they are not democratic. That may sound crazy but everyone is over extended in what they have invested in. Your elephant may be the harbinger of doom. All those early imperial fortunes built on the African slave trade. All the wealth you see is just a show. Like the old castle wall. It was mostly re-built about twenty years ago and I hate it. That is the sort of thing our grubby American friend might do."

"He would have built a castle."

She giggled as I ate a chicken leg and then another.

"But your fortune, Alexei, even if you never see power, is considerable. You are rich beyond your wildest dreams. I feel like the devil showing Christ all the realms spread out before him." She casually stroked my arm with the riding crop.

"Was it your husband who took you to the ballet? Took you to the ballet to see my mother?"

She selected a chicken leg and bit into it. "No, it wasn't. It was an actor. As I said, I used to be an actress. Most of the family do not know that. I acted my way in here to all this. None of this is real . . . In a way . . . I can help you with the financial side of things. You'll be the most eligible bachelor in the world."

"With an elephant." I said.

To put it simply, I was a prisoner. Just as much as if the new Soviet government had sent me to Siberia, or the Tsar had sent me to one of his road building camps there that I had heard talk of in the circus. Rosie took me riding or hunting most days after that and I let her. If I tried to go about alone, even in the grounds, several servants with soldiers always appeared. No explanations were offered and I did not complain for fear of making things worse and being parted from the elephant and Anna. There always seemed to be a soldier not far away, but with Rosie I was free. I did not like hunting with dogs but that was the way the landowners met and gossiped and could conduct their "secret" romances, much the same as in my homeland, which also spread to the house in a cloud of dried flower trails. We went onto other people's estates and farms, but you did not have to ride far from the ancient oak woods before you saw the yellow, sulphur smoke belching from the chimneys or the winding gear of the mines.

One day soon after our first ride, a lovely orange-red fox, a magnificent dog fox with neat, dark brown paws, turned and appeared to open its mouth and laugh at the hunt before getting through a small hole in a fence into the vegetable allotments by the houses of one of the pit villages. The hounds milled around and the huntsmen in their red coats they called pink stopped, almost embarrassed, as large women with folded arms came out and laughed and stared at them. A couple of match-thin, dirty-faced children snatched up sticks and chased one of the hounds and the dog retreated.

A young girl turned and looked straight at me. She had been cleaning out a grate by one of the cottages. She was very pretty but her skin was chapped and red-raw with the cold and she had a look of utter hopelessness on her face. She was pregnant. She was coughing, as was I, even though I felt better today.

"Lost that foxy?" said a smooth voice behind me.

The girl went inside her cottage.

"Rosie says you prefer it when they get away?"

I turned and there was Billy, Earl Fitzwilliam, on his own in his top hat and hunting pinks, as most of the others, including Rosie, rode off to the sound of the horn. Billy pulled out a silver and crystal hunting flask and offered it to me. He was smiling from ear to ear in a detached sort of way, showing his white teeth, as if everything in the universe was a joke, his joke. I refused the flask and he then took a drink before putting it back into his pocket. He sat very straight in the saddle and his moustache looked more splendid than ever, but the most striking thing was the amusement in his cold blue eyes.

"I don't like to see things torn apart,' I said.

He edged his horse closer to mine. "That's always the last act of any hunt, any tragedy, isn't it? You have to have the catharsis. The kill. The sacrifice. It's the basis of our culture and religion. Rebirth in the next hunt. Thought you Russians were meant to be a . . . tough lot."

"Were you going to say cruel?"

He laughed and, leaning forward, peered into my face. "What do you think of my Wentworth?"

I steadied my horse again. "I had no idea, where I was brought up, about all this industry. All this . . . wealth."

A worried middle-aged woman came out of one of the houses with steaming cups of milky tea which we both refused and she curtsied. I could see there was real fear behind the politeness. When she was gone Billy, in his assumed absent-minded, dreamy way, said: "Are you not worried about your own plight? There are those in the government that wonder why you've not asked . . . for things. Perhaps you should. Many are the sort of men who are more comfortable with a little greed rather than grace and modesty and the way of the stoic."

He was making me an offer. My horse, sensing the changing mood underneath the smiles, began to buck his head and I calmed him as one of the miner's children came too close. The child darted in again with a bunch of grass and the horse took it and tossed its head as it ate. The child went back to his mother, gleefully.

"I'm very grateful for your hospitality, Earl Fitzwilliam," I said. "But I am not in a good position to ask for anything, am I?"

He looked pleased but was silent for some time.

"You really should have brought your hefalump on the hunt."

I shook my head. "She'd not have come. We have both been hunted enough."

A small crowd of women had now gathered to look at us. They were giggling and whispering to each other while still being cautious. This seemed to please Earl Fitzwilliam.

"Good answer, my boy. I'm going to do what I can for you. What I can. These are very difficult times. Things go wrong very quickly when they do, as you well know."

Having made his threat so politely, Billy then rode off and a group of fashionable young men and women who had been holding back their horses under a spreading oak tree rode with him. They spurred their horses into a gallop. His wife Maude was there with a young Argentinian polo player and a blonde-haired woman now rode by Billy Fitzwilliam. Rosie had come galloping back from the ridge above the village where the hounds were now, and pulled up her horse beside me. Like the other ladies, she wore a black coat today and looked so pretty with her curls peeping out from under her riding hat.

"He likes you and that's good. Billy is in many ways the most powerful member of government who isn't in the government."

I had no doubt of his power.

It was also obvious, even to me, that Rosie was very much in love with Billy but that he was not in love with anyone at all. He was a Tsar. He was the winner of the world war. There was more trumpeting that a fox had been found but we did not follow the rest. They just seemed to accept me as one of them and there were no questions. They were not the sort who asked questions of themselves. "I want to go down to Cannes, the Riviera . . ." I heard one woman shout on a blast of cold wind. I thought of the mother they had decided I had, there, taking lemon tea and vodka and pickled tomatoes with the other exiles. I held the reins very tight. Not for the first time I felt a pang of homesickness for Russia, an immense country that had never wanted me.

Rosie was quiet as we rode a long way back and then, under another magnificent old tree that must have been there since before the house, we saw a red deer stag and his hinds. The stag did not give way or move an inch. He was a monarch with sixteen-point antlers. He was a magnificent creature there on the ridge beyond a fence, looking down on the desolation of a mine spoil-heap below. I turned to Rosie and there was a sadness in her eyes. She reached over and put her hand on mine that was holding my reins. It was as if she wanted the moment to be frozen there and then.

She kissed me tenderly on the cheek and rode away. When I turned back there was no trace of the stag or his hinds.

A few days later, I had just finished breakfast, porridge and kippers and toast and raspberry jam and Anna had left with one last kiss when in walked Billy himself and Rosie. I was surprised that they had not gone to London.

She was laughing too loud and Billy was holding a cricket bat and a small red leather ball. I had heard about the ritual of cricket from books and magazines and had watched the boys playing in the horse yard with an ancient bat and ball. I had seen pictures of men in white clothes and knew it was a complicated game that was played over many days. "It is the real English religion," said M. Hippolyte. "There is something positively Druidic about the game. It's how the English convince simple peoples of their superiority. It does not seem to be treason, until it is too late." Antov had refused to believe there was anything so tedious.

"C'mon, my boy," said Earl Fitzwilliam. "I'm going to show you the finer points of cricket. If you understand this game you'll understand how to seize everything under heaven, intact."

Rosie was wearing a white dress. She gave me a smile but it was in no way a true one. She was back acting the part of the grateful ornament to Earl Fitzwilliam while her husband was off somewhere else, as was Billy's wife. I had heard one of the women say at a hunting party, "Even the mistresses have their own lovers in this set." It was no different in this than Russia and amid the rumble of industry there was not a hint of pretence. But Rosie sometimes forgot she was an actress and I saw the pain in her eyes. I had the impression she and Billy had had a row and like the thunderstorms that used to appear from nowhere out of the steppe at the Potemkin House, there was going to be another flash and then that strange flinty smell before the ground-shaking detonation and downpour.

I wanted to talk with her, just the two of us, about many things that morning. I was very fond of her and growing more so each day.

I was quickly dressed by Ibbotson in a white shirt and trousers and deck shoes with a tie as a belt around my waist and followed them. We arrived in the great Marble Hall and I hardly believed my eyes. I laughed.

The furniture had been put against the wall and on the semi-precious stones of the Italian floor two cricket wickets had been inserted into blocks of wood. Three footmen were in the room in their full livery and gave a little bow when I came in. I saw that Rosie's white skin had gone red on her neck and the base of one ear.

"This is the wicket," said Billy, pointing to the three pieces of wood and the two bits on top, called bails. Ibbotson, who was also in the room, had given me a crash course as he had dressed me. I think I was meant to try and catch the ball.

"Now, if I bowl, you can see at least how to defend a wicket," said Billy. "Who is going to bat?" he said, and none of the servants rushed to answer. I was going to say I would have a go, but Rosie snatched the bat from his hand. She took up a position by the wicket. I wondered where he had decided not to take her. They were meant to have left for London over a week ago. The servants watched her every move and she was reflected in the Venetian mirrors, being in the centre of the room.

"I will bowl underarm."

"You can bowl how you like," said Rosie.

He then, from a few steps behind the other wicket, strode up and hurled the ball down at her with a straight arm. I was worried. But I had forgotten in my growing affection for her that Rosie was also Miss Emily of the flying trapeze.

She hit the ball before it bounced and no sooner did I hear the sound of the leather against the bat than there was a shattering of glass in the mirror above the fireplace that had framed the images of Popes and Doges, then silence. No one moved.

"I'm not going to play your stupid fucking games anymore, Billy. Fuck you! Stick your stupid cricket bat up your tight arse," she said, and threw the bat at him as she walked out. Billy stayed where he was for a few moments.

"Bad fucking luck," he said, kicking a piece of mirror glass and rushed out after her.

Three days later I was allowed to ride out with another hunt, not the Wentworth, chasing over the dry-stone walls. I was hanging back planning to sneak off home to the stables and see the elephant when suddenly ahead of me was Rosie, on her white horse, stopped in a ploughed field. I could see the hunt charging off in the distance and made out Billy in his top hat. They still had not left.

"Let's go back," she said. "You come with me."

"I can ride back on my own," I said. "I promise I won't slip away."

She smiled, but I saw she was upset.

"Billy is off to a house party with a new tart. All the pretty ladies come and go at Wentworth, don't you know?" she said, and whipped her horse into a gallop back towards the stables.

When we got back she kissed me on the cheek and there was devilment in her eyes. She was furious.

"I want to show you something. A secret. Promise you'll not tell?

We went through the Marble Hall.

"I never told you that Pavlova danced here. Pavlova! In the Marble Hall where I smashed that mirror. Look, they've already replaced the fucking antique Venetian glass. Goodness, how efficient, how tiresome. Your mother taught Pavlova all that she knew. Did you know that? Did you realise that? Pavlova danced here in this lovely room. I'm sure you would have liked to have seen that. As a dancer I'm sure she was made to give you up. But her star pupil, the greatest dancer of all time danced here. Whatever has happened, that lives on. Do you realise it was the balcony of your mother's house in St Petersburg where Lenin made his first speech after returning from exile? That's not long ago. Perhaps you should be careful with mummy, too."

Rosie did not mean to hurt me, I am sure. I stood very still and looked around me, thinking of the ballet dancer at the Christmas Ball, the SUGAR PLUM FAIRY, but Rosie was already rushing ahead and I followed her through two other galleries. She stopped by a small door in one and pressing on the wall a box sprang into her hand. In the box was a key. She then opened the door and we went inside.

Before I could protest she kissed me on the lips and probed my mouth with her tongue. Her kiss was hard and violent and totally Rosie and I took her in my arms. I was fond of her, I had begun to love her, but then I thought of Anna. I wanted a world that was different from all this deception. I wanted the world of the elephant. Rosie then broke away and twirled around:

"Behold, the inner sanctum of the Fifth Earl who rarely spoke to anyone. He liked to come in here and be among his precious things. He loved these more than diamonds or his family. He called them his enchanted forest. They are lovely, aren't they just? This is what we dig out of the ground at such great cost to the poor men. This is what pays for and powers our world. It is different when one sees it as a thing of beauty. The Fifth Earl hated art but loved to be in here."

She turned on more electric lights and I looked at the six-foot pieces of coal in glass cases on plinths around the room. In the coal one clearly saw the delicate impression of leaves and branches from millions of years ago. They were perfectly preserved. The tracing was as delicate as any drawing and reminded me of the frost pattern on a window.

"Look at this one, you can see an insect. Millions of years ago that insect was alive. Alive around here. Before the house. A paradise jungle for your elephant. Before bad Billy. Before man. What do you think?"

"I think they are exquisite. Like you."

She came up and kissed me again.

"The Fifth Earl lived in constant fear of his son's secret. Billy's father, the Fifth Earl's son was an epileptic. That can fuck up inheritance. So Billy's father went off and discovered the land North West Passage in Canada, but still the old man had no time for him. Billy was born out there among the natives. That's why his aunt Alice says he's a Red Indian. But they were out there for something else, an ore that will power the future. Or blow it to pieces. Look."

She took my hand and led me to a lead-fronted door with a small, glass observation window. I looked in and jumped back. Rosie laughed.

I peered in again. Painted on a dark background was a half-naked figure of a native with a tomahawk in glowing paint. It was very well done. It was flickering and seemed to be alive and rushing at the door.

"That, of course, is radium paint from the ore they brought back. But what Billy's father found was more than that and a silly trade route. He discovered a whole village in north Ontario over that ore that was kept warm by a process going on underground. The Indians were growing grape vines and peaches nearby. Wines and peaches! Peaches eaten by polar bears! A few miles away a mountain had been destroyed where the reaction had gone amiss, killing a whole tribe. Thousands. In a blinking of an eye. Goodness, how sad. There's a picture I have seen of an enormous rusting anchor before the blast and a perfectly clean one embedded in rock like a fossil afterwards. Such puissance. The same thing happened when they tried to mine the magic rock with black powder. Bang! There is a fortune in harnessing such a process that might replace all other fuels. And weapons. And political power.

And the poor people would not need to do a thing. Just like us. Imagine that."

She paused looking at the ferns traced on one of the pieces of coal.

"Masterson got to know of this . . . He does not know it all . . . I don't. But he tried to blackmail Billy. Billy has world-sized dreams. That's why I was there, at the circus. Screwing Masterson. To find out how much he knew. But then the government wanted to know too. I like the dare of things, you see. I'd do anything for Billy but he's a ruthless man. That's an understatement. And on the surface we all lie around doing fuck all but fuck and drink and eat and hunt. Oh, I've made such a mess. He keeps telling me he wants to leave all this and go away with me. I am telling you this because Billy is not your friend. At times I doubt whether he's mine."

She then grabbed me and before I could say a word she was kissing me and pulling me down and we were unbuttoning each other's clothes until we were naked on the floor, surrounded by a fossil forest in the coal and the radium warrior, and we made love and I thought of nothing, nothing, nothing else, surrounded by her kisses and the fabulously expensive perfume Billy bought her.

About a month went by at the great house and I worked trying to get my story down on the pieces of blue paper in my room. I wrote very fast with a fountain pen I had found on the first day in the drawer of the desk of what came into my mind about the journey and people and the elephant rather than making an exact record like a scientist or a clerk. I glanced out of the window at the bare oaks and now and again I saw the huge stag and his does standing under the spreading branches, gazing at the house. I wanted to convey what it was like on the road with the elephant. My friend, the elephant.

I read in *The Times* of the election in London and Lloyd George seemed to have survived despite his fears, Rosie told me, about lots of new women voters. She and Billy remained at Wentworth and I saw Rosie every day, as well as Anna. I made love to them both. I did not intend that. I did not want to be like the rest of the house guests. I did not feel guilt with Rosie. It was like being in the circus. It was outside the life of meaning.

But I worried Anna might find out and be hurt.

I had plans, if anything happened, that the large cigar humidor now used to hold the manuscript was going to be given to Anna.

Carefully, I tied each bundle up with thin, pink lawyer's ribbon I found in the desk.

It was the intelligence services that scared me most. They had the power to erase even a Tsar from history if they so wished. They had the power to erase my story without trace. However much I might long to disappear, I wanted a record of my being alive, of my drawing breath. I wanted a person years from now to read of the last Tsar.

Most of all, I wanted the story of the African elephant to be known.

One morning I had been riding with Rosie and, back at the house, we stood on a wide balcony overlooking the deer park. She bent down and picked up a handful of confetti and threw it into the wind: "All these trails of confetti. Like there's been a wedding, except adultery and orgies are the opposite. Goodness, how sad. Do you lay false trails, my dear? Prince Felix Yusupov said he has had word there is a great imposter in England who declared himself at a ball in the country."

"Only one?" I said, and she attempted a laugh.

"Do you think Billy's tired of me? Are you?"

"God no!"

"Do you know what the grand ball was for?" She was looking up into my face.

"It was anticipating the peace, someone said."

She laughed again. "No. Good King Billy said it was for me. In honour of my glorious cunt."

She took my arm. "He does love me, you know. In his way. It was to celebrate my return from a Swiss sanatorium and my cure from TB. That's what he told people in my absence at the circus. My chest is entirely better now. Don't you agree?"

I pretended a laugh. There was an unsure note in her voice. "You certainly convinced Mr Masterson."

She nodded. "Masterson's not a wholly bad man. He has his dreams and enthusiasms. He is always looking for what's coming next. Here, in this house, I can see things are beginning to fall apart. I may well have to find myself new surroundings, a new circus, before that happens. I cannot bear things to be less than today, a fading. I'm sure you know that better than I. Lots of other estates have been broken up and sold off already. You have to know where it's all going next. Goodness, how sad! Listen to me. I learned those words in a play. Goodness how sad! I'm just another ornament."

She stood very close to me. She then held onto me with both hands.

"Of course, the ball was a perfect cover for the men, the King and his advisors to talk. They were expecting defeat, you know. No one had a fucking clue. The peace and you and that wonderful elephant came as a complete fucking surprise. And talking of surprises, I don't want you to worry but . . ."

As she was speaking, the stonework by her shattered and I heard the sound of the shot echo in the distance.

I pushed Rosie inside.

Several footmen ran out onto the balcony and below on the lawn a soldier levelled his rifle and fired at a line of trees.

Rosie was shaking and I put my arms around her. There was plaster dust on her face and in her hair and a small cut on her cheek. I was shaking too. I began to cough and Rosie recovered. She kissed me briefly and very tenderly on the forehead.

A cloud of servants had formed around us. "Stop fussing," she commanded, and walked towards the staircase before looking back at me both passionately and sadly. "Thank you, Your Highness. I'll say goodbye now . . ." Her voice faltered, and then, in control again, she turned away.

People were running everywhere and I had to slip down and see if the elephant was alright. She was not where I thought she was and a stable boy guided me.

The elephant ruffled my hair, concerned. The problem was how to leave in a hurry.

I heard a step behind me and turned. It was Patrick.

"Are you all right, sir? I heard about the shot. As you see I moved the elephant, sir, and when I left she was sleeping. The Marchioness, Rosie, told me to do it. I think she was looking for the Earl who often takes a car to London in the middle of the night to see more lady friends. We keep the cars in the garage the other side of the barn. They say he has not slept proper since the trenches and don't want to in case he finds himself back there. There are lots like that. He'll do his ticker a mischief one day. Hope I don't speak out of turn, sir. But it helps to know the form."

I nodded. "Yes, thank you." Patrick smiled.

"The soldiers are guarding the wrong barn and you can get here from the main staircase and follow it down to the stables. I have also told a friend of yours where the elephant is when she came with our lunch."

"Thank you very much, Patrick."

We both knew who he meant.

"And this American who came uninvited to the ball, we have in one of the lockable stalls where we keep difficult horses. He was moved from the ice house. He's been asking for you. The grooms have been pelting him with horse shite but he still keeps asking for you or the Marchioness. He offered me a job in a film he is making about the outlaw Jesse James. He's a very strange man and it's hard not to believe him. He's in the old stable block if you want to see him."

Patrick must have seen my surprise. "I don't think they know what to do with him. Or they've just forgotten."

I nodded and followed Patrick. I was so glad he had told Anna.

Mr Masterson was sitting on a stool by a manger. His white suit had been well and truly plastered with horse dung and there was even evidence of it on his face and in his hair.

"Ah, the boy! The Imperial fucking Tsar. I wish to hell that I had never seen you. I wish I'd have had the good sense to leave you back in Riga. Well, they're shipping me out to face the music in America, that's what they are doing. I don't think I'll face anything of a legal nature, there being the distractions of the peace and all and no one wanting to make a fuss. They don't want the business about the fake corpses coming up, I bet. That's what's going to kill you, boy. The peace. You're in the centre of one hell of a fuss and they are going to bury you and the elephant. I might make a film out of it one day in Hollywood. Well, aren't you going to say something? We had good times together. I dearly tried to be honourable with you and that cold, vicious woman we knew as Miss Emily. Say something to me boy. I did help you. I am a man of my word. I rode with Billy the Kid."

He looked a pathetic figure in his stained white suit, squatting, gigantic, on a milking stool. But I had no doubt he would rise again.

I felt sorry for him but I kept seeing the picture he had of the hanged elephant on the steam crane in Erwin, Tennessee. The atrocity he wanted to emulate in Hull.

I turned on my heel and left him. There was too much between us for me to say another word more.

"Too good for me now, are you? Well, I'll get out of this jail but you'll die here. You will die here. Do you hear that, boy? It's the only thing they can do in the circumstances. You're an embarrassment to the peace."

I left Mr Masterson without a word and slipped back into the new hay barn and saw that the elephant was now standing and I went over and hugged her leg. But she snorted and blew air out of her trunk and I knew something was wrong. She pointed her trunk towards the shadows and then the spy called Cleethorpes stepped into the light.

"Sorry, hiding. Force of habit, what! Such a glorious creature. She is suspicious of me."

I stared at him. "I wonder why." At times he seemed genuinely surprised about his appalling actions, as if someone else were responsible.

"She did not make her famous hypnotic sound, her vibration or communication."

"She has to be relaxed."

"I really mean it, she is a wonderful creature. I had a spiffing ride on an elephant once at the zoo. In a wooden box, a sort of howdah, with seats that they put on its back. It cost sixpence with an ice cream. I understand you do not call her anything as that would take away from her wildness and her dignity. I do applaud that. And with all of your problems and responsibilities you have devoted yourself to her. Devoted yourself to her! It would be so much easier without her. Can I touch her? I understand she ripped her keeper to pieces after he sold her child to be cooked and eaten. Man is capable of such horrors. Horrors. No animal would do that, ever. Can I touch her?"

"Oh, yes. It was another elephant that killed the keeper. They communicate, you know. She could not kill."

I led him forward.

"I came as soon as I heard about the shot. We have the man. He's a Russian."

I placed his hand on the elephant and she did not draw away. She blinked. I was not quite sure what might happen if she tore Cleethorpes in two. I had no doubt she knew who he was, what he was. Whatever I thought of him, he was a brave man and showed no fear.

"Thank you," he said. "The man who shot at you was from one of the pro-White groups who want you killed on English soil thinking that we will then attack Russia. They say your very existence led to the death of your father and family, which I think is pretty damn harsh and a bit too King Oedipus for me. There are also pro-White groups who want to rally round you and then attack Russia. Some of the Reds want you to attack Russia so that they will have an excuse for what is happening there. The other Reds just want to kill you because of who you are. But, as your friend, the cowboy, keeps telling everyone who'll listen, the real danger comes from within. She's a lovely elephant and we've kept you alive this long, so you have the support of Weston and I."

I stared at him without emotion. I could feel the fever I had returning.

He then shook my hand hard. "Stay on your guard and we'll see what we can come up with. Don't worry, I'll not double cross your elephant. I'm sure they never forget and I've become rather fond of you both. I can be quite sentimental, you know."

When he left I felt a shudder of fear run through me. I do not think it was being shot at. I began to cough. It was the kind words of the new head of domestic intelligence. He was the British equivalent of the old Okhrana or the new Cheka under Lenin. The men with long, black leather coats and amber beads and paler eyes. What he had said about my being responsible for the death of the Tsar and the Imperial Family was horrible. I was so upset for a few moments I could not even remember the name of the stupid seaside town he was called after. If that was his name. In coming here I had not gone forwards in terms of civilisation's time at all.

The elephant touched my forehead with her trunk. I wanted to go away with her right now.

Later that night I told my guards I was going to the library and then went down the main staircase and into the stables and from there across the small courtyard and into the hay barn. It was warm inside and Anna was already there. She had been crying.

"I heard someone tried to assassinate you."

She flung her arms around me. We kissed and kissed. I

should have felt guilty about Rosie, but I did not. I loved them both. I told myself it was not betrayal but a kind of innocence.

"I may well have to get away from here. I may well have to get out in the next few days. I will send for you as soon as I am safe."

"Let me come with you. Please. We could go now. I have no one."

Her words had a frantic sound. NO ONE.

"It will only be for a day until I can get the elephant to a safe place. Then we can be together, I promise. We can just disappear."

She looked at me helplessly and then laughed.

"With your elephant?"

Anna began stroking my hair and we moved into the back of the barn and our passions overtook us. Afterwards we lay together naked, caressing each other. I then took the silver elephant from round my neck with its poem by Pushkin, with the tear stain on the third line. Was it my mother's tear or the Tsar's.

"The Tsar gave this to me and I want you to have it, my love. It is yours. You are more precious to me than life." I told her where my writings were.

She cried and her tears wet my cheek.

But Anna did not take the silver elephant. She refused. Perhaps because it was already the witness of a love lost. Then she said: "No one has been so kind to me as you. No one. If anything bad happens, please do not wait. You'll have to get out. I'd rather you be happy with someone else like in the poem you read me. We will find each other." She then started to kiss me again.

I looked at the face of Anna and was so glad, just glad to be there and alive. The elephant started to make her music that changed one's thoughts and I lay there seeing a much better world after the ruins of revolution and war.

"We should be getting back. I love you, Anna."

"I love you," she said.

The warmth and stillness of the barn conspired to shield us from time and parting. She grabbed my arm. "Promise you'll not leave me? I know what I said but don't leave me. Come and find me," she said.

"I promise."

TWENTY-FOUR

NATASHA IMMEDIATELY UNDERSTOOD why Pushkin had said Moscow was like Babylon. There was conspiracy in the air. There was beauty and there was the scent of blood. It excited her. She got up and jogged from her faded old hotel, The Hotel Budapest, recommended by a Russian friend, where Lenin had his only affair. The room had not been cleaned and was too hot and you had to bring your own drinking water, but you could hear the strange mediaeval clang of the Kremlin bells. As if history was pealing into her room. Past all the designer shops and bars she found the Bolshoi and then Red Square where she gazed and gazed at the dream-like beauty of St Basil's, whose builders had their eyes put out so they could not build another, and close by, under the Kremlin walls, was where the Strelsky, the first rebels, were buried alive, silent and defiant. The story of the boy had somehow brought back the rebel in her. In the blue sky the ravens wheeled and danced.

She marvelled at the boy's dream of a white hotel on a windswept beach. Her father had purchased such a hotel near Monterey as part of his obsession with Steinbeck and the novel *Cannery Row*. Perhaps the boy saw her father's future as well as the Tsar's.

Natasha went for dinner in the Bar Moloko, a place that could easily be in London or New York, except the food was better. She met a man who she had contact with in her Pushkin studies from the Moscow School of Economic Sciences, that also now included writing. He brought his wife and another man, and they talked about the boy and the manuscript, but she was met with a lack of enthusiasm. "There have always been so many of these pretending princes," was the distracted reaction from her host, who had to go early because he was leaving the next morning to open a new school in Yekaterinburg, formerly Ekaterinburg. "They are sending me to the start of Siberia, where they killed the Tsar," he said, trying elaborately to make a joke, and she was left with the young professor he had brought, drinking coffee and then iced vodka that tasted like electric snow. He was a tall man with sleepy, unhappy, dark blue eyes and floppy dark hair. He had been in the army and was a talker. He told a tale of making martinis in his tank with eau-de-cologne when they could not get vermouth, and drinking the perfume when they ran out of vodka. There was something about him, a determination perhaps, that reminded her of the man in Paris. The Russian suddenly grabbed her hand hard to make a point about Gogol and was about to apologise, but she smiled in a way he could not mistake. He lived way out in the feral suburbs and in the park next to his house there were four bodies found every week. He said it with a shrug. The next moment they were outside in the cold of the street and he had his arm around her and they were heading back to her room at the Budapest. They walked past the pole-dancing bar next door and a girl on horseback, who the man explained was selling her body in that way because streetwalking on foot had been forbidden by the tidy new mayor. Perhaps it was the cold air, or the mounted prostitute, but whatever Natasha intended she could not see it through. Outside the hotel she kissed the surprised and disappointed academic goodnight and went upstairs to read in bed.

It was only later in Natasha's dreams that they giggled along the endless corridors that were so big and brightly lit they were surreal. They began to kiss by a table with a vase of dried flowers. Once inside the room she started to take off his clothes and, after a moment's hesitation, he did the same for her, and they fell down on the bed and he was inside her. She wanted to feel, really feel, to be the butterfly of her dreams in the eternal, unreflecting instant. The Kremlin bells began to clang. He made love to her again harder this time, brutally, and she came and she went for him with her nails, biting and scratching until he cried out and tried to push her off. But she did not let go and had her arms around his throat and she was laughing as there was blood on the pillow, and the bells from the Kremlin clanged, the empty sound that the Streltsy had heard, and he was fighting her now and he kicked out and burned himself on the radiator by the bed and she laughed more. She reached for the heavy ashtray on the bedside table as again the man tried to get up. Only then did she realise it was the man in Paris, and woke.

Why was she trying to kill him?

TWENTY-FIVE

THE UNEXPECTED MANUSCRIPT: PACKET XIII

"LE TSAR DOIT MOURIR!" The shout in my dream woke me. It was me who was shouting. It was what I predicted years before. The Tsar must die.

I was lying in bed in between the starched sheets, listening to the owls in the deer park, trying to plot an escape, which kept coming up against obstacles however well I thought it out, when there was a noise from the chimney. Soot fell out into the room and one of the firedogs made a scraping sound against the stone. I reached for the dagger under my white pillow but suddenly a face-blackened butler, Ibbotson, stood before me.

"Hush, sir. Don't make a bloody sound. Got to get you out. The Marchioness, Rosie, says so. They're making plans to kill you in the cabinet, whatever that is. Sounds like a mahogany thunderbox. All on account of the peace. Dangerous stuff peace. And you being sick and likely to die on their hands. They are making plans to kill you and your elephant, which they are extremely suspicious of. We got to move fast, sir. Will you put on these nice overalls and there's some combinations and thick socks and boots in this bag? Thank god it's a wide chimney. Good thing we've not got to get the elephant up there."

I hesitated. "I can't leave Anna."

"You must sir, you really must. There's not time. They could come any moment."

"I love her . . . We love each other."

Ibbotson looked frantic. A smile line at the side of his mouth twitched slightly. There was a sound outside the door where the soldiers were.

"I'm not leaving, not without her. It was a promise. A sacred promise. What will she think of me if I break my promise? I'll just be like all the rest."

Ibbotson took a deep breath. "She'll understand, sir, and we'll get word to her." He laughed. "I promise. I'm sure Anna would rather have you live and not be with her for the present than have you with her and dead. And the elephant who you saved."

I had promised I was not going to leave her only a few hours ago. Still I lay there.

"If you dither you will die," said Ibbotson. "That's what my old sergeant used to say at the front and he was right. There are plans to kill you and stuff you in a hole. Then a warrant will be put out for you for killing a man on a lock near Goole. They're not playing around. Come on, sir, you trust me. Patrick's already taken the elephant down to the castle wall. Then we have several miles to go before dawn and there's a place to hide where no one will find you. When you get to safety eventually, out of this country, the Marchioness says all the finance things will be done and a deal made with the government. But it's too dangerous now. The politicians are terrified of anything that will damage the peace that they did not cause. Like a lost Tsar turning up."

All I could see was Anna's face when I dressed in the overalls. I took only one picture of my mother. I had no picture of Anna and that made me tremble. I looked at the Cossack dagger and then pushed it into Ibbotson's hands.

"I want you to have this," I said. "It belonged to a friend."

"You keep it, sir. Anyways, I'm coming with you. If you don't mind, that is. I have never really fitted into this profession but am very handy at many things when it comes to it. You asked me to keep my ear to the ground when you came, to help you, and now here I am, at your service."

He then produced a revolver from his coat and put it away again, like one of his disappearing tricks with chickens and eggs. It occurred to me that he was taking a considerable personal risk for me. I also realised that once I left the country house, if the threat was not real, then my claim to being the Tsar was going to be weakened. I had to decide and thought of the large hole the soldiers had dug and what I owed to the elephant and one day informing the world about her gifts and revelations.

Minutes after that, I was following Ibbotson into the chimney and up metal hoops to the roof.

It was a starry night and I could see Sagittarius and the Belt of Orion and Aldebaran and many other brilliant constellations and galaxies in the night sky that M. Hippolyte used to point out to me. There was a cold wind and a bright waning moon and I climbed out of the chimney to find there was a road of lead from one end of the huge building to the other. Slate roofs went up to the parapet on both sides, but they drained to the middle. We kept low and hurried along the light grey road until we saw the ancient-looking wall.

"It doesn't join on at this height," said Ibbotson, worried.

"I can make it," I said. It meant jumping out about three feet from where the house ended in an elaborate glass and stone winter garden. "But what about your leg, Ibbotson?"

"I'll give it a go. My dancing days are probably over anyway."

I took a deep breath, went back several feet and looked across at the old wall.

It was much further away than I had thought.

I knew if I hesitated any more I was never going to make the jump. I flung myself across the void and bashed my head on a stone as I landed. Part of the wall started to crumble.

"Get back," I shouted, but it was too late and in a moment Ibbotson had joined me, and the wall partially collapsed. We scrabbled for a hold as falling stones seemed to make a thunderous noise and for perhaps five minutes we remained very still but no one came. The wall was not at all well built and we felt part of it moving under us. Very carefully, we started to climb down.

"My fucking foot, sir. It's not even hurting. I think I was so scared it's stopped hurting for good," said Ibbotson. "I never liked old walls."

Soon we were in the shadows at the bottom of the wall. Ibbotson made a hooting noise like that of an owl that Antov had taught me to do and it was answered. A few moments later the elephant, blocking out the moon and stars, was beside us and we began making our way to a nearby spinney.

My entire body was tensed for a shout or the rifle shot.

Then Patrick was talking in his low, soft voice. "You follow the lane to Thorpe Hesley, skirt around it and then up to Wortley and then the Winter Hills. It will take you a couple of hours. The soldiers are all on the other side and there are police at the Thorpe Hesley gate so go around them softly now. There's a wood there, so it should be grand. Good luck to you."

I took his hand. "Thank you, Patrick and tell Anna I will send for her. You will tell her?"

"That I will, sir. Don't you worry for nothing."

Then we were away, sticking near the black hedges of the moonlit fields. I looked back at the house and could not help thinking that I had betrayed Anna. It felt like I had betrayed a sacred wedding vow. There was a tear on my cheek.

"Don't fret, lad," said Ibbotson. "She'll wait for you. I can't tell you where we are going because I don't bloody know. But we have to go now."

Everything did go well, at least until we approached the police post and found soldiers were there too and when we went into the wood we saw soldiers at a brazier, drinking tea and smoking and saying what they were going to do when they were civilians again. Then, out of the darkness, there was the sound of a bolt cocking on a rifle and someone said: "Advance one and be recognised. What the bloody hell you got there?"

All I could see was the end of a cigarette. I stood still and so did the elephant. I thought it was all over and expected the soldier to call to the other men and be taken back to the house. I held on tight to the ear of the elephant. Then I heard a heavy blow and a man falling to the ground. Ibbotson had knocked the man out, who luckily for us was not wearing his helmet. But that was not the end of our worries. A barbed wire fence had been put up in the wood and we had to search the soldier's pockets for wire cutters and cut through it for the elephant to pass. Ibbotson tied the man up and gagged him and left a small open bottle of beer by him as if he had been drinking and someone had robbed him.

"Most likely he will keep quiet," said Ibbotson, and we

went on. "Or he will be on a charge for not keeping a proper watch for elephants and Russian spies."

We crossed one large road but there was no traffic and no soldiers or police and we were quickly into a lane at the other side and climbing up a wooded hill.

"This is Wortley where Robin Hood and his merry men came from," said Ibbotson.

"Perhaps we can join his band," I said.

"I am sure he needs an elephant."

The moon went behind clouds for a while and the going was more difficult as we skirted an edge which fell away. In the distance I could see the lights of Rotherham and Sheffield and the glow and flare of the furnaces and the coke ovens. Even in the fields it smelt of burning.

Ibbotson stopped to make sure where we were. I had begun to feel lost again in many other ways. In the short time at the great house I had almost thought that the hardships were over and that the journey had finished. In fact, it was only a pause. I blamed myself for not being more convincing to the King, the King who looked exactly like the Tsar.

"There should be a field ahead and after that we cut left into Mary Brummet's Lane and then we get to the entrance."

We found the field easily enough, and the lane, but we spent the best part of an hour searching for the entrance to the place.

Then there was a whisper from Ibbotson. "Found it! Here she is! She's a beauty."

I had thought we were searching for the entrance to an abandoned house, but in a tangle of trees and blackberry bushes was a large hole and a sign that in the moonlight said Danger: No Trespassing. The word DANGER stayed in my mind.

It was a hole that could just accommodate the elephant if she crouched down and almost crawled.

Ibbotson struck a match and lit a small lantern he kept in his pocket, the kind that miners use. The chamber above us was echoingly large. We were in an extensive, dry, circular space.

"This was one of them old bell pits the monks who started mining coal here left. I've known of this one for years. We used to come and play here when we was kids. We'd get knocked into the middle of next week if our mothers caught us. The roof holds up because it is dome-shaped like an Italian church. At least, that is what the theory is and what I was told. Plenty of them collapse over time because of all the workings below. I'll disguise the entrance but we will be safe here when the hue and cry starts. They will hunt you up hill and down dale."

I was silent. Focussed on the lamp.

"Where do we go from here? The elephant needs food." I eventually said. Ibbotson pointed to a sack.

"There are some potatoes. Patrick brought them last night. But no, sir, I do not know what happens next. I don't know what our destination is or how we may get there. My bloody foot hurts now, though. I don't think I'll be playing for England at football in a hurry. I've some food with me and the best thing we can do is take turns to watch and the other one sleep. The prime minister will be told about your escape if he don't know already."

I lay there trying to sleep but there was no way I could. When I closed my eyes I saw Anna's face before me and heard my promise, clear and sincere on my lips. Was this what it truly meant to be an adult? I wondered if she would even remember about the manuscript. She was never going to trust anyone again. I looked around at the darkness and it also occurred to me that if anyone wanted to kill me and the elephant they had us where they wanted us again. I did not suspect Ibbotson for a moment, I was sure he was a good man. But it was just the sort of thing that the clever Cleethorpes might engineer. All one needed to do was block up the small entrance and we would suffocate or starve in time. There would be no need for shooting or field guns. We would be out of the way forever. The treacly, dank smell of the coal was overwhelming, we were surrounded by the fossils of a forest of long ago, a tropical forest that had gone cold. Like the miners who worked every day in the dark, we were invisible. I started to cough and then held my breath in case I was heard outside. I rested my head against the elephant's trunk. They could not kill her, not now.

I shook myself out of thinking that way and started to cough again, hard. When I closed my eyes the darkness flashed. M. Hippolyte used to say that thinking of the universe and how vast it was and how random, full of millions of stars, was the cure for black moods.

He said to think of such vastness and then realise that in all of it you were a totally unique and individual creature. Antov then said that imagining eating ice cream always cheered him up for the somewhat opposite reasons. It worked for everyone he knew and he didn't know or care why.

My thoughts turned to the clarity of there being only power, the river of dark fire, and what we invent on its banks. I remembered my bargain with the Holy Man, Rasputin. He was not going to crunch me down with French marzipan cakes, MUNCH, MUNCH. I knew the meaning both of meaning and no meaning, the good and the bad, the negative and the positive, and the eternal flow between one and the other, the LIFE of the world. It was ENORMOUS as

Rasputin had said. Even more so than my enormous elephant!

I had fulfilled my promise, but it was almost funny. I had the answer all along inside me. I heard it in the song of the elephant. I saw it instantly in Anna's smile the first time we met.

Rasputin had known that. He had known that awesome simplicity of everything.

It helped me slowly get control of myself.

Then there was a noise outside and Ibbotson motioned for me to come to him and put the light out. I heard the elephant move in the dark and then she stopped. I held out my hand and her trunk was there. I edged towards Ibbotson. I felt his coat and outside we could clearly hear men talking. They were not local.

"If they came up this way with an elephant then where the fuck is it?"

"There were tracks back there that could be made by an elephant."

"Or big horse tracks that's got washed out by rain."

"Or someone with a paint tin taking the piss."

"So where's it gone, then, if it came up here? It's disappeared into thin bloody air. Therefore, it never came up here. If it's this side of the house at all they are sticking close to the road and heading for t' coast. The boy's like as not, not with the animal anyway. Who would try to escape with a gigantic bloody elephant? If he's a Russian spy he'll be legging it in t' other direction."

"Maybe it just flew away, Sarge."

"Shut up, Diggle."

There was a groan from another of the soldiers.

"So you want us to go back down that hill, Sarge? Can't we have a smoke?"

"That boy can't be a Russian spy. They don't employ boys."

"He could be older and look younger. Like you, Sarge."

"Well, that's brilliant thinking, my lad," said the sergeant, irritated. "We should have you in the fucking government. I suppose the elephant is only dressed up as an elephant and they've gone off to the pub. The only fucking circus is you lot. Pick up those rifles and we'll go back down to the road. It's a good thing you never got to go to France. You can't even find a ginormous African elephant and a boy!"

They moved off and I was elated, even though they had called me a boy.

We had vanished like a fox into a hole, but there were main roads all around us and these were blocked. I took the next watch and became very cold and despondent in the night.

I began to dream of chocolate ice cream, as Antov advised, when Ibbotson roused himself.

"You let me sleep longer than I should have."

"Does your foot still hurt?"

"Yes, but 'tis a noble wound. I banged it on an old castle wall saving a young Tsar."

We laughed.

I curled up in the crook of the elephant's trunk and when I woke it was dark outside again.

I went to where Ibbotson was and looked out into the night. We could hear the sound of movement on a nearby road. The soldiers had probably joined up with others and were sticking to the roads, thinking that's what I might do. There were trucks but they were going away from us. I wondered who was leading the search.

Ibbotson got out his watch again as the moon came from behind a cloud. "I was told to be out and watch all round and above at exactly eight and it's coming up to that now. It's a nice still night, sir. There is no signal, I'm just told there will be no mistake. That's all they'd tell me."

I was shivering and accepted his words without question. I was still thinking of Anna and how she had found herself so alone at that railway station.

"What's that?" said Ibbotson.

I heard a low noise approaching from the west. It sounded like a car engine, but that was impossible for behind us were woods and shale heaps. The sound grew louder and the moon disappeared behind a cloud. Most of the stars were out but as the noise increased I noticed that they began to vanish. I thought for a moment that the elephant had come out with us.

The engine stopped. Around us there was a rustling as there is in leaves on a windy night. But the night was completely still. The engine started again, getting closer.

I do not know why but I thought of the trenches and the gas attacks I had been reading of in *The Times*. It came as a yellow choking fog and there was the smell of petrol or something pungent in the air. I felt the blood beating in my temples.

But it was more of a wonder than that.

TWENTY-SIX

N ATASHA STOOD AT the bar of the pub near the
great English house where Alexei had written the story
of the elephant, and the elephants he had met with the Tsar.
"If you want to go round Woodhouse then gu' wi' me son,"
said the owner of the Huntsman pub in Wentworth, as he
presented her with steak pie and chips, a dish and a smell that
was one colour, brown. It was the only thing left on the menu
on a warm day. "Don't wait for folk who runs yon house to
answer you. They never do, whoever it belongs to now. It's
done up inside but there's miles o' pit workings underneath.
One day, whole bloody lot will fall through and good riddance.
End of story. And you must see Ann Copley. Local historian.
Was a teacher. She's a case!"

Natasha nodded and smiled. She had taken the plane from
Moscow to London and then come to Wentworth. She was
officially obliged under Covid rules to isolate for a number
of days, but the friendly girl on her hotel reception said no
one bothered.

The village was small and built of a dark and pinkish stone.
It had a church and flower baskets and rolling hills nearby. It
did not seem part of the exhausted, rust belt towns and cities.
The story's magic must be still here, somehow, the evidence,
Natasha thought. Men watched her and drank slowly from
pints of mahogany dark beer. They were like her neighbour
staring when he found her naked in the garage. They did not

embarrass her, only make her feel a species apart. Natasha had a half of bitter and the warm, foaming liquid tasted of sweat and metal. The pie was better, but she could only finish half of it. "Don't worry, duck, we'll put it in't dog."

The son of the landlord turned up on the doorstep in what looked like a new jacket and drove Natasha to the house in a Japanese sports car. There were deer grazing under an immense tree; the car juddered over a cattle grid. The park was lovely.

"We'll just go on a bit further and look back at house," said the son.

They went past what she thought was the house, but a quarter of a mile along the road there was another cattle grid and the car stopped. "That's it," said the son. "No one built one bigger. No one."

She looked back, amazed. It was, as the boy said, enormous. She knew now why they gave guests dried-flower confetti to find their way back to their rooms. But there was scaffolding on a few of the walls and corrugated iron covered holes in the roof; it now seemed lost as well as abandoned.

"What we drove past first were stables," said the son. "Come on, I'll show you some of the main rooms and the Whistlejacket room. I know one of the caretakers. They've even got a copy of the painting the horse went for and tried to eat."

She walked through damp-smelling dingy room after dingy room, where the once white dust covers on the remaining pieces of furniture had turned a dirty grey, while the son tried to chat her up and find out what hotel she was staying at. He was clumsy and sweet and harmless and, in the end, kept his distance. But the forgotten house did not keep its distance. Even more than the Tsarskoye Selo palace outside

St Petersburg, where the boy found the silver elephant at the Christmas ball, there was a sadness one could almost taste, a continuing message from the cracked mouldings and the pillars and the paintings and the faded painted silks, of a horror and a surprise, a shock that such magnificence had been passed by, had been snatched from the centre of things and now existed as a to-be-restored ghost, mainly for business conferences and wedding parties, a piece of Imperial nostalgia. The son did not know where the Bedlam Room bachelor's quarters were, but he took her up to the Whistlejacket room, where the copy of the Stubbs painting lived up to expectations. It was not even the original copy but a cheap photographic print. She went up to the picture and the horse seemed about to leap out at her, as if escaping from the doomed house. The image still had its power. Natasha did not blame the horse. If an artist painted a picture that showed the true her, all of her life and dreams, she would attack it. Natasha then went to the window and looked out over the park and tried to imagine the miners appearing from the fog and scaring the King and General Haig. She tried to imagine a Russian boy on an elephant.

"Are you here long?" said the son.

"No. Do you know where Ann Copley lives?"

Ann Copley, a small and thin, white-haired lady, fixed the son with such a stare that he left Natasha at the cottage. The sports car roared away. "You must be careful o' that sort. That landlord's son wants castrating and that'd be too good for him. I've never had a use for men, Come in, love. Have a cup of tea. You want to know about the family? Just ask."

Natasha entered the low cottage that still had an old, iron, coal-burning range which heated the house. Ann Copley brought her a cup of tea and a plate of thickly-buttered scones, even though she asked for coffee. Natasha enquired about the boy and just let the woman speak.

"There were talk of a young man at the end of the First World War, but there's nothing much written down. By some accounts, namely a Methodist preacher at the time, if we are talking of the right person, he was a little shit. Got more than one girl in the family way, though the whole house was at it day and night. It were their sport more than hunting. But this lad and one of the grooms, an Irish boy from Greasborough, where they used to bring in extra servants from the estates near Wexford, they were notorious. It's said orgies went on and them two were not above blackmail. Then they burgled the place and buggered off, probably to America. The lad said he was Russian but there is a doubt to that as well. He rode an elephant, they say, at one of the miners' demonstrations. That is word of mouth handed down as is the fact he was bone idle, a dreamer, and lived on the stories of him being related to the Tsar, or something. He never got out of bed except to get into another one. Yet he could spin a tale of dreams like you wouldn't know. I only have that from hearsay from the love letters and diaries that went up in smoke, or most of them, when they burned all the documents of the house in the Seventies to keep their secrets, secret. Of more darkness than Ancient Rome. Later on some were in league wi' Hitler. I think the boy you are talking about may have been a gypsy. And that Anna he got in the family way was no angel. She was foreign too. They found her on Masbro' station. She died having that wicked boy's baby. A nice young man who came and bought some of the papers about a year ago was interested in that. He bought a bundle of papers that might have been ̶ boy's diary, which I never saw and I would have doubts ̶ ̶ man who bought it could have been foreign. Then

352

again he might not. All I can remember about him was that he was tall. Tall. Funny how some folk don't stick in your mind. Soft-spoken and well-mannered. He got fleeced though. Paid double what they were worth. But not the sort to care. He asked about a silver elephant on a ribbon. He was very fashionably dressed which made him look odd round here."

"An elephant with red eyes?" said Natasha.

"Yes. Rubies. How did you know that? Are you all right, love? Do you want a drink of water?"

The taxi came and Natasha got in: "She's a mad old bat, that Ann Copley. She's paid by Wentworth, tha' knows. Don't believe all she says. It's all stories."

At the hotel, in a desolate nearby town, where she had a room for the night, Natasha turned to the boy's book again.

TWENTY-SEVEN

THE UNEXPECTED MANUSCRIPT: PACKET XIV

T HE SPLUTTERING ENGINE noise ceased. I blinked
and then my heart jumped like a salmon.

There was a craft above us that had almost stopped on the
windless night. There was a rushing sound and cables from
whatever it was trailed over the blackberry bushes on both
sides of the lane.

The moon came from behind a cloud and I saw above us
a thing both of beauty and of terror. It was a vast silver ship,
a perfect bullet-shaped construction that was entirely of this
new century, but did not seem at all real. I felt both its weight
and lightness in the sky. It could not possibly be real. In the
moonlight it reminded me of a suit of armour. I heard it as a
choir's song, a cantata.

It was the stuff of dreams and fairy tales and far beyond
that.

My first thought was to run to the elephant for this was
the army and they had finally caught us. The craft had been
sent to find us. But I was rooted there, staring up at the ship,
for it looked at times like a boat seen from directly under the
water. It was the length of a small farmer's-field and had the
letters and numbers RS 33 on the side and the red, white and
blue roundel of the Royal Flying Corps.

The fact that it was real and of this world was even more of a wonder.

I glanced at Ibbotson who was as surprised. His mouth hung open.

Then all around us there were men running. They were dressed in black and were pulling on the ropes and a man secured a line to a gatepost. Another man came up to Ibbotson and cupped his hand to the butler's ear and whispered words I did not catch.

"Go and get the elephant, please sir," said Ibbotson. "Go and get her now. There's not a minute to lose. They've got to haul this contraption up to that field. Go and get her."

I obeyed, although when I came out again I half-expected to have dreamt the whole thing. I knew the craft was an airship, or as the Germans called them, a Zeppelin. ZEPPELIN was a good word. It hung inside me. I knew they flew a long way, even across the Atlantic, it was said. They had bombed London, and fighter planes had been sent to attack them and blow them up, but some got away. Inside the larger ones there was great capacity for people and goods and, perhaps, even an elephant. I had read all this in magazines like the *Illustrated London News*, but I was still wary of a trap, an ambush.

The elephant was at the door and she ruffled my hair with her trunk. Slowly, I led her outside and already the craft was gone from overhead and was resting in the nearby field. Close by the hedge there was a group of cows that did not seem disturbed by the sight and a door at the back of the craft was open and a ramp down. Then, although I was with the elephant, I started to cry. Tears ran down my cheeks.

I was leaving again, always leaving, always going somewhere else, into another future, and always without a family. Ibbotson saw me and handed me his handkerchief.

"Come on, sir, you've been marvellous. Bloody marvellous. Nearly home now."

I shook my head and smiled and pulled the elephant after me.

She was my only HOME.

Then a tall, athletic man came bounding down the ramp and gave me a big smile. I froze.

It was the spy who called himself Cleethorpes. I thought it was all over.

"Well, my boy, they are hunting for you everywhere again, just like old times. There's been a secret meeting of the cabinet and it's deemed unnecessary to take you alive. Lord Northcliffe, who is now minister for propaganda, is putting out a story that you are really a Russian spy for Lenin himself. That's so funny! Really, it's because they don't want to upset the new Soviet government who they don't want to fight on behalf of some young and exiled Tsar. The King and Lloyd George are too busy flag waving and kissing babies in peace parades. No one wants to spoil the party. And God knows what King Billy is up to. It's bitter men far down the chain of command that have taken this decision and they did not ask me, or even my brother, Weston. The cheek of it. They do not realise this is the intelligence age. I'm here to help and before you think I've become a pansy and a softy I have my own dark reasons, one of which is to get back on my brother. I had also never been in one of these things."

I stumbled forward and intended to take his hand, but he immediately went off to the captain of the craft who came over and looked at the elephant. The captain shook his head.

"When you said elephant, I thought it was going to be one of those you see at the zoo. This one is more like a double-decker tram. I'm sure she'll not fit, and if we do get her inside and she was to step off the platform and the skin was to tear, we would all be finished. I don't think we can do it, old man. You'll have to leave her. Sorry. Hard cheese."

Cleethorpes turned to me and saw that any attempts to persuade me to leave the elephant were not going to work. He dashed after the captain and I followed.

"Look captain, you've a very strong worsted harness that you demonstrated carrying a truck. I was there and I saw you do it and some major said he reckoned you could carry a tank slung underneath. A tank weighs more than our elephant, even this one, so we could sling her underneath, couldn't we?" He turned to me. "Do you think she'd be up to that? If she started to swing about it might be curtains."

The moon lit all of us up and I still remembered exactly what this man had done to my family and probably to M. Hippolyte and Antov, my tutors, as well, whatever he said. Yet here he was trying his best to help me and the elephant.

I went up to her and put my face against her trunk and she made that ethereal sound, her music, that I saw had an effect on all around us.

I took the sound as an affirmation.

"She'll be pleased to be slung underneath," I said.

At first this was anything but true, but I hugged her trunk and kissed her and finally she was strapped securely into the harness.

I wanted to be strapped on with her, astride her neck if possible, but they said there was too much danger of my falling off. "That would indeed upset the elephant," said Cleethorpes, who was positively jumping up and down with excitement at flying further in the airship.

"Where exactly are we going?" I asked, as they were fixing the strong material under the elephant. The captain was saying that it was not a chilly night and, as we were not going high, he thought she would be alright with the cold. It was vital to get the elephant away to show there had never been a problem in the first place, only unsubstantiated rumour.

"Where are we going?" said Cleethorpes wistfully. "I haven't known for years, old chum. That's all part of the fun."

I do not know how long it took us to load but the wind was getting up and the men in black were weighing on the ropes.

I went with Cleethorpes and Ibbotson and the captain onto the mostly glass bridge of the control car that was slung beneath the aircraft and the elephant was in front and a little below us, directly in the middle of the ship. All the propellers which drove the ship were behind.

The ropes were let go and we drifted upwards and there was a pull as the harness of the elephant tightened and then she was flying with us out over the valley that led down to the furnaces of Sheffield. I craned forward and was relieved as I saw her raise her trunk and spread her immense ears slightly

"I think your elephant is making a joke," said the captain.

We then started the engines, which did not work the first or even the fourth time and then exploded into life. I thought the elephant was going to be disturbed but she was not. We began to work our way slowly up over the dark Pennines where there was hardly a light below.

The captain and his first officer kept consulting their glowing compass and chart to make sure we were exactly on course and I looked, repeatedly, to see that the elephant was all right. Most of the time, like us, she was peering down into the night at what was below her. There was one point when, at the highest peak of the hills, which were not exactly mountains, there was a low bank of pearlescent cloud and the elephant could no longer be seen.

"If anyone looks up now they'll see a flying elephant," said the captain, and everyone laughed.

Ibbotson, who was having a cup of tea, said. "A magistrates' court at High Moor near Holmesfirth heard today that a man walking home from the Pig and Whistle saw a flying elephant but that it was grey. It was on a wire beneath the clouds and it went up into them before he could show it to the constables. The magistrates gave him thirty days' hard labour for repeated drunkenness and lying to the court."

I felt so tired in every part of my body and being, but I could not eat and would not sleep as I watched out for the elephant below me. After another pearly bank of cloud she moved her trunk again and there, ahead in the distance, I saw the sea.

It was lit silver in the light of the moon and was so beautiful that I gasped.

Here and there were wisps of cloud, but I could see from England to Ireland and our own shadow as we eased out over the water. I saw a lone boat or two, but most of the sea sparkled in surreal light. The first officer pointed out to me the mountain of Snowdon and the mountains of Wales, but my eyes were on the great shimmering highway of the sea.

When I crossed it before, I was in darkness with my friend, the elephant, but now I was above the waves and was able to appreciate the ocean in full and from an angle unimagined.

The captain was talking of a rising in Ireland and that it was because of the war and it seemed so strange that we could all be up here in this ingenious machine, made by men, looking out on such a scene as any painter or poet might treasure and still be capable of slaughter on an industrial scale.

That was the thing that was so incredible about the world: that we never bother really to see the BEAUTY. That was what the elephant had taught me. That and we should try and love it all, good and bad, with a passion.

I peered down on her and saw from the playful way she held her trunk and ears that she was also enjoying the immense view from coast to coast with, here and there, indications of waves, bordering the silver of the sea and breaking on the black land. She weighed perhaps seven tons and floated above the ocean like a piece of thistledown. It made me want to laugh with joy at how she had been saved, why these men, some definitely not good, had risked their lives for her, because there must be a different way.

We kept out over the sea in the darkness until after Dublin when, for an instant, a searchlight shone up into the sky near us and then was turned off. We hummed on over a group of fishing boats below.

I wondered if they saw us and what they might have said if they had.

I so wished Anna were beside me, on that deck with the crew about a business they did not need to be involved in. It was not just the beauty that would have moved her, but the complex nature of all our souls.

The captain and first officer were suddenly very busy with the chart and we turned inland before we got to a fishing town.

Below us was completely black for miles, there was not a streetlight nor a lamp at a window. There was nothing. Then, right in the far distance, there was a single tiny glow of a light, a pinprick, and the first officer looked at the chart and leaned out of the one opening window and took our position with an instrument that measured the angle of a star. The cold air rushed in and I worried about the elephant but saw she was moving her trunk.

She knew, saw and felt, that we were descending.

The light in the distance was brighter. The captain handed me some binoculars and I saw a line of bonfires through them.

Behind the fires was a great house, not as large as the one we had left but substantial and with Grecian columns at the front.

A white flare was fired up into the sky and came down with a magnesium glare. We were lucky there was no wind.

"Gently now, we must bring her in very gently towards that haystack, away from the bonfires," said the captain. "Cut engines and drop ropes fore and aft. Drop her nose, helmsman, but just a little. There now, we are coming about. Release the auxiliary hydrogen, tanks three and five, we are going down. Drop the earth wire . . . Brace! Brace! We are going down . . ."

I was biting my knuckles. I began to cough. I felt the craft become lighter as the elephant landed on the dark grass below.

We still were moving and she was running and was in the air again and then running, but men on the ground were pulling on the ropes and we were down. That was all the welcoming party there was.

Everyone on the deck cheered and patted each other on the back and the captain came over and shook my hand.

"I think we made it, young man." But then he was busy again.

I do not imagine he had any idea of who I was. He was the sort who did not complicate his life with questions.

We waited for a time, something to do with electricity, and I hoped the elephant was not affected by it. When I was let off I ran towards her and hugged her trunk, which was cold and wet but she was happy and did her little dance and I did mine and the crew laughed at us but I did not care. No sooner had we landed than the airship was turned around to fly home.

"I think the army might miss this if we don't get her back. Lots of luck, young man," said the captain. "I don't think I'll be doing this again in a hurry." The crew then cheered the elephant.

Cleethorpes came over to me. He clasped me gently on the shoulders. I was still not sure of him or his motivations, but there was a huge smile on his face.

"My brother Weston will never, ever forgive me for this. Don't worry, we'll be watching over you. I'm leaving Ibbotson here to help you, though he thinks it's his own idea. The Marchioness sends her love. You're a very unusual person in these uniform times whatever you come to do in your life. You also may be onto something with this song of the elephant. I spent more time watching her the night before last, in case those ordered by Whitehall came for her, and I heard the strangest thing and saw . . . Well, you know . . . She is . . . Everything. Reminded me of those singing bowls in Tibet when I went climbing once with Weston. Gets you right inside. I will be in touch. Bye for now, young man. Be seeing you. God save the . . . Elephant!"

With that he ran to the airship.

"Goodbye," I shouted. But the engines had started and the door had closed.

⚜

We watched, waving at first, until the airship vanished behind a cloud. We were free. I kissed the elephant again on her trunk. The men who had held the airship's mooring ropes had disappeared back up to the house.

"Perhaps we should go in for a cup of tea and meet the Earl's cousin. He had his hand in this. The house is called Coollattin," said Ibbotson. "Colonel Cleethorpes told me."

I nodded, breathless with the cold air, and took hold of the elephant's ear and we walked towards the house.

There, men in military uniform and girls in white dresses were dancing under great chandeliers. We had arrived for a Christmas ball. There was a huge tree with glass globes and an angel on top. Or, perhaps, the SUGAR PLUM FAIRY. Things were starting and ending again. Old words tumbled through my head. I AM EVERYTHING AND EVERYTHING IS ME. I laughed. LE TSAR DOIT MOURIR! The Tsar must die! I no longer needed to hide in WORDS. I was at the ball. The orchestra was playing. The orchestra was playing a waltz. It was another time to dance.

LE TSAR DOIT MOURIR!

TWENTY-EIGHT

S IX MONTHS AFTER the wedding and on her return from Russia and Europe, Natasha still had in her mind the joyful image of the enormous elephant flying to Coollattin. In the spring she finally went to Jelena's summerhouse on Long Island. To call it a summerhouse was somehow understating the Regency style, stone-fronted mansion with its swimming pool and grounds sweeping down to the ocean. It was the sort of house Frank Sinatra and Grace Kelly lit up in *High Society*. The rooms were not in mothballs and the furniture was not covered in drapes and the place was full of Jelena's dogs and cats. Natasha had arrived early and she spent a long time gazing at the steam rising from the leafless swimming pool.

Natasha had put off this meeting several times, using the excuse of her job at Columbia that she had been skipping. She had been writing poems again. She dreamed and she wrote. She did not like what she felt she had to say. It upset her.

Last night she had read the manuscript through again and been in uncontrollable salty tears because everything in her life had become focussed on the book. She turned and looked out at the ocean and walked down towards the rocky shore. The sea stretched away into INFINITY.

The universal scale and pearl-grey indistinction between water and land only accentuated the human problem, to make the story she had to address even more heroic but strange.

What these good people had asked her to do had made

her look back and that had been so painful. She took a last gulp of the seaweed-scented air and strode up to the mansion.

More cars were now in the drive, expensive foreign ones, Jaguar and Mercedes.

There was a crowd of people in front of the house: all of those from the wedding and a few more that she did not recognise. No one was wearing masks. She saw Sergei, who was holding his whippet, and he waved to her like a long-lost friend. Several others had brought their dogs and wore their usual ancient orders on pretty ribbons. They were all dressed up and she had on a smart black suit she had bought for work under a red wool coat she had borrowed from her friend with the apartment. There was an air of excitement but also of reverence, as one would expect at a reading of a will.

"Little one!" said Nadya, kissing her three times, followed by Jelena. "Little one, we are looking forward to this. We are all looking forward to this so very much. It is important to all of us. And you are one of us now, little one!"

Natasha did not reply. She could not reply. She rushed into the house and there was a maid standing by a huge blue and white Chinese vase.

"Do you know where the room . . . ?"

"It's along there, ma'am."

The room was already set out with rows of chairs. There was a screen for her PowerPoint presentation and a lectern. She wanted to maintain a professional distance, but that was immediately undermined by a painting of a magnificent herd of elephants walking into an African sunset above the malachite fireplace.

The lines of expensively-upholstered chairs filled up and Jelena introduced her.

"All of you know how this lovely girl, this princess, Princess Natasha, is connected to us and our story. She is a poet and is also so clever, being educated at the Harvard that she has done her own researchings into the story and to where the prince and the elephant ended up. I do not know, none of us know, the findings of Princess Natasha's investigations. But I am sure she has discovered much! So please listen patiently until she has finished. Please begin, Your Highness."

There was an immediate round of applause and smiles and Natasha adjusted her notes and connected her computer. She put her copy of the manuscript on a little table and held her hand on it for longer than she should have. She felt a very real emotional connection with those pages, but was dreading what she had to tell her audience.

"Firstly, let me thank Jelena for inviting me here and Sergei for letting me examine the original manuscript. The story of the prince and the elephant is a very affecting one and I have read it many, many times. I don't think I'm over stating when I say it has changed the way I look at other people and the world for the better . . . The journey is an epic one, not only physically but emotionally and artistically. It is a delight . . . and so sad."

There was approval at this and certain people, the priest and Sergei, began to clap. One of the dogs started to bark. Jelena held up her hand and scowled at them. There was quiet.

"But, as Jelena has so very flatteringly pointed out, I am an academic as well as being a poet. The main questions we want to answer are: is the story true and, if so, where did the prince and the elephant eventually find a home? Was that the real meaning of the word on Pushkin's crest, *Fumoo?*"

A couple of people sitting in the front rolled their eyes at the first suggestion as if it was already established. Natasha cleared her throat.

"Let us consider the first question in terms of the manuscript. There's every likelihood that there was a second illegitimate son – one is already documented - of the Tsar and a St Petersburg ballerina, the boy then being brought up in the Imperial Nursery. The Imperial Nursery was full of the court's illegitimate children and others they took a fancy to. I found that an Antov and a M. Hippolyte had been sent into exile in 1905, but it occurred to me I was looking at the wrong things. I should concern myself first with the manuscript itself. It is written in an exquisite, educated schoolboy hand on blue paper, which, and my researches confirm this, is the same blue vellum paper supplied to guests at Wentworth Woodhouse, England, in 1918-20."

There was a gasp at this and murmurings of pleasure. A page was displayed on the screen behind her.

"But there are certain of these pages that are not blue but white, and the white pages for the most part are towards the end of the story and after the meeting with 'the disappointing King'."

There was a ripple of laughter.

"The blue pages bear the crest of Wentworth at the top. They also have a clear watermark of the Wentworth crest, a winged griffon and two coronets and the motto *Mea Gloria Fidea*, my glorious faith, half-way down the sheet. You can see this on the screen. The white ones do not. You may think this a small point and that the prince merely asked a servant for more paper and that servant was not able to find any so-called blue vellum. This struck me as unlikely because there was a very large order for this paper in records that exist and fifty sheets in the desks of the principal rooms. In a house with three hundred and sixty-five rooms there surely would be enough blue paper. So I compared the ink and the writing between the white pages and the blue. I thought I had found a slight change in narrative style in some of the pages but could not see a ready difference in the writing or the ink. So I sent them off to a handwriting expert I know who also sent the ink to be analysed by a scientist at MIT who works with the police. The ink is a more expensive kind than that used on the blue paper and likely to have been bought in London, in Holborn, from an ink manufacturer who supplied the legal trade. The white paper came from the same shop, Hanley and Sons. They also made fountain pens until the shop was destroyed in the Second World War. The white sheets of paper are manufactured possibly two or three years after the blue. The expert said white paper was used not only because of the difficulty in getting an exact match with the blue from Wentworth, but to distract from the difference in the hand-writing. The ink on the white sheets dates from exactly 1920 and the hand is close but belongs to another. Tests showed a fifty-seven per cent correlation that the handwriting on the white sheets is not that of the prince. The white pages at least could therefore have been done by a contemporary, or even by a person quite recently. The materials are all obtainable from antiquarian sellers and auctions, albeit very expensive. The last pages concerning the airship, which are all white, must have been written later, anyway."

She paused and took a sip of water. Her audience were not as happy now.

"So what if some of the pages have been re-written. The original probably went mouldy or something,' said Sergei. "The prince must have added the last pages later, with another pen. And other white pages. Maybe he rewrote. Then some servant took the white papers back to put with the blue papers." Those around him nodded.

Natasha cleared her throat and moved on.

"Well, you can read all of this forensic investigation in my report, of which I have brought several copies. So, let us consider historical fact. Because of the explosion of media and increasing skill in the manipulation of such historical truth, establishing historical fact has become almost impossible. Not only was a spin put on events at the time, but also by interested people looking back at history they did not like. We have leaders nowadays who refuse to believe anything but their version of the truth. Anything else is 'fake news'. We have Eisenstein's totally inaccurate film of the Revolution . . . So I was well aware that I was peering through a dark glass, though hopefully not darkened by my own agenda. Always at the point where the story, the popular story, the seductive myth, takes over is it easy to hide the truth. Successive Russian governments have set up departments devoted to the destabilising power of fiction. Telling a favourable story afterwards is as important as winning the battle. And sometimes a story, a fiction, is all that is needed to win."

Images of armed men storming the Winter Palace in Eisenstein's film played out on the screen. The red flag was raised. "None of this ever happened," she said. "The palace had been taken without a shot."

A dog barked. The room was silent now, people sat on the edges of their handmade chairs. Natasha felt hot and did not want to go on. She had another drink of water. Nadya had an agonised expression on her face and appeared to be saying a prayer and moving her hands across her chest. Natasha fixed her eyes on the light blue curtains at the end of the room and continued.

"We do know that a deaf-mute youth of the prince's age came through Riga and went across the North Sea to England with a circus owned by an American called Sam Masterson, who went on to be a successful film producer and director under another name. I have testimony that our prince came to Wentworth Woodhouse at the correct time and that the King was there for a secret meeting with Earl Fitzwilliam. To confuse matters further, a gypsy boy may have pretended to be Russian. Other facts, however, do not tally. The mass demonstration of miners, on white pages, seems to have occurred a year later, although there might have been one at the time of the pit disaster. But, most of all, I cannot find any mention of a specifically African elephant. There were Indian elephants in the circus and posters of a show to hang one of them for killing a trainer. We do not know if this took place. There are pictures of an Indian elephant working at Park Gate forge, but not at the right time. The Wentworth stables records, copies of which were at the Fitzwilliam estate in Ireland, show that no elephant was ever there or hunted for by the military or police, unless, of course, these are fake. I consulted an eminent psychiatrist and he thinks that the poor boy may have invented the elephant entirely following the dreadful traumas of his journey that are most probably understated or omitted in the text. But it was not just to help himself. He creates the elephant as a good god universally to counter wickedness and anarchy. In the story the elephant's curious song or vibration inspires positive dreams and love. One must not forget that this boy set out effectively motherless and fatherless into the world in every emotional sense and then was banished into exile with bright, if questionable, companions. As Pushkin says, better the illusions that exalt us than ten thousand truths. The psychiatrist confirmed in his opinion the little prince was autistic and probably at least borderline Asperger's at the start of his journey. Or it could be a more extreme personality disorder, formerly known as schizophrenia, with hallucinations such as the river of dark fire, though this has been linked with Schopenhauer's description of the anarchic, artistic *Wille*, the raw power behind creation. The boy hides in words that are like jewels to him, mirrored halls of meaning. The psychiatrist concluded the image of the elephant therefore can be seen as a progression and externalisation of this novel use of language. It is important to stress that the elephant here, in the manuscript, is not, I repeat not, the clichéd 'elephant in the room', the obvious problem no one wants to talk about, unless it is a roomful of dreams. Rather it is fundamental to humanity as, the prince writes. The elephant represents all that is good in the boy and the world in a ruined landscape of evils and falsehoods and war that must be embraced. Everything, good and bad. The god that Alexei invents is a receptacle for his hopes and dreams, his innocence, his transgressions and the instinctive goodness that was his angel and his undoing. The elephant is infinite and is as infinite as human love. I think he found a paradise, an enchanted forest for his elephant, but not in any physical way. It was in his heart."

She saw several horrified men in the front row shaking their heads.

"It may be the little prince died at Wentworth, was quietly murdered. Or he died of the Spanish Flu. It may be that is the reason for the white pages. I do not think they killed him because he was an embarrassment. They were too powerful to be embarrassed, though he may have found out something or heard something he really wasn't meant to. Or they murdered him just from a British sense of neatness. No one was going to investigate. This was the richest house in England at the time. In a way, it was the epicentre of world capitalism and the war machine. The wealth of that family was astounding. The entire British coal industry that was worth twenty-five million in 1914 had yielded a hundred and sixty million pounds in profits by the end of the war. This is well over two hundred and fifty billion dollars now. There are rumours of a secret meeting with the Bolshevik government and payments of Moscow gold to influence non-intervention in Russia. There are the dark plans of Earl Fitzwilliam. There are secrets that have been guarded into modern times. All the private records of the family were destroyed in 1972 in a bonfire on the estate that lasted for three weeks. The house was just as much a closed society as the Selo palace and the people who lived in the tied cottages on the estate hardly better than freed serfs. No one ever found the little prince because where he both started and stopped writing is where he disappeared. The whole thing may have been engineered by British Intelligence, who fancifully completed the manuscript rather than destroy it so the prince's entire story would be presumed to be fiction. Then there is the powerful and enigmatic figure of King Billy, Earl Fitzwilliam. It is only my opinion, but I think Alexei never stood a chance. Perhaps he guessed his fate, I do not know. He has left us a strong sense of freedom and spiritual homeland in his writing, which is the meaning of *Fumoo*, a word which originates in Cameroon, the birthplace of the ancestor of Pushkin, the prince's ancestor. The timeless nature of Africa and its abstract art in this story cannot be over-emphasised, the elephant's song changing our perceptions directly as all good art does. Slavery and African gold were the magical drivers of the industrial revolution. The boy's story of the elephant is a counter to the inhumanity of our digital age. He means us to take this story to our hearts as he took words into his head as a lost child. It is a story very much of today."

Natasha felt tears coming to her eyes and took a deep breath.

"I cannot be certain as to what happened, but my advice is to stay with this beautiful story as a beautiful story. To me it is like a gospel story. It has a greater truth to tell than that we can discern in the muddied history and the downright lies of the politicians."

A man at the back began to shout in Russian.

"Lies!" shouted someone else, bewildered.

Jelena stood up slowly from her chair and then flew screaming at Natasha and hit her on the side of the head with a pot robin she had scooped up from a small table in front of the lectern on which rested a pitcher of water.

"Get out of here! Get out of here with your lies!'

Natasha began to move and then almost run towards the door as someone threw a glass. It was the little priest.

"She's not a princess. She's an imposter."

The idea was absurd. It annoyed her. She turned and paused.

"I do not think of myself as a princess. Even if the family tree you sent me is correct and I am descended from the boy. That has all gone, can't you see? Others helped themselves to the money and lands long ago. They're not going to give it back."

If anything, her words sounded even more insane than the story of the boy.

She strode down the hallway and out onto the drive. She asked a young man for her car as people started to gather, furious, outside the house and one hurled a stone. A mist had rolled in and shut off the vastness of the sea. There were only the angry, well-dressed people in front of the house yelling at her.

"What have you done to us, little one?" were the words she heard as she drove off. A stone hit her rented car but she did not stop.

When she got back to the borrowed apartment on 20th she collapsed on the sofa and began to weep again. She could not stop herself. The next day a letter arrived containing a cheque for her services, ten times her university wages, and a blurred black and white picture. It was of a laughing little boy in a sailor suit clutching a toy.

The toy was a tiny silver elephant.

Natasha stayed all day in the apartment with the curtains drawn and occasionally the telephone rang but she did not answer. The most dangerous thing in life is to play with another person's dreams and illusions on the bank of the river of dark fire.

The man in Paris, the man she loved more than anything in the world, had called her princess. He was very like the boy in the story.

She quit her job at Columbia and, months later, had thirty messages mounted up from ChiChiChica when a letter came inviting her to a hotel in Monterey, to take part in an environmental poetry programme. The hotel looked very like the one-time cannery factory hotel her father had bought and died at, but was in the wrong place. She didn't care why she had been invited. She just needed to be anywhere but where she was. What was wrong with her? Tears ran down her cheeks. She had lived in the boy and the elephant's story for so long now, it was like saying goodbye to them. They were shouting something to her across a great chasm. She saw them in her dreams. She saw them in the dream of the rebellious butterflies. She could not quite catch their words. That night she dreamed of the river of dark fire the boy had talked about and smelt a rank smell as it rushed at her to engulf her, while on the banks men played dice and women danced fandangos with giant flowers. She woke with a start and sent an email to ChiChi that just said:

To: (ChiChiChica) Froment@fas.harvard.edu
From: NatashaA@gmail.com

Soon: I fucked up. We have to. Don't we? We have to get through the night to see the dawn and all that stuff. x

Natasha drank too much of the Beluga vodka she had brought from Moscow and went back to sleep. She went to sleep with the elephant sonnet on her lips.

The next day there was an email.

From: (ChiChiChica) Froment@fas.harvard.edu
To: NatashaA@gmail.com

You have ignored my other emails but please, please reply to this one. The Feds still want to talk to you about Paris. I want to help, Natasha. But you have to stay where you are. I am saying that as Professor Froment. You have a brilliant future. Columbia said you quit your job and they have been calling and calling you. And, yes, in my opinion, and that of the head of the Slavic section here, that elephant poem you have discovered from later in the book may well be by

Pushkin. That's worth a paper on its own. And to think it is part of the book. I read your new poem in the Paris Review, which is wonderful. You don't have to prove to everyone most of what we do in life is all an illusion, all a big lie. The boy's story is remarkable. And we can guess what happened to the boy and the elephant in the story, if they are real. But you have just become too involved in it. Sure, maybe all this business with the manuscript is your green light at the end of the dock. Like in Gatsby. Your chance for your hopes and dreams and freedom. But is someone manipulating you? Who is there for you? Ask yourself that, my darling. The man in Paris? I really don't think so. I love you no matter what, love minus zero. Yes, Love. Everything that matters. Pushkin's Elephant. Stay where you are. I am so frightened for you. It is in my dreams and I never dream. Is the man in Paris' mixed up in things? Or have you done all this yourself? Did you fake the whole thing? Please tell me? Are you the author x?

TWENTY-NINE

NATASHA LOVED THE boy's first pages. When he found the silver elephant at the ball. She read them again in the car before walking to the hotel. It was not big, painted white and was out on a rocky point that plunged into the sea after the pines let go. It was like the one in the boy's dream when he boarded the train. A wide beach stretched away north to another rocky point with a small lighthouse. The powerful waves surged up the bay and out again with a rolling thunder. She felt like a child at the seaside.

Natasha parked her rented station wagon in the car park blown with the white sand. She blinked. It was as if she had parked the car there before.

The Pacific rollers were coming in and seething around the wooden piles the rambling shutter-board hotel was built on.

An old hand-painted sign just said HOTEL and the place was hard to find in any guidebook. A sign on the beach said DANGER in red. *Beware surge tides in stormy weather and there is a danger of the lighthouse on the promontory to the north being cut off.* Out at sea there were dark clouds and a storm was coming in with the tide. The bell in the lighthouse began to clank and clang. She climbed the wooden steps into a lobby and smelt fish cooking somewhere and there was a radio playing on a floor above and the sound of flutes and old West Coast music came and went with the crash of the rollers outside. On the wall behind the reception was an autographed photo of Marlon Brando and half a page about a cowboy film she had never seen. There was an envelope with her name on the counter and a red ribbon trailing from it. Her hands shook slightly as she turned over the envelope and pulled on the ribbon. Out fell a silver elephant with rubies for eyes.

Natasha was so shocked she backed away.

Outside the waves boomed. The tide was coming in hard. It was there, the elephant.

Someplace in the old wooden hotel that creaked with the sea like a boat she thought she heard a laugh. It may have been the radio. Another song played. Her whole body seemed to vibrate with the timbers as the white wooden structure was hit by another wave. Why had the powerful sea never swept the hotel away? She wondered if she was in danger, but she did not care.

The wooden counter of the reception was made from the pines that surrounded the bay. She picked up the elephant and held it in front of her eyes and just stared and stared. It was old and the word *Fumoo* was written on one side in English script. Natasha could hardly breathe though every window in the place was open.

"Hello!" she shouted. There was no one.

She pressed the trunk and a little roll of paper shot out. She read the Pushkin sonnet. There was a tear stain on the third line. She put it back.

Away to the left a shutter banged in the wind.

The wind in the shutters and the old ironwork and the trees sounded like the elephant's song. Natasha wanted her poetry to act on the reader directly, just like the elephant's song. That was what she wanted.

At her feet was an old waste-paper bin.

She turned and looked out of the open window down at

the perfect crescent of white sand, punctuated here and there with rocks. On the next headland the cluster of sea pines had been blown into strange, processional shapes, and before it met the sea there was the lighthouse, a small one built of white stone, among rocks that almost looked like elephants bathing.

The waves came rushing up the beach and then she saw the pattern in the sand.

All the way along the shoreline there were the footprints of an elephant.

Her foot touched the waste-paper bin and she laughed. It was the regulation green bucket of a wastepaper bin that had once been in every office. There was fresh, wet sand on the bin.

The bottom of the bin had been used to make the footprints that led to the lighthouse. It was just the sort of thing the man in Paris would do.

It was as if an earthquake went though her from her belly and up her spine. How could she let herself fall for this? She wanted to kill him. Kill him!

The man in Paris.

She stared down at the prints. Elephant tracks in California. Elephant prints in the Monterey sand.

He had done the whole thing. The whole thing with the book. For her.

If it was meant to be an apology . . . it had got her writing again.

Natasha bit her lip. She knew. She knew the poetic meaning of all this, not just as a cold idea. She recorded the words on her phone to send to ChiChi.

"I have to sing like the elephant. It's that simple. I am nothing without my poetry. The man in Paris made me realise this. History is dead. So is prediction and dreams. There is only action. I must sing my song, that's all."

Natasha gripped the silver elephant hard. The man in Paris had used the boy's story he had been researching to make Natasha continue with her poetry, a love she probably thought she loved more than him. He did this even though she had split from him. He was like the "mute offender" in the Pushkin poem. The words of Pushkin's sonnet were in her head.

> "I loved you without hope, a mute offender;
>   What jealous pangs, what shy despairs I knew!
> A love as deep as this, as true, as tender,
> God grant another may yet offer you."

The man in Paris had done all this for her.

It was wrong, she knew, to love him. The man in Paris. She knew exactly what ChiChiChica would say.

He bought the blue pages. He wrote the white pages. He set it all up. He conned those poor Russians.

She knew what it was about now. He loved her without limit and he was forcing her to choose. It was a choice between poetry and the ordinary. It gave Natasha a wonderful freedom.

THIRTY

NATASHA KICKED HER shoes off and ran fast towards the lighthouse, that place of constancy and light, which had revolving mirrors to warn and to reflect the whole of creation. To follow the elephant tracks. That's what the boy who led her here would have done. She ran so fast she thought her lungs were going to burst. One of the waves hit her legs, like the ladies' dresses hitting little Alexei in the face at the Christmas Ball at Selo. SLAP-ONE-TWO-THREE . . . SLAP-ONE-TWO-THREE . . . Ahead of her was a pine that could be the Christmas tree. There was a smell of pine needles and scented candles as the sea nearly knocked her off her feet.

She ran in the elephant tracks as fast as she was able. The sea swirled over them. He must be here. The man in Paris. She was going to make it. It had all come good from the bad, like in the boy's story. She was going to make it. She must.

Nothing was as real as the wet sand beneath her feet.

She believed in the elephant. She believed things could be good.

This was real.

ACKNOWLEDGEMENTS

I WANT TO thank my wife Alice for her encouragement and for proof-reading this book, Jennifer and Christopher Hamilton-Emery, Emma Dowson and all at Salt. I would like to thank Balraj Khanna, Jonathan Pegg, Andrew Kidd, Richard Cohen, Brice Marden, Gerard Malanga, Polly Samson and David Campbell of the Hawthornden Foundation, who supported this book with a Hawthornden Fellowship at Casa Ecco on Lake Como. Also, the staff at Bath Spa University and the PhD Forum, in particular Professor Gerard Woodward, Richard Kerridge, Steve Hollyman, Tracy Brain, Katie Rickard, Ian Gadd and the Global Academy of Liberal Arts, which allowed me to present my PhD thesis and the concepts behind this novel to the Bulgakov Society in Moscow, and those at Corsham Court Library. I would also like to thank Nadja and Jelena Poderegin, Nika Velt, Masha Melnikova and all my friends in St Petersburg and Moscow.

This book has been typeset by
SALT PUBLISHING LIMITED
using Neacademia, a font designed by Sergei Egorov
for the Rosetta Type Foundry in the Czech Republic. It
is manufactured using Holmen Book Cream 70gsm, a
Forest Stewardship Council™ certified paper from the
Hallsta Paper Mill in Sweden. It was printed and bound
by Clays Limited in Bungay, Suffolk, Great Britain.

CROMER
GREAT BRITAIN
MMXXI